DIRT

Evil in the Heartland

To James & Mary Lou
Love ya!
Enjoy Dirt.

John P. Goetz

This book is a work of fiction. Names, characters, places, and incidents are either the product of the author's imagination or are used fictitiously. Any resemblance to actual persons, living or dead, or to actual events is entirely coincidental.

Dirt: Evil in the Heartland

ISBN-13: 978-1523408832

ISBN-10: 1523408839

ALSO BY JOHN P. GOETZ

Doorway to Your Dreams

The Protocol: A Prescription to Die

Souls of Megiddo, Book 1: The Caretakers

"Farmers plant their heart and soul year-after-year, using tears and sweat as rain."

The Book of Lost and Forgotten Dreams

DEDICATION

To Arvilla.
No matter where I am, you will always be home.

DIRT

Evil in the Heartland

John P. Goetz

Prologue

"A race begins with the blast of a starting gun, and ends joyously with your arms raised at the finish line. Life is a race too, but ends with your arms crossed in a casket."

The Book of Lost and Forgotten Dreams

Arvilla, ND

June 22, 2012

*

The sun fell behind the horizon two hours ago. In the sky above, there were stars. The waxing crescent moon was in the blackness too.

Somewhere.

No one could see a twinkle of a single star, or the shine of the moon. The seemingly ordinary farmyard was illuminated by dozens of spotlights. It looked more like noon, instead of ten in the evening.

At first, the story warranted a single photographer and reporter from the *Grand Forks Tribune.* The story had to be a hoax, because things like this didn't happen out here. As the story grew legs, and became reality, the once small trickle of cars became a flood of every type of newsroom vehicle. The single reporter from the *Tribune* called his editor who then called a friend at the television station. The floodgates opened.

"It's true. They found human body parts in the pigpen. Yes, I said human. We need more feet on the ground. This is going to be big. Front page stuff. Above the fold. Get this stuff online ASAP."

Now there were cars and vans littering the circular gravel driveway, and leaking onto the main dirt road that intersected the farm's entrance. Every local station from Grand Forks and Fargo, and even the big ones that drew a national audience, was represented. The throng of cameramen, photographers, producers, and reporters packed the farmyard. No one cared where they parked, or what they drove over. No one cared that this was someone's home.

It was now a crime scene and nothing else mattered.

The only thing they grudgingly accepted as off-limits, was the perimeter of the crime scene defined by stripes of bright yellow DO NOT CROSS tape, and guarded by three stone-faced sheriff's deputies who were told to keep their mouths shut if they valued their jobs.

But that's what telephoto lenses were for, and news crews knew how to push limits.

The story was alive and needed feeding.

A producer, wearing blue jeans, sandals, and a tank-top, held cell phones against each ear. He was trying to hold two simultaneous conversations. He was from one of those national news channels, and was trying to explain where Arvilla, North Dakota was in the big scheme of things.

"South of Canada. West of Minnesota," he said into one phone.

"Yes. It's confirmed, they found body parts," he said into the other. "Human parts, yes. Likely female."

A brunette reporter wearing a blue dress and matching heels, ordered her cameraman to make sure he got a good close-up of her standing holding her microphone in front of the big red barn next to the pigpen.

"Does my hair look ok?"

The guy behind the camera, surely tired of dealing with the reporter's ego, thought, "Does your butt look too big?"

The reporter wanted to make sure she looked good on camera and started to fluff her hair and barking orders.

"Be sure to get the pigs in there too. Oh my God, I just stepped in something! It stinks back here. How do these people live like this," she asked as she smoothed her dress. "Are we on?"

The locals were there too, of course. It didn't take long for word to travel the six miles from the farm into town. Once the story's seed was planted at the bar, the facts were stretched and warped. The essence of what happened was tangled within every version of the story depending upon who was telling it, and how many beers he or she already had.

"He murdered some girl."

"It was only one girl."

"No, you're wrong. I heard it was dozens."

"But they found body parts, right?"

"Oh yes. I heard they found a lot."

Nothing like this ever happened before, and everyone was eager to get a few seconds or minutes of fame in front of the camera. Their cars and trucks added to the growing lot at the farm.

"Yes, damn right I knew him. Can I say that? Can I say damn? Well, anyway, I went to high school with him. I never thought he'd do something like this," said a former high school football star as he showed a news anchor how he could chug a beer. "I saw him last week as a matter of fact. Me? I work at my dad's gas station."

The same former jock, now rotund, bald gas station attendant, ended the interview with a fist pump, and a loud "who-ya!"

"He is a good boy! Everyone loves him," said a buxom woman who was being ogled by several cameramen because she wasn't wearing a bra. "I don't understand how he could have done something like this."

Arvilla was in the news. On every single channel.

They were famous.

This is how it all started, but a story is better told from its roots. You have to understand the story's players of course, and one of the most important is the town.

*

Arvilla, North Dakota.

Zip Code 58214.

Its area code is the same one used for the entire state: 701.

Arvilla is an eye-blink town twenty-two miles west on Highway 2, from one of North Dakota's largest cities, Grand Forks. Grand Forks, "Forks" to the locals, is on the Red River that defines the border with Minnesota, and is seventy-five miles south of the Canadian border. The Red River flows north into Canada, empties into Lake Winnipeg, and eventually into the Hudson Bay. Arvilla is three miles west of the decommissioned Grand Forks Air Force Base. In its heyday, the airbase was home to B-52's, KC-135's, and B1-B's.

Like everywhere else, Arvilla's population varies from year-to-year, but on average there are 313 souls residing there. Mathematically, that is five people per square mile.

Most locals think that's urban sprawl.

New York City averages more than 27,000 per square mile.

Although its streets have names like Hartford, Hersey, Washington, and Hughes, you really don't need them if you are going to send someone a letter. The postmaster knows everyone, and knows what mailbox to put the letter in. If one of those big shipping companies needs to deliver a package, and the driver doesn't know which house to go to, he stops at the bar, maybe has a pop, and then asks for directions.

"Where does Marleen Johnson live?"
"It's the white two-story next to Junior's."
"This town is full of white two-stories."
"The one with the deck over the garage."
"Trampoline in the front yard?"
"No. The other one."
"Got it. What's the special today?"
"Liver and onions."

You can't get lost in Arvilla. Its perimeter is not measured in miles, but blocks. The blocks can be counted on one hand. They are not New York City blocks, but country blocks. If it takes you more than thirty seconds to drive by the town in its entirety, you're going to slow. After all, the day to take your pickup for a walk is Sunday.

There are only three businesses in Arvilla: a bar, an accountant, and a grain elevator. The bar is Arvilla's ad hoc municipal hall. It's the primary dissemination point of all information: good, bad, and rumor.

There are no gourmet coffee shops in Arvilla. But if it's early enough, you can get a cup of hot coffee at the bar. They don't serve decaf, and they will laugh at you if you ask for a spritz of one of those fancy flavorings like almond, hazelnut, or toasted marshmallow frappe. Coffee comes in one flavor: Folgers.

There are no fast food restaurants either, but you can get a California burger with extra jalapeños at the bar as long as it's after eleven, and before two. They'll even put a T-bone on the grill, and serve it with a baked potato, the veggie of the day, and a roll.

And ketchup, of course.

The only spices ever needed or used, are also at the table: salt and pepper.

Arvilla's streets are not paved. That means for a few weeks in the early spring, the roads become virtually impossible to traverse. As the winter's frost escapes, the ground expands, heaves, and leaves hundreds of frost boils in every direction. The boils turn the roads into a war zone with hidden landmines cars and trucks must maneuver around else be lost up to their axles. When the thaw is complete, the frost boils retreat, the roads are leveled, and the residents simply adapt to the never-ending dust until winter.

Unless it rains.

Then they deal with mud.

Despite preconceived notions about outdoor toilets, corncob toilet paper, and lights by candle, people in Arvilla do have the modern conveniences of life including, plumbing, running water, electricity, and even the Internet.

Most residents of Arvilla don't lock their front doors, and probably don't even have the keys if they wanted to.

So why bother?

Some people who live on either coast, are positive that North Dakota is somewhere north of Siberia, and definitely not part of the United States, but it is. Regardless of what those big city people may think or say, you don't need a passport to visit. Despite over-hyped news reports that happen at least once a year, the "North" of "North Dakota," will never be dropped.

The bar is more than happy to take your Washingtons, Lincolns, Hamiltons, and Jacksons. You can get a beer, a burger, an order of fries, and be given a few dollars of change from a Hamilton. In the big city, the same meal would require at least a Jackson.

Maybe a Jackson *and* a Lincoln.

It gets cold in North Dakota.

Most believe the winter keeps the riffraff out.

You accept the cold. You embrace it. You bundle up, and learn to not feel your extremities for a few months. It's easy, once you learn how to walk with five additional layers of clothing.

You get used to starting your car in your boxers and work boots in the middle of January, because you're simply too tired to get dressed. If anyone asks a local, "What's that cord sticking out of the front of your car for?" he will instantly know you're not "from around here."

Some tell the truth.

"A block heater. Warms the engine a bit so it starts when it's really cold outside."

Some spin a tale.

"It's a special device used to get electricity from the car's battery to the house, because, as everyone knows, North Dakota doesn't have electricity yet. That special plug provides the only way to run the refrigerator that keeps the milk cold that was just taken from the Holstein cow that everyone has in the spare bedroom that was recently converted into a manger."

The first spring day when the thermometer barely kisses forty degrees, is special. It means bare feet, short sleeves, and cut-offs. Those heat waves are relished, as the next day may require you to bring out the parka, gloves, and stocking cap again.

Arvilla doesn't have a traffic problem. It doesn't have smog or a single traffic light. Residents don't suffer from road rage. A bad day in Arvilla is when you have to wait until the beer truck finishes unloading the forty cases of Pabst Blue Ribbon because the cooler is empty after the weekend's dance featuring the local boy who formed his own band and is now the talk of the town.

Families have lived in the area for generations. Most are those ensnared, by choice or not, in the generational pull of family farm. Some have dreams beyond the tractors, cold and dust, and bolt the gravitational pull.

They don't return.

Those who remain are lifers. In time, they are ultimately buried in the local cemetery.

For lifers, leaving the family, or the farm is never seriously considered. Tending to the same thick, black dirt that their father's worked, and their grandfather's before them, is an integral part of their being. Planting seeds, watching them grow, and reaping the harvest, is what provides a sense of pride and accomplishment.

It's what they love.

It's what they are good at.

It's what they know.

Most everyone in Arvilla and the surrounding farms has earned a nickname. Very few are called by what their parents intended. The nicknames are not plain. They are not the simplistic, shorted versions of Robert, Daniel, Susan, Bradley, or Richard.

That would be too easy.

Arvilla nicknames are unique and colorful. They are names like Tubbs, Red, Dirt, Booger, Bud, Junior, Skip, Buck, Skunk, Chub, Sis, Butch, or Squirt. Many never know a friend's birth name. They only learn of it at his funeral, or when reading his obit at the bar while drinking a beer.

"Says here that William Kinnear died."

"Yeah. A few days ago."

"Says that he was from Arvilla?"

"Yup."

"Any relation to Tubbs?"

"That's him. William Kinnear. Tubbs Kinnear. One and the same."

"His real name was William? Jeez, I knew him for thirty years. I didn't know that. He was always just, you know, Tubbs."

"Want another beer?"

"Make it a Windsor water."

Everyone knows one another in Arvilla.

Everyone helps one another.

When good things happen, everyone hears about it in time, and everyone is happy. Congratulatory beers are bought and shared. When bad things happen, everyone immediately knows, and everyone talks. Beer to drown sorrows are bought and shared.

Good news remains concise and compact.

Bad news grows in all directions, and achieves a life of its own.

Book 1: Spring

Sowing

"It's not one's life that's good or evil. It's the heart that turns as black and sticky as tar."

The Book of Lost and Forgotten Dreams

"The lesser of two evils is still two evils."

The Book of Lost and Forgotten Dreams

1978 – 2010

July 4, 1978

St. Joseph's Hospital
Grand Forks, ND

*

The two new fathers regarded one another while simultaneously looking through the window at the squirming newborns in the small metal cribs on the other side. The two men knew each other all of their lives. They were friendly, but not exactly best of friends. They lived a mile from one another. In North Dakota, that was considered close. Each lived on his own family farm, and minded his own business in order to feed his family in his own unique way. In rural terms, they were neighbors who drank a beer every now and then and commiserated about the price of grain, beef, and pork.

He wasn't supposed to be smoking in the hospital, but William "Tubbs" Kinnear didn't care. No one was going to tell him when or where he could do anything. They were his lungs, and he chose to do whatever he wanted to them. Tubbs savored the smoke in his lungs, slowly let the smoke trickle out through his nose, dropped the spit-soaked stem of the smoldering inch-long Camel onto the hospital floor, then smashed it with the heel of his tattered leather work boot that was smothered with layers of pig shit. By the time Tubbs looked back into the nursery, he pulled another fresh cigarette from the pocket of his bib overalls, pushed it between his lips, lit it, and blew another fresh stream of smoke at the glass.

*

"Tubbs," said Tom "Skip" Carlson as he nodded to his neighbor. "I hear you have yourself a boy. Congrats."

"Skip," said Tubbs with a return nod. "Hear the same's for you."

"Back row. Third from the right."

Tubbs responded with another exhale of smoke from the corner of his mouth and nostrils.

Skip smiled a proud, new-father smile.

Tubbs nodded again, but didn't further any conversation or even look in the direction that Skip pointed. He pinched the new cigarette between his thumb and forefinger as he took a long, deep drag. While holding his breath, he pulled a small metal flask from the other pocket of his bibs, opened it, and took an exaggerated draw. He knew he probably wasn't supposed to be drinking either.

It was his liver, too.

"Skip?"

Skip turned his attention from his son to what Tubbs was offering.

"Thanks."

Skip took the flask, and winced as he swallowed a mouthful of Canadian Club whiskey. He handed the flask back, and pointed his pinky finger towards his son.

"Daniel Scott Carlson. Came in at almost five and a half pounds. Eighteen inches. 3:05 this morning."

"Irish?"

"Sis' grandfather's name."

"Hmmmm."

A fresh stream of smoke spewed from Tubbs' nose and flicked the cigarette. The air conditioning swirled the ashes, blew them against the wall where they tricked down, and added to the growing pile against the grey rubber wall guard.

"How about yours?"

"My what?"

"Your son. What's his name?"

"Dirk or something dumbass like that. Don't really give a shit what she calls him. Could be Jackass for all I care. Just need another set of hands," he said while taking pulls from both the cigarette and flask at the same time.

"Which one is he?"

"Which one what?"

"Crib. What crib's he in?"

Skip watched as Tubbs scanned the nursery.

"Three down from yours. To the left, I think. Hadn't really paid much attention to the squirmers. Watching the nurses. More interesting."

Skip moved his eyes down three rows of cribs, and found the baby Tubbs pointed to. It was five down. Not three. The baby's name was Dirk Valoise Kinnear. 21 inches. 7 pounds. Born July 3 at 3:22 pm. He had jet-black hair covering an oblong head. He wasn't an attractive baby. Skip didn't know what the average size of a newborn was, but Daniel was tiny in comparison. He could do the math.

"Big boy. Tall."

"Who?"

"Dirk. Your son."

"So she named him Dirk. Fuck me. Dumbass name. Her grandfather's."

"He's definitely tall. Or seems to be."

"Trude's family's tall. Lanky jack-a-bitches."

"Sis said that Buck and Winnie had a boy yesterday. Should be here somewhere."

"Who?"

The cigarette bobbed between Tubbs' lips, and added more ashes to the pile on the floor. Some were still red and landed on his boots where they smoldered against the layer of dried pig shit.

"Buck and Winnie. Thorson. Just down the road from my place? They're living on the old Cumberland place. He's an MP at the base. She subs at the elementary school every now and then."

"Larimore or Emerado?"

"Both, I think. She goes wherever they need her."

"Thorson. Another Norwegian. Shit. They're everywhere."

Skip snorted a laugh. He was half Norwegian himself.

On his father's side.

"Probably serve lutefisk at the baptism," said Skip.

"Never understood how they can eat that. Fish soaked in lye. Who woulda thought of doing that? Dad always called it "Loota-shit," he said as he grimaced, and turned back to the sightseeing.

"Your dad was a good man."

Tubbs nodded, then pointed his chin towards the glass, and scratched his crotch.

"That one there makes my willie twitch. The tall blonde."

Skip slowly shook his head, further understanding why he and Tubbs had never become close friends. He'd probably just heard and experienced the longest continuous conversation that Tubbs had ever been a part of. One for the record books. Skip returned his attention to the nursery and scanned the rows of cribs in search of a card with "THORSON" written on it.

There were twenty-five cribs, and Skip stopped by each one.

There were lots of new skulls of mush to populate the world.

Lots of Olsons, Swensons, and Paulsons.

Plenty of lutefisk to be eaten.

Even better, more lefsa.

Skip's stomach growled.

He loved lefsa, but found lutefisk nauseating.

Then he found him. The fifth row down, and the only boy in the group.

The only "THORSON" in the batch.

"Found him. Booker John Thorson. July 2nd. 4:19 am. Nineteen inches. Seven and a quarter pounds," said Skip as he pointed to the crib. "Good looking boy, too."

There was no response.

Not even a grunt.

Skip turned.

Tubbs was gone.

All that remained was the sour smell of sweat, stale cigarette smoke, and a pile of ashes on the floor next to six smashed butts.

Skip turned and studied the three boys and smiled. He was looking at the next generation.

April 17, 1987
4:00 AM

The Kinnear Kitchen
Arvilla, ND

*

Despite having been released from the hospital two days ago after suffering her third miscarriage since the birth of that boy, Gertrude Kinnear, who everyone called "Trude," and sometimes "Rhymes with Rude," behind her back, still woke at 4:00 every morning.

She'd never been able to sleep, the ruptured disc in her lower spine she'd suffered since her teenage years made sure of that, and this morning she woke barely able to move. To compound the pain in her back this particular morning, she woke up with a headache. It was a banger that made her want to rip both of her eyes from their sockets and obliterate them with a twenty-pound sledge, just to feel a little bit better.

There was no hope that the muscle relaxants the doctor prescribed, gargantuan yellow and green capsule filled with something called Dantrolene, would help. This morning it was already too late for any pills, as they only worked if she took one when the pain was at the steak knife level. Once the pain turned to ice picks, as it was now, it was too late. The doctor suggested losing weight, but she dealt with that with a dismissive wave of her thick hand.

“Damn witch doctor doesn’t know what he’s talking about,” she always said. “I don’t need to lose any weight.”

The only thing Trude could do was ride out the storm, and hope the colors didn’t start, as once that happened, she’d be back on the couch staring at the ceiling. For now, she had work to do. And lots of prayin’.

Her work was important, and she enjoyed it. It helped her relax. It brought her closer to her Savior. She felt that as she polished a crucifix, she was also cleansing her blackened soul.

Trude was still a little slow. She was still sore “down there,” but she knew, deep within the depths of her dark, tarnished soul, that Jesus’ hand and his unconditional love would sustain her each and every day. She held one of her stomach rolls with one hand while her other massaged her back.

“Jesus, save me,” she whispered.

She’d bled a lot during the second miscarriage. The third was even worse. Her heart had stopped and they had to charge-up those paddles she always saw being used on TV.

She almost died - she had, really. She'd stood at the gates of Heaven, and was turned back by Him. She learned there was a reason for her torment, and why she was being denied access to her salvation. Her Savior told her what she must do, and why she was being made to suffer – she had to save her son from the fires of Hell. He sent her back down with a plan, and three holy words to guide her new life.

Prayer, Penance, and Pain.

The Three P's of Christianity.

Trude understood that saving her son's soul would be difficult – if not impossible. It would be a very long road to travel. Three hours of prayer and bible study before breakfast, a full day of either work or school, then another two hours of bible recitation and prayer before bed. Penance and pain were used as needed – which happened to be frequently at this point in the process as he was a rebellious, sinful boy with a coal-black soul.

She'd save his soul by any means necessary, as despite his evil nature, he was her son. The Almighty didn't forsake his children. She would try not to forsake hers. She would endure. She would have to make him suffer, as the Almighty had made his Son suffer.

She was positive that the boy was the cause of her inability to sustain a life within her womb. Almost nine years ago, he left something behind in her womb. Something wicked. An evil, poisonous seed that killed any other life it came in contact with. That seed had tarnished her soul in the eyes of Jesus Christ. The boy, Dirk, was the result of two minutes of pleasure. A name she regrets, as now everyone called him Dirt.

It was probably appropriate, really, as it described the boy perfectly. He was filthy as dirt. He was ugly as dirt.

Perhaps the fault was hers by choosing the name of her grandfather. After all, he was an evil man. Liked his whiskey too much. Smoked too much. Cursed too much. Fornicated too much. But her mother had insisted.

"Name your boy, Dirk Valoise. After your grandfather."

So she did.

And had been paying for it ever since.

Trude was nothing, if not obedient.

Dirk turned out to be an evil seed from an evil man. Now she was being punished for the forty-second act of fornication that had been forced upon her. There wasn't going to be any more of that any time soon – if ever. She didn't want to get married in the first place, but her father forced the situation when she couldn't hide being pregnant any longer. Hers was a shotgun wedding.

Trude pressed the small of her back with her thumbs, arched backwards, moaned, and balanced her smoldering Virginia Slim in her mouth. The smoke curled up above her head, and formed what she thought looked like a halo. She took deep breaths, and tried to think away the pain that was growing in intensity with each passing moment. She felt guilty letting the pain control her.

"Hail Mary, full of grace. For art thou' and deliver me from evil. Amen."

Slowly, she pulled down a small cedar plaque from the wall above the empty spice rack in her kitchen, softly kissed the small cross etched on its corner, and gently began dusting. The plaque was engraved with one of her favorite verses.

"For I consider that the sufferings of this present time are not worth comparing with the glory that is to be revealed to us. Romans 8:18."

"Praise the Lord," she whispered as she reverently placed it back on its nail. She stood back, adjusted the left corner down a bit, closed her eyes, and prayed.

"It's about time you got up," she screeched when she opened her eyes.

*

On television, the call of the American bald eagle is made to sound majestic and powerful. It's America's emblem after all, so it has to sound regal. In reality, its call is a high-pitched screech reminiscent of a dozen two-year-olds in the grocery store checkout aisle when the candy they are demanding is denied. When a young bald eagle is learning to use its voice, it has a very good role model.

Trude Kinnear.

Trude, wearing a white nightgown with blue and pink flowers and tattered white slippers that were at one time fluffy, walked to the table and looked down at the boy. She noticed that he didn't move as she approached. He didn't look up at the sound as she cleared her throat. She was glad. She didn't relish looking at him. She would have preferred a face closer to that of Clark Gable. Instead she gave birth to a tall Don Knotts with round, sunken eyes, an over-sized mouth, and ears that needed a strip of Velcro to hold them back. His wide gaze remained focused on empty Joseph and Mary salt and pepper shakers in the middle of the round Formica table.

He was learning.

Progress.

"Indeed, all who desire to live a godly life in Christ Jesus will be persecuted," she said as she tapped the table next to the boy's arm with her long, painted fingernail. "Elbows off of the table. Where is that from? What verse is that?"

Eight-year-old Dirk hesitated, moved his arms to his lap, and looked down at the floor.

She flicked her cigarette, and watched the smoldering ashes drizzle into his greasy, dark brown hair, which cascaded over his eyebrows. Some of the ashes floated over the collar of his pajama top and onto his bare skin.

She saw him wince as they landed, and burned out.

They were miniature angels.

She knew he wasn't going to answer correctly.

He was too much like his father. A lazy ass, dumb fuck.

She apologized to Jesus for the vulgar thought and word in her mind, and then nudged the boy with her knee. She didn't want to touch him with any bare skin.

"Boy? Where is that from? Confess to Jesus how you are tormenting your mother. Tell me. Tell Jesus."

"Corinthians?"

"No!" she seethed. "You're so stupid, boy. No wonder Jesus has forsaken you."

She would endure.

She pressed her temples with both thumbs, and prayed the colors would not come before this morning's lesson was complete. She would do her best to save her son's soul. But it would be difficult.

She kicked the chair, and even with the weight of the boy on it, it still slid an inch across the cratered linoleum floor.

"Corner. Under the crucifix. Go," she said as she pointed to the hallway. The cigarette she was holding between her fingers swung in the air and its burning end lighted the dark kitchen like a 4th of July sparkler.

The boy didn't move as she'd directed. Instead, she watched Dirk frantically thumb through the bible she'd put in front of him. He'd pay for his disobedience.

"Isaiah."

She sucked on the cigarette, grew the flaming, red glow, took it from her mouth, and smashed it into the back of the boy's neck.

He grabbed at the new wound, and squealed. Before he could turn around, she beat his hand back, and then twisted and ground the butt further down to the filter. The smell of burning hair and flesh overtook the rancid smell of the cigarette smoke.

"No! It's not Isaiah. Next time, listen to me, boy. When I say move, you move. Now go!"

She heard him begin to whimper.

"I don't want to hear a sound, boy."

She kicked his chair again, and watched him scurry to the corner.

"No. Not that one. I haven't polished that yet. The one in the hallway."

Dirk, still in his father's hand-me-down pajamas that were way too big, walked down the hallway with his hand on the back of his neck, and stood facing the wall. He was getting tall she thought, almost eye-level with the suffering figure of Jesus nailed to the wooden crucifix. She noticed a flight of tears streaming down his face, and smiled. His knees quivered.

"Stop your cryin', boy," she paused to let her next word hurt even more. "You piece of dirt. You'll never amount to anything. You know that, boy?"

Maybe it would work after all. She might be able to exercise the demons living in him after all. She turned up the radio that was re-broadcasting last week's sermon from the Reverend Billy Joe Langley.

“Praise the Lord,” she said to the voice coming from the radio. “You listen to Reverend Langley, boy. You listen and think about your evil ways. Pray for your sorry soul. Tell Jesus how sorry you are, boy.”

The colors began to flash behind her eyes as the nerves in her spine expressed their anger over her movements. Trude held her back, and limped to the sofa where she would likely spend the rest of the day.

April 17, 1987
6:00 AM

The Carlson Kitchen
Arvilla, ND

*

It was a gorgeous April spring morning. The sun had just come up, and was glistening off of the dew on the grass. There was a slight, cool breeze just strong enough to sway the layers of half-naked trees that circled the Carlson farmyard, and blow the scent of the blossoming lilacs into her kitchen. Right now, she could see through all of the trees to the eighty-acre field that circled the farm. If she looked at a certain angle, she could still see through the cluster. In a few weeks, that view would be erased as the leaves would smother the scenery. This morning, like most mornings on the farm, she didn't even need the alarm as she woke up at 5:30 sharp.

Sis had an extreme case of spring fever, and the first thing she did was open every single window on the first floor of the farmhouse. If it were a bit warmer, she'd be out planting her annuals and tomato plants – but that would have to wait a few more weeks. The weatherman said there was a possibility of frost each night this week. Too soon to put anything in the ground – unless she wanted to have to replant everything. The rule her mother drilled into her psyche was, "Wait 'til after Mother's day, and your flowers will never sway."

A terrible anecdote, but a rule she still lived by, and one that seemed to work. She had a month to go to release the energy she'd kept caged all winter.

Back in the kitchen, she filled up Mr. Coffee's water reservoir, turned him on, and listened as he started to chug and spit. Within minutes, the kitchen smelled of Folgers. And, as the scent made its way up the stairs, around the corner, and into the master bedroom, she was sure Skip would begin to stir.

The scent of coffee was his alarm clock.

On weekends, she let him sleep till 6:30. She relished the half-hour she had to herself. The curtains she'd embroidered, the ones with the lilacs and roses and red trim, were billowing in the slight breeze. Sis pulled her auburn hair into a ponytail, tied it with a rubber band, and turned on the radio. The morning Ag report was a must each weekday morning.

Spring wheat, the staple of the Carlson farm, was up three cents on news that the Chinese were halting any further purchases of wheat from the U.S. Sunflowers were up a penny. Barley was down two.

As predicted, she heard the toilet flush, and then her husband's heavy trod down the stairs. Sis got up from her chair, pushed the box of Kellogg's Raisin Bran, and the quart of two percent towards the bowl she'd already put at his place, poured him a fresh cup of coffee, and topped off hers. She felt his breath against her neck.

"Good morning, Gorgeous," said Skip as he kissed her neck. "Looks like a beautiful morning out there."

"Breeze feels good."

"Mind turning that up?" Skip said as he filled his bowl with cereal, and pointed at the radio with the box of cereal.

"What's wrong? Your legs not working this morning?"

Skip rubbed his back and grimaced.

"Not after what you put me through last night. Can hardly move."

"I don't remember anything going on last night. I have no idea what you are talking about."

*

"It's almost seven," said Skip as looked at the time on the microwave. "Kids are gonna be up."

"Skip," said Sis as she wiggled her finger while pointing to her husband's chin. "And yes. I can hear them now. Sounds like Danny."

"How do you do that?"

"What?"

"How can you tell who is who from down here?"

"I'm a mother. It's my job."

Just as he was about to say, "I think it's Bekks," Danny came bumbling down the stairs."

"It's Dan-The-Man. We heard you clomping around up there. Knew it was you."

Sis looked at her husband and shook her head.

"What now?"

"You're amazing. You know that?"

Skip pushed up the brim of his lime-green Steiger cap, and looked up from the bowl of Kellogg's Raisin Bran he was eating. He raised his eyebrows as he had just shoveled a spoonful into his mouth which was therefore pre-occupied and couldn't say "what?"

"I just told you! You have more milk on your chin than you do in your bowl. It's going to drip onto my tablecloth and I just washed it."

Skip wiped his arm across his chin, and used his sleeve to soak up the pool of milk that had accumulated in his cavernous chin dimple.

*

Knowing he had the same gully that seemed to capture milk just as easily as his father's did, and knowing that he too was eating cereal, Danny adjusted the red Case cap on his head and slowly maneuvered his chin to his right shoulder. He slowly wiped it against his t-shirt before his mother had a chance to turn her attention his way. Of course she'd tell him to use his napkin, but it was easier to do what he'd just done.

"I saw that."

"Wha?" he asked as a bran flake flew from his mouth and landed on the salt shaker.

"Use your napkin, young man."

"But dad..."

"Your father doesn't have manners. I'm not raising a caveman, so use your napkin," she said as she pushed his napkin towards his cereal bowl. "And wipe that off of the salt shaker before you think of leaving this table, young man."

Danny looked at his father, and was rewarded with a slow, almost imperceptible, wink.

"I saw that."

Danny exhaled an exasperated breath.

"There's my baby girl!"

Bekks, the youngest Carlson, came around the corner still in her onesie Wonder Woman pajamas, and sat down at the table in her usual spot.

"What's going on?"

"Your father and brother don't know how to eat their breakfast, that's what."

Bekks, who looked like her mother with her bright, hazel eyes, auburn hair, and a small, perky, button-sized nose, and didn't suffer from the chin dimple dilemma, giggled and started wiping her chin against her sleeve puppeting her brother and father. Danny resembled his father with his green eyes, and dirty-blonde hair.

And chin dimple.

"Aren't you going to get after her?"

"She's not old enough to know she shouldn't be copying her father and brother."

"She's seven years old!"

Dan knew better than to continue the argument when his mother gave him, "the look."

Skip swallowed what was in his mouth.

Danny knew his father was going to say something to piss off his mother.

He did that a lot. Most of the time it was on purpose, like now. Sometimes, by mistake.

His father may run the farm, but his mother wore the pants.

"We'll have time to teach you though. Won't we Bekks? You'll be burping at the dinner table just like your ol' man."

"Like hell you will," said Sis as she pushed back her chair from the table.

"Like hell you will," said Bekks.

Danny laughed and coughed as milk leaked from his left nostril.

Sis looked at her husband and son. To Danny, it seemed as though she had one eye on him and the other on his father. She must have super powers.

"See what you've done? What you two have created?"

"But I didn't..." said Danny.

Before he could finish his sentence, his mother put up her hand while reaching for the coffee pot. The "putting up of the hand" was the equivalent to getting "the look."

Danny looked at his father who was grinning from ear to ear. Evidently, very proud of his daughter.

And himself.

"Don't you two have work to do? Something to grease? Something to take apart? Something that needs to be done? Preferably something outside?"

Skip took his cereal bowl in his hands, brought it to his mouth, and drained its contents in one gulp.

"You're right, Hon," he said as he pushed his chair back.

Danny noticed the large dollop of milk sloshing on his father's chin as he watched him walk towards the stove where his mother was standing. His father stopped, but his arms around her waist, and nuzzled her neck.

"Love ya, hon! "

"You! Now I have milk dripping down my neck! Get out. Now. Before I assault you with Mr. Coffee here. Go feed those pigs of yours, would ya?"

Both Danny and Bekks laughed at their parents.

"Slurp that up, Dan. Let's get out of here before your mother brings out the shotgun."

"I'm making meatloaf for dinner. Be sure you're back by noon. And don't forget that Buck and Winnie are coming over for supper. Pot roast and pinochle."

"Noon it is, Ol' Wooomin. This man loves your meatloaf," said his father as he patted his stomach, and then ducked towards the screen door.

Danny heard his mother squeal followed by the thud of a wet towel hitting the screen door as its rusty spring slammed it shut behind them.

"Don't call me that! "

As he and his father walked towards the tractors they were preparing for the upcoming planting season, his father turned and blew his wife, who was watching them through the kitchen window, a kiss.

"Did she blow one back?"

"Yup. And she's still watching us."

"Good. That means she's not mad. I hope you find someone just like her, Dan. Isn't no one better on this Earth."

Dan watched his father grab a stalk of crab grass, tear it in half, put one piece in his mouth, and hand the other piece over.

“Chew on that.”

“There. Now you look like a real farmer,” said Skip when Dan put the piece of grass in his mouth.

April 17, 1987
8:00 AM

The Thorson Home
Arvilla, ND

*

Wendy "Winnie" Thorson, sat down on her son's bed then gently kissed both of his eyelids. It was something she'd done since he was an infant and always seemed to have a calming effect on both of them.

"How's my boy? Why aren't you up? It's a beautiful day out today."

"My head hurts. My eyes."

Winnie pushed his dark brown, almost black, hair up off of his forehead felt for a fever with the palm of her hand.

"You don't feel warm, Booker."

"It's really bad."

"Where does it hurt?"

Booker pointed to his temple.

"Behind my eye."

"Both?"

"Just my left. Is Dad still home?"

Booker closed his eyes, and winced as another jolt stabbed his eye.

"Did I hear someone ask for me?" asked Buchanan "Buck" Thorson as he walked into his son's bedroom.

Buck was an MP at the air force base. He was dressed in his uniform and ready to head out the door. "What's going on in here? Some sort of party that I wasn't invited to?"

"Book has a headache. Says it's bad."

"It *is*, Mom. It's really bad."

"Where does it hurt, Book?"

"He says it's behind his eye."

Buck sat down on the bed next to his wife, grabbed Booker's foot, and gave it a heavy squeeze.

"Well, the key is the dark. No light. No noise. No food. Just some 7-Up if your stomach can handle it. Got it, kiddo?"

Buck got up from Booker's bed, and pulled down the shade tucked at the top of the only window in his bedroom. It was an east-facing window so the sun was coming straight in.

"Feel better?"

Booker didn't open his eyes, but nodded.

"Good. Mom and I are going to head downstairs. I'm going to go to work. She'll bring you up some pop. Ok."

Booker nodded, rolled over, and buried his head into his pillow.

*

Winnie and Buck stood by the refrigerator while Buck poured a can of 7-Up into a glass.

"You had these when you were his age, right?"

Buck nodded.

"The pain is intense. Feels like ice picks behind the eyes."

"That's the way he described it. Ice picks. Can they do anything?"

"No. Hopefully he'll out-grow them. I did. Had to wait for puberty to finish reengineering my body though."

Winnie held up the glass of pop.

"This will help?"

"Not really."

"Then why?"

"It will put something in his stomach in case he needs to throw up. Better than the dry heaves. Those aren't fun when a migraine hits."

"The dark?"

"Definitely. Keep him in the dark. No noise."

Winnie pulled out a chair from the kitchen table and sat down. She looked at her husband.

"Do you think we should take him in? You remember what the pediatrician said when he was born, right? When we had that scare?"

“It was jaundice, Winnie. That’s all.”

“But that spot on the x-ray. On his brain?”

“That was nothing, remember? They took another x-ray, and it came up clear. He had jaundice. We put him in the sunlight like they said, and it cleared up.”

Winnie took a sip of the 7-Up.

“I’m gonna take this up to Book. You get to work.”

Buck hugged his wife, held her tight, and gave her a kiss on the forehead.

“Don’t worry, Hon. He’s having a migraine. That’s all. I had them when I was his age.”

“You sure?”

Buck crossed his heart with his finger.

“And hope to die.”

May 22, 1988
9:00 AM

The Kinnear Fields
Arvilla, ND

*

Tubbs glanced up and checked his rearview mirror for the fifth time since he first noticed the ancient, Allis-Chalmers coming up behind him. It was an ancient model, at least forty years into semi-retirement that many farmers had and used for menial tasks around the farm like hauling equipment from field-to-field, running augers, or pulling a rock skid around the field. The old tractor was gaining on him, and its big orange nose was beginning to fill up his mirror. He pulled over to the far right side of the dirt road, took a gulp of the beer he held between his legs, saluted the driver as he passed, and let the tractor that was going much faster than he was, leave him in a cloud of dust.

"That's Mr. Thompson," said Dirk.

Tubbs nodded, took a drag from his Camel, and flicked the ashes on the floor of the pickup. It was a typical Sunday afternoon. He and Dirk were checking the fields, and taking the pickup for a walk.

Tubbs wasn't in a hurry.

He never was.

Tubbs didn't see the benefit of rushing. After all, the longer he was out checking the fields, the more beers he could have without that woman's constant haranguing about the abundance of sins he was committing on the Lord's Day.

"Did grampa farm this field too?"

Tubbs grunted a yes the best he could despite having a mouth full of beer, and lungs full of cigarette smoke. He cranked the wheel to the right, and pulled the pickup into the entrance of the eighty-acre field. This was the first time he'd asked Dirk to ride along.

The kid wasn't so bad after all.

Ugly as all get out.

But not that bad.

"Along with all of the land around the farm," Tubbs said after he swallowed the beer, and let the smoke stream out of his nose.

"What we gonna do?"

"Checkin' the fields."

Tubbs popped the center console, grabbed another beer, and popped it open.

"But it's right there. What's there to check?"

Tubbs didn't answer. Instead, he got out of the truck, walked into the field, and knelt down into the black dirt. He didn't tell the boy to follow him, but when he heard the passenger door open and close, he knew the boy wasn't far behind. He heard the boy fall as he tripped over a large, black clod of dirt left over by the plow.

"Shit," said Dirk as he spit dirt out of his mouth.

Tubbs ignored him, but laughed a bit inside, and drilled his beer can into the soil next to his knee.

"What we checking?"

"Seeds."

"The ones we planted?"

"See if they've sprouted."

"What if they haven't? What if it hasn't been long enough? How do you know where the seeds are?"

Tubbs finally looked up at his eight-year-old son who was already almost as tall as he was.

"It's what we do."

To keep his hands free, Tubbs used his tongue and pushed the nub of his cigarette into the slot where a front tooth used to be. He hadn't been to a dentist in thirty years, and wasn't about to start now. He'd lost the tooth last year and actually found that not having one in that particular spot was rather convenient. He rather liked having a place to stick his cigarette when his hands were busy.

With both hands free, he dug a small divot into the earth, grabbed a handful of soil, and brought it too his nose. Tubbs closed his eyes, sniffed, then let it drizzle down between his fingers, and fall back into the hole.

To city boys, it was just something they were afraid to get too much of under their fingernails. To him it was gold. Black gold that, when properly cared for, kept his family and thousands of others fed year-after-year. It was his father's land, and his father's before that. He was the third generation Kinnear to tend this land. Tubbs looked over at Dirk who was mimicking what he'd done.

Eventually the land would be Dirk's.

He wasn't the laughing type, but he thought the sight warranted a stifled grunt.

"Not supposed to eat it, boy. Don't breathe so deep. Otherwise you'll be coughing it up for days. Just smell it."

Dirk looked at him, and wiped the rim of spit and dirt from around his mouth with his arm.

"Like this?" said Dirk as he held his dirt-filled palm a few inches from his nose and took a slow, deep breath. He didn't choke or eat any this time.

"Like that," said Tubbs. "What do you smell?"

Dirk took another slight sniff, and wrinkled his brows.

"Dirt."

Tubbs took a large pinch of soil from the divot he'd dug, and placed it in Dirk's palm.

"Close and squeeze. Hard as you can."

Dirk squeezed his hand closed. The muscular stress stretched across his small face.

"Don't hurt yourself."

Without having to use his hands, Tubbs took another long drag from his cigarette.

"Now open up your palm. What do you see?"

"A clump."

"What does that tell you?"

"It's wet?"

"Yup. That was from a few inches down. The moisture is by the seeds. Right where we need it. If it just blew away, we'd be in need of rain."

Tubbs grabbed another small handful of soil from a spot next to his knee, and poured it into the palm of Dirk's other hand.

"Squeeze it again."

Dirk repeated the exercise, opened his palm, and the slight breeze blew his palm clean.

"That's the soil at the top where you see things every day, but the seeds aren't there. Never judge just by looking at the surface. You gotta look deeper."

"Where are the seeds?"

"Down there."

Tubbs dug into the ground another few inches until he found what he was looking for; the line of seeds he'd planted two weeks ago. He grabbed another handful and gently brushed away the soil. There were five seeds. Tubbs selected one with his fingers.

"Are they growing?"

Tubbs nodded.

He put one seed in his palm, and moved it so Dirk could see. He let the others fall back into the small trench.

"Starting to sprout."

"Right on time," said Tubbs as he put the seedling into his mouth, bit it in half, and spit both pieces back into his palm. The seed was soft, but not rotted.

"Can you tell what it is?"

"Wheat."

"Sure?"

Tubbs moved his palm closer to his son, and watched him look at the two halves of the sprout. Dirk looked him straight in the eye.

"Yup. That's wheat."

"Not durum?"

"Too short for that."

Tubbs nodded.

Two weeks ago, he'd sown almost eleven thousand pounds of wheat in this particular 80-acre field. The eleven thousand pounds represented more than one hundred and twenty million individual seeds. The seeds were germinating on schedule, and in mid-August he'd be harvesting one hundred and ten million wheat plants that would hopefully yield more than one billion seeds.

It was the life of a farmer.

Tubbs clapped the excess dirt off his hands, brushed them against his bib overalls, and flexed his fingers. His arthritis was bothering him today. His hands were large, worn, and perpetually dirty. His knuckles resembled cauliflower florets and resisted movement, but he didn't make a living with excuses. Calling in sick, and saying "it hurts" was for city boys who worked in offices, sat behind desks, and put sugar, cream, and a squirt of that hazelnut syrup crap in their coffee each morning. If he called in sick, nothing would get done because at this point in his life, he accepted the fact that everything hurt. Tubbs liked his coffee black and wet. He washed his cup with a jolt of whiskey each morning.

"Come on," he said. "Let's go check the barley across the road."

Journal Entry
Of Dirk Kinnear

April 2, 1992

Dear Friend:

You don't know me yet, but my name is Dirk Valoise Kinnear. Everyone calls me Dirt. I know it's a weird middle name. Maybe even a weird first name – my real name, not my nickname. I know that one is definitely weird. But it's my name, and there's not much I can do about it at the moment. Evidently Dirk Valoise was my mother's grandfather's name. He died before I was born. I think he was in one of the World Wars. Probably the second as I don't think he was old enough for the first.

You may be wondering what the story around Dirt is. If you think about it, and once you know the story, it makes sense. It happened back in kindergarten.

Maybe it was first grade. I can't really remember.

My friend, Danny Carlson, misunderstood my name on the first day of school when we were introduced. When his mother came to pick him up, he turned to her and said, "His name is Dirt. He's my new friend." Instead of "His name is Dirk."

It stuck.

The rest is history.

He wasn't really my friend back then, but now we are. We had really just met. Our dads know one another, but we hadn't had much of a chance to get to know one another even though our farms are only a mile from one another. We're neighbors but not like neighbors in town are. You know, the kind who can walk across the driveway, knock on the door, and ask a friend to come out and play.

I don't want to walk a mile to ask Danny to hang out.

So, everyone calls me Dirt now – all because of some kid didn't really know how to distinguish a "K" from a "T." I don't really like it, but it is what it is, I guess. It's just a name and I'm used to it.

So a little bit about me besides how I got my name.

I was born on July 3, 1978. I'm 13 years old now, but will be 14 in a few months. I go to school in Larimore. I'm a Polar Bear. I'm not in any sports, so I guess I'm not a "Polar Bear" really. That's only for the jocks. I couldn't dribble a basketball or throw a football if my life depended on it. Gym is definitely my least favorite class. I'm very uncoordinated and always the last to get picked.

What's my favorite?

English.

I got this idea of writing down my thoughts from my English teacher, Mrs. Beck. She also teaches Spanish, but I'm not taking that. She's cool. I really like her. She told me that I was a good writer, and that I should write all of my thoughts down, and pretend that no one will ever read what I write. That way, she said, "You'll be more honest and talk about things you wouldn't talk to anyone else about."

"Write it like you are talking to yourself in the mirror," she told me.

I must admit that I typically don't talk to myself, and definitely not in front of a mirror, but it was the best advice I've ever received.

She also said to address it to no one in particular. Maybe use, "Dear Friend."

So I am.

That's you I guess – even though you really don't exist.

As I said, Mrs. Beck is one of the best teachers I've ever had. She has really bad arthritis, and when she points at someone, her finger doesn't go in the direction she wants. Some of the other kids laugh behind her back.

She gives me things to read, and she doesn't call me Dirt. She gave me Grapes of Wrath *by John Steinbeck a few weeks ago. I love it. She's said I could take as long as I need to finish it. That it might be a tough read for someone my age.*

I love it.

I have to hide it under my mattress, as my mom wouldn't like the fact that I'm reading something other than the bible. I wouldn't want her to ruin Mrs. Beck's book.

Do you want to know about her? My mother?

Are you sitting down? She's a doozie.

And I think I can tell you this.

I really hate her.

Mother thinks I'm evil, that I poisoned her, and that's why she hasn't been able to have any other kids since I was born. She seems to always have a backache. Plus, she's always wearing the same thing. She's always in her nightgown. A white one with blue and pink flowers. It's really ugly. Honest though, that's all she wears. I think she has ten of them in her closet.

When the pain in her back is really bad, she gets headaches. I know it's "migraines," but the way she says it, the word comes out "My Grains." She makes it sounds like she's looking for a box of Kellogg's or something.

Kellogg's My Grains. Make your morning GRRREAT!

She has some big pills she is supposed to take when her back flares up, but evidently they don't work too well, as I catch the brunt of things when her back is especially bad. She spends most of the time lying on the couch staring at the ceiling and smoking cigarettes. I don't remember a day when her back wasn't *hurting her. I know if my back had to support all of her weight, it would hurt too.*

I don't think her baby issues are my fault.
At least I hope it wasn't.
Sometimes I have to wonder though.

Sincerely,

Dirt

Journal Entry
Of Dirk Kinnear

April 9, 1992

Dear Friend:

I know I just talked to you, but I had to tell you about something. I found an old paper in the back of my closet. It was a drawing I'd made a long time ago. It doesn't have a date, but I'm guessing because of the crayons I used, it was about the time I was in first or second grade. So that makes it around 1986 or 1987. I'm surprised that it was still in the house as mother typically burned or tossed anything I brought home from school. She didn't look at anything I brought home.

I just stopped showing her anything, as I knew for certain nothing was going to be taped to the fridge.

Especially not this drawing!

She would have punished me big-time for this one.

The picture I drew was me with a crucifix above my head and mother standing behind me still in her nightgown and slippers. The crucifix was greenish-blue and it had yellow lightning bolts coming out of it. She was drawn in red and had one of those jagged smiles like a pumpkin. Her eyes and the smile were in black. I drew her with a cigarette in her hand, and it had a red fire coming out of it. I drew myself in orange with a sad face and tears. I also had bumps on my shoulders. I'm guessing those are the burn marks. My tears and the bumps on my back were in black crayon. At the bottom of the picture, kinda slanted downwards to the right, with a turquoise crayon, I wrote:

Why does mommy hate me?

Would I get in trouble if I killed her, chopped her up, and fed her to the pigs? Is that a mean thing to do to the pigs? What if I hit her with one of her bibles, and broke her neck? I hate to admit it, but thinking of her dying makes me feel good inside.

I bet if a psychiatrist saw the picture, he'd probably have a field day and recommend years of psychoanalysis.

For both of us.

Sincerely,

Dirt

June 3, 1993
Arvilla, ND

The Kinnear Fields
Arvilla, ND

*

Dirt glanced at his broken, barely readable, Casio watch that was tied to his wrist with an old shoelace. The symbols on the watch showed that the time was 88:88, so he had to shade the watch with his palm in order to see which areas of the display were darker than the others. The only thing that was readable was the AM/PM indicator, and it told him the obvious: it was morning. After he deciphered the time through the cracked crystal, he determined that it was probably 7:15 in the morning – or somewhat close to it.

He'd already been hard at work for a bit more than two hours with about an hour of that time in the field. He twisted around in the seat of the white, twelve-year-old Case 2290 tractor and looked out of the cracked rear window to see the line the twenty-foot cultivator he was pulling was cutting in the rich, black dirt. It hadn't rained in a few weeks so the cloud of black dust billowing around the cab made it difficult to see his work. He tapped the lever controlling the depth of the cultivator and heard the growl of the tractor's diesel engine deepen at the extra work he'd just given it. He pushed the throttle control to its stop. A black stream of smoke erupted from the exhaust stack, and then cleared as the engine accommodated for the additional fuel he'd just fed it.

"Goin' balls to the wall," he said.

Dirt's vivid imagination had plenty of ideas of what "balls to the wall" meant, but he just couldn't untangle the picture created in his mind with the words. It didn't make physiological sense. Nonetheless, his father said it every time he pushed the throttle forward, so he did too since the first time he was put in the driver's seat of a tractor.

He was eight then.

Dirt swung back to the front, pegged a tree at the other end of the field, turned the steering wheel a quarter inch to the left, and ensured the front of the tractor stayed true to the tree.

It was a trick his father taught him to keep the cut straight.

A trick that worked with words that made sense, and didn't need any untangling.

"Pick a point in front of you and stick to it."

Besides being shown how to turn the tractor on and off, that was the only lesson he ever received. Everything else comprised of getting thrown into the deep end of the pool and figuring out how to find the steps.

"How deep do I go?" he remembered asking.

"You'll know it when you feel it. Just keep the cut straight."

Dirt remembered the slap across the back of his head and the thud of his father's wide knuckle on his temple when he turned the steering wheel too far.

"You're over steering. You numbskull. Look how crooked the cut is now. Looks like a drunk is driving this cocksucker," his father yelled as he put the tractor back in line. "Well, are you?"

"What?"

"Drunk!"

"No, sir."

He remembered wanting to cry, but he knew better and fought against any visible quiver of his lip.

Crying wasn't acceptable.

"Small moves. All you need. See?"

"Yes, sir."

Five minutes later, his father was gone. He was an eight year old alone in a forty-acre field driving several thousand dollars' worth of farm equipment.

Now, fourteen-year-old Dirt, who would be fifteen next month, was very good at what he did. Better than someone with decades of experience as a matter of fact, and definitely better than any other kid his age. Even with his bigger and better equipment, his best friend, Danny, couldn't cut a straight line if his life depended on it.

"You're over-steering, butt-head," he always laughed. "Those sunflower look like they were planted by a drunk!"

Dan never listened, and his typical response was, "So? What's the big deal?"

Tractors, his dad told him, were like women. Little nudges here and there, and they'd listen to you. Eventually. Give them too much attention and they go berserk. Dirt, however, took his father's advice regarding women with a grain of salt. From his point of view, his father's track record was nothing he ever wanted to emulate.

Dirt reached for the Thermos of warm water at his feet, took a long pull, and dried his face with his arm. Even though it was only a bit past seven in the morning, it was already becoming a toaster oven in the tractor's cab and black, dirty sweat was drizzling down his forehead, and dripping off of the tip of his nose. It made sweaty mud on his shirt and pants. The tractor's air conditioner hadn't worked in for as long as he could remember, so all he could do was open the tractors two windows and use was the vent that blew hot, dusty air in his face.

It kept the dirt-infused air moving in three speeds.

As he wiped his face, he could feel the dirt smear against his lips, and could already taste the grit in his mouth – he'd be blowing black snot rockets for days. He missed the radio more than the A/C though. The radio stopped working last year, and his father refused to put in a new one.

"What do you need a radio for? You're supposed to be paying attention to what you are doing, not listening to your music."

Dirt could really use some Metallica or Guns N' Roses right now. But there was only an empty hole where the stereo used to be, so all he had to do while going up and down the forty-acre field was further ponder what "balls to the wall" meant while humming *Welcome to the Jungle*. Dirt wanted to have his own band one day and play rock and roll.

The classics.

All he needed now was a guitar.

Dirt felt his shirt pocket and pressed it against his heart. His small notebook, his security blanket, was there and he could feel the pen against his chest. He'd take a break in an hour or so and write. For now, Dirt's sight-line tree remained dead ahead, and his cut remained straight and true.

June 3, 1993
Arvilla, ND

The Carlson Fields
Arvilla, ND

*

This was Danny's first year of driving the six hundred horsepower, lime green, Steiger Tiger ST470. The four-wheel drive Tiger was a behemoth of a machine. His father had bought it off of the lot two years ago, and, from Dan's point of view, it was the biggest thing he'd ever seen. It took him fifteen minutes to top-off its three-hundred-gallon tank with diesel. Each of its eight wheels was taller than he was, and he needed to use their treads as rungs to even reach the first step of the Tiger's ladder and climb into the cab.

The Tiger wasn't exactly engineered for a fourteen-year-old.

"It's your machine this year, Danny. Take care of her. Treat her like a beautiful woman," his father told him when he took Danny out to his first field to show him how to operate the monster.

"Dad, it's a tractor."

He remembered his dad laughed and pushed the brim of his baseball cap down below his eyes.

"You're young. You'll know what I'm talking about soon enough."

Once inside, Danny imagined that this was exactly what the space shuttle Columbia's looked like from the pilot's perspective. Gauges and dials lined the panel above his head, and the dashboard around the steering wheel was littered with toggle switches. The levers to control speed, power, and the hydraulic systems were lined up to his right. Even his seat had controls and levers to adjust his comfort and height, and despite all of the adjusting he could figure out, he couldn't lower it enough to allow his feet to touch the floor. When he lowered the seat all of the way down, he just created another problem. He couldn't see over the steering wheel to watch where he was driving. His father told him that reaching the floor with his feet would have to wait.

"Seeing where you are going is more important. You'll be fine by next year. I promise. I didn't start growing until I was fifteen."

Dad was always right.

As the entrance to the 80-acre field approached, Danny pulled back on the throttle to slow the 8-wheeled monster, and carefully maneuvered the Tiger and the cultivator into the field. Dan couldn't fully engage the clutch, steer the tractor, and sit at the same time, so when he needed to change gears, he had to stand up, use the entire weight of his fourteen-year-old body to engage the clutch, and then reach over the large steering wheel to maneuver the gear control to another slot. Luckily, when he was in the field, he didn't have to worry about speed to any great extent as the tractor was good in first, maybe second, gear. All he had to do is control the throttle, and the depth of the forty-foot cultivator behind him.

Dan put the Tiger into neutral, pulled back on the primary hydraulic control to release the pressure of the cultivator's wings against their locks, grabbed the small sledge hammer, hopped off of the seat, and climbed down the ladder. He didn't use the treads as rungs on the way down, he just jumped the last three feet and sunk into the black dirt of the field. He felt the dirt sift into his shoes and was sure his feet, despite wearing socks, would be totally black by the time his day was done. The Tiger's Caterpillar engine quietly rumbled above him as Dan adjusted his cap, and walked to the cultivator to remove the pins securing the wings.

Journal Entry
Of Dirk Kinnear

July 1, 1993

Dear Friend:

Tomorrow I'm going fishing! I don't think mother knows I'm going, but Dad actually came through. He surprises me some times. I don't think he really hates me like mother does. He just doesn't care. I'm "manual labor," not necessarily his son. Oh well. I guess Danny's father, Skip, approached Dad about having me come along on the trip. I really like him. He's always nice and I like to watch how he and Danny act. It's amazing to see how a real father and son live. Danny's mom, Sis, is also really nice. She's very pretty. I like Booger's folks too. His dad is an MP at the air force base and his mom is a substitute teacher. I've had her once or twice.

She always says hi to me.

I wish I could live with them.

Either of them.

The fishing trip will be just us guys. Minus my dad, of course. He doesn't do anything social except have a beer at the bar as long as someone else is buying. It will be Dan, Booger, Skip, Buck, and me. I'm so excited. I'm glad Dad won't be there. He doesn't fit in so it would be very awkward. It will be the first time I've ever been fishing. Hell, it will be the first time I've seen a body of water bigger than the old sandpit. Second, I get to be away from HERE! I think, I hope, it's going to be fun.

I'm sure it will be.

It's all Danny and Booger have been talking about since they invited me and I got the green light to join them.

The only thing that concerns me is that I don't know how to swim. I'm a bit afraid as a matter of fact, as the lake is pretty big.

But get this. It really makes me smile when I think about it and I'm sure you will think it's just as ironic.

That woman would have a heart attack if she found out where I will be: Devils Lake. Maybe I should tell her. I can't wait to tell you how it went and how many fish I caught.

Sincerely,

Dirt

July 2, 1993

Devils Lake, ND

*

It was birthday weekend times three and today, specifically, was the day Booker turned fifteen. Tomorrow was Dirt's day. And on July 4th, Dan turned the big one-five. The five men, two dads and three teens, were on Highway 2 heading west from Arvilla through Larimore to Devils Lake where they planned three days of camping, fishing, and frivolity.

The trip of about seventy miles would normally take an hour and a half. With Buck driving, and managing the Ford Explorer as if it were a starship with warp drive, the seventy-mile trek would take no more than an hour.

"Good thing you're a cop," said Skip as he eyed the speedometer. "Eighty-five in a sixty?"

"Wouldn't matter. I don't have jurisdiction off-base," he pointed to a small black box on the dash. "This thing is telling me there's nothing out there. Hasn't chirped since we left the farm. We're good."

"Mom says he likes to pretend it's an F-16, Mr. Carlson," said Booger from the back seat. "Just wait until he has to turn, and switches on the afterburners. Hold on tight."

"That's enough from the back seat, Birthday Boy. What happens in the Explorer, stays in the Explorer."

The three boys, Dirt, Booger, and Danny laughed. They were sitting in the back seat of the Thorson's Ford Explorer. Buck was in the driver's seat piloting, and Skip was busy reading the current issue of Sports Illustrated in the passenger seat and hanging on the best he could.

Behind the boys, stacked in the Explorer's cargo area, were three coolers filled with food and pop that was, according to Danny's mother, enough to "feed you five men for a month." There was a fourth cooler, that neither wife knew about, reserved just for the dads. It contained enough Miller Lite to quench the thirst of a small town. The tents, camp stoves, fishing rods, tackle, and life jackets were all secured in what the Explorer was towing. It was Buck's pride and joy, a Bayliner bowrider.

Skip turned down the radio, put the magazine in his lap, and turned towards the boys.

"You boys are awfully quiet back there. What trouble are you brewing?"

"We're trying to teach Dirt how to play cards."

"Go Fish."

"I can't believe he's never played it before."

"Mom won't let me have cards," said Dirt. "Plus there's no one to play with."

"My dad plays cards with me all of the time," said Danny.

"Mine too," said Booger.

"Not mine."

"Well, having any success?"

"He can't count past five, he can't shuffle without spilling them all over himself, but he'll do fine. Next year. Maybe he'll make it past seven," said Booger.

"Give me a break. You're the one who doesn't know a queen from a king," said Dirt as he snapped Booger's ear with his thumb and middle finger.

"Ow!"

"That's enough guys. We have four days together. Don't kill one another yet. Wait until we've been there a few days, ok? Then you can do whatever you want. For now though, no fighting," ordered Buck with a low growl from the driver's seat.

"Captain Buck has spoken, guys. Listen to him or he'll put you out with a photon torpedo or something from this jet he's piloting."

Booger shoved his elbow into Dirt's side.

"Are you all ready to have fun?" asked Skip a little too enthusiastically.

There was no immediate reply. He just saw each boy look at one another, and then roll their eyes. Danny was the first to break the silence.

"Dad. We're not babies. We're going to be fifteen."

Skip looked at each boy and realized they were growing up.

Fast.

Dirt was already a head taller than the other two.

"You're right, Dan. You're all old men now. You know what that means?"

"What?" said all three boys simultaneously.

"It means you'll all be able to clean your own fish."

Dirt was the first to speak up.

"Clean the fish? What do you mean?"

"All men clean their own fish."

"Clean them? How are they getting dirty? They live in the water?"

"They don't come out of the water as fish sticks, Dirt. They have scales and guts and eyes and, well, everything. You know. Things that don't taste too good on the grill. Things they use in dog food."

Skip used his hand as a knife and demonstrated how to clean a fish.

"Of course, now that you're fifteen, it will be easy. You just take the knife, slice through the gill, turn it, cut down to the tail, turn the knife again, and cut off the skin. Bingo you have a filet."

Skip looked at the amazed look from each face.

"Don't they try to get away?"

"They don't squirm much. You drive a nail through their head to keep them down. And they only squeal a little bit when you do that. Make sure you don't cut their tiny stomachs though."

"What happens if you cut the stomach?"

"You have to eat what's in it. Part of the rules from the government. It says it on the license."

Skip reached into his pocket, and pulled out his fishing license.

"Yup. Right here. Section 5. Paragraph 2. It says if the stomach is inadvertently cut during the cleaning of any fish caught within the confines of North Dakota, said cutter must consume the contents of the fish in question. Right there in black and white, guys," Skip folded the piece of paper and put it back in his pocket. "You gotta be really careful when you're cleaning the fish. Happened to a friend of mine once. He was sick for days. Diarrhea everywhere. Made a big mess."

"What's it taste like?"

"Don't know. I've never cut a fish's stomach before. Come close. But never made a cut. The worst part is the eyes. They look at you when you're cutting them in half. It's like they are trying to talk you out of it with their little fishy eyes."

"I don't think fish squeal, Mr. Carlson."

"That's gross, Dad."

"You really put a nail through their head? I want to see the eyes."

"We'll worry about cleaning the fish later. I think we can appeal to the President or maybe the Secretary of Defense if you are in the Air Force if either of you cut a stomach. We have to catch them first. You guys go back to your card game."

*

Dirt looked at his hand, pulled out his three fives, and laid them down on the makeshift table that was spread across his and Booger's lap.

"No. You need four of a kind in order to lay down. That's three," said Booger.

"You need to ask one of us for a card first though."

Dirt nodded, picked up his cards, put them back into his hand, and held them close to his chest.

"Ok. Do you have any fives?"

Danny and Booger rolled their eyes.

"You have to ask one of us."

"Booger. Do you have any fives?"

"Go fish."

"You should have asked me! I have one."

"Now you have to pick one from the deck."

"What was it?"

"Why do you want to know?"

"If it's a five, you can lay down the set, and take another turn. Otherwise, it's Danny's turn."

"Oh. It was a nine."

Danny grinned.

"Cool. Dirt, do you have any nines?"

"Nope."

"What? You just said you drew a nine."

"I lied."

"Bull. Show us your cards."

Dirt set his cards out on his table, looked up at Danny, and grinned a toothy grin from his wide mouth.

"See. No nines. Three fives, an ace, and a two. Go. Fish."

Danny growled.

"You cock..."

"Daniel! Don't finish that."

"But you say it all of the time."

Skip looked over at Buck, and saw the smirk growing across his face. It was going to be an interesting four days.

If they survived the next seventy miles unscathed.

*

It was dusk, and the rays from the setting sun were creating water diamonds across the top of Devils Lake. Earlier in the day, the wind had made the lake choppy with whitecaps rolling towards the shore. As the sun set, and the air cooled, the lake began to calm and slowly turn to glass. A full moon was rising and already touching the top of the trees on the opposite shore.

Half a mile away from their campsite, Buck was at the controls of his red and white twenty-one foot, Bayliner Classic bowrider. With its I/O 220 horse motor, he could pull all three boys at once on the giant, yellow "Big Bertha" tube and make all of them airborne using a few sharp, whiplash turns without the slightest exertion from the boat. Big Bertha was on the schedule for tomorrow, and probably the day after that, and the day after that. Fishing wasn't what the boys were focused on, especially after Skip's description of having to clean them. After the even more vivid descriptions from Booker of how fast they would go across the water and how high they'd fly, all of the boys were looking forward to it, and now had a singular focus that didn't include walleye, perch, or northern pike. They tried to talk him and Skip into getting Bertha out tonight, but both dads agreed it was too late, too dark, so too dangerous. He and Skip promised to pump up Bertha first thing in the morning after everyone ate some breakfast. The boys were already taking bets on who would be the first to go airborne and land in the lake.

Dirt was the odds on favorite at 70/30.

With the electric trolling motor, and fish finder he'd installed, his Bayliner was also the perfect fishing boat. The walleye couldn't hide when Buck was on the hunt. He'd bought the boat used two years ago with grandiose plans of using it every weekend. That wasn't working out as he'd wanted, as life was only allowing him to get it on the water two or three times a season.

"You never get to use it. Why not sell it?" Winnie would ask at least twice each year when she grew tired of looking at it wrapped in a blue tarp sitting on its trailer in the middle of their yard.

"Hell no," was his standard reply after each request. He didn't want to admit that it was an expensive toy that he should have waited a few more years before purchasing.

Maybe when he retired, he'd live the dream. Until then, he'd get out on the water whenever he could.

Buck stood up and stretched. He kept his right hand on the trolling motor's small throttle, and his right knee on the captain's chair. He didn't bother steering too much as they were barely moving across the water.

"How you doing over there, Skip?" said Buck as he pointed his elbow towards the special cooler.

"Just fine. Don't you think we should turn the lights on?"

"Nah. Can you throw me one? There's no traffic out here so we're good. The lights would scare the fish anyway."

"Dad says they don't like shadows in the water and the lights make shadows."

"Shadows?" said Skip with a perked eyebrow towards Buck.

"Oh. Yeah. You know. They don't like shadows."

Skip tossed a beer; Buck caught it single-handedly, and popped it open.

"You want to take a break, Buck? I can drive for a while."

"Hell no. I know where the fish are. And you boys have to catch something before we head in."

Buck took a couple gulps out of the can, then did a double-take as he looked towards the back of the boat where the three boys were fishing.

"Hey, Dirt. Where's your life vest? You gotta get that on, corporal."

*

Bradley Rostbach was hot-rodding his Kawasaki Jet Ski across the glassy waters of Devils Lake, with his girlfriend Emily holding on tight behind him. He could feel her tits against his back, and found that if he quickly changed speeds, she had to hold on even tighter to stay on board, and press her chest even harder against his back. From what he could feel, she was cold. Bradley may have been able to control the speed, but he was having trouble controlling his crotch, and at nineteen he knew it was an effort in futility. He gave up trying to hide anything a while ago. At first, he tried to keep things under control by thinking of nuns and English bulldogs, but his imagination kept morphing into a teddy-clad cheerleader holding a golden retriever puppy. There was only one remedy, and he had plans of dealing with that later, if he got her drunk enough.

"Here, finish this off," he yelled back as he took the can of beer from between his legs, and passed it back to Emily.

Emily took the can, and pressed it against his back.

"Fuck! That's cold!"

With one hand, Bradley reached into the ski's side pocket, pulled out another beer, popped it open, and gulped half of it down.

He'd lost the precise count a while ago, but he thought this was his seventh or eighth.

It was no big deal, he wasn't feeling anything yet. It typically took at least ten before things started to get blurry. Seven just made him horny. Beers eight and nine created the situation he was in now.

"I'll head over to the rocks. By the power lines," he said as he pointed in front of him with his beer hand.

Emily replied with a nuzzle against his neck.

Bradley smiled.

He'd be able to park the Jet Ski by the rocks, and convince Emily take care of that problem between his legs after all. With his luck, the nuns and bulldogs would kick in and kill everything.

"Want another beer?"

*

Buck was astounded.

He wasn't mad, and he definitely didn't intend to be too gruff, but Dirt looked like he was on the verge of tears. The boy was clearly scared to death that he was in trouble. It was such a small thing, he was only fifteen, but the kid looked as if the world was about to end, and he was going to be beaten to a mere inch of his life.

"I don't have one, Mr. Thorson."

Buck thought he saw Dirt shaking, and he wouldn't look him in the eye. Buck was a big guy with a big, booming voice to match. He knew he could be intimidating – especially to a kid – so he kept the tone of his voice, and its volume as unintimidating as possible.

"Didn't you grab one when we left shore? I'm sure I gave you one."

Dirt kept his gaze on his feet, and shook his head.

"I had it. I think I left it by the tent. I'm sorry, Mr. Thorson."

"What a dumb ass!" said Booger.

"Book," said Buck as he looked over at his son. "Pay attention to your line, and mind your own business."

Buck turned his attention back to Dirt.

"You can call me Buck, ok? It's just us guys out here. None of this mister stuff."

Buck knew the kid had it hard, and wasn't going to make a huge deal of it. He wanted all three kids to have fun this weekend, and it was too early to have things go downhill. He'd heard about the cigarette burns. He'd heard stories about Trude. And he knew Tubbs.

The kid didn't have an easy home life.

Buck had a hard time believing it could be true, but hell, the kid was afraid to take his shirt off.

"It's no big deal, corporal. Here, take mine. You'll need to adjust the straps though, I'm a lot bigger than you," said Buck as he unsnapped his life vest and tossed it over to Dirt. "Just pull the straps to tighten it."

"You are one skinny, corporal, Dirk."

That made the boy smile.

When Buck saw that Dirt had the vest on, and had pulled the straps as tight as they'd go, he turned his attention back to the matter at hand.

Fishing.

Or, in their case, the lack thereof.

Buck took another gulp of beer.

"Guys! Come on! It's getting dark, and we need to catch some fish. We can't go back to shore skunked."

"Hey Dad, let's head over to those rocks. You know, where the power lines are? We always catch some over there."

"Good idea, Book. Good idea."

Buck tapped the throttle a bit, tweaked the steering wheel, and pointed the bow towards the high-tension poles.

“Do you think Walter is there?” asked Booger.

“Who’s Walter?” asked Dirt and Dan.

“Walter. The One-Eyed, One-Ton Walleye. Yes, he’s there and waiting just for us. I can feel it.”

*

“Faster!” yelled Emily above the howl of the Jet Ski. “I want to go faster!”

The sun was down, and the sky was quickly darkening. Even though Bradley could barely see the lights of small campsites along the shoreline, he was more than happy to oblige. He’d grown up on the lake and knew its shoreline by heart.

“Hang on!”

Bradley pressed the throttle to the hilt, and started another loop around the small island of rocks created for the high-tension line poles.

*

“Dad! Dad! I got one! I got one,” yelled Danny as his pole bent towards the water. His line started whirring as a fish starting pulling it out. “What do I do?”

"Hang on. I'll be right there. Don't pull it too hard, you might break the line. Go slow. You don't want it to drop the hook either."

Skip looked over at the others. Booker was concentrating on his line. Dirt seemed totally amazed at what Danny was doing, and had left his line unattended. Buck was still standing at the controls with a beer in his hand, and also watching the excitement at the back of the boat.

"Buck, where's the net? This could be that Walter you were talking about."

"Book. Get Skip the net would ya? It's in the side well. Skip let me know if you need help."

"But Dad, I felt something on my line too. I don't want to lose it. It's Walter. I know it is."

"That's ok. I see it," said Skip. "Hang on Dan. Let me reel mine in. I'll be right there. Just keep doing what you are doing. Slow moves. Let it take your line."

Skip finished reeling in his line, put his pole on the deck, and reached down for the net.

"Oh fuck," yelled Buck. "They're coming straight towards us."

Skip had the net in his hand, and looked to where Buck was staring.

"Boys! Jump. Get off the boat. Head to the rocks. Fast!"

*

Bradley kept the throttle pressed against the stop, and kept the Jet Ski headed straight for the pile of rocks he knew was there. He could see the red beacon lights at the top of the poles that told airplanes the poles where there. When he followed the shadow down, he could make out the rocks. His left hand was getting tired of holding down the throttle, but the anticipation of what lay ahead kept the blood flowing.

Everywhere.

Emily said she wanted fast.

She was getting it.

“This fast enough?” he said, as he turned a bit, and handed Emily another beer. “Here. Finish this one off.”

Emily wasn’t paying attention to him or the beer headed in her direction. Instead, she was yelling something incomprehensible, and pointing straight ahead.

“What?”

Bradley turned around, and saw what Emily was focused on.

The words “Bayliner Classic” were two feet from his face.

*

Unless it was to the sandy bottom of Devils Lake, Buck knew he and the boat were going nowhere fast.

The small prop of the trolling motor was the only thing moving the twenty-one foot fiberglass Bayliner, and he knew there was no way in hell his boat would get out of the way as fast as he needed it to. No matter how hard he twisted its throttle, the electric trolling motor just didn't have the power to move any faster. To get out of the way, he'd have to lower the boat's main prop, start the engine, and hammer the throttle down.

"Get out! Everyone. Just. Get. Out!"

Physics and time were not in his favor at the moment.

"Now!"

There was nothing else he could do.

Buck felt the Jet Ski slam into the starboard side of the Bayliner, and tear through the fiberglass next to his captain's chair. The point of the Jet Ski's streamlined body connected with his chest, pushed him across deck of his boat, and through its port side. He saw just a glimmer of the two human shapes that were on the Jet Ski, fly over his head. He felt his body become engulfed by water, and his lungs begin to burn. He could hear the faint buzz of the trolling motor's prop, but as the water pressure increased as he descended deeper and deeper, the sound disappeared. Buck wished he had another beer, and hoped Skip and the boys made it to the rocks before the Jet Ski hit.

*

Booger didn't make it to the rocks. He jumped into the water on the other side of the boat when his father yelled; he sank a few feet, and then bobbed to the surface thanks to the jacket he was wearing. Once he surfaced, he grabbed the rail on the port side of the boat, and worked his way around the bow to where his father had been sitting when the Jet Ski hit; his captain's chair.

"Dad! Dad! Where are you?"

He could hear Skip yelling for him, but ignored his calls. He could even see Skip, Dirt, and Danny sitting together on the rocks, but he couldn't go where they were. He had to find his father before he did anything. He had to be around here somewhere.

"Dad! Dad!"

"Book."

Booker looked towards the boat's stern.

"Dad!" he yelled again.

"Book. Over here. Stern side."

The sound was almost imperceptible, but Booger knew it was his father. No one else called him "Book" besides his mom and dad. And his mother was at home enjoying the peace and quiet without a husband and son horsing around the house.

The sound was coming from the boat's stern.

Booger held on to the boat's side rail, and worked his way around to where his father's voice seemed to be coming from. The boat was taking on water and listing to the port so as he made his way around the starboard side, it became harder and harder as that side of the boat was a bit higher.

"Dad!"

"Book. Back here."

It was definitely his father.

"Dad, I'm coming."

When Booger reached the stern, he saw his father hanging on to the engine cowling. The engine was still idling, but was in neutral, so the prop wasn't engaged. The water was churning from the engine's exhaust, and made the water look as if it were boiling. The trolling motor wasn't where it used to be, so Booger figured it had been ripped off, and was likely at the bottom of Devils Lake.

The full moon provided enough light, so Booger could see his father. He was struggling to hang on to the cowling. Blood was pouring from an open gash in his forehead, and even though the impact was only minutes before, his father's left eye was swollen and barely open. The worst injury though was his right arm. That's where the Jet Ski must have hit him. It was gone. His father was hanging onto the boat with only his left arm.

"Crawl inside. My seat, Book. The cushion. It floats. I need it, Book."

Booger had forgotten that his father had given Dirt his life vest. Evidently he didn't have time to grab the cushion before being hit and thrown. Booger pulled the small ladder down, and climbed into the boat as fast as he could. Normally the ladder he used would be used to climb in after spending a day on the tube.

Now he had to use it to save his father's life.

He knew exactly what his father was asking for, crawled as fast as he could to the captain's seat, and ripped the cushion off. It made a tearing sound as he separated itself from one-half of its Velcro pair.

"Got it Dad. I got it," yelled Booger as he headed back to his father.

"Book! Watch out!"

"I'm coming Dad."

Booger saw his Dad's eyes grow wide. He didn't understand why his father was reacting the way he was.

Then he heard the click.

Booger realized exactly what had happened, and what his father was trying to tell him.

It was too late.

He heard the click, and ka-thunk as the transmission engaged the propeller.

The cushion's strap was tangled around the throttle. The strap that his father was supposed to be able to hang on to, and keep floating. The strap that was supposed to save his life. As Booger rushed to his father, he pulled the throttle to its stop, put the boat's engine at full RPM, and engaged the propeller. There was nowhere for the boat to go though. It was already stranded on the rocks.

Booger saw everything.

He saw his father sink into the water with his one arm flailing; trying to grasp the ladder that his son had just used to get onto the boat.

Even in the moonlight, Booger saw the water of Devils Lake churn red with the blood of his father.

*

It was seven in the morning. Half of the sun had made its way over the lake's eastern tree line, and the blinding glare off of the water was making it hard to keep track of everything going on at the accident site. The police had left an hour ago after talking more with Skip and the three boys.

"How much beer did he have?"

"Two."

"Was he going fast?"

"Us or the bastard on the Jet Ski?"

"You."

"No. Using the trolling motor."

"And you told everyone to jump?"

"I knew it was going to hit us. Saw it coming."

The police asked the same questions to Skip and each of the boys. All of the stories all seemed to match.

A couple of drunken teens on a Jet Ski collided with a red and white twenty-one foot, Bayliner Classic bowrider.

Case closed.

The police were on the scene within an hour of the accident, and had carried away the three bodies by two in the morning. Skip saw the faces of the guys who pulled the bodies of the Jet Ski riders.

One of them puked in the lake.

No one had slept in more than twenty-four hours, and everyone's eyes were telling the same, exhausted story.

Winnie, Skip, and Sis sat at picnic table by the campsite. Skip noticed that Winnie, who had her arms wrapped around Booker, and periodically drying her tears in his hair, was a seesaw of emotion. At times she was stoic and unemotional. She talked about what needed to be done. The funeral. Packing Buck's clothing. Being a single mother. Then, with a quick flip, she'd be inconsolable. Sobbing and barely able to catch her breath as she expressed how she couldn't believe that her husband was gone.

Skip shielded his eyes from the sun with the palm of his hand, and looked across the lake towards a floating crane.

"I can barely make it out, but it looks like they are getting Buck's boat off of the rocks."

"The police said they'd be doing that. They asked me if I wanted it delivered to the farm."

"They can bring it over to our place, Winnie."

"No. That was Buck's pride and joy. We'll figure something out," said Winnie as she squeezed Booker. "Won't we Book. We'll figure things out."

"Did anyone try to call Tubbs? Tell him what's going on?"

"Dad doesn't have a cell phone, Mr. Carlson. Mom doesn't answer the phone."

"I guess that answers that," said Sis.

Skip looked at his watch. It was approaching 7:30.

"We should probably head home. Everything is already packed."

"Mom, can Dirt and Danny ride back with us?"

Winnie looked at Skip and Sis.

Both nodded.

"They'll keep you company on the drive home, Winnie. We'll follow you, and take Dirk home."

"Why don't I drive the Explorer, Winnie. You, the boys, and me. Skip can follow us."

*

Booger, Danny, and Dirt sat in the same seats, and in the same order as the trip to the lake. It was a lot quieter on the trip home. Instead of Skip and Buck in the front, it was Sis and Winnie.

Moms instead of dads.

Dirt sat between Booger and Danny. He had his arms wrapped around his entire body.

He felt cold.

Guilty.

Out of the corner of his eye, Dirt saw Danny's mom turn around and survey the three boys in the back seat.

"Dirk?"

Dirt slowly looked up at Danny's mom. He was sure he was going to get into trouble. The shoe was going to drop, and he'd be blamed for everything.

"Honey. Are you ok? Would you like a bottle of water?"

He'd never been called honey before.

Maybe he wasn't going to be blamed after all.

"No thanks."

Dirt relaxed his arms a bit, looked back down at the floor, and studied the white Ford logo in the middle of the rubber mat.

Journal Entry
Of Dirk Kinnear

July 3, 1993

Dear Friend:

Today I turn 15, and I really don't know if I want to live another day. What was supposed to be a fun weekend turned into a horrible nightmare.

I feel so bad, and I don't know what to do or say.

Booker's dad is dead.

He's dead because of me. For no other reason than my stupidity.

I didn't have a life jacket on. I don't know how to swim so he gave me his jacket. And paid for it. When that Jet Ski slammed into the boat, Booger's dad was right there. I saw it hit him. He saved us all. Told us all to jump. But he didn't have time to do anything. I saw him go under, and then we couldn't find him after that. We yelled and yelled for him. They found him eventually. He was all bloated, and he was really cut up from all of the jagged rocks. He was missing an arm.

I wish it had been me.

I don't blame Booger if he never wants to see me again.

His dad is dead because of me.

And his dad loved him. He actually enjoyed doing things with him. During that trip, I actually saw what it was like to have a dad who enjoyed the company of his son.

Skip and Danny.

Buck and Booger.

I was so jealous that I would never have what they have.

Had.

Now Buck is gone. Booger is like me now, kinda.

His mother called me Honey. Her voice was so sweet and gentle. Nothing like my mother's voice.

Maybe everything mother has been saying all of this time is true.

Maybe I am evil.

I should have killed myself when I first thought of it.

Today I really feel like my name.

Happy birthday to me.

Fuck that and everything else.

Sincerely,

Dirt

July 7, 1993

Larimore, ND

*

The weekend had been a total bust, his birthday was all but forgotten with all of the commotion, his family didn't go to a single 4th of July picnic, and now he was at a funeral on a hot July day.

Even though the sky was overcast, it was still muggy. It was hard to breathe the thick air, and Danny could feel the sweat running down his back and chest. Danny wanted to be any place on Earth other than in the second row of folding chairs looking at a flag-draped casket that contained the mangled corpse of his friend's father.

Danny sat with his parents behind Wendy, Booger, Booger's grandparents, his aunts, and uncles. Everyone was dressed in his or her best black dress or black suit. Buck's casket was directly in front, unopened, draped in a flag, and surrounded by four white-gloved soldiers in full military attire. Having retired from the Air Force after serving twenty-five years, Wendy wanted to make sure there was an honor guard. Wendy had a big pair of sunglasses on that covered her entire face. All of the women in the front row, except Wendy, were crying, but Danny could tell when he saw her without the glasses that she had been.

The men were being men. Stoic. Yet, when Danny really paid close attention and studied their faces, he could see the corners of their mouths quiver when the priest spoke about Buck, his legacy, and everyone he left behind.

Booger was different.

While the older men were stoic, trying to hold their emotions at bay, Danny didn't see any emotion at all behind his eyes.

There was nothing to hold back.

He was lifeless.

His mom and dad told him that he was probably still in shock.

Booger didn't acknowledge Danny when he walked by. Booger didn't even hug his grandmother when she sat next to him and they were very close. Danny watched Booger recoil when she took his hand, and tried to hold it with hers.

Danny looked around at all of the people, hoping to see Dirt somewhere in the crowd, but he wasn't there.

At least Danny couldn't see him.

He really didn't think he'd show up anyway.

When the priest concluded the short mass, the soldiers assembled around the casket, took the draped flag, and precisely folded it into a small triangle. One solder saluted the others, walked to Wendy, and presented her with the flag.

Danny heard her mumble a “thank you” when she took it in her hands.

The soldiers raised their rifles and fired several volleys in rapid succession. The ceremony ended when the one soldier who didn’t have a rifle, began to play Taps.

*

Booger and Danny sat on the porch while all of the adults mingled inside and tried to hide how uncomfortable they were. They all nibbled on homemade buns with roast beef, spooned tuna casserole onto small plates, and left everything uneaten in the kitchen before they gave Wendy a hug and tried to leave without causing a stir. Danny could hear them talking every now and then when the screen door was open far enough.

“I heard he would have lived if he had a life vest on.”

“Why didn’t he have one?”

“I heard he gave it to one of the boys.”

“Probably that Kinnear kid. I hear he had it. He’s always been trouble.”

Danny really wanted to go scream at all of them. Yell at the top of his lungs.

"It's not his fault!"

But he didn't.

"I think you're going to have a lot of leftover tuna casserole."

"I hate tuna casserole."

Booger surprised Dan when he laughed, smiled, and repeated even louder.

"I hate fucking tuna casserole!"

"Shhh," said Dan. "They'll hear you."

"Who the fuck cares. Wanna go hang out in the barn? Get outta here?"

Danny looked at his friend.

An hour ago, Booger looked more like a department store mannequin. Now he wanted to go hang out in their barn, and was yelling about how much he hated tuna casserole.

"Maybe we could ride our bikes over to Dirt's?"

"Don't have my bike."

"We'll double-decker on mine to your place. You ride on the handlebars; it's only a mile. Then go to Dirt's from there. Come on! It'll be fun."

"I need to change clothes."

"You can wear some of mine. Close enough."

"But shouldn't you stay here with your mom? You know. The funeral and all?"

"Fuck that," said Booger as he ran to his bike. "Come on. Let's blow this peanut factory."

January 13, 1995
8:30 PM

The Ice Cream Shoppe
Larimore, ND

*

The three sophomores sat in the corner booth at the Ice Cream Shoppe. Danny and Booger had walked over from the high school after having watched the varsity Polar Bear's boys' basketball team totally embarrass the Hatton Thunder. It was a blowout with the Bears scoring 56 points to the Thunder's 12. Now there was talk of the Bears heading all of the way to State this year. Dirt was already waiting for them when they came in, had saved a booth, and was already eating what looked like a triple-decker burger.

Danny was in the middle of the bench facing the door, and despite it being only ten degrees and snowing outside, had decided on eating ice cream. He was nervously picking at the whipping cream on the top of his hot fudge sundae. Booger and Dirt were sitting together on the opposite bench trying to keep Danny from going insane as he impatiently waited for the events to start. If everything happened the way he was hoping it would, tonight was the night he was going to make his move.

He wasn't going to propose.

He wasn't going to sing or dance.

He just wanted to say three simple words, "Hi. I'm Danny," and hope she didn't start to laugh or just completely ignore him.

The girl that had Danny so enthralled was only a freshman, but he didn't care. Carolina Holmes had caught his attention the moment he saw her walk down the center isle of the school bus. At the time, Danny was in the eighth grade, and she was in the seventh.

Now they were in high school.

He'd caught her eye and actually smiled at her once while walking between classes.

He was positive she'd smiled back.

That or it was a grimace.

He remembered his stomach had performed a series of acrobatics, and his face flushed with that slight, quick display of teeth.

But they were such beautiful teeth.

Danny knew that her father was stationed at the Grand Forks Air Force Base, and flew B-52s. And, according to sources, they had lived in Germany before coming to North Dakota. Someplace in Japan before that.

"Do you think she's coming? You heard she'd be here, right?"

"That's what I heard."

"Do you think she'll talk to me?"

Booger shrugged.

"Don't know. Don't see why not."

"Probably kick you in the nuts, if you ask me," said Dirt.

"I didn't ask you."

Danny tried to change the subject, and talk about something other than his anxiety. If he didn't calm down, he might pass out at her feet before he got a chance to even utter the first of his three introductory words.

"Dirt. Why didn't you come to the game?"

"Not much for basketball. You know that."

"Or football or anything," added Booger.

Dirt shrugged, and slid out from his seat.

"I'm gonna get some more fries. Want anything?"

Booger shoved a couple of singles towards Dirt.

"Yeah. Fries. None of that cheese stuff though."

"Danny?"

"I'm good," said Danny as he drilled his red plastic spoon into his ice cream. "You said she'd be here, right?"

"Dude. You've asked me that six times now. Chill for fuck sake. I heard Kristie and Carolina talking in study hall.

Said they were going to hang out after the game, and they might stop by here. That's all I know. Ok?"

"Now it's 'might?' But before the game, you said they 'would.'"

"No I didn't."

Danny exhaled, and nervously clenched his hands into fists.

"My dad will be here in an hour to pick us up. There's not much time."

"Dude. Look. I think your wish has been granted," said Booger as he pointed towards the window as a car pulled up.

Three girls got out of the back seat of a Volvo station wagon. The blowing snow glowed in its headlights. The girl wearing a white coat and a red stocking cap, waved to the man sitting behind the wheel.

Carolina Holmes.

Danny thought she looked practically angelic standing in the blowing snow in front of the glow of the headlights.

"That's her. That's her."

"Down boy. Jeez! Calm down!"

Dirt returned holding a tray with two red and white paper baskets of fries. He slid one over to Booger, and kept the tray in front of him with his paper basket of fries. Dirt took a handful of fries from his basket, dipped them in a small container of cheese goo that he loved, and stuffed them into his mouth.

"I think she's here," said Dirt as a pulverized mixture of cheese goo and fries fell from his mouth.

"Man! That's so gross."

Dirt scooped up the blob of orange fry mixture, and popped it back into his mouth.

"What should I do?"

Booger and Dirt looked at one another, and then shook their heads in unison.

"You have got to be kiddin'," said Dirt.

"You are such a pussy," said Booger.

Danny ducked as Dirt threw a cheese-tipped fry at him.

"Ok. Ok. I'm going."

Danny swallowed another spoonful of his sundae, and slid out from the booth.

Danny stopped and turned back to his friends.

"What!" they both said. "Get out of here!"

Booger tried to shoo him away.

"Just go, would ya!"

"But."

"No buts. Just go," interrupted Booger.

Danny smiled, and wiggled his finger at his two friends.

"One of you should move to the other side. Where I was sitting," said Dan. "People will think you're gay or something sitting by yourselves all close and cuddly like that."

Booger and Dirt looked at one another.

Dirt shoved another half-dozen cheese fries into his mouth, and shuffled to the booth's now vacant bench.

*

The three girls walked into the shop, stomped the snow off of their sneakers, and then headed for the counter. Carolina Holmes, who everyone called Lina, unzipped her coat, took off her stocking cap, and stuffed it into her pocket. The static it left behind caused strands of her light brown hair to float and dance above her head. She cut her eyes over to the booth where she saw Danny Carlson sitting when she got out of the car. He was there when she walked in, but now he was gone.

She felt her heart sink.

"Hi Lina. What can I get you?"

Lina turned her attention to the girl behind the counter.

"What?"

"Do you want anything?"

"Oh. Um," Lina looked up at the menu. Her attention was elsewhere, and she let her disappointment veto her desire for ice cream.

She'd missed him.

"Nah. Maybe later."

"What's wrong?" asked one of the girls of the trio who was also at the counter. "You were so eager to get here."

"Nothing's wrong. Not hungry anymore. I'm gonna go sit."

Lina shoved her hands in her pockets, and turned around. She'd intended on heading to the booth, but stopped before she moved a single footstep.

It was him.

She hadn't missed him after all.

Danny Carlson was right in front of her.

"Oh. Excuse me."

He was staring at her, and didn't move out of her way. She noticed that despite his mouth being open, he had incredibly dark, brown eyes that matched his hair.

She could see her reflection in his pupils.

Her mouth was open too.

She thought she looked like a troll, and quickly closed it.

"Excuse me," she repeated as she tried to walk around him.

"Hi. I'm Danny."

Lina pushed her hands deeper into her pockets, but stopped and looked straight at him.

"Yeah. I know.

"Wanna have a sundae with me?"

Lina wasn't sure how to respond. Yes, she was excited when she saw him, but she was here with her friends. Lina looked over at the girl sitting at the booth she'd saved for them, then over to the other girl standing next to her at the counter.

"Uh. I'm here with my friends."

"She'd love to," said the girl at the counter.

"What?" said Danny.

"I said, she'd love to."

Lina turned back to Danny, shrugged, and smiled. She didn't want to be too obvious.

"Sure. I suppose."

Lina focused on Danny's face, squinted, and then giggled.

"What's wrong? What's so funny?"

"I think you have some hot fudge on your nose."

January 21, 1995

The Forx MegaPlex
Grand Forks, ND

*

Danny could hardly breathe.

He was so nervous, he was positive he could feel his chest quiver when he exhaled. He could feel the sweat crawling down his neck, and the dampness growing in each of his armpits. He thought about taking his coat off, but he was too embarrassed to display the growing sweat stains.

He did unzip it at least.

He wanted his hands free and clear, so he took off his gloves, and stuffed them in his coat pockets.

And his stocking cap.

That came off right after the gloves.

His dilemma was simple.

Should he ask permission, or just do it?

Should he hold her hand?

Would she slap his hand away, or let things happen?

Danny felt cold droplets of sweat cascade down his arms.

He shivered.

*

"What time is the movie?"

"6:00."

"And what movie is it?"

"*Dumb and Dumber*. A comedy. Jim Carrey's in it. You like him, Daddy. You always laugh."

"And who are you going with?"

"Danny Carlson from school."

"What grade is he in?"

"He's a sophomore."

"Don't you think he's kinda old? You're only a freshman. Why is a sophomore asking a freshman to a movie?"

That's how the day started for Lina after she hung up from talking to Danny. If it weren't for her mother intervening, she would have never made it. She understood that he was in the military, and that she was his only child, but she was fifteen after all.

"Daddy. I like him."

"What do you mean by that?"

Lina couldn't back-pedal fast enough, but her mother came to the rescue, and stopped the inquisition.

"Frank. She'll be ok. I know Danny's parents. They're good people. I'm sure he is too."

"I don't know. He's older than she is," he looked at his wife. "I know how boys can be. What they're thinking of day-in. Day-out."

Lina watched wordlessly as her father looked back at her, then at her mother.

"I want you home by ten. Understood?"

"Thank you, Daddy!"

Lina wrapped her arms around her dad's neck, and looked up at her mother who winked at her.

Now she was sitting next to Danny in the middle of the theater with a medium Coke in her cup rest. They were sharing a large bucket of buttered popcorn. Lina was enjoying the movie, but her attention was elsewhere.

Out of the corner of her eye, she saw him reach into the bucket.

She reached in too.

"Oh. Sorry," he said as he pulled out his hand, and let Lina grab a greasy handful of popcorn.

Lina slowly, and as imperceptibly as possible, shook her head and looked up at the ceiling.

She'd done that on purpose.

*

Danny wasn't sure.

Did she do that on purpose?

Did she reach into the popcorn bucket at the same time to send him a signal that it was ok to hold her hand?

He thought he was about to hyperventilate.

Then he'd pass out, spill all of the popcorn in her lap, and hit his head on the seat in front of him.

He didn't want that.

Very bad first impression.

It was his first date.

Ever.

He'd never been so stressed.

He wasn't sure what the rules were.

"Be a gentleman," his mother had told him.

His father wiggled his eyebrows at him, and slipped him two twenties as he walked out the door.

"Is she cute?"

"Skip!"

"Well, is she?"

"I guess so. Yes."

"You men," growled his mother.

Parents sent very contradictory signals in his opinion.

He was the quarterback of the JV football team, yet he couldn't decide whether to hold his date's hand or not.

He heard Booger's voice in his head.

"Pussy."

Then he heard Dirt's.

"Go for it."

Then he saw his father's eyebrows wiggle at him, and then flash his toothy smile under his cheesy mustache.

Then he heard his mother telling him to be a gentleman.

Danny cut his eyes over to Lina. She was watching the screen. Her right hand was on her Coke. Her left hand was on their shared armrest.

Danny took a deep breath, and made his move.

He slowly moved his hand over to reach for the popcorn then went in for the kill.

He took her hand.

She held his back.

She didn't pull it back.

She didn't yell.

She didn't call for security as she made her way out of the theater.

"'Bout time," was all she said.

His face was immediately warm, and he felt his heart beating out of his chest.

She liked him too.

Danny smiled.

And wanted to puke.

Journal Entry
Of Dirk Kinnear

August 22, 1996

Dear Friend:

It's getting weird calling you just "friend." So I thought of a name for you. How about Sam? Sam is a good name, isn't it? It's not male and it's not female. You are just you.

From now on, you are Sam.

But on to more important things...

I can't believe I've been writing to you for four years now.

It's been so nice to have someone to talk to.

Today was the first day of my senior year in high school. Dan, Booger, and I have a few classes together this year. We are in Mrs. Erikson's biology class. Mr. Vogel's history class. And Ms. Kingston's social studies class. Basically second, third, and fifth periods. We don't have lunch together. Dan and Booger go to the first lunch: 4a. I'm in the last group: 4c. I'm glad we at least have the classes together that we do.

They're my best, and only, friends.

Mrs. Erickson stood next to me and put her hand on my shoulder. It scared me and I squealed because that's what mom does before she puts her cigarette out on my neck. Everyone laughed. I turned really red. Mrs. Erikson said she was sorry for scaring me. The only bad thing is that Vince Grier and Kip Smith are in her class too. I really hate them. They are jocks and since I'm not a jock, I'm basically sub-human to them. Even the teachers treat them differently.

They miss tests, and no one says a word.

They're constantly picking on me.

Vince walked by my desk in history class, and pushed my books onto the floor. Kip was right behind him, and he kicked them further and they slid to the other side of the room. They both said they were "oh so sorry," but I knew better – it was too planned. The bell hadn't rung yet so Mr. Vogel hadn't arrived. Danny got up, and pushed Vince into a row of empty desks. He told him to grow up. I think Kip was going to try something, but Danny turned around before he had a chance. Danny told them to pick up my books. I think Kip was going to wet his pants. Danny is the quarterback for the football team. Vince and Kip are on it too so they know better than to mess with Danny. He's kinda like a Pharaoh as the team and school treat him like a God. The bad thing is that both Vince and Kip looked at me when class was over. I could read Vince's lips. He said, "Fuck you, Kinnear." Kip looked at me, started rubbing his eyes like a baby, and then bumped me into the row of desks.

I wanted to run away. It's been the same now for eleven straight years, and it doesn't appear that the last year will be much different.

But enough about school.

We started harvest last weekend.

I love the smell, plus harvest has a sense of accomplishment to it. I remember planting most everything, and now we get to see what it all became.

Sincerely,

Dirt

August 26, 1996

Arvilla, ND

*

The colors on the farm are vivid and ever-changing. At the beginning of the year, the fields are a simple black. Within a few weeks after planting, a carpet of deep green begins to take hold as the seeds of wheat, durum, oats and barley begin to sprout, and break the surface. Throughout the summer, the green grows deeper until the carpet begins to ripen. When the wind blows, the oceans of deep green undulate, as their stalks grow stronger and taller. As summer moves to fall, the fields become a gradient of greens and golds until the green is completely enveloped by seas of gold.

*

Dirt's favorite season is fall, and harvest is his favorite time on the farm. To Dirt, harvest provides a sense of accomplishment, after months of toil and anticipation. Farming is a gamble, his father always told him. It's Russian Roulette in the dirt.

The one thing Dirt doesn't look forward to during this time of year, is harvesting barley. Barley is typically the first, but always the worst. Dirt learned his lesson years ago when he made the mistake of taking off his t-shirt. It was ninety degrees and muggy, so he didn't see the harm. It was too hot for clothing. If he could have, he would have stripped to his boxers.

"You're gonna scratch your damn skin off, boy. I'd put that shirt back on if I were you."

His father was wearing a long sleeve shirt with sweat stains that reached his cuffs.

Dirt didn't listen, but he never did take his shirt off during barley harvest again. No matter how hot or muggy it was outside, he kept his shirt on. Typically he wore something baggy with extra-long sleeves.

He didn't want any exposed skin.

He scratched for days that year as the chopped, porcupine beards from the barley stalks made their way onto his sweaty skin and stuck. He couldn't move without forcing them deeper into his skin, and no matter how many showers he took, he could never wash all of them off.

"Dumb ass. Told you to keep your shirt on."

That was years ago when Dirt was only allowed to sit in the truck, and move it from place-to-place in the field.

He'd been managing the entire harvest since he was fifteen.

Since 1993.

His father rarely worked on the farm any more. His constant combination of beer and whiskey made it dangerous for all involved. So these days, he sat on his metal folding chair in his workshop, and told Dirt what needed to be done. Do this. Do that. Not that, you dumb ass.

Dirt didn't need direction.

He was managing a 2,000-acre farm on his own.

Not bad for a seventeen-year-old.

October 11, 1996

Larimore High School
Larimore, ND

*

Homecoming at Larimore High School is a yearly testosterone-filled exposition that brings the entire town out to the football field to drink hot cocoa, eat hot dogs, munch on salty popcorn, and commiserate about the year's harvest. Dirt always thought it was ironic that the football field was not by the high school, but by the elementary school. What makes things even worse, in his opinion, is that he has to explain why it was a perfect example of irony.

Dirt wasn't on the football team, and therefore not out on the field in an orange and black uniform being hailed by the crowd, and cheered on by girls in short, pleated skirts who thought they were getting the crowd revved up by jumping on each other's shoulders when in fact most of the crowd was either ignoring them, or trying to see what lie beyond the pleats.

Despite his love of music, and knowing how to play the guitar better than anyone he knew, he wasn't with the marching band preparing for the half-time entertainment either.

Dirt wasn't a joiner, as he preferred a relatively solitary existence.

He didn't want to be here, but after hours of hounding and discussion, he gave in more to end the conversation then because he accepted their premise about the evening's potential frivolity.

"You'll have fun."

"No I won't."

"But we're playing Hillsboro!"

"What about them? I haven't been to a single football game in eleven years. Why should I start now?"

"Give it a chance. It's homecoming."

"That's not a good reason."

"Come on! Come and cheer for the Polar Bears, Dirt. It's our last homecoming. Our last one, Dirt! Can you believe it?"

Dirt remembered rolling his eyes at that last entreaty, as the only reply he could think of was, "Thank God for small favors."

But now he was here, sitting in the cold trying to make the best of things by watching the pleated skirts fly up. Dirt doubted that homecoming would be the blast everyone said it would be. The bag of popcorn and a diet pop he was sharing with Lina, were the only things he was enjoying at the moment. He pulled his notepad and pen from his pocket, and started writing.

"What's that for?"

Dirt pointed at his notepad, and looked up.

"Yes. What's the notepad for?"

"I'm bored."

"But what is it?"

"My journal. I just write things down. Been doing it for years."

"Why aren't you watching?"

"I am."

"Yeah. You're watching the cheerleaders. That's about it."

"Big deal. They have shorts on under their skirts," said Dirt as he swirled his index finger in the air.

"What?"

"The cheerleaders. They are wearing shorts under their skirts."

"That's because of people like you. And because it's twenty degrees out here."

"Why aren't you one?"

"A cheerleader? Me? Yeah. Right. That's the last thing I'd be."

"Homecoming queen?"

"Even worse."

"They crowned Danny king, didn't they? Why aren't you queen?"

"Do I look like I want to be homecoming queen?"

Lina's breath puffed from her mouth, and she put her hands in her armpits to warm them up.

"Yeah. I guess you're right. The homecoming queen wouldn't be seen using her armpits as hand warmers."

"I can't believe how cold it is tonight."

"S'posed to snow."

"Like my hat?" Lina said as she tipped its floppy brim down below her eyes.

Dirt shoveled a handful of popcorn into his mouth, and looked over at Lina.

"Looks good on you. Brings out your blonde highlights."

"I can't believe you said that."

"What?"

"Blonde highlights. Didn't know you knew what highlights were. You're full of surprises, Dirt."

Dirt shrugged, breathed into his cupped hands, then took a sip of pop using the straw he'd bent to identify it from Lina's.

"Number six gave it to me."

"Number six?"

"You know, Danny. Your best friend? Mr. Homecoming King? The quarterback hottie in that orange and black uniform out there," she said as she pointed out onto the field. "Has a big number six on his back?"

"He gave you a hat. How romantic."

"He knew I wanted it."

"You should have asked for a new car or something then. At least I would have."

Lina jumped up and started screaming at the top of her lungs. The rest of the crowd was also on their feet. Dirt remained silent, sitting, and writing.

"Go! Yes! Go Booger Go! Get it! Go! Yes! Did you see that?" Lina turned back to Dirt. "Did you see that? Did you see that?"

Dirt didn't look up, and shook his head.

Lina looked through the crowd.

"Danny threw a pass to Booger. Two yards to go. Amazing."

"That's what they're supposed to do, isn't it? Get that ball from over there," Dirt pointed to one side of the field then to the other. "To over there?"

"I wonder if there are scouts here. Danny said there might be some here from the U. Watching him and Booger. Maybe they'd get a scholarship."

"Girl scouts? From the U? They sell cookies, right? But isn't it a bit early for that? I thought that was in March. I like thin mints the best."

"Sometimes I can't tell if you are serious or not," said Lina as she slapped Dirt across the top of his head. "Why aren't you wearing a stocking cap?"

"Don't have one. And you know I'm the last one picked in gym, Lina. I don't exist here, remember? How would I have any idea of what is going on out on the field. All I really know is that they are chasing that brown, egg-shaped ball for some reason."

"But that had to have been at least forty yards," Lina shook her head, took off her hat, and started waving it. "Dan's the man! Dan's the man!"

Dirt bared his teeth, and started to pick popcorn kernels from his gums. If sitting in the cold trying to avoid the frigid breeze, cheering for a bunch of jocks as they threw a ball across a field was supposed to be fun, then he was having the time of his life.

"Dan doesn't want to go to the U anyway. He wants to go to UCLA."

Lina hopped down from the bleacher she was standing on, and sat down. She pushed Dirt with her elbow.

"Hey! I was writing. You made me mess it up."

"What did you say?"

"Dan wants to go law school in California. Wants to get out of here and be a big time lawyer. I want to escape too. And Booger, I think. Don't you next year? I can't believe you don't."

Dirt stopped writing when he sensed the overt silence from Lina. He looked up, and saw that Lina's eyes were suddenly wet.

"What's wrong? I thought you knew?"

Lina violently shook her head, and caused the tears that were pooling in her eyes to stream down the side of her face.

Without saying another word, she got up, ran down the crowded bleachers, and disappeared into the throng of excited Larimorians.

Dirt shrugged, and wiggled the tip of his pen.

“Go Polar Bears!” he whispered as he put his head down, and resumed writing.

October 12, 1996
8:30 PM

The Ice Cream Shoppe
Larimore, ND

*

Danny and Lina sat at the same booth at the Ice Cream Shoppe they always did. It was the same booth where they'd shared their first sundae. Until now, they always sat on the same side of the table. They would hold hands under the table and fed each other ice cream with their free hands. Tonight, Lina chose to sit on the opposite side.

Danny had a sundae in front of him.

Lina wasn't in the mood for ice cream.

"Why did I have to hear about your plans from someone else?"

"I was going to tell you."

"You should have told me first. I heard about it from Dirt, Danny."

"Keep your voice down."

"Don't tell me to keep my voice down."

"Lina, come on. Don't be mad."

Lina had told herself that she wouldn't get all teary and start to cry. She told herself that she wasn't one of *those* kind of girls. The kind that cried the minute anything went wrong. She was strong and independent, and intended to stay that way.

It wasn't working.

She felt her eyes getting wet as the tears welled up. She wiped them dry with her shirt, and pulled the brim of her hat down.

"So it's true? You want to leave?"

*

Danny knew the night wasn't going to be fun. Dirt had warned him about what had happened at homecoming, but he didn't seem the least bit phased.

"She just left the stands."

"Why?"

"I mentioned something about your plans to leave for California after graduation. What's the big deal?"

"You said what?"

"That you are leaving for school. Doesn't everyone know?"

"No. No one but you and my parents, Dirt!"

"Well, now she does too."

Dirt had been Danny's friend since kindergarten. They'd had some rough patches, but this was the first time Danny ever felt like throwing a punch and giving the guy a black eye.

Danny reached for Lina's hand and held it.

"Lina. I'm sorry. I should have talked to you first. Dirt was there when the application came in the mail. That's why he knew so early."

She didn't respond.

"I was hoping you'd join me."

She finally looked at him.

"In California?"

"Yes. After you graduate. I was hoping you'd come out there with me. I want to go to UCLA. They have a great law program. Did Dirt tell you about that?"

"He mentioned something. But after the first couple of sentences, I wasn't hearing anything."

"I want to be a lawyer. Not a farmer. I'm not cut out for this."

"Sounds like you have big dreams."

"My head is full of them, Lina. Really. And I want you to be part of them."

Danny could see in her face and eyes that she'd softened. The anger had dissipated a bit.

Danny moved to her side of the table, held her hand in his, and kissed her fingers. He scooped a dollop of ice cream and hot fudge onto his red spoon, and brought it over to Lina.

"Want some?"

Lina unenthusiastically took the spoon of ice cream being offered.

"So, Mr. Bigtime Lawyer. Tell me about these dreams of yours."

Journal Entry
Of Dirk Kinnear

November 23, 1996

Dear Sam:

I honestly don't know how much more of this I can take. It's Thanksgiving today, but I don't have much to be thankful for at home. I know mother is not cooking any dinner – never has. Dad can't toast a piece of bread without burning it, and I doubt she wouldn't eat anything I made. If I had a place of my own, I'd at pop a Swanson's turkey dinner in the microwave and be thankful by myself.

This year it will be a bit different and I'm really curious to experience my first Thanksgiving.

Danny invited me over to his house.

He said he would be over on his snowcat by noon to pick me up. He has one of those Arctic Cat El Tigres that can go so fast it feels like you can fly.

Booger and his mom will be there too.

Danny said it would be a great day, and the three of us could go out riding the snowcats and pull an inner tube like we do at the lake.

Except this is on snow and in the cold.

When I told him that I didn't have any heavy winter clothes, he laughed and told me it was no big deal.

"You can wear some of my snow pants. Might be a bit short, but we won't laugh."

He laughed even harder when I told him I didn't know what snow pants were.

Danny told me what his mom always makes for dinner. It sounds so incredibly good; my stomach is growling just thinking about it as I'm writing. I've never had a real Thanksgiving dinner before. He said there would be turkey, mashed potatoes, corn, sweet potatoes with toasted marshmallows, homemade rolls, stuffing, and whatever kind of pie I wanted for dessert.

I can't wait.

I hope there's apple pie. I love apple pie.

He told me it was no big deal when I sounded so excited.

"It's just a traditional meal, Dirt. Nothing special. My mom's a great cook though"

Wow. No big deal? It sounds absolutely incredible.

But back to the strangeness of my life.

Home.

That woman went on a tirade yesterday about the whole Thanksgiving thing when I told her and Dad that I was going over to Danny's.

"They should mind their own business. Leave us alone. Gluttony is a sin. One of the seven deadlies. Our savior didn't sit around and eat like swine on one day of the year. Neither will you."

She's one to talk about gluttony, but I guess Cheetos and frozen waffles don't count.

Then she started reciting bible verses about gluttony, and how I was instigating evil for even saying the word "Thanksgiving" in her presence.

"You're evil. You're blaspheming our Savior," she told me.

Dad left in the middle of her speech, and left me alone with her. I know if she had anything to do with it, I would be locked in my closet of a bedroom, and not allowed to go over to Danny's.

I'd crawl out my window if she even tried it.

I look at myself in the mirror now, and only see the burns. It's so embarrassing. And they are really sore today for some reason. I put some aloe on them to cover up the oozing red sores.

They sting like a son of a bitch.

I've let my hair grow long to cover the burns on my neck. In the locker room after gym, the guys notice the ones on my back, but they've started to just look away. Danny and

Booger know what's going on, but don't say much. There's nothing they could do anyway. I've learned not to cry when she burns me, because that makes things worse. Crying was replaced by anger a while ago. Once in a while, though, it comes back. If I do cry, or even try to move out of the way, she lights another cigarette and snuffs that out on me too. I get a twofer.

Yesterday she wanted me to recite Leviticus 26:40. I used a wrong word, and that set her off. I think the end of the world would be quieter than one of her eruptions. The burning smell made me sick. I really want her to die. I wish dad would do something, but he just grunts and shakes his head if I say anything to him.

"Don't talk that way about your mother," he says.

I really don't consider her my mother anymore. A mother wouldn't do this. The fact that he doesn't do anything makes everything worse.

Maybe I should just kill myself. That would teach them.

What if I killed both of them?

I doubt if anyone would notice.

I should try to have a good day today with everyone, and forget about this place.

Sincerely,

Dirt

Journal Entry
Of Dirk Kinnear

January 5, 1997

Dear Sam:

I can't call her mother anymore. She's "that woman in the house" or just "that woman." Sometimes she's, "that fucking bitch." I really hate her. I know I used a bad word.

I'm sorry.

I just don't understand.

She's always saying how good God is. How merciful. How wonderful. How incredibly powerful he is, and that everyone is supposed to fear him – especially me since I'm Satan's son.

But it doesn't make sense. Why would she say I'm Satan's son as that would mean she'd had sex with Satan? I wonder if she'd ever thought of that.

I doubt it.

She's not that smart.

And I don't think Satan could stand spending more than a few seconds with her. He would probably look at her in that nightgown, back off and say, "I ain't touchin' that!"

I've noticed that her back and My Grains are worse. Even after all of these years, she still says it that way. When she's not praying or tormenting me, she's laying on the couch in a fetal position with a cigarette dangling from her mouth, or from her hand. She screams if Dad or I make too much noise. She stands at a ninety-degree angle whenever she gets off of the couch.

She's gained a lot of weight, and I'm quite frankly amazed the couch still supports her. And yes, she still wears that same nightgown with the same slippers day-in and day-out. Both are getting thread bare. The slippers lost their pink fuzz years ago.

I hope she blows a blood vessel.

If God exists, and he's supposed to be good, why is he letting her do this to me? She says it's because he wants it. That it's because I'm evil and my tarnished soul needs to be cleansed of all of its evil. I'm "Satan's Spawn" as she describes it.

To me it sounds like a bad horror flick.

This entire thing about me being the son of Satan doesn't make sense. I don't think there is such a thing as God. And since there is no God, there can't be a Satan. Right? Don't they come in pairs? Good and bad? Salt and pepper? Ketchup and mayo?

I've decided that I'm an atheist.

She made me that way.

My view is pretty simple. We are born then we die. There are good people. There are bad people. That's it. No heaven. No hell. You die. It goes dark. You decompose.

I almost forgot to tell you, she won't be burning me anymore.

I finally fought back. I hit her. Hard. It felt so good. I was so happy inside but so angry at the same time. I didn't think those two emotions could happen at the same time. But they did. I have to admit that I made her mad on purpose. I knew what she wanted me to recite. After all of these years, I know all of the psalms by heart. I said it wrong just to piss her off. I wanted this to happen. When I felt the cigarette get close, I grabbed her wrist, and twisted as hard as I could. She screamed, and dropped the cigarette.

She called me an, "Evil son of a whore."

I said, "Yes, maybe I am. And that makes you the whore, doesn't it?"

It took her a while to untangle my logic. It was fun to watch when the reality of what I said hit home.

The cigarette burned a hole in the old linoleum. I called her a "fucking bitch" too, then told her that if she ever touches me again, that I'd kill her. She called me names again, and said I'd go to hell for blaspheming in front of her and in the midst of her bible. She tried to grab me as I started to walk away, and as I twisted out of reach, I elbowed her in the face. It was kind of an accident, but when I saw where my elbow was heading, I put more force behind it. I hit her right below her left eye. She'll be sore for a while. Hopefully swollen. She must have told Dad because he was really mad later on. He got really drunk, and threw a full can of beer at me. I can't believe he'd waste a can like that. It's so important to him.

Anyway, the can hit me on the back of my head. I picked it up, tossed it back to him, and told him dropped something. He could barely open his eyes, when he called me a son of a bitch.

I said, "You finally realized that? It took you long enough."

It was worth it though.

I'm serious.

She'll never touch me again. If she does, I might kill her. I have that hunting knife, and it's sharp. I can almost imagine it sliding into the back of her thick skull.

Sincerely,

Dirt

Journal Entry
Of Dirk Kinnear

January 25, 1997

Dear Sam:

Senior year is half over. Graduation is in May.

Thank God.

I can't believe I made it for so long without killing someone. Just five more months to go. I'll be able to walk out of the doors of this prison for the last time. They can all kiss my lily-white ass. I don't really understand it, but being an absolute prick must be a requirement for high school.

Teachers AND students.

I really miss the old days. I heard Mrs. Beck had a heart attack and passed away.

Maybe it was cancer.

Remember her? She's the English teacher that got me writing to you back in '92. She let me keep that old copy of The Grapes of Wrath. *I still keep it hidden, as I do with any of my books, because that woman in the house would slice my balls off if she caught me reading something other than the bible. I keep it wrapped in an old pair of boxers. I don't think she'd ever bring herself to be able to touch those. She would think her fingers would burn off.*

But back to school.

It's been a real bitch lately. I'd like to shove a basketball up Mr. Roman's ass, but it would fall out. I hate gym class. Always have. Always will. Not everyone is a jock. Why can't they realize that? Not everyone lives and breathes football. Not everyone can dribble a basketball. Not everyone likes to wear an orange and black onesie, grab his opponent's ball sack, and yank when it's wrestling season.

Something happened in gym that I have to tell you about though. It was the day before Christmas break started. Vince Greir and Kip Smith dragged Cindy Brady, she's a cheerleader who thinks her shit doesn't stink, into the locker room.

Remember those guys? They were the ones who threw my books on the floor. Danny took care of them.

Cindy was acting like she was protesting, but I don't think she was. Most everyone was either in the shower, in a jock, or naked and drying off.

"Hey, Cin! There's Dirt. Don't bother opening your eyes. He's hung like a hamster. Nothing to see there."

Kip laughed as Vincent continued saying something about my inability to dribble a ball, and what I had in my jock. Cindy laughed too, even though she was faking having her eyes closed. I always thought she was a bitch. Now I know she's just like the rest of them.

I hate all of them.

Maybe I should feed them to the pigs right after that woman in the house. They could be dessert. Every time I think of them, my stomach turns in knots and I feel like vomiting. I wish I could be someone else. I'd make them all pay.

When he heard all of the commotion, Mr. Roman came in to the locker room, yelled at them, and told them to get out. Before he left, he turned towards me, and then grunted, "What are you looking at Kinnear? This is the boys' locker room, remember?"

I wish they would all get hit by a train.

Or shot.

Or stabbed and cut to pieces.

I've never had gym class with either Vincent or Kip, so they've never seen me naked.

They'd be jealous – believe me.

I'll get back at them.

Don't know how.

Don't know when.

But I will.

Sincerely,

Dirt

April 7, 1997
6:00 AM

The Carlson Farm
Arvilla, ND

*

Danny could smell the fresh coffee and, despite the fact he didn't really like breakfast, the bacon his mother always fried to a perfect crisp and had waiting for him with a glass of orange juice and a tall glass of milk each morning. He was still under the covers contemplating getting up and dressed, but he wanted to hear more. His parents were talking about him, and it was on the verge of becoming an argument.

His parents never argued.

"Don't you dare ask him, Tom."

His mom was serious because she was calling him Tom, and not Skip. It was like being called Daniel Scott Carlson. When the name given at birth was used, it wasn't good a good thing in the Carlson household.

"But why?"

"Because farming isn't what he wants to do."

"But he always said it was."

"When he was ten, yes. He's eighteen now."

"But if I ask him..."

Danny heard his mother cut his father off before he had a chance to finish his sentence. She was very good at doing that, and Danny had suffered her method of interrogation more than once. No one debated Sis Carlson, and came out unscathed.

"No. You. Won't."

"Without Dan, there's no one to take the farm."

"We'll think of something. He won't say no to you, Tom. You know that. Then he'll resent you. Resent me. And I can't have that. Don't you dare ruin this for him."

"But..."

"No. You will not ask him to take the farm, Tom. Let him spread his wings. Maybe he'll come home, maybe he won't. But you have to let him decide."

Danny thought the conversation ended, so he pushed back the covers, and reached for his pants that were still in a pile where he'd left them the night before. It was time to get dressed, but he stopped with the pants at his ankles, when his mother started again.

"Did you see this?"

Danny couldn't see what his mother was referring to, but he was positive that it was his acceptance letter to UCLA he'd received yesterday along with the information about the academic scholarship he was being offered.

A full boat.

That letter was exactly what Danny wanted. That piece of paper provided a means to escape the dirt roads, the grease, the cold, and the overall drudgery of being a farmer.

He was headed for someplace with life.

Someplace with excitement beyond wondering about how the crops were going to turn out year-after-year, listening to the farm report day-after-day, and sitting on a stool at Butch's drinking and over-abundance of beer, whiskey, vodka with all of the other farmers in cowboy boots, Wranglers, and flannel shirts.

"Top it off?"

Danny heard grunt, a cup slide across the table, then the tinkled splash of coffee being poured into a cup.

"Why does he want to go all of the way out there? I heard something about a football scholarship at the U."

"He doesn't want to go to the U. He wants to spread his wings, Tom."

"I didn't need to do that."

"Well, he does. And besides, he's not you."

"They're talking about you."

The new voice startled Danny. He tripped on the legs of his jeans, and fell to the floor in his boxers. His jeans wrapped around his ankles in knots.

The voices in the kitchen suddenly stopped.

"Next time try knocking, Bekks."

"Mom's calling Dad by his real name. That's not good."

Bekks sat down on his bed, seemingly unaffected by her older brother's tangled predicament, and current state of near nakedness. Bekks, who was already dressed in her typical spring wardrobe of cut-offs, cowboy boots, and a flannel shirt, was running a paddle brush through her long auburn hair that was slowly becoming a more red as she meandered her way through puberty.

"What are you going to do?"

"I'm getting out of here, Bekks. I'm going to UCLA, and Dad's just going to have to accept it."

"But the farm."

"I don't want to be a farmer, Bekks."

"Well, it doesn't sound as if Dad knows. He thinks you're here to stay."

"Well, I'm not."

*

Danny walked down the stairs and into the kitchen holding his boots in his left hand and gym bag over his right shoulder. As he expected, there was a plate with five pieces of bacon, a glass of orange juice, and a tall glass of milk on the table at his usual place.

His mother was sitting in her spot next to the window facing the yard. The radio was on, but she wasn't listening to the typical farm report that would be on if his father was still there. Instead she had her classic rock station on, and they were playing Fleetwood Mac or something like that.

Her kind of music all sounded the same to Danny.

His mother amazed him. It wasn't even seven in the morning, yet she looked as if she'd been up for hours. She was the epitome of a morning person. She was wearing blue jeans, a black shirt, and had a grey, sleeveless crocheted sweater vest that, when she was standing, hung down to her thighs. She wore the small necklace his father gave her on their fifth wedding anniversary. Its small white pearl, wrapped in a gold and diamond net, dangled in the pit of her neck.

There was an envelope placed next to his plate.

His letter from UCLA.

She was staring out the window, so Danny didn't think she knew he had come down. He should have known better.

"You'll need to talk to your father," she said without turning around.

"Figured. I heard you talking."

Sis turned towards Danny and nodded while taking a sip of coffee.

"Where is he?"

"In the shop. Said he wanted to get an early start."

"Mad?"

"Not mad. Confused."

Danny looked up at the clock. It was 6:45. He had half an hour before Booker picked him up. Summer football practice was the shits.

"You have time," she said as she handed him his UCLA acceptance letter, and gave him a kiss on the cheek. "I'm proud of you. And so is he. Don't forget that."

*

Unless contemplating the construction of his shop, Skip wasn't getting an early start on anything. Danny found him sitting on a brown metal folding chair, staring at the rafters, and fiddling with the greying hair of his thick mustache. His mug of coffee was sitting on a small table next to the radio a crowbar, a grease gun, and three crescent wrenches. It was a lot like the scene he just left in the kitchen, except his mother didn't allow tools on the kitchen table, and the radio had the farm report on instead of music.

Spring wheat was down a nickel at the opening bell.

Soybeans were up a penny.

The Secretary of Agriculture was at a conference in Minneapolis, and then would be flying to Des Moines to discuss the future of corn ethanol subsidies.

"Dad?"

Skip slowly turned, looked at Danny, and smiled.

Danny could tell the smile was strained.

"Dan the man."

"Can we talk?"

"Anytime. You know that."

Danny pulled the UCLA letter out of the envelope.

"Mom says she talked to you about this?"

Skip took the piece of paper from Danny's hand, unfolded it, and started reading it again.

He didn't say anything.

He just nodded as he read.

Danny slid another chair over from the wall, and sat next to the table.

Oats were up two cents.

Barley was down eight.

"What's the 2325 mean?"

"My SAT score."

"That good?"

Danny smiled, as he knew it was *really* good.

"Yeah. It's not bad. The best score is 2400."

"You've always been smart, that's for sure."

Danny started rubbing the palms of his hands against his thighs. A nervous habit he'd had for as long as he could remember. He didn't really know what to say next.

He went for broke.

"I want to go to law school. Be a lawyer."

Danny knew his father was never one to talk too much. Like Danny, he was more of the contemplative type. But when he had something to say, people listened. Danny didn't say a word as his father started combing his mustache with his fingers again – his version of the palm against the thigh thing.

"So they want to give you a scholarship?"

Danny nodded.

Skip folded the letter, and handed it back to Danny.

"Looks like you have everything planned out. I'm proud of you."

"I know you wanted me to take the farm."

"It's not about what I want. You're a man now. Gotta spread your wings," he said as he looked at the old beat-up clock that used to hang in the kitchen and rescued from the garbage. "You better get going. Bus will be here in a few."

Durum was up seven cents.

Sunflowers were down three.

"See you tonight."

"See ya," said Danny as he turned back, and waved with his palm.

*

Skip watched his son leave the shop.

Yes, he was proud. There was no way to deny that.

To be certain, he was proud of both of his kids.

Danny had turned out. He wasn't a felon, and he didn't do drugs. The kid was smart, and was being offered a full scholarship to college that proved it.

Then why wasn't he happy?

Skip took a sip of coffee, pulled a crescent wrench from his back pocket, and started to dismantle the manure spreader.

Pinto beans were down two cents.

Corn was up one.

Journal Entry
Of Dirk Kinnear

May 9, 1997

Dear Sam:

Graduation is two weeks away. I can't wait.

I'm going to talk to the recruiter as soon as I can.

I'm getting out of this hellhole, and I can hear the clock ticking down.

I made the mistake of telling Danny and Booger about the incident in the gym with Vince, Kip, and Cindy. Danny gave them hell. Booger just smiled and kept looking in the distance as if there was someone out there he could see and no one else could.

It was weird.

He looked different – like another person.

But the good news is that I have a plan. I know what I'm going to do to Vince and Kip. It took a while, cost me seventy-five bucks, and a trip to Fargo, but I figured it out. It will be epic. I'm going to do it right before graduation so it will hopefully be "the talk" when all is said and done. Vince and Kip will regret the day they crossed my path.

I'll leave Cindy alone for now, but Booger thinks I should do something to her too. He knows what I'm going to do, but doesn't know all of the details.

It feels good to have a plan.

The woman in the house keeps telling me "God is the source of all beauty, boy." Since I don't believe in God, I have trouble making sense of what she's saying. To me, the source of all beauty is the Internet.

Sincerely,

Dirt

May 12, 1997

Larimore High School
Larimore, ND

*

Principal Arnold Roebych stood in front of the two seniors. Seniors, he'd been told, who hid alcohol in their lockers for a little soiree after school. He'd been the principal at Larimore High for decades. When he started, he had a full head of hair – albeit short and cropped. Now Principal Roebych was bald except for a small patch of short hair around the sides of his head. He was always dressed in a suit and tie.

Over the years, he had seen every trick the outgoing class had ever tried. There were some good ones. As of yet, no one had ever been hurt. Some were actually quite ingenious. In 1981, the seniors picked up Mrs. Henderson's tiny, roller skate-sized Honda Civic CVCC, and put it in the middle of the gym. A picture of that one landed on the front page of the

Larimore Gazette. Principal Roebych admitted to a select group that it was, in fact, kinda funny.

This year there wasn't a prank on the calendars that he was aware, but he'd been told there was a party being contemplated. A party with lots of alcohol. He wasn't a prude, but Principal Roebych knew that teenagers and alcohol did not mix. He didn't want any dead students on his watch.

"If you open your lockers, and give me the alcohol, nothing will happen. If I have to open your lockers, and find anything, you won't be graduating with your class. That's a promise."

Principal looked around at the gathering of students. He could send them all back to class, but didn't. This would be a good lesson for all of them.

"You can't do that."

"Trust me, Mr. Grier. I can. This is my school."

"But those are our lockers. Our private lockers," said Kip Smith.

"Wrong again. They belong to the school. Now. Will you open them or not?"

Neither Vince nor Kip moved.

Principal Roebych looked over at Paulie, the school's maintenance man, and nodded.

"All yours, Paulie."

Paulie used a bolt cutter, and sliced through the combination padlocks on each of the lockers.

"Last chance guys."

When neither Vince nor Kip moved, Principal Roebych walked to the lockers, pulled up on the latches, and let the doors swing open.

*

Lina squeezed Danny's hand, then pulled her backpack's straps up closer to her neck. They were some of the last students to join throng gathered by the lockers outside of Mr. Lingerman's chemistry classroom. Lina was standing on the tips of her toes trying to make out what was happening.

"What's going on?"

"Someone reported that Vince and Kip had bottles of booze in their lockers. For some party tonight," said Danny.

"Who could have done that I wonder," asked Booger.

"Yeah. I wonder," said Dirt.

Lina saw the look Booger and Dirt shared.

"What's going on? I saw that."

"Saw what?"

"That look."

"I don't know what you are talking about, Lina. I'm here to see what's going on just like you are."

"Me too," said Booger.

"Idiots. They aren't going to open their lockers," said Danny. "Paulie's going to use the bolt cutters."

*

A collective intake of gasps and laughter erupted as the locker doors swung open.

There were full bottles of booze in each locker: Canadian Club and Smirnoff vodka.

But that's not what caused the commotion.

It was the pictures that were taped to the insides, and the paraphernalia that fell to the floor that caught everyone by surprise. These were two jocks from the football team. The pride and joy of the XY chromosome.

Principal Roebych half expected to see pictures of scantily clothed fashion models taped inside of the boys' lockers. Most did. He didn't expect to find pictures of naked men in various states of arousal.

But he did.

And VHS tapes.

Not of the Disney variety.

And magazines.

Not of the *Sports Illustrated* variety.

"You two," he said as he pointed to Vince and Kip. "In my office. Now."

Principal Roebych looked over to Paulie.

"Get this cleaned up. Bring the bottles to my office. Incinerate everything else."

Principal Roebych looked over at the boys.

"That is unless you want it returned. As Mr. Smith said so eloquently, these are your private lockers after all."

Neither boy responded.

Each was looking at the group of students with his mouth open.

"That's not mine!" yelled Kip. "Honest. Someone put that there."

Everyone laughed when his left leg became wet, and a puddle of piss pooled at his feet.

"But that's not my stuff! Honest!"

*

Dirt and Booger quietly smiled at one another as the crowd of students returned to the classrooms they were scheduled to be in. Dirt felt absolutely wonderful.

It was his plan.

His revenge.

He didn't want to share the feeling. He wanted to keep it all to himself, as what they did to him and the emotions it caused were his only. Dirt vividly remembered the words from that day in the locker room.

"Hey, Cin! There's Dirt. Don't bother opening your eyes. He's hung like a hamster. Nothing to see there."

Vince and Kip looked deathly pale as they walked away with Principal Roebych. Their masculinity was in question, and they were both probably wondering how life could continue.

Larimore was a very small town.

Everyone talked and it didn't take very long for rumors to start, grow, and become viral. Vince and Kip had been a thorn in his side since junior high.

For six, long years.

Now their reputations were tarnished.

Regardless of their pleas, there would always be doubt. Whatever else happened before graduation, everyone would remember the time at Larimore High School when the principal found the gay porn in the football players' lockers.

"Who were they again?"

"Vince Grier and Kip Smith. You don't remember them?"

"Yes! That's who. What ever happened to them?"

"Vince is fat and bald. Works at his father's gas station. Recruiters caught wind of what happened, and wouldn't touch either of them. I heard they lost their scholarships."

"What about Kip?"

"Shot himself the next summer."

"Oh. That's too bad."

Dirt liked the way he imagined their demise. His reverie was interrupted when Booger elbowed him.

"What about the other thing?"

"What?"

"You know. That *thing*?"

Dirt finally figured out what Booger was referring to. A grin formed from ear-to-ear.

"The black dildo?"

"Yeah. That."

"It's in Kip's backpack with a picture of Vince. For his dad to find."

"Was it worth it?"

Dirt looked up at the yellowing hallway ceiling, and pondered the seventy-five bucks he'd spent versus the torment the two had caused.

"Every. Fucking. Penny."

May 18, 1997

Larimore High School
Larimore, ND

*

"You boys look so handsome!" squealed Sis and Wendy as they stopped in front of the three boys and kissed each one.

Dirt, Booger, and Dan were standing with the rest of the graduating class of 1997 on the sidewalk in front of the high school. It was a big class this year. Almost forty graduates. They'd just received their diplomas, and were standing in the reception line shaking hands and giving cheek-kisses as people walked by to congratulate them. Dan was the valedictorian and had to give a speech about the future, its promise for each and every one of the graduating class, and how they would all be exemplary citizens and represent their families to the best of their abilities.

It was all bullshit.

Dan knew most of the class would be stuck on the farm, be pregnant within the year, or head off to the military.

Booger received a scholarship to the University of North Dakota.

Dirt barely made it.

“You’re men now,” said Skip. “Didn’t think you’d make it alive, really.”

“You’re making it sound like we all lost our virginity,” said Booger.

Wendy gasped.

“Booker Thorson. You watch that mouth of yours!”

Dirt and Booker laughed. Both elbowed Dan under their graduation gowns.

“Well, just one of us,” whispered Dirt. “Hey Dan. That hickey is really bright. Can you dim it a bit?”

Dan blushed.

“Be quiet.”

“I saw Lina before the ceremony,” said Booger. “She used a lot of makeup on her neck. Gonna start calling you Hoover instead of Dan.”

“What’s so funny?” asked Sis.

“Nothing, mom. Nothing. These jerks think they are being funny. But they’re not.”

Skip made a point to shake Booker's hand and then Dirt's.

"Your dad would be very proud," he said to Booger. "Don't ever forget that."

He embraced his son.

"Proud of you too, Dan."

Dan could tell it hurt his dad to say it. He may have been proud. But he wasn't happy. His dad couldn't really look him in the eye for any length of time.

May 19, 1997

The Kinnear Farm
Arvilla, ND

*

Dirt looked up at the blue sky as he walked to the latest addition to the Kinnear family, a John Deere 8870. It was a four-wheel drive, big green monster with eight tires, almost four hundred horsepower, air conditioning, and a working cassette player that Dirt was eager to get using. He'd been jealous of the four-wheel drive tractor that Danny had been driving since he was eight. Now, at eighteen years old, he finally had one of his own.

But that's not why he was looking at the blue sky. It was not why he had a relaxed smile across his face. It was not why he thought the lilacs that grew along the perimeter of the farm smelled especially sweet.

No.

It was much more than that.

Dirt was positive this had to be what the first day of freedom felt like for a wrongly-convicted man who'd been locked away behind bars for twelve years. Besides the occasional holiday, today was the first Monday in a dozen years that Dirt wasn't required to be in school.

It felt absolutely wonderful.

Besides that woman in the house, there was no one to torment him. No teachers. No jocks.

Absolutely no one.

He could easily avoid the woman in the house by just staying outside and working all day. He learned to manage breakfast, lunch, and dinner by having his own groceries and keeping a microwave and mini refrigerator in the machine shop. As for showers, he had learned to use the garden hose. Very fast, cold showers were commonplace for a while until he'd contrived a small propane burner to heat enough water for a quick, warm shower. His bed was the only reason to have to walk through the front door. And he was trying to figure out what he could do to change that.

For the moment, however, he had a job to do. He had to prep the new tractor for its first day of work on the Kinnear farm. That meant changing the oil, the oil filter, the air filter, and getting it greased. It might have been new to him and his father, but he had no idea how its previous owners had treated it. His father taught him many things over the years, and one of the most important lessons was keeping care of the farm's tools and equipment. Treat your tools well, and they'll last forever. His father's Dodge Ram was proof of that. It was vintage 1980's, and had close to 250,000 miles on it. It would likely have a longer life than his father.

Perhaps even Dirt.

He was under the tractor loosening the tractor's oil plug when his father drove into the yard pulling another new piece of equipment. Except it wasn't a typical farm implement. It was a silver Airstream camper that had to have been at least twenty feet long. Dirt watched his father pull past him, stop, and then slowly back the silver tube into a small clearing in the trees next to the workshop. Dirt pulled the plug loose and let the old oil drain onto the gravel. He crawled out from under the tractor, and walked to his where his father was now standing.

"What's that, Dad?"

"A camper."

Dirt wanted to say, "No shit," but thought better of it.

"I know it's been rough in there. You can live in here if you want. For graduatin' and all."

Dirt was astounded.

He stood next to his father, his mouth agape.

"Here's the key."

Dirt didn't move.

"Do you want it or not?"

All Dirt could do is nod.

"Thanks," Dirt looked at his father who had already started to walk away. "Dad."

Tubbs turned around. He had the look of having been at Butches for three beers too long. The filterless Camel that he'd been sucking on, stuck out from the gap where one of his front teeth once lived. His eyes were barely open.

"Thanks, Dad. Really."

"Been sitting in the Gunderson's pasture for a dozen years. He wanted to get rid of it. No funny business in there. None of that silly weed stuff. If I find out you're doing that, I'll burn it to the wheels with you in it."

He turned around, and started to walk away.

"Get that 7780 in the field by noon."

Dirt threw the keys up in the air, fucked the catch, and had to fish them out of the stream of dirty oil leading back to the tractor. He wiped them off on his pants, and went to see his new home.

*

Dirt pulled down the rusted metal tread that was folded under the frame of Airstream, stepped up, and pulled the latch on the silver door. It opened with a loud protest, but to him, it was the glorious sound of independence.

It was nothing a squirt of oil wouldn't fix.

Dirt walked into his new home.

His silver castle on wheels.

It had a single hallway down the center. As Dirt looked towards the back, to the single bedroom, the kitchen was on his right and his dining room, a small table with a bench, was to his left. The kitchen had a small refrigerator and a three-burner propane stove with a small oven underneath. The only available counter space was a small square between the stove and the fridge and two feet to the right of the stove.

"Microwave goes right here," he said as he pushed an inch of dust and an empty mouse nest off of the counter between the stove and fridge.

Dirt continued exploring. He found the hot water heater hidden in one of the closets. The bathroom was on the left side, and was his only concern. Not because it lacked anything, but because it was on the curved side of the camper. His head was only an inch below the roof when he walked down the hallway. In the bathroom, he had to hunch down to even walk in.

Standing in the shower would be a pipe dream.

But Dirt didn't care.

"A shower with hot water. I can't wait," he said to his reflection in the crusted mirror. "Will have to figure out where to drain things."

The back of the camper was just as perfect as the rest. There were two twin beds separated by a small dresser, but he was sure he could re-engineer things to put both beds together and move the dresser to the other side. He'd outgrown his twin bed years ago.

Dirt sat down on the mattress in his new bedroom, looked back towards the front, and saw something he'd missed.

Not only was the camper his graduatin' present, but his father had left something else on the small couch at the front of the camper.

A new guitar.

Dirt had asked for one years ago, but was told by the woman in the house that Christmas was the Savior's birthday not his. When he asked for one on his birthday, that woman told him that he didn't deserve anything.

"You're eat'in our food. That's present enough. Now get to work."

He walked to the couch and strummed the strings as delicately as he could.

To his ears, the sound was as angelic.

Dirt did another visual tour of his home and smiled. He picked up his new guitar and sat down. A cloud of dust filled the front half of the camper.

"Sweet. The guys are gonna love it," he said with a cough.

Dirt's reverie was interrupted when his father pounded on the silver shell of his new home.

"That tractor won't put oil in itself boy! Get to it."

Dirt put the keys in his pocket, walked out, and locked his door behind him. He brushed his hand against the sleek sliver skin as he walked back to his work.

It was a great day.

Journal Entry
Of Dirk Kinnear

May 21, 1997

Dear Sam:

It's been very busy on the farm. Now that I'm out of school, Dad has me working even more. But I'm back to tell you about something that happened the other day. Something my dad did. I hope you are sitting down because you will be as surprised as I was.

Sometimes Dad surprises me, and does the strangest things. Most of the time I think he hates me, then out-of-the-blue he does something that totally freaks me out but is fucking cool at the same time. I didn't even know that was possible. Yesterday he came driving into the yard pulling an old, beat-up Airstream behind the pickup. He said it was from the Gunderson's pasture. Now that I think of it, I do remember seeing it out there. Never thought for a minute that I'd be calling it home.

I don't know which made more noise. The pickup, the silver torpedo behind it, or his coughing. He has been coughing a lot lately. It looked like the camper had to have been at least a hundred years old. I was changing the oil on the 8870, and watched as he backed the rickety old thing into the trees behind the storage shed. I looked up as he walked over to me. I thought I was in trouble for something again. Maybe he hit a tree that I should have known to cut down before he came home. Who knows. It's always something, and generally always my fault whether I knew about it or not.

But I wasn't in trouble.

He called it a "graduatin" present.

He just handed the keys over to me and mumbled, "Here. I know it gets tough in there. If I find out you're smoking silly weed in there, I'll torch it with you locked inside."

And he just walked away.

I have to admit that I was practically speechless. I could tell from the look in his eyes that he was on the downward spiral from a kick-ass bender. Plus he was mumbling – not that that's unusual behavior from him. He's never given me anything in my entire life. And by, "it gets tough in there," he meant in the house with that woman he married. As for "silly weed?" I've never smoked in my life.

So believe me, that came out of left field.

He's the one that drinks Canadian Club like bottled water and chain smokes Camels. They are the kind without filters and smell like acid. I'm not that stupid. Sure, my hair is long and all, but that doesn't mean I smoke "silly weed."

I'm a pot virgin.

I've never even heard it called that before! I think he must have had some of that "silly weed."

Ok. I do admit taking the whiskey that one time, but that was different.

And it made me puke my guts out.

He just handed me a key on an old Dodge keychain. He loves his Dodges and John Deere – that's for sure.

I'm sure he has a spare, but that's ok. He bought the thing, after all so I guess it's his prerogative. When I opened the door, there was a second surprise. A guitar. I had asked for one at Christmas last year but that woman vetoed any gifts as she said, "This is His birthday. Not yours." So Christmas at the Kinnear home is usually spent reading the bible.

I tend to just hide.

But not anymore!

I didn't realize the old man was paying attention. It does get tough "in there." I honestly don't know how he has lasted for so long being married to that woman. Coming up on twenty years I think. I have trouble calling her mom as the only type of mother she's been is of the fucker variety. Even after all of this time, she still thinks I'm Satan's spawn. She reminds me of it multiple times a day as a matter of fact. Now that I have a home of my own, I won't have to get up at 4:30 for bible study. Some days I used to want to beat her unconscious with her bible, but I learned to just deal with it. I've learned to pick my battles. I can't sleep through her moaning and groaning anyway.

She has trouble with her back, but I think she's sick beyond that.

I'm serious.

There's something wrong with her.

I'm counting the days until I can leave for good. If I leave after harvest and join the Navy as I want to, I have about 3 or 4 months left. I'll be nineteen by then so they won't be able to stop me.

Technically I think I can join at eighteen, but I'll stay for harvest.

I won't come back either.

Never.

The last either will see of me is my white ass as it drives off into the sunset. Since the "biggie" last year, she hasn't tried to burn me with her cigarette. I think she knows better now – that or she's afraid of me since I'm now more than a foot and a half taller than she is.

That, by the way, happened really fast.

It was like boom!

All of the sudden I was tall, and she had to look up at me.

To her, I probably look more like Satan every day – especially with the zits and all. Yes, I still get zits even though I'm eighteen. Good ol' puberty definitely came late for me, and seems to still be rearing its ugly head.

Maybe I should really cause a stir in her bowels before I leave. Make the last thing she sees of me really, really memorable. I'll cut off all of my hair and glue some horns to my head. Really freak the shit out of her!

Maybe she'd have a heart attack and croak.

Wishful thinking, I know.

I already know most of the passages she quizzes me on, so that's a good thing. I don't have to sit in the corner any more when I don't know the answer. I can finish her sentences before she does and that really pisses her off.

It's fun.

I thought she was going to blow an O-ring yesterday. She started with something from Proverbs.

"Folly is bound up..."

I knew exactly what she was going to say, and I finished it.

"....in the heart of a child, but the rod of discipline drives it far from him. Proverbs 22:15."

Her face turned all red and she brought her hand up like she was going to hit me. I just stared at her. She brought her hand down, and called me evil and told me to go do my chores. For some reason she likes the passages about discipline.

Fucking bitch.

I'd like to discipline her with an iron pipe across her forehead.

Like I said, only four more months until I'm out of here. With my luck, she'll die the day before I leave, and I'll have put up with all this shit for nothing.

But now I have an Airstream I call home.

And a guitar.

Life is sweet right now.

Sincerely,

Dirt

July 26, 1997

The Carlson Farm
Arvilla, ND

*

Tomorrow was the big day.

Danny was California-bound.

His 1990 red Ford Escort was packed, filled with gas, and ready to go. His parents had given him a small going-away party that afternoon filled with grilled burgers, potato salad, pop, friends, presents, hugs, good lucks, and good-byes.

Booger, Dirt, and Lina were all there. Booger gave him a book that listed all of the California nude beaches. Dirt gave him a lamp for his desk.

"You'll have to study at night, won't you?"

"You are always so practical, Dirt," said Lina.

Lina gave him a necklace with a golden ring. She'd had it inscribed on the inside of the band.

Lina and Danny - 1997

At seven, his parents left for town. His mom wanted to hear the band at Butch's. Danny was sure that it was because she didn't want to be at home to watch her son pack his car. Bekks had gone along, and was spending the night with her best friend. She said goodbye in-between sobs. She gave him a pencil holder she'd made in pottery class, with a haiku she'd written about little sisters and big brothers etched in the clay.

He and Lina had the house to themselves.

She'd come back after he texted her giving her the, "all's clear" message.

Now they were in his bedroom, under an old blanket.

Naked.

"This is the only blanket you could find?"

"Everything else is packed."

Danny ran his finger down the bridge of her nose, across her lips, down her throat, and between her breasts.

"You are so incredibly beautiful, Carolina Grace Holmes. You know that, right?"

Lina smiled.

"That's what you always tell me."

"I have to tell the truth. I'm a law student, you know."

"You don't watch much television do you?"

"You'll join me, right? Right after you graduate?"

Lina nodded.

"You'll come home during your breaks?"

"To see you. Yes. And you can fly out next summer. Spend the summer at home?"

"It will be fun. I promise."

*

Lina rolled onto her side, and felt Danny hold her waist.

He was the big spoon.

She didn't want him to see her face.

She was crying.

She was being the girl she didn't want to be.

Lina had accepted things the night at the Ice Cream Shoppe.

Danny had dreams. She knew he had to leave.

She knew it was good-bye.

There wouldn't be any semester break visits.

There wouldn't be any summer break vacations together.

Lina grabbed Danny's arms and held him tight for one last time.

July 20, 1998

The Kinnear Farm
Arvilla, ND

*

The decision to escape the trap he found himself in was easy, and one that he came to when he was a freshman in high school. He wanted to leave then, but knew he had to wait until he had a high school diploma in his hand.

High school graduation was now history. Two days after receiving it, Dirt threw away the little piece of paper framed in the small black case that proclaimed he'd met all of the educational requirements of the great state of North Dakota and was officially an adult. However, even after a year, he still found himself traveling dirt roads, eating dust, and calling a silver tube on wheels home. The farm and everything life could throw at him erected roadblocks that he felt obligated to handle.

But now it was time.

He'd let everyone else control him far too long. Danny left. So could he.

Yes, Dirt cared about the farm, but he had a life of his own to live. Nothing was going to stop him now. Dirt knew that if he didn't leave before harvest started, he'd simply resign to his situation, and never leave.

He'd be stuck in this place forever.

Dirt watched his reflection as he approached the glass door, and saw his shoulder length hair fluff in the breeze. He realized he neglected to have it cut to something a bit more audience-appropriate.

It was too late now.

At least he remembered to wash it.

Dirt opened the door to the office in a small strip mall on South Washington St in Grand Forks, and walked in. A chime let the four men sitting at their desks know that a potential recruit was there to visit. Dirt looked at all of the posters hung throughout the office. They all made his decision seem so adventurous.

Almost glamorous.

He'd walked through the door. The only thing remaining was the decision to make. Army? Air Force? Navy? Marines?

*

Tubbs rinsed his coffee cup with whiskey, swirled it with the dregs of his coffee, and then poured it down his throat. It was his technique of keeping his cup clean. It was his fourth cup, but his first with whiskey. He tossed the nub of his fifth Camel onto the kitchen floor, and ground it to a pulp with the heel of his boot. It was time to get back to work. Lunch was over, his favorite soap opera, *Days of Our Lives,* ended with another cliffhanger to be resolved tomorrow. Tubbs grabbed two beers from the fridge, and headed back into the yard.

This year's Farmer's Almanac claimed there were at least four, maybe even five, weeks before harvest was supposed to start. His crops told a different story. His barley would be ready in three weeks, with oats following close after that. Crops trumped anything the Almanac said, so it was time to get things ready. Things were moving fast this year, and delays in harvest cost money.

Tubbs always worked on the trucks first, as they were the easiest to get ready. All he had to do is charge the battery, and change the oil on each of his two trucks. Tubbs convinced the GMC Sierra 6500 grain truck to start, and parked it in the center of the yard where he'd change its oil. It surprised him when he didn't need to use starter fluid, as it hadn't been started in months. He knew the other truck, the 1950's-era Dodge that didn't have brakes, wouldn't be as cooperative. It always resisted the first start of the season, and seemed to be getting more tired and stubborn year-after-year.

Just like him.

Since both of his trucks sat parked in the pasture most of the year, their beds filled with leaves and dirt that decayed into a two-inch thick black slurry that would have to be cleared out before a single gain of barley was poured into it. It didn't take grain long to rot once it became wet, and there wasn't a market for rotten grain.

When he parked the GMC, he opened its hood to reach the dipstick, and raised the bed to let the sludge slide out. The bed would still need to be swept, washed, and rinsed. For now, he left it in the sun to completely dry.

Cleanup work for the boy.

What Tubbs wanted now, what he needed right this moment, was another beer.

Tubbs took the last drag of his cigarette, flicked it into the pigpen, and glanced at his watch. The boy said he'd be back by one, and it was almost twelve thirty. The boy didn't bother to tell him why he had to run into Forks at the last minute, and he didn't bother asking. All Tubbs knew was that the boy washed his hair, put on good shirt, clean jeans, and a pair of black shoes he didn't know the boy even owned.

He'd have to check out the Airstream to see what else the boy was hiding.

Probably some of that silly weed.

Instead of his normal, greased-smeared t-shirt, the kid was wearing a fancy one with buttons. Tubbs figured there must be a set of tits he was sniffin' after. Tubbs didn't give a flying rat's ass what the kid was doing, or who he was doing it to, but he better get back when he said he would or there would be hell to pay. Tubbs doubted that it was a set of tits. He didn't think there was a chance in hell the boy would ever find a woman.

He was so tall and lanky. Not an ounce of visible muscle. Those big ears. Those fucking weird, round eyes that always seemed to be staring. That long hair.

Tubbs cringed.

The boy was such an ugly thing.

Got it from his mother's side.

Tubbs held his aching left arm at the elbow, and wiped the sweat from his forehead with his shoulder. He fired-up another Camel, and stuffed it into his tooth-gap. There was rarely downtime on the farm. Maybe an occasional Sunday afternoon where he could rest and enjoy a six-pack or three, but those were few and far between. One season lead to another, and when one was done, preparation for the next immediately followed.

There was always work to be done, but Tubbs believed there was always time for a cold refreshment. There was no need to rush too much. The boy would pick up the slack. He always did. Tubbs started to walk to his workshop, where he and the boy shared an old fridge. He kept his beer. The boy kept his food. Tubbs stopped when his foot landed into a pool of greasy, black filth. He followed the wet, dark line to its source – the red and white GMC Sierra 6500 grain truck. It was leaking hydraulic fluid.

"Shit. Goddamn bastard thing is leaking again."

The GMC's hydraulic support arms were fully extended. They were trying to keep the box upright at sixty degrees, but with a leak in the hydraulic system, it was a losing battle. As he approached the truck, he saw the fluid spraying from the hydraulic fluid case, and pair of cables tucked under the box between the frame's twin I-beams three feet in front of the rear axle. He could hear the hiss of the arms slowly losing pressure, and lowering the box as more fluid spilled onto the ground.

Tubbs felt a wave of nausea take hold, and steadied himself against the frame of the truck's box. The sweat he thought he had under control, and wiped off his forehead a short while ago, dripped onto his nose then down to his boots. For reasons unknown to Tubbs, his chest began to feel tight.

*

Dirt studied the posters, and the literature each recruiter gave him. After twenty minutes, he sat down at the desk belonging to the United States Navy. The Navy always intrigued him. He wanted to be on an aircraft carrier. Perhaps be on the ordinance crew. Maybe operate the catapult, and be responsible for launching the jets. After talking for an hour, filling out the initial forms, and shaking hands, the recruiter gave him all of the necessary paperwork in a white folder with the words "GO NAVY" in blue letters across its front, ceremoniously presented him with a blue t-shirt with "NAVY" in big, white letters, and walked him to his pickup.

"You drive this?" asked the recruiter as he commented on Dirt's rusted Toyota pickup with its cracked windshield. "You are one brave man."

"Gets me to where I need to go. Can't have anything really nice on the farm."

It couldn't be opened from the outside, so Dirt reached in through the window, and pulled the lever to open the driver's side door.

"I'll give you a call, and send you an email when everything gets scheduled. Once you're past those hurdles, you'll be good to go. You'll be a Navy man. Welcome aboard."

"I'll get my hair cut before then. I promise."

The recruiter smiled, and nodded his head in agreement.

"Good idea. Otherwise the drill sergeants will do it for you. That won't be fun."

Dirt shook the recruiter's hand again, and headed home. He smiled at the thought of never having to travel the twenty-one miles on Highway 2 between Grand Forks and Arvilla again.

As the recruiter said, there were two small hurdles to clear. He had to pass a physical, and get a qualifying score on the Armed Services Vocational Aptitude Battery test. He definitely wasn't the least bit concerned about the physical. Although it couldn't be seen, his arms were pure muscle from working on the farm, and he even had a six pack that he was pretty proud of. What Dirt didn't know was what a "qualifying score" meant.

"You'll be fine," the recruiter had told him when he asked about the tests. "Don't worry about a thing."

He still would, it was in his nature.

Life didn't have a good track record of going in his favor.

But if fate would look away for just once in his life, then in two weeks, Dirt would be in basic training at the Naval Station Great Lakes in North Chicago.

Dirt could hardly wait.

*

Tubbs barely had the strength to climb into the truck's cab. It felt as if it took hours to climb into the truck, but once inside, he started it, and pulled the lever to fully extend the box. He needed it all of the way up if he was going to fix the leak. Tubbs knew better than to work on the truck's hydraulics without using a wooden wedge placed between the truck's frame and the box. The blocks he needed were by the fuel tanks on the truck's passenger side, and he could see them sticking out of the tall thistle growing behind the tanks.

He turned the truck off, wiped another gallon of sweat from his forehead, and crawled back down as he held his arm even tighter against his chest. The wedge wouldn't necessarily stop the box from falling, but it would slow it down enough for him to get out of its way. A two-ton steel box fell lightning-quick, and would crush a man to death before he had time to say, "Oh fuck!"

Tubbs only knew one person who was stupid enough to work on a truck's hydraulics without the safety blocks. He was a pallbearer at the guy's funeral.

As word had it, the mortician couldn't figure out how to sew the two-piece of his body back together and make the guy look good at the same time.

They kept the casket closed.

Once on the ground, Tubbs' leaned against the back of the truck's cab to catch his breath, and wipe his drenched face. He was getting dizzy, and the nausea was becoming worse with each passing moment. Despite having raised the box again, he could hear the hiss as it slowly crept back down. The spray of hydraulic fluid was becoming heavier minute-by-minute.

He had to get those blocks, and put them in place.

Tubbs pushed himself away from the cab.

His knees wobbled.

A spike of intense fire-like pain flashed in his chest as his heart was being slowly starved of blood. He reached to the side to support himself on the truck's cab again, but instead fell forward. The truck's driver's side I-beam support kept him from falling on the ground.

A spray of hydraulic fluid hit his face.

The hiss of the falling box triggered panic in his brain, but his heart fluttered to an abrupt stop before Tubbs could will his arms and legs to move out of its way. Tubbs didn't hear or feel the crunch of his spine and rib cage as the truck's box finished its slow decent.

*

Dirt slowed to a mere crawl as he pulled into the farm's driveway. The lilacs on its west side were in full bloom, and hid his pickup from being seen from the farmhouse. He wanted to be as quiet as possible, and hoped his father didn't see him drive in.

It was a quarter after one, which meant he was fifteen minutes late. If he could park, get changed, and out to the trucks without being seen, there would be no way to tell what time he'd actually arrived.

A seemingly solid plan.

When his truck passed beyond the security of the bushes, his stomach flipped. He wasn't going to be able to disguise his tardiness. The GMC was in the center of the yard with its hood up. The box was askew, but he could see his father's legs on the driver's side.

"Fuck," he said to his reflection in the mirror.

He shouldn't have stopped for the three Big Macs he ate on the twenty-two mile drive home.

But he was hungry.

It wasn't the first time his stomach got him in trouble, and he was sure it wouldn't be the last. Not only would his dad be irate about his tardiness, but he'd probably have a coronary embolism when Dirt told him about his planned departure in two weeks' time.

Dirt smiled.

He was actually looking forward to having that discussion.

There was no point in trying to hide, as he'd surely been noticed by now. It was easier to just rip the bandage off with one fast pull. He'd tell his dad now instead of this evening after he'd finished his first six-pack of Schlitz. Dirt parked next to the green diesel tank, grabbed his white "GO NAVY" folder, and walked around the GMC to where he saw his father's legs.

"Hey, Dad. Sorry I'm late," he said as he walked past the driver's side door. "Have a minute? I have something to talk to you about."

Even though his eyes and brain knew that there was no way his father was going to respond, Dirt still finished the sentence. Dirt dropped to his knees, and stretched forward to see his father's face.

"Dad?"

Dirt didn't know why he said that either.

At least he was still in one piece.

His father's eyes were open, a drizzle of hydraulic fluid dripped from his forehead, swirled with the blood that was oozing from his mouth and nose and added to the pool directly below his face. The Camel that was stuck in the tooth-gap, was barely a smolder and the smoke was slithering into his nose. Since there was nothing inhaling the smoke it simply lingered and wafted away in the slight breeze. His tongue was swollen and purple. It stuck out between his lips about an inch as if he were trying to lap up the bloody hydraulic fluid as it dripped.

Dirt crawled back, stood up, and brushed the gravel from his knees. He still had the "GO NAVY" folder in his left hand. He looked over at the farmhouse, to his Airstream, to his pickup, then to his dead father.

He could leave now.

Call the recruiter, and beg to get things moving faster.

Get his physical done this afternoon perhaps.

Let that woman in the house find her dead husband.

Let her handle it.

Claim he was never here.

Dirt looked over at the farmhouse and screamed. He didn't realize there was so much trapped anger contained within his slight frame.

He wasn't angry about the death of his father, but at fate's intervention. He screamed because of his life. The only emotion remaining within him now was rage.

Dirt threw the white folder in the pigpen.

“Go ahead, motherfuckers. Eat it.”

Dirt pounded his fists against his thighs, and then leaned against the fence with his head down on the top support. He pressed his forehead hard against the rail. He wanted to cause pain. He needed to feel something. He wanted something to replace the rage.

He watched as the pigs’ curious snouts push the folder into the shit-filled, gray swill. His eyes become wet, and Dirt felt tears drizzle down and burn his cheeks.

He assumed the sheriff would need to be called.

Harvest was right around the corner.

The crops would need to be brought in.

Dirt dried his face, and walked to the house.

Journal Entry
Of Dirk Kinnear

July 28, 1998

Dear Sam:

Don't have much to say today except that Dad died.

His funeral was yesterday.

I know I didn't give you much preamble to that, I'm sorry. Not because he's dead, but for telling you that way. I'll miss him, I guess. We weren't that close, but he brought a speck of sanity to the farm, even though he didn't do much.

He was a drunken, son-of-a-bitch, but he taught me a lot.

I was told by that woman in the house that I wouldn't be welcome in the House of the Lord. She said if I showed my face at his funeral, the police would be called. I have no idea what they would do, but I decided not to test her. I'm sure there will be lots of talk about the fact that I wasn't there.

I stayed in my Airstream.

Practiced my chords.

Taught myself a new Eagles song.

I don't mind, really. As I've said before, I don't believe in God. A funeral is just part of that whole "God-thing," and all of the rituals surrounding that concept. That woman told me that Jesus would not allow someone like me in His house and that I should be the one in the casket instead of her dear, loving husband.

I had a hard time not laughing.

Loving husband.

Those were definitely not words to describe Dad.

I spit in her face.

She screamed and acted as if she'd been covered in acid.

I wish.

As soon as word got out about Dad's death, some people came by the farm. The visits were all the same. Everyone gave that woman a stand-offish hug; she spouted something from the bible about death, sinners, and redemption. I thought perhaps she might dress in something other than her nightgown and slippers. But she didn't.

The sheriff, Gordy Albrecht, came by to pay his respects. That woman in the house didn't come out, but Gordy came by the Airstream. He's a good guy. Has gained some weight though.

When others stopped by, they saw me by the Airstream, came by, shook my hand, told me how they knew my dad, then went back to the house, and gave that woman a tuna casserole.

What is it about funerals and tuna casserole?

Is it a rule?

I tried to be polite to everyone.

Most left as quickly as they came.

Booger spent most of the day with me. I appreciated that. Now we have even more in common. Both of our dads are dead and buried.

Everything and everyone seemed so plastic. My dad didn't have a lot of friends. He wasn't a social animal. So their condolences were rather hollow in my opinion. The woman in the house? I don't think she has any friends, so they definitely didn't come to see her. It's just a thing farmers do regardless of how they really felt about a person.

Everyone goes to the funeral.

As for me, I'm not feeling anything anymore. No rage. No anger. I'm just numb.

I don't understand the emotions.

Maybe I don't have any.

Did I tell you that I found him?

I did.

It wasn't pretty.

He was dead. Crushed like a bug.

I told you he taught me a lot. For one thing, he instilled a fear of grain trucks that I'll always have. He practically ripped my head off one day when he saw me checking the hydraulic fluid on the truck with the box up.

"Use those Goddamn blocks! You wanna get crushed?"

Then he told me about his friend who was stupid enough to do what I was just about to do and didn't survive. Apparently Dad was a pallbearer at the guy's funeral and, unlike Dad, he was found in two pieces.

But it wasn't the truck that killed him.

He's dead because his heart stopped.

He'd dead because he smoked, and drank to excess.

They performed an autopsy. It listed the cause of death as a myocardial infarction. Big words for a heart attack. He was dead before the box turned his heart into a pancake.

The booze and never-ending Camels got the best of him in the end.

Doesn't surprise me at all.

The box crushing him was fate trying to be funny.

I don't think he's in Heaven. But he's also not in Hell. He's just gone. Evidently that's not the way I'm supposed to feel. So I have been faking it. When I thought people expected me to be sad, I thought of some of the burns on my neck and shoulders.

I thought about my lost chance of escaping.

That didn't make me cry, but it did make my eyes water. I tried harder to look sad. In my head, I kept wishing it was that woman who was dead instead of him. But I caught myself smiling at times when I thought of that. I think some saw me smile as they talked to me about Dad and before they dropped off the tuna.

So I stopped, and thought of nothing.

I suppose I saw it coming.

Things just don't work out for me, Sam.

I threw the Navy papers in the pigpen. They had fun sniffing them. In the end they were just trampled into the muck. I guess I can file that dream away under, "Dirt's Life of Missed Chances."

Unlike the Go Navy folder, my missed chances folder is getting rather full.

I keep thinking, "If one of them had to die before I left, why couldn't it have been her?"

I haven't found an answer yet.

I'm stuck here on the farm, as that woman in the house definitely can't manage anything. I could see it now, she'd be trying to baptize the cows and pigs in the mud hole and hitting them with one of her crucifixes if they didn't oink or moo when she was expecting a "Praise the Lord, Sister Trude."

Sometimes I make myself laugh.

It's the only thing that keeps me sane.

Sincerely,

Dirt

February 10, 2009

The Law Office of Bancroft, Simpson, and Associates
Santa Monica, CA

*

Daniel was dressed in a black Brooks Brothers suit, white shirt, and a red tie. His hair was perfectly coiffed, and there wasn't a microscopic hair visible on his face.

The cologne he used this morning was Clive Christian No. 1, which cost him almost two grand for a small, one ounce bottle. He was sure anyone here in the office, specifically the partner he was scheduled to talk to, would recognize the scent of the cologne he was wearing, and would definitely approve.

Daniel was in the standard power uniform for all California attorneys. He made sure there wasn't a thread out of place.

The other part of his uniform was in the parking lot. A black BMW 640.

Convertible of course.

He was on the third visit to the law firm trying to court him from the group that hired him out of college. It only took a few years to make a name for himself, and to out-grow his current employer.

It was time to move up a few rungs on the ladder.

The partner's assistant, a gorgeous brunette named Ashley, led him into the now-familiar mahogany-furnished conference room, and pulled a tall black chair out from the table for him.

"Have a seat. Here's a bottle of water, Mr. Carlson. Mr. Bancroft will be right in."

Daniel watched the woman's curves as she walked out of the conference room. Her black dress defined every nook and cranny of her body.

"My daughter," said Andrew Bancroft as he walked into the conference room. "Isn't she a beauty?"

Daniel fumbled with his folder, and feigned straightening his coat.

"You can say she is. I know what I have."

"She's very beautiful, sir."

"Maybe you two can hook up. Once you accept my offer, of course. I wouldn't allow it otherwise. She needs to find a good husband, and you appear suitable."

Andrew Bancroft sat down, and slid the leather bound portfolio he'd been holding over to Daniel.

"I think you'll find the offer very fair. And lucrative. It's our final offer."

Daniel calmly and slowly opened the folder. He read the offer the firm's founding partner presented.

$450,000 per year.

"As requested, there is a bonus structure with that too. It's outlined on page three."

"I appreciate the offer Mr. Bancroft. It's a nice counter."

This was Daniel's third visit.

The first offer was low.

$275,000 without a bonus plan.

The second offer was a bit better.

$325,000.

But it still lacked a bonus structure or plan for becoming partner.

"And you'll see what it will take to become partner. We've outlined a very detailed plan. That's on page four, paragraph five. If you follow it to the letter, which I do not doubt you will, you can expect to have your name on the door in short order. We don't make that offer to anyone."

"I see that. What's this on page five, paragraph six?"

Inside, Daniel was doing a dance at the field goal stanchions.

On the exterior he was stoic and cautious.

Daniel tapped his pen on the paragraph he was referring to.

"It's a name clause. Common for actors and actresses who come from your part of the country. It happens to apply in this particular situation."

"My part of the country?"

"Fly over country. You're from the Dakota's I believe. There's an image on the west coast that has to be maintained. Your name is a little too ethnic."

"Carlson? Ethnic?"

"Yes. Very Scandinavian. Not too many of those here. In our business with our clients."

"I never thought Carlson to be ethnic."

Andrew Bancroft nodded.

"It's very ethnic as a matter of fact. Brings on an assumption of lesser intelligence. Our clientele is Hollywood's upper echelon. They expect intellect and the utmost discretion. Carlson doesn't convey that. It wouldn't portray the right image on our door, either."

"So in order to become a partner in this firm, I have to change my last name."

Daniel tapped his pen against the folder again. This particular request had taken him by surprise.

"Who chooses?"

"What?"

"My new last name."

"Lucky for you, I've talked it over with Ashley. We both think Carpenter would work. Daniel Carpenter, Attorney at Law. It has a very nice ring to it, and it's a very subtle modification. We feel it would be very easy for you to transition to. And not the least bit Scandinavian. Very intelligent sounding. Perfect for our firm. Carpenter would look good on the door."

Daniel played his trump card. If the partner and his daughter were already talking as if he were a member of the team, then they could up the ante.

"Make if half a million, and I'll sign right now."

Book 2: Summer

Fallow

"Unless you know what seeds have been sown, you can never know what will take hold and grow."

The Book of Lost and Forgotten Dreams

"The weed, a misplaced plant. The murderer, a misunderstood man."

The Book of Lost and Forgotten Dreams

JOHN P. GOETZ

2010

May 3, 2010

Outside of the Opera House Lab
Arvilla, ND

*

The act of torture and the murder of random women, quickly became a group effort. Albeit small, he had an audience. He stopped whistling long enough to shake the bone shards and sinew off of the newly severed left hand before he threw it into the orange bucket to the right of his worktable. The hand twirled three times, and hit the side of the bucket on its way down. The bucket tilted, almost spilled the entire contents, but then righted itself.

"That was close. Almost had one hellava mess."

"I'd give you a hand, but you just threw one."

"That was funny."

"I try."

The man laughed, popped a handful of blood-smeared sunflower seeds into his mouth, plucked one with his tongue, placed it between his teeth, and bit down. The crack of the shell echoed in the darkness as it split in two.

He laughed again.

"Now what's so funny?"

"The crack. Sounded just like her leg. Didn't it?"

"S'pose so. I don't know how you do that?"

"Do what?"

"Eat those seeds like a fuckin' squirrel."

"It's easy. All in the tongue."

He deftly touched the nut with the tip of his tongue, pulled it into his mouth, and spit the two shell halves onto the growing pile at his feet.

"I'm feeling down. I'm starting to feel like a dwarf."

"A what?"

"Sorry. I shouldn't talk while I'm chewing."

"I thought your mother taught you better."

"Shut up. Leave my mother out of this," he said as he cracked another shell. "I said I feel like a dwarf."

"I heard you, but I still don't understand."

"A dwarf. You know, from that old Disney cartoon. *Snow White*. The little guys with the white beards. I'm whistling. I'm working. Get it? Don't tell me you don't know about that."

"I know what a dwarf is. And I know the cartoon. I just don't know why you feel like one. You just don't look like a dwarf is all I'm saying."

The man regarded himself despite the darkness and shadows thrown by the surrounding trees. It was a calm evening with barely a breeze. A few clouds floated by and occasionally blocked the moon's light. The clouds were nothing ominous that foretold of approaching thunderstorms – just typical puffs that in the black sky were gray instead of white. In the distance he could hear the dull, constant, deep growl of a tractor still running at full bore. He stopped his work, and cocked his head in the direction of the rumble.

"That's a John Deere."

"And why is that important?"

"It's not. But I can tell by the sound of its engine. Like the commercial says, 'Nothing runs like a Deere.'"

"I'm not especially fond of green. And I think you should get back to what you were doing."

He could barely see the tractor's lights in the distance, but he could still detect the earthy smell of the black dirt being kicked up by the tractor and the drill it pulled behind it. Even from this distance, his keen sense of smell picked up the faint whisper of diesel exhaust.

He liked the smell.

"They should bottle that."

"What?"

"Diesel exhaust. They should bottle it. I'd definitely buy it. Splash it on like Old Spice."

"You and no one else, I'm sure."

"Oh, you be quiet."

"I wonder what he's planting."

"Probably wheat."

It was planting season after all, and the wheat had to be sown. And the barley. And the oats. And the durum. And the sunflower. And, well, everything. Everything had to be in the ground by the end of May in order for harvest to happen on time.

There was a schedule for everything.

Everyone knew farmers' lives depended on a successful planting season. The seeds were the first dominos in a long line to be felled.

"Well? Are you going to get back to work or what?"

"Ok. Ok. Quit being a dick, would ya?"

"That wasn't nice."

"Then why don't you help?"

"That's your job. Not mine. Remember that."

He used a battery-powered reciprocating saw on the right hand, cracked another nut, and tossed the shells and hand in the bucket.

"I know. You're right. I can't be a dwarf. I'm not short. Not fat. Don't have a white beard."

"No. Definitely not fat."

"Big boned," he said as he started whistling the same tune again.

But still, he considered, he *was* working hard. He *was* enjoying it. He *always* enjoyed *this* work. And he *was* whistling.

It seemed to make sense.

"That's quite a snappy tune."

"It's from the movie too."

"The one with the dwarves."

"Exactly," he giggled as he gave a bloodied thumbs up. "And I also have a beautiful woman working with me. Just like on the cartoon."

"She's not really working with you, you know. Like the one in the cartoon did. She could twirl and dance. This one? Not so much."

"She could before."

"Before doesn't matter."

"Cartoon girls aren't alive, anyway. They're not real."

"Smart ass. You know what I meant. Now you are being a dick."

"I know. She's not much help now. She's still fun though. Plus the movie girl had dark hair. This one was blonde. Used to be a cheerleader back in the day," he hesitated and looked up at the moon. "At least I think she was blonde. Maybe a ginger. One of them was blonde, anyway."

"Doesn't matter."

"No. You're right. Who cares what color hair she had."

"Not me."

He had to admit the reality of the situation. She really wasn't with him. She did put up a fight, and was really being a bitch before she went away. He still had the scratches on his arm. Now, she was more just here *with* him while he worked.

While he worked on her, to be more precise.

Her eyes were open though.

Watching him work and whistle.

He'd take them out soon enough.

The eyes were always the last he worked with. He liked eyes the best.

"Pretty eyes."

"What color?"

"Blue, I think. They're kinda cloudy now."

"You let her sit outside too long."

His lips were tiring of the whistle-pucker, sunflower nut-crack exercise, and his arms were numb and exhausted from the constant motion required by his work. He hadn't taken a rest in a few hours. He stopped his labor and musical ramblings to think about just which dwarf he'd be.

"Which one am I? Doc? Grumpy? Happy? Sneezy?"

There was no reply.

"Come on! I need a name. It didn't take so long to name the others. Why is it taking so long to name me? Doesn't it matter that we've been doing this for so long? I'm a key member of the team, right?"

The man looked around in the darkness. Confused. Almost scared at the black silence. A small bank of clouds covered the moon, and there wasn't even a faint shadow cast against the ground.

"No, not Sneezy," he said as he stifled a laugh. "I don't have any allergies. Where are you?"

"Or Sleepy."

"You scared me. I thought you'd left."

"I was just gone for a while. Pussy. Scared of the dark?"

"I'm not a pussy," he said indignantly to the waxing gibbous moon, balled his hand into a fist, and beat it against his thigh. "I don't need much sleep, so Sleepy wouldn't work. Nothing seems to fit!"

The man continued to beat his thigh in disgust with himself.

"Those names are too cartoony for you, anyway. Calm down. You get so excited over the smallest things."

The man calmed a bit, but continued to pound against his leg with his fist.

It would definitely be bruised later on.

"I feel so left out," he kicked his shoes in the blood-sticky dirt. "I just want a name is all. I *want* a name."

Then it came to him.

"Why should I be something that someone has already made? I should create something unique. A new name that no one else has."

"You've been doing this a long time now. What is it? Five years without a name?"

"Six."

"Ok. Then you should have a name. It's time. Be original. I mean your name, of course."

"I couldn't be the Original. We're only here because of him."

"Exactly."

"Yes! I'll be eighth dwarf."

"You're not short though."

"It's a metaphor, dummy. You know the song."

"Don't call me a dummy. You know better. You would be nothing without me."

"Sorry," the man looked down at his shoes and beat his leg harder. "I was just kidding."

"Calm down. Or I'll leave again."

"No. Don't do that. Please stay. I like talking to you."

"Are you going to behave? Calm down?"

"Yes. I'll try."

His name had to be powerful. It had to evoke fear. It couldn't be cute or cuddly. It would have to be something special. He provided a valuable service after all. He helped the women transition to a better place.

"What was her name?"

"What does it matter? I want a name for me?"

"I'm just curious."

"Cindy, I think. Maybe Tara. Can't remember."

"I like Cindy. Pretty name. Do you know for sure?"

"I don't know. Like I said, it may have been Tara. I can find her stuff. Should be around here somewhere."

"Don't bother. She doesn't need it anymore. What should we call you though?"

"Pestilence?"

"Sounds like you're a mosquito. Or a wood tick. You need something better. Less itchy."

"Yeah. Something evil. I like where you are going."

"Remember your Latin from Sunday school?"

The man stopped kicking the dirt. His fist beating slowed to a dull thump. His leg would be sore.

"Yes. I do. I still have the scars from where the nuns hit me when I couldn't count backwards from ten."

"You probably still can't."

"Decem, novem, octo,"

"Ten, nine, eight. Not bad. Still know the mass in Latin?"

"No shit."

Then it came to him.

"Evil. Malum. You are so smart. I would have never thought of that. Malum. Latin for evil."

"Sounds perfect."

"Malum it is. Definitely a strong name."

"Do you think he'll like it?"

"Who?"

"The Original, who else?"

"I'm sure he'll be fine. Can we get back to work now? We still have to get with Boots, grind everything, and feed it to the swine."

Malum laughed.

"Damn pigs. They'll eat anything."

Another wisp of clouds covered the moon and its light faded. The glow through the clouds, however still cool as it approached midnight, warmed his soul.

"I'm so happy you like my name."

There was no reply.

May 4, 2010

Larimore, ND

*

Sheriff's deputy Booker Anthony Thorson was on still on duty, but he had a special errand to run. Something he did twice a week without fail. His holster hung at his hips with his gun on his left. His radio hung off of his right shirt pocket. His silver nametag with THORSON engraved in black letters was placed above his left pocket. The creases on his pants and shirt were stiff and ironed to perfection. His shoes were buff-shined to a blinding sheen.

Booker stood at the front door, and pressed the doorbell. There was a small wreath hanging on the front door that said, "Home Sweet Home." When there was no answer, he rang the bell again, and knocked three times.

He looked at his watch and then turned around to double-check the parking lot.

Her car was there.

Finally, he heard the deadbolt turn, and the door ease open.

"Booker. You are so handsome in your uniform. I was in the bathroom."

"Thanks, Mom."

It was their standard lunch date. Every Tuesday and Thursday at noon, his mother cooked him his favorite meal: grilled cheese and onion on sourdough with Campbell's tomato soup made with milk, not water. His grilled cheese was, as always, cut into four equal-sized triangles.

His mother moved from the old farmhouse into a small apartment two blocks from the high school shortly after he graduated from the police academy.

Now he had the old farm to himself.

It was Deputy Booker's Bachelor Pad.

"I have lunch all ready," she said. "Take that holster off, and sit down. That thing scares me."

"Dad wore one all of the time, ma."

"I know. And it scared me then, too."

Booker unclasped his holster, and laid it lengthwise on his mother's floral couch.

*

Winnie Thorson turned sixty-one in March. She was slowing down a bit, but nothing significant in her opinion. Her naturally auburn hair didn't have a single strand of gray. The only telltale sign of her age was the set of crow's feet extending from each of her eyes. The reading glasses she had to keep on the top of her head didn't help though.

In three years, she will have been single for twenty years. Even though she had received several offers, she'd never dated. Buck was the irreplaceable love of her life.

Now her days revolved around her son, and she cherished every minute she could spend with him. They sat across from one another at the kitchen table in her small kitchen. The single, small window that she had fully opened, looked out to the small playground.

"Kids playing much yet?"

"After school mostly. They're pretty good. They keep it quiet."

"If the noise gets out of hand, let me know. I'll shoot them."

Winnie hit her son across the top of his head.

"You be nice!"

Booker gave her a wide grin as he took a bite of his sandwich.

"Did you sub any last week?"

"Once. For an English teacher at the high school."

Booger took a spoonful of his soup and followed it with the cold Dr. Pepper his mother always had ready for him.

"You're having your headaches again, aren't you honey? I can see it in your eye."

"I'm fine. Just tired."

"You're lying. A mother knows."

Booker smiled at his mother, and tried to change the subject.

"So what's been going on?"

"You are just like your father. You change the subject when you don't want to talk about something."

Booker smiled.

"I learned from the best."

She pushed the paper in his direction.

"Did you hear about this? It's just terrible."

"What?"

Winnie unfolded the *Grand Forks Tribune,* and turned the picture that was above the fold towards Booker.

"I remember her. She was in your class, wasn't she? Cindy Brady. She was a cheerleader. Everyone called her Cin."

Booker glanced at the newspaper, and the photo of the blonde. He crinkled his mouth, and shook his head.

"She doesn't look familiar. That was so long ago, Mom."

"She was in your high school class. 1997, right? With Danny and Dirk? That wasn't so long ago."

"What happened? Why's she on the front page?"

"She's been missing for a week. Found her car abandoned at the taco shop in Forks. Her parents still live here in Larimore. By the water tower. Across from the elementary school."

Booker sopped up the soup with the last triangle of his second sandwich, then washed it down with his pop.

"I hope they find her. Five days though?"

"That's what it says."

Booker shook his head.

"What's wrong?"

"Stats. Generally missing persons have forty-eight hours. After that, the news is never good."

"Oh jeez. I'll have to bring something over to Frank and Linda. See if there's anything I can do. Maybe a tuna casserole or something."

"I'm sure they'd like that, Mom."

Booker looked at his watch, and then wiped the crumbs from his mouth with the precisely folded square of paper towel that his spoon was sitting on.

"Thanks for everything, Mom. Gotta run. Excellent lunch as usual."

As she always did, Winnie took her son's face in her hands, and kissed each eye.

"Love ya, kiddo."

"Love you too, Mom."

"Same time Thursday?"

"Same time Thursday."

May 5, 2010

The Opera House Lab
Arvilla, ND

*

He felt complete, finally felt like a man with a purpose.

He was Malum. A man with a name.

It had a nice ring to it, and not the least bit wimpy.

Or itchy.

He'd been around for too many years without a name. He didn't know why it took so long for him to finally push the subject. He'd asked Marco so many times he'd lost count.

But he knew it wasn't Marco's decision.

"He's not ready to give you a name," he always said. "When he's ready, you'll know."

It hadn't taken so long with the others. The others were baptized, and named quickly. Sometimes within hours of appearing. Sometimes a few days. A week at the most.

Never years.

Never.

Except for him.

He assumed it was because he was the special one of the team.

He didn't know why he was different. But in the end, it didn't matter, for now he had a job to do. He had to bring the newest member of the family up to speed.

Someone who came to live with them two days ago.

He had to let him know about the others. To teach him the ins and outs of being the newest member of the family.

Malum pulled a chair out from the kitchen table and sat down.

"You're the sixth, you know."

Malum saw a faint nod.

"That's ok. Being the new guy can be scary. Be the quiet type if you want, but you'll learn to speak up after a while. Otherwise you'll just get run-over. Stop me if you have any questions."

"It's scary here."

"You're scared?"

The new one nodded.

"There's no reason to be scared. No one's going to hurt you. Just do what you're told and you'll be fine. Try to keep your mouth shut about our little operation here. Understand?"

"Yes."

"Good. Now, you're Zeke, right?"

"Zeke."

"Speak up. Can't hear a word you are saying the way you are mumbling."

"I'm Zeke."

"That's what I thought I heard. Zeke it is. Welcome to the family, Zeke."

The family was growing. They were now a party of six; things were getting very crowded. Malum didn't know if there would be room for any more, but that wasn't his decision. If more were needed, more would come. And when that happened, if that happened, he'd just have to make room like he did with for the others.

Malum turned his attention back to the new guy.

"Let me give you the low-down on the family you are joining. We are a team. There's Marco, Jimmy Boy, and Clint. They've all been around for a while. Marco is the oldest. The first. Came around in 1990. Then it's Jimmy Boy. I'm the fourth. Joined up probably fifteen years ago, but I can't really remember. Everything kinda mushes all together. Then Clint. Now you. Boots is like a member of the family and comes around when we need him. He's our engineer of sorts. You'll like him."

Malum reached for a piece of cheese he'd sliced and put on a small plate on the table for them to share.

"What? You want to know about Jimmy Boy? Why him?"

"I like the name. Better than Zeke."

Malum grabbed a handful of crackers.

"I agree. He has an odd name. Not like the rest of us. Most want to know about the Original. Why he brought us here and everything. But you asked. So here you go. Jimmy

Boy. That's a tough one. Well, he's definitely the talker. He's kinda cute in that baseball cap, he just never shuts up. Never stops cleaning. Fucking annoying if you ask me. Royal pain in the ass, but someone's gotta do what he does. All of us have a job. Even you, my friend. Even you."

Malum filled two glasses with cranberry juice; drank from one, and pushed the other to the new guy.

"Who's Marco?"

"Marco? You want to know about Marco? You like to play with fire don't you?"

"Why?"

"Asking about Marco. That's why. Just remember these four words and you will be ok: don't fuck with Marco. It's very simple. He has a hot temper. No patience whatsoever. Don't talk to him. Avoid eye contact. If he asks you to do something, just do it. He doesn't like newbies, and you are the newbie until someone else comes along, and I really don't know if we have room for anymore if you ask me. He really doesn't like anyone. He tolerates The Original at times. He does respect Boots though."

"He runs things?"

"Yes. For the most part. He's the boss."

Malum shook his head. He felt goose bumps crawl down his back. Even he didn't fuck around when Marco was involved.

"That's a lot to remember."

"Yes, I know that was a lot, but I'm serious. Don't fuck with Marco. He's the closest to the Original, and what he says goes. He's very smart. Now do you want to know about the others or not?"

"I'm a little sleepy."

"That always happens. The new ones are always tired for a few days. Battery gets drained. Don't know why. But you'll come around. Have more energy."

"Who are you?"

"Me? I'm Malum. Just got my name the other day as a matter of fact. It's Latin, you know. Means evil."

Malum puffed his chest.

"Why'd it take so long?"

"You're preaching to the choir, my friend. I don't know why it took so long. Maybe I just wasn't ready until now. But I like it. I like my name."

"What's your job?"

"Well, I um. It's hard to describe, really."

Zeke shrugged.

"I'm not going anywhere."

"You're funny for a newbie. Don't you dare talk like that to Marco. Trust me. He'll kill you. And if that happens, we all get hurt. Have you ever seen the Brady Bunch? You know, that old sitcom?"

Zeke nodded.

"Good. Then you'll know what I mean when I say to think of me as Sam the Butcher. Charismatic. The ladies love me. Sweetness covering something sharp."

Zeke imitated a stab though the heart.

"You're funny. Yes. I know all of the best cuts and even how to tenderize. We have a pretty good setup down in the Opera House Lab. I'll tell you about the others later. We have a lot to get done, and not a lot of time."

"What is it?"

"We have to go slop the pigs," Malum laughed. "With our own special feed. You might meet Boots too, if he's around."

"What was her name?"

"Cindy Brady."

"Like that sitcom?"

"Yes. Just like the sitcom."

JOHN P. GOETZ

2012

Journal Entry
Of Dirk Kinnear

April 13, 2012

Dear Sam:

Are you sitting down? Remember a while back when I mentioned that the woman in the big house said that, "All things beautiful come from God," and I said that, in my opinion, "All things beautiful come from the Internet?"

Well, I was right. And for once in my life I'm actually feeling pretty good about it.

Are you curious?

Well, I met someone. We haven't met officially yet as it's all been virtual, but I'm hoping that we can meet in person.

How you ask?

It's a dating site just for women who are interested in dating farmers. For some reason, some think we are sexy. Yes, I know, it's an online site, but there's no one around here that I'd consider dating. Everyone around here is too old, already seeing someone, or smokes.

Sometimes it's all three.

Anyway, I joined the site the other day. It's called luvafarmer.com. It costs $9.95 a month for guys, but it's free for the girls. I, for one, think that's sexist, but it's their business model, and it appears to be working. The funny thing is that they are based out of Miami. I honestly didn't know there were farms in Florida – coulda fooled me! And Miami is a long ways from Arvilla, ND. They have a slew of other sites: luvalawyer, luvadoctor, and luvamechanic. Luvafarmer caught my eye right away. Plus they have billboards everywhere now. What's amazing is that there are hundreds of women on the site. I've chatted with four women so far. One from Rhode Island. One from Oregon. One from North Carolina. The one I'm most excited about is from Grand Forks. Yup. Just twenty miles east. And get this.

Are you ready?

She says I'm cute despite my profile name: DIRTYFARMBOY.

It's not what you think. Maybe I'll change it. But really, it's just a takeoff of my nickname.

I have to admit though, it does pique the curiosity of some of the ladies.

She's from St. Paul. She's a senior at UND studying mass communications. She works in a dentist's office in Grand Forks now and is taking summer classes.

I know. I know. You can stop your laughing now. I know what you are saying.

"Your pigs are cute, too."

Her name is Holly Newcomb, and we are going on our first date on Saturday.

Sincerely,

Dirt

May 29, 2012

The Carlson Farm
Arvilla, ND

*

It was six in the morning. The sun was just rising and a slight breeze was floating through the open window and fluffing the curtains that Sis had made more than twenty-five years ago. Their home was a wealth of memories. Art projects the kids had made in junior high were still hanging on the upstairs hallway. The hand prints that both Danny and Bekks made when they were in fifth grade were hanging next to the front door on loops of yarn.

Skip and Sis sat at the kitchen table wordlessly drinking coffee. Even though both of their children had left the nest years ago, the silence was unnerving.

They were getting old.

Skip turned up the volume on the radio. The farm report was on. Even the radio was getting old. Its white plastic case was now more yellow.

Skip thought he could still hear Danny's heavy, clodding footsteps as he hopped out of bed, and headed into the bathroom.

Those were wishful thoughts.

"Want to top it off?"

Skip pushed his coffee cup towards the center of the table.

"Sure."

"If it's bothering you this much, why don't you wait? Do it next year? Maybe the year after?"

"Because we are almost sixty-five now. Both of us. We're too old to be managing three-thousand acres."

The radio was on its normal station and the monotonous voice of the morning farm report's announcer was telling them the current state of affairs and the rollercoaster prices of farm commodities.

Wheat was up a nickel.

Barley was down two cents.

"Can you turn to the news? I can't listen to that voice any longer."

"You have two hands, don't you?"

"Can't find my glasses. I can't see the damn dial."

Sis pointed to her head.

"Up there."

Skip felt the top of his head and laughed. His cheaters were where they always were when they weren't on his nose. On the top of his head.

"Shit. I'm getting old."

"You're still handsome as all get out."

Skip smiled.

"And you are still drop dead gorgeous. You'll look great in that bikini on the beach."

"You made up your mind then?"

"Auction in October. Florida in November. Sell everything. Just like we discussed yesterday."

Sunflowers were up a penny.

Corn was down a nickel.

Soybeans were up two.

Another college girl was missing.

"I hope they catch whoever is doing this. Everyone is so scared."

Skip nodded.

"Read about it in the Tribune yesterday. Some girl from St. Paul. I think her name was Holly Newcomb or something like that. They had her picture on the front. Pretty girl."

"Things like that aren't supposed to happen here. That's big city stuff."

"Proves that it's time for us to leave."

June 1, 2012

The Law Office of Bancroft, Simpson, and Associates
Santa Monica, CA

*

The Pacific was three miles to the west. He couldn't see it, but even in his air-conditioned, humidity-controlled makore-furnished office off of Wilshire Blvd in Santa Monica, he could smell it. The salty air of the California coast was so much different from what he grew up breathing in North Dakota. California air had an exotic thickness to it. It had a constant, acidic flavor that stuck to the back of his tongue with each breath. He'd grown used to it, had learned to like it, and now couldn't imagine life without it. California air flavored everything. He needed the acidic burn in his lungs just as much as he needed a five-shot latte each morning.

North Dakota air was thin and light. Rather flat. Flavorless. Unless you were standing next to a tractor and getting the diesel fumes fed directly into your lungs. A person can see what he is breathing in California. It has character and swirls when you drive through it. The North Dakota air he remembered was boring. It didn't swirl and burn his throat.

Daniel's problem was that the more he thought about it, the more he found that he actually missed home. Despite the seemingly constant internal struggles to deny it.

But Southern California was his home now. North Dakota was almost two thousand miles, and a decade, away. Senior Associate Daniel Carpenter of Inglewood, formerly Danny Carlson of Arvilla, was well on his way to becoming partner. Soon, if everything worked according to his plan, the firm's large, frosted-glass front doors, would be changed to include his name:

The Law Offices of Bancroft, *Carpenter*, Simpson, and Associates

He'd been at the firm three years now, and he was the star he'd advertised himself as. He didn't want anything to jeopardize his trip to a corner office on the building's fifth, and topmost, floor. He'd worked too hard to let his plans go awry. The spreadsheet he was preparing had to be spot-on before his meeting with the firm's founder, managing partner, and future father-in-law, William Bancroft.

*

A chirp from his desk phone interrupted Daniel's concentration. Even though its tone was acoustically calibrated for his office, he jumped at the noise, and quickly pressed the blinking button to silence it.

"Yes?"

"Sorry to bother you, Mr. Carpenter, but I have a Rebecca Peterssen again. She's on line two. Should I tell her you are with a client?"

His sister, Bekks.

Her third attempt to talk to him since he sat down at his desk at 7:30.

He looked at his watch.

It was 9:30.

She was nothing if not persistent.

Daniel looked at spreadsheet on his computer screen, jotted E14 on sticky note, and tossed it in the folder in front of him. He wanted to start exactly where he'd left off.

"Put her through."

"Who is she?"

"No one."

He pressed the blinking button on his phone, and began nervously weaving his black Monteblanc Meisterstück Classique pen between the fingers of his right hand. He could sit in front of humorless judges and a dozen lawyers and not be nervous. His sister calls, and he turns into a basket case. Daniel shook his head in amazement but continued twirling his pen.

"Hey, Bekks."

"So you finally decided to tell your little blonde gatekeeper to let me through."

"Her name is Hanna. She's not blonde. She's a red head, and she'd actually quite good, as a matter of fact."

"Hanna. Sorority girl. Kappa Imma Slut, I'm sure. And a ginger? You know they don't have souls."

"Come on, Bekks."

"Does she put out?"

"She's a great assistant, if you must ask."

"So is a poodle with proper training."

"You called me, remember?" said Dan as he tried, probably unsuccessfully, to hide his annoyance.

"I still think she sounds like a Zappa progeny."

"Bekks, I'm very busy."

"Whatever. Am I talking to Daniel or Danny. Carpenter or Carlson? There's like four of you now, right?"

"Depends. If you are going to bitch at me for not coming home, not calling, not sending a post card, not being a farmer, not being the perfect son, not ensuring the sky is constantly blue, then it's Daniel Carpenter and my rate is $700 per hour. If you called because you want to talk to your big brother, and tell him how much you love and admire him for getting out while he could, then it's Danny Carlson and there's no charge."

"What if it's both?"

"My rate goes up to $800. Your choice," Daniel looked at the Rolex Platinum Pearlmaster on his wrist. "I bill in fifteen minute increments. So the minute Hanna put you through, you were at two hundred."

"You're an ass, you know that?"

"That just cost you another five Jacksons."

"You're still an ass."

"I'm a lawyer. It's my job. If I fart while thinking about a client, I bill it. Part of the game, Bekks," Daniel decided that he should lighten up. It was his sister, after all. "What's up?"

He was met with silence.

"Bekks?"

"It's dad."

Daniel stopped weaving his pen. He could tell she was crying.

"What about him?"

"They've decided to sell the farm. Mom and Dad. It was supposed to go to you. To us. You weren't supposed to leave, Dan."

"I can't worry about that, Bekks. You know that. I'm here now. I'm a lawyer. Not a farmer."

"He doesn't look good. Mom's worried."

"I can't worry about that, Bekks. Mom and Dad will do what they need to do. You know that."

The line went silent for a while.

"Bekks?"

"You're an ass, Dan. A real ass."

Dan heard a click as the line went dead.

June 1, 2012

The Opera House Lab
Arvilla, ND

*

Jimmy Boy adjusted his Minnesota Twins baseball cap, and stopped his furious polishing. He wiped the sweat from his forehead with his arm, sat against the doorframe of his bathroom, and peered down the stairs into the basement. There were too many lights on, and they were starting to affect his concentration.

He stretched his legs out and released a loud groan. A voice called up from the Opera House Lab.

"What's wrong?"

"Oh. Nothing," he lied. "I was getting a cramp. I'm not as young as I used to be! But it doesn't matter does it. The home can never be too clean."

"What?"

"I'm polishing the floors. Like 'em to shine, you know. Had to stop to stretch my legs. And the "getting old" thing was just a joke, by the way. I'll always be here for you."

If he extended his toes, Jimmy Boy could almost touch the hallway's opposite wall. He leaned forward and rubbed his sore knees and looked down hallway.

He saw a smudge.

"Damn it. I missed a spot."

When Jimmy Boy heard what he thought was a thump, he looked down the stairwell. He could see the shadows thrown against the cinderblock wall and the blue painted concrete floor from the small night light he bought at one of those dollar stores last year.

"Was that you? Clint? Zeke?"

"It's Clint. And I dropped the knife."

"Oh. Ok. Just wasn't sure. Excited for movie night?"

"Of course."

"Yeah. Me too."

"Do you want popcorn? I have an unopened bag of Old Dutch plain the half-bag of Old Dutch white cheddar we started from last week."

"Fresh? Or stale like it always is. I hate chewy popcorn."

"Yes, they are still fresh. I used a chip clip. Quit your complaining."

"Any pop?"

"Oh. Just a sec."

Jimmy Boy eased himself up from the floor, walked back into the kitchen, and opened the fridge.

"Damn. Just a second," Jimmy Boy slapped his forehead. "I forgot about that smudge."

Jimmy Boy walked back into the hallway, bent down so the light was just right, and found the spot on the floor that he'd missed.

"I gotta get this cleaned up, first."

*

"Sorry that took so long. I ended up doing the entire thing over again. But we have Coke and Sprite," yelled Jimmy Boy on his way back to the stairwell after triple-checking the sheen of the hallway's hardwood floor.

"Sprite."

"Want ice? I'll bring both bags of popcorn. I know how you like to mix it up."

"I want my own bowl."

"Yes. I know. I know. I'll bring a bowl for you. I know how you make a mess and it's easier to clean"

Jimmy Boy eased back onto his hands and knees and re-started his polishing. He suddenly stopped, and skidded backwards to the stairwell.

"Almost forgot! I have a couple of VHS' that I hope you'll like."

"I suppose they are those Disney ones you like."

"Of course they are Disney. What else is there?"

"Something good? A crime drama perhaps? I thriller?"

Jimmy Boy looked at the only two VHS tapes he had. The only ones in the house.

"*Lion King* and *The Rescuers Down Under*."

"Shit. I'm so tired of those. *Lion King* I suppose."

"*Lion King* it is. We just watched that last week, but if you want to see it again, fine with me. Love that one."

"Hurry it up though. Quit the cleaning and get the movie going."

"Just give me a few minutes, and I'll be down. This floor still isn't right."

Jimmy Boy re-adjusted his baseball cap, sprayed more Liquid Gold polish on the dust rag, and resumed polishing the hallway's hardwood floor.

"Kills my knees, but we can never be too clean! Can't be a dirty-birdie like you!"

*

Even though the flickering television provided some light, Clint wanted even more. He didn't like being in his basement without lots of light.

He was afraid of the dark.

He normally didn't do movie night, but no one else showed up.

Just him and Jimmy Boy.

He really didn't like being in the basement.

The shadows.

The smells.

The equipment.

The dark.

The screams.

Sometimes Clint would see unexplained shadows of the corner of his eye as he walked down the stairs. As soon as he'd turn to look, they'd disappear into the dark corners of one of the special rooms. Sometimes, when he was in a hurry, he could hear something whisper his name in the dark.

"Clint."

He'd feel the hairs on the back of his neck crawl whenever that happened.

He hit the light switch with his elbow and waited for the first two rows of florescent shop lights hung from the basement rafters to flicker on. He hit the second switch and another set of fifteen lights turned on.

As each light flickered on, the shadows of the tree-shaped air fresheners that hung from the lights twirled on the floor. They were a conglomeration of scents: pine, new car, cherry, and even leather.

At this point, they all smelled the same.

His roommates weren't too keen on personal hygiene, so it was Boots who devised the air freshener trick to make the room smell better. Except for Jimmy Boy, his roommates were beyond hope, and always smelled bad.

Clint yelled up to the first floor.

"The air freshener supply is getting low. I really don't like the leather scent."

“Get more pine then. The green tree ones.”

“Yeah. I’ll be sure to order more of those. You can get anything online these days.”

Finally, when all of the lights were on, and he could hear their distinctive hum, he made himself comfortable on the couch.

Clint heard Jimmy Boy.

“Come up and help,” Jimmy Boy yelled. “I can’t carry everything.”

*

Jimmy Boy adjusted his baseball cap and walked down the stairs. He deliberately skipped the fourth step as that one was cut down the center and was supported by a mere sixteenth of an inch of wood across its top. A small five-pound bag of potatoes would be enough to break through the plank. Under the step was another piece of wood with dozens of nails with the business end up. It was a little deterrent that Boots devised.

The tray was stacked with the movie-night snacks: bags of popcorn, 2-liter bottles of pop, a bowl, and two glasses of ice. The two VHS tapes were balanced on top of the popcorn bowl. *Lion King* was on top. That’s what Clint had said he wanted to watch.

Jimmy Boy sat the tray down on the couch and turned around to see if Clint was following him.

"I have one of those. Really!" said Clint as he turned the corner into the small alcove where the TV was positioned against the wall. He'd furnished it with a love seat, a small table, and a 30" flat screen television. The TV was always on. Most of the time just a blue screen but sometimes there was the flicker of static. Right now, at two in the morning the networks weren't showing much of anything but infomercials.

Clint loved infomercials.

They always were selling something cool.

Something worthwhile.

New gadgets and all.

"Really! I have one of those automatic knife sharpeners. It's pretty slick. Works like a charm. Marco and Malum love it."

"Where is it?"

"It's right over there. Malum used it just the other night as a matter of fact. Well worth the $19.95. Or so I'm told."

"We should get another one in case that one breaks."

"Should I? Do you think so?"

Jimmy Boy nodded.

"You're right. I will."

Clint picked up the phone, dialed the number on the screen, and ordered another knife sharpener.

June 15, 2012

Butch's Bar
Arvilla, ND

*

"Deputy Booger," yelled Dirt. "Get over here, and sit your ass down."

Dirt watched his friend walk over to the table. He was still in his blues and his holstered gun bounced against his leg. The clasp on the leather case hanging from his belt on his hip was unsnapped and his stainless steel set of cuffs peeked through. Booger looked pretty good in his uniform and never had any trouble landing the ladies.

Dirt accepted long ago that of the three musketeers, he was the one hit with the "not so pretty" stick. While Dan and Booger were potential fodder for the cover of *GQ* magazine, his was a face more suited to the back pages of *Mad.*

"Have time for a beer? Or are you still on duty."

Booger tapped his silver badge with his hand.

"On duty. If this is on, anything more than club soda could get me in trouble. Gordy would cut my balls off."

"So it's Deputy Booger for now. Good enough. Can I at least buy Deputy Booger a club soda or a can of pop?"

"Sure," said Booger as he turned to the bar. "Lina. Can I get a club soda with lime?"

"What's the magic word?"

"Please?"

"Nope."

"Fuck you?"

"That's two words."

"Kiss my ass?"

"That's three. I said one. You had old, drunk Mr. Swenson for math, didn't you?"

"Shit. I don't know. All I want is a glass of club soda."

"That's it," smiled Lina. "Sit down. I'll bring it right over."

"Lina. Can you bring me a shot of Windsor?"

"Sure thing, Dirt."

"Why didn't you ask him for the magic word?"

"Because I like Dirt. You? Not so much. Plus he has nice hair. All tied up in a ponytail. Sexy."

Booger scooted his chair up to the table, rocked it onto its two back legs, and leaned against the wall.

"She loves me."

"Lina? I don't think so."

"Why not?"

"I think she's still waiting for Dan."

"Not gonna happen. She is so fucking hot in that leather cowboy hat," growled Booger as he and turned back to Dirt. "Dan doesn't know what he left behind."

"Dan gave her that hat. She always has it on."

"She needs to get a life. Get over him."

"Hat or no hat, Booger, Lina is hot all of the time. Those blue eyes. That blonde hair. Enough to make a man beg. And as for Dan, he knows exactly what he did. He had dreams. Wanted to escape. He's not worried about anything here in North Dakota."

"I'll help her forget him."

"Did you hear the latest?"

Booger crinkled his eyebrows and pursed his lips.

"No. Haven't been around much. Been busy."

"I heard from Bekks that he's on the road to making partner."

"Good for him," nodded Booger. "He's too good for us now, I suppose. He'll never come back here. Voluntarily, anyway. Makes more in a day than I make in a mother-fucking year. A funeral's about the only thing that he'd come back for at this point."

The two stopped talking when Lina brought the whiskey and glass of club soda.

"Here you go, guys. I'll put it on your tab, Dirt. Anything else?"

"A table dance? Maybe a lap dance?"

Lina looked at Booger, and rolled her eyes.

"I'd back-hand you Deputy Booger, but you'd probably slap those cuffs on me."

"Promise?"

"I'll leave you *boys* alone," Lina said. As she started to walk away, she turned around back to her friends. "And yes, I know I look hot in this hat. I get better tips that way."

Lina slid the brim of her hat below her eyes, turned around, wiggled her butt, and slinked back behind the bar.

"I'll give you more than the tip," said Booger.

"Keep it up, Deputy. Keep it up. And, by the way, I need more than this," said Lina as she wiggled her pinky finger.

Dirt and Lina laughed.

Booger turned pink.

"She's feisty. I like 'em like that. Still single?" asked Booger.

"Yes! I am," yelled Lina from behind the bar. "And I want it that way."

"Fuck. She's got good ears."

Dirt poured the contents of the shot glass into Booger's club soda.

"Hey! I'm on duty."

"Fuck it. Did I tell you what Dan did?"

"No. Like I said, I haven't been around much."

"Buying a house I guess."

"What?"

Dirt nodded.

"And engaged to the partner's daughter. Bekks told me. I don't think Sis and Skip know, so don't say anything."

"Still going by Carpenter?"

Dirt nodded.

"Don't say anything to Skip or Sis. That would kill them. I don't think they know. At least not Skip."

"How's Skip doing? Heard he was selling the farm."

"Heard the same. This fall I think. He's having an auction after the harvest. It will be his last."

"Bekks say when?"

Dirt shook his head.

"No. She's kinda leaving it be. Says he's changed a lot. Called him a royal prick the last time she called him. Guess he's thinking of buying a big fuck-ass mansion too."

"Screwing the boss's daughter. Smart move."

Dirt cut his eyes over to Lina. Even though she wasn't looking at them, he was sure she'd heard everything he said. He didn't intend for that to happen, but he was sure it wasn't anything she didn't already know.

"One lucky son-of-a-bitch. Got out when he could. We should have all left."

"Some of us are prisoners here," Dirt lifted his hand. "Me for one. I don't even think about it anymore. It's easier that way. Probably you, too."

Booger took in a deep breath, and slowly exhaled as he nodded and took long drink from his spiked club soda. When Booger put the glass back down on the table, Dirt noticed that except for a few cubes of ice, and the green rind of a lime, the glass was empty.

"Your band playing tonight?"

"Yeah. Thought I'd have a few before everyone showed up. Helps loosen the chords and fingers."

Booger pointed at Dirt's chest.

"Love the shirt. That new?"

"Yup. Jenny designed it."

"Jenny who?"

"Jenny from high school. Remember her?"

"Sounds familiar."

"Good in art. Kinda short. You have to remember her. It wasn't *that* long ago."

"Sorry. Drawing a blank on that one. Must not have made much of an impression on me."

"Doesn't matter, I guess. Well, she made the design. Just came in the other day," Dirt smiled and looked proudly down at his shirt.

"Wait. Think I remember now. You tried to date her, right?"

"*Tried.* She didn't like my long hair. Said I looked too much her cousin Veronica."

"Yeah. I remember her. Dark hair. Pug nose. Big tits. Always had a camel toe."

"She was very nice."

"Whatever. They're always 'very nice' but 'I'm very nice' does not mean 'I put out.' "

"You're such a pig."

Booger shrugged, and bobbed his head as if to say, "Yeah, tell me something I don't know."

Dirt's black t-shirt had the name of his band, "Dirty Deeds" scribbled in a multi-colored crayon font over caricatures of him and the two other members of his band. Each was covered in mud.

"Can I get one?"

"A shirt?"

"No. Your dick. Of course your shirt. They're cool. I'd wear it everywhere. Advertise your band."

"What size?"

"Large."

"Our first set ends at 8:00. Come back, and I'll have one ready for you."

"You still playing every Friday?"

"Yup. As long as Butch makes money, he still has us play. Go till closing. Might start to play Saturdays too, but I gotta run that by the guys in the band before I tell Butch anything. Want that shirt autographed? "

"Ummm. Let me think about it," Booger looked up at the ceiling and held his chin between his thumb and forefinger. "Hmmmm. Fuck no."

"Bastard."

Booger brought the front legs of his chair down, pushed back from the table, and stood up.

"See you at eight. Catch ya later, Lina," Booger kissed the palm of his hand, and threw spit-kiss towards her.

Lina caught the kiss, spiked it into the sink, and turned on the garbage disposal.

"Oh. That hurt, Lina."

"See ya later, Boog," laughed Lina. "Be safe. It's a jungle out there."

"Oh yeah. Highway 2 between Arvilla and Larimore is a regular kill zone. Best get my flak jacket on."

*

Dirty Deeds finished the first set, and Dirt delicately placed his guitar on his stool.

His throat was dry, and he needed a beer.

Or two.

"Gonna play my song for me tonight, Dirty?"

Dirt smiled as he recognized the sultry voice, and smelled the all-consuming aroma of Charlie – the woman's favorite, and always over-used, K-Mart perfume.

Julie Walker was leaning against the bar making sure it didn't fall over and make too much of a mess that Butch would have to clean up. Julie was thirty-five years older than Dirt, but when she had enough beer in her, she seemed to think that Dirt was the sexiest man on the face of the earth. They'd hooked up once.

Once.

They were both drunk, and he was five years younger then. She hadn't let him forget that night, and she'd never stopped begging for a repeat performance.

It wasn't going to happen.

Julie had huge breasts that overflowed the too-small bras that she always seemed to wear. She loved to present them to anyone who would look, and would sometimes reach underneath and push them up with her fists. She never missed a chance to thrust them in Dirt's direction whenever he and his band were playing. The moment her blood transitioned from having red and white blood cells to being pure malt barley, she started to not only push up her boobs, but nuzzle them with her face.

From what he'd learned listening to the lore of Arvilla, his father dated her in high school before he met that woman he eventually married.

That made his memory of that single night with Julie even worse.

"You could have been my mother," he once said to her.

"Oh. That turns me on," she slurred and threw a wink.

A seductive wink from a drunken woman who could hardly walk was extremely comical as her cheeks crinkled up, forced her mouth into a grimace, and closed both eyes.

Julie was always at the bar when his band played.

Tonight was no exception.

"Hi Julie. How are things?"

"Just fine," she said as she thrust her chest at him.

She wiggled her shoulders, and started to talk in a throaty voice she surely thought was the ultimate of sexual come-ons.

"These aren't for milk any more, Dirty. They're for fun. And just for you."

She did the fist trick, and pushed her boobs up to her cheeks.

"Leave the kid alone, Julie. Why don't you ever ask me to play with them?"

Dirt turned to see Jimmy Morgan slumped on his bar stool, picking rectangles of paper off of a stack of pull tabs. He was sucking on a Winston that had reached its filter, and had died hours ago.

Julie gave Jimmy the finger.

"Fuck off, Jimmy Morgan. Why don't you go play with yourself?"

Dirt started to walk up to the bar. Julie grabbed for his shoulder but her hand landed at his waist.

"I was distracted by your crotch, Dirty."

Julie licked her lips.

Watching a drunken woman try to seductively lick her lips was almost as comical as watching her wink. Julie's lipstick smeared across her mouth, and up to the bridge of her nose.

Dirt felt a wave of red embarrassment work its way from his toes to his forehead. He tried to inconspicuously look down at what was evidently distracting her. He hoped it wasn't what she thought it was.

Then he saw it and a wave of relief washed over him.

He dug his hand into his pocket, and pulled out a wad of tissues and his phone.

"Just my phone," he said to Julie.

"I'd like to find out for sure, Dirty."

Dirt made eye contact with Lina who was working behind the bar. He put up two fingers.

Lina nodded.

"Want me to play *Take It Easy* for you Julie?"

"I love the Eagles, Dirty. And you do them so well."

Dirt kissed her on the cheek.

"Just for you then, Julie. We'll play it during our next set, and I'll dedicate it to you. Ok?"

Julie bent forward and almost fell to the ground.

Dirt reached out, guided her upright, and leaned her back against the bar.

"Be careful. You'll hurt yourself."

Julie planted a wet, red-lipsticked kiss on his neck, and patted his cheek.

"You're such a good, boy Dirty. Such a good boy."

Julie looked down at the floor then back into Dirt's eyes.

"What big feet you have! You know what they say about big feet!"

June 17, 2012

The Opera House Lab
Arvilla, ND

*

Sundays at the Opera House were tedious yet vitally important to the family. The checklist of chores was always the same, and needed to be completed in what had become a very fast-moving, sometimes chaotic, eighteen-hour day. Preparation for the next guest was critical, and Jimmy Boy even made a checklist to ensure everything was done according to his plan.

When things needed cleaning and organization, he lived and breathed by checklists.

Wake at 5:00 on the dot. Check.

Ensure the bed is made, pillows fluffed, and the bedspread wrinkle-free by 5:23. Check.

Complete the four s's (shit, shave, shower, and shampoo) by 6:00. Double-check, check, check, and check.

Scrub and bleach the lab's sinks by 9:00. Check.

Ensure the stainless steel worktables and equipment glisten and are all germ-free by noon. Check.

Ensure the "Spot Free Rinse" is ready for the next guest and all electronics are in proper functioning order by 2:00. Check.

Hand-wash the floors with bleach and ammonia by 3:00. Check.

Fumigate the house with Old Spice by 4:00. Check.

Make sure the light dimmers work and the lights are dimmed as low as possible. Marco hates bright lights. Check.

Welcome the next guest by 8:00 for her stay. To do.

The chores were always the same. Day-after-day. Week-after-week. Month-after-month. Unlike the others, who tended to be less systematic, Jimmy Boy's forte' was organization and cleanliness. He wanted to impress the guests after all, so he was the one that ensured everything was done to industry standards.

For what industry?

He wasn't quite sure.

But if there was some sort of documented set of guidelines available for what they did, he was sure his work would be written about in all of the journals and talked about in all of the seminars. The others had different skills, just as important he had to admit, it's just that they didn't appreciate the need for an organized, germ-free, sparkling work environment as he did.

It was technically just the basement. Jimmy Boy was the one who came up with the some of the names – including the “Opera House Lab” and the "Spot Free Rinse.” He’d come up with that name after running the car through a wash and watching the sign blink and tell him each stage the car wash was in. His favorite was "Spot Free Rinse" and he thought it was a perfect name. Besides being the most fastidious of the group, he was also the group’s most creative. Clint made the wooden signs with "The Opera House Lab" and "Spot Free Rinse" routed onto their fronts. Boots did all of the engineering. He was great with tools and putting things together. But it could have been Marco since he had a demonic creativeness to him and also was rather good with power tools – he just used them differently.

Although he doubted it.

Marco just didn’t do things like that.

Jimmy Boy really didn’t care who made the signs – he just knew he liked them. The lab’s sign was painted blood red and hung above the lab’s entrance.

Welcome to the
Opera House Lab

The sign for the rinse was painted just like the car wash's with a different color in each letter and was hung on its trap door's latch with by a black shoelace.

You Are Now Entering the
Spot Free Rinse

The others balked at naming the lab and some of the equipment, but Jimmy Boy thought it made perfect sense. After all, women who visited were always screaming something incomprehensible, the event always had the same tragic ending, and in the end, they always needed to be cleaned. Someone, typically the female love interest, always died.

Just like an opera.

Two-horned helmets and breastplates were the only missing props.

Jimmy Boy would have to consider how to incorporate those and make the atmosphere a bit more jovial.

*

Boots was the group's tinkerer. He assembled most of the lab, but his pride and joy was the Spot Free Rinse. Macro wanted his guests to be clean before they were put on his table. When he explained to Boots what he wanted to do, it didn't take Boots long to engineer the rinse's ingenious design.

"I don't want them on my table until they are spotless."

"Hot water?"

"No. Not worth it. Can you electrify it inside? I need to be able to get their attention if they disobey."

"Sure. Whatever you need, Marco. Pretty easy."

The Spotfree Rinse was an amazing contraption, that became an integral tool in his assembly line.

The Spot Free Rinse was an eight-foot tube of corrugated, galvanized steel that Boots acquired from a construction site. It had been intended for a ditch, but now it was theirs. The tube was set upright upon a wooden frame and placed directly above the stainless steel worktable. A set of straps hung from the ceiling and was fed into the top of the tube. A circular piece of 1/4" wrought iron was welded onto the bottom of the tube and provided its floor. When the Spot Free Rinse was filled with water, the bottom leaked a bit, but it held the water long enough to do the job. The leaks were easily managed with a line of caulk along its perimeter –

inside and out. Jimmy Boy fussed incessantly over the leak, but the others had learned to live with the constant trickle of water. Directly above the table, Boots had cut a 2X3 foot door with a latch that could only be opened from the outside. Even though he lined the door with a rubber gasket, it leaked just as much as the bottom did. Inside the tube was a wooden platform made of teak set on the bottom that was angled at forty-five degrees so that when the door was opened, the remaining water and everything contained inside slid out onto the table as slick as shit out of a goose.

Boots also engineered the electronics of the Spot Free Rinse and even Marco had to admit that it was a "shit-fuckin' impressive example of human ingenuity." Marco rarely complimented anyone, so when he said that, everyone knew they'd hit a home run.

Even Boots.

Boots pulled a wire from the light switch closest to the stairs to a new box containing a simple light dimmer switch. Power was turned on and off by pressing the button and the current was controlled by turning the knob left and right. Except that Boots' electrical work didn't turn on a light. He ran fifty feet of Romex from the dimmer box to the Spot Free Rinse. He drilled two holes, inserted a bolt into each one, sealed them with silicone gel, and then connected the wires, one hot, one neutral, from the Romex to each of the bolts.

"See! You press this, turn the dimmer, and it's electrified. You control the current."

"That's fine, but what happens when one of us touches it on the outside?" asked Marco. "We end up like the bitch we put inside."

Boots thought of a solution fast though. Spray-on rubber. Within a day, Boots had the outside of the Spot Free Rinse coated with a layer of rubber that created an electrical barrier between the metal, and anyone on the outside. Any one of the group could hug the tube, and not feel a thing.

"Watch this," said Boots as he pressed the dimmer and turned it all of the way to the right.

Boots then walked over to the Spot Free Rinse, wrapped his arms around it, and smiled.

"See Marco? Completely safe."

"Does it work?" asked Marco as Boots walked back to the switch and turned off the current.

"Fuck yes! Trapped a couple of rats from the barn. Fried them in seconds. Worked like a charm."

"Use water?"

"Yup. Filled it to about here," said Boots as he reached to a few inches above the door.

"Good. The new valve work better?"

"Perfectly. Drained the water into the floor. Just a bit left when I opened the door. Much better now."

That was three years ago and since then, Boots had made several improvements one of which was a heart monitor that allowed Marco to easily check the status of their guest inside and how much life she had left.

Again, Marco was impressed.

"How in the fuck did you find that?"

"Thank God for the Internet. You can get anything and everything there. If you know how to look."

"And you know how to hook it up?"

"Fuck yes. It was easy. I put connectors on the outside for you. Just match the six colored wires. Red to red. Blue to blue. Black to black. White to white. Green to green. And yellow to yellow."

"Not bad, Boots. Not bad."

"Thanks, Marco."

"How about a window? I'd like to watch what's going on. Can you put a window on it?"

The next day, there was an 8 X 10 piece of 1/2" think clear acrylic. Boots placed it on the inside and sealed it with silicone.

"Placing it on the inside. Good thinking, Boots."

"Pressure keeps it on that way. Otherwise, it would come flying off with a hundred gallons of electrified water behind it."

Marco nodded and smiled.

He had to admit, the lab was coming along nicely.

It was the perfect man-cave.

Then he looked up and saw it.

"Jimmy Boy! Get that fucking Viking helmet out of my lab!"

*

Of the group, Malum considered himself Mr. Charisma. Besides being the finisher, he knew how to use words, his voice, his smile, and his eyes to get what he wanted. Malum knew how to dress, and how to move. He was right out of the current issue of *GQ* and, in his opinion, the ladies found him irresistible. He was the Pied Piper of the Y chromosome. If he left it up to the others, they'd never have friends over. Marco would, quite frankly, scare them before they walked through the front door. Jimmy Boy, despite being boyishly cute with his little baseball cap, would be too worried about the mess they were making and would be constantly brushing crumbs or pieces of hair off of the guests while they sat in the chair of honor. Clint, and Zeke? Well, they would just bore their guests to tears or completely gross them out when they started farting, scratching their ass, picking their belly button and smelling their finger, or eating their own snot.

Malum was the group's front man. He enticed the ladies on the dating site luvafarmer.com, set up dates, met them at the taco shop on Gateway drive in Grand Forks, and then brought them home to meet everyone.

Tonight was no different. He was meeting Monica Hammond. A twenty-year old, originally from Santa Monica, in her junior year at UND.

That made him laugh.

Malum couldn't fathom why someone from California would come to North Dakota to get a degree in Women's Studies, but he wanted to find out.

He opened the door to the restaurant, and saw his prey sitting in one of the multi-colored booths next to the front window.

June 17, 2012

Brentwood, CA

*

The three were standing in the expanse of the gourmet kitchen. A kitchen that was bigger than the entire first floor of the North Dakota farmhouse he grew up in. The realtor, a power-brunette named Lumin Hawthorne wearing a navy blue pant suit, black heels, and sunglasses resting on the top of her head, was leaning against the built-in refrigerator holding a Coach briefcase in her right hand, a Coach purse over her left shoulder, and was texting using her free left hand. Dan and his fiancé, Ashley, were standing next to the black granite-topped center island. Dan put his hand on Ashley's shoulder and gently squeezed.

"How many bathrooms does this place have again?"

"Six and a half," answered Lumin. "Two and a half on the first level. Two on the second, and separate his and her bathrooms off of the master suite."

"Two and a half? How do you have half of a bathroom?"

"A toilet and a sink. No shower or bath."

"You can take the boy out of the country, but you can't take the country out of the boy. You're in California, now Daniel. Don't embarrass me like you usually do."

"Oh," nodded Dan as he turned to his fiancé. "We need six bathrooms, Ash?"

"Six and a half," corrected Lumin.

"We really need six *and a half* bathrooms?

"Daniel, you're going to be a partner. We, *you*, need this. To fit in. Five thousand square feet is on the small side if you think about it. I'll need it to entertain."

"Five thousand square feet is small?"

"Compared to what the other partners at the firm have. Yes. I'm amazed you don't realize that," nodded Ashley. "It is small. It will be a good starter. Daddy would expect nothing less."

"But six and a half bathrooms? How many places do two people need to shit? That's a lot of Charmin to buy," he whispered before turning back to he realtor. "Four point six mill?"

"Don't be so crude," said Ashley as she kicked Daniel's ankle.

"You have it backwards. Six point four," said Lumin as she scrolled through text messages on her phone.

Daniel winced.

"It's Brentwood, after all. Your neighbor to the east is Rubert Timmons. To the west is Dominique Willa."

"Dominique!"

"Yes. Dominique will be your neighbor," Lumin smiled.

Even though he'd been in Southern California for more than a decade, he still didn't have all of the names down.

"Rupert Timmons?"

"*Deadman's Secret*," both women said in unison.

"Won an Oscar last year for that. Can't remember. Best picture. Best editing. Something like that."

"He was in *Red Heads* in 2011. That one won Best Picture," said Lumin.

"Yes! That's it. I loved that movie."

"Didn't O.J. live in Brentwood?" asked Daniel.

"Other side. Not even close."

Ashley turned to Daniel, wrapped her arms around his waist, and pulled him to her.

"We need to buy this."

"I think they'll be reasonable," interrupted Lumin as she looked up from her textual conversation.

Daniel shook his head.

He lived in a condo in Union City worth six hundred thousand that he bought four years ago for four fifty. He couldn't fathom owning something this expensive. And in Brentwood.

"Garage?"

"Six car."

Now he was really interested.

"I suppose I could rent out the condo for a while. See what the market does. Maybe sell it in a few years."

Daniel saw Ashley's eyes brighten as she smiled. It was a familiar smile. One she wore whenever she won.

Ashley always won.

He always had trouble resisting her. He turned to Lumin.

"Four?"

"Not *that* reasonable."

"What then?"

"High fives. Low sixes. Let's start at five-eight be happy with six-one."

Daniel looked over to Ashley. Her smile was wider and he felt her hand move stealthily toward his crotch.

"We need this Mr. Carpenter," she whispered in his ear.

She knew how to get his attention.

"I sure hope I make partner, Ash."

"You will. I'll talk to daddy tonight."

"Let's start at five-five, and be happy with six."

Debra raised her eyebrows then shrugged.

"All we can do is ask."

Daniel watched Lumin pull out what seemed to be a ream of paper from her briefcase, and set it on the island in front of them. It made a distinct thud against the granite. She went back into her bag of wonders, and pulled out three Monte Blanc pens.

He only had one.

"Now if you are done fondling him, we can get this offer done, and over to the seller's agent. We should hear something tonight if we can get this done. What are you willing to put down for earnest money?"

"Five hundred?"

"Can you do seven and a half? If the seller sees that, they're more likely to accept your offer. Show's you're serious."

Daniel looked at Ashley.

"Are you sure, Lina?"

Dan realized what came off of his tongue the minute it happened.

Lina was becoming a regular memory lately.

As was home.

He tried to cover his mistake with a loud cough. Ashley was talking with the realtor. If she heard him, the next few seconds would tell.

"Ash? Are you sure?"

Ashley turned towards him. He could tell from her eyes that she'd heard his slip.

"Just write the fucking, check, Daniel. Do you think you can handle that or are you just too damn stupid?"

Daniel nodded, and pulled out his checkbook. His stomach was trying to convince him to escape – to not even begin writing the numbers. He'd thought he'd escaped a prison when he left North Dakota so long ago, but he found that he was trapped again.

At this point, he wasn't sure what it would take to be happy. Perhaps the decision to leave wasn't the right one after all.

His ambition took hold and pushed his indecision back to where it belonged. He put the pen back in his hand, and started writing the largest check he'd ever written.

Then he stopped.

"You know. Let's look at a few more. Let's see what's available with beachfront."

Daniel tried to buy time.

June 17, 2012

The Opera House Lab
Arvilla, ND

*

"Dim those fucking lights!"

Marco didn't like bright lights on in the lab. He had Boots install dimmers on each and every light switch in the house and had specifically told everyone to keep the lights on at the lowest setting. Of course no one ever listened, and the lights were surface-of-the-sun bright.

"Dim the Goddamn fucking lights! Is no one listening up there?"

When no one answered, Marco walked to the dimmer, and slid it down. He could feel the faint beginnings of a headache and hoped it wasn't too late.

Marco generally didn't work in teams; he didn't like the distraction others brought. He was more creative when he was alone.

He liked to experiment.

Collaboration slowed him down, and when he got going, he preferred to work fast. There was an art to his work, and trying to teach the nuances of what he did was difficult if not impossible.

There was emotion.

A creativity that couldn't be taught or explained.

You either had it or you didn't.

Marco had it.

There's not another Picasso wandering the streets; he worked alone, and in the end created works of beauty that were priceless.

Like Marco.

"You're late. The lights were bright. Do you know that? They were fucking bright!"

"Sorry, Marco. You ok?"

"Just shut the fuck up."

Today, Malum was in the room with him. If Malum wanted to learn the tricks of the trade, so be it. He was willing to give it a try.

But nothing more.

"Are you ready," said Marco as he looked across the room. "Better yet. Are you sure?"

"I'm ready Marco. I want to do this. I want to learn how."

Marco shrugged, and pressed a button that engaged a pulley that tightened the rope connected to the harness he'd strapped around the guest before her spa treatment started. Of course she was knocked out during her preparation, but had regained consciousness an hour ago. He'd added an ample dusting of Special K when he brought her ice cream over to her when they stopped for dessert last night.

She ordered maple nut ice cream.

He hated maple nut and ordered chocolate.

When he walked back to the table, he sprinkled the special ingredient on top of her detestable light brown scoop of ice cream and handed it to her with a smile. It was enough to knock out a horse.

"I have to watch my figure," she said. "I can't eat all of that."

"Fucking bitch," he thought. "You'll be watching a lot more very soon."

"Eat what you can. I'll finish the rest. Maple nut is my favorite."

"We should share."

"I have my chocolate. Eat up."

A scoop of chocolate was a boring choice, yes, but cheap. By the time he reached the Grand Forks International Airport on Highway 2, she was out cold. The name always amused him – *International*. There was nothing *International* about Grand Forks, North Dakota. The only reason it was international was the fact that it had a single flight that went to Winnipeg. Travelers didn't get from Grand Forks to Mexico without a stop in a "real" international airport.

Like Minneapolis.

As the pulley tightened, his guest floating inside the wash thrashed and screamed as she was involuntarily lifted into the air. Boots built the rinse chamber relatively soundproof. Not totally, as he could hear the obscenities she was screaming, but good enough so that nothing was heard outside of the Opera House Lab. He'd never considered himself a mother-fucker or a faggot, but evidently his guest thought she knew more about him than he thought. This wasn't the first time he'd been called names, and wouldn't be the last. The dose of Special K he'd given her was definitely wearing off, and she definitely hadn't fallen into a K-Hole. She was completely aware of her surroundings. A K-Hole had only happened once, and he had to shorten her spa treatment to just a few hours as she caused way too much damage to the equipment than any amusement she provided. She kept screaming that she was being eaten by snakes and spiders when, in fact, it was Marco who was tormenting her.

"What's her name? I can't remember. Look in her purse."

Marco connected the wires he'd placed on her chest to the heart monitor next to the table and turned it on. Her heartbeat was fast. Extremely fast. The rhythm, however, was normal. Blood pressure was on the high side at 140 over 110. If he were a doctor, he'd be concerned.

Marco wasn't a doctor and he knew exactly what the cause was. Blood pressure on the high side was normal given the circumstances.

"Holly Newcomb. Minnesota driver's license. Student at the U. Looks to be in her senior year."

Marco pressed the intercom button.

"Hello, Holly. I'm Marco. That's Malum. A trainee."

He didn't care to listen to her screams and pleas, so Marco turned off the intercom as quickly as he turned it on.

"You always talk to them?"

"Sometimes. It lets them think I care when I call them by their name. Psychological stuff."

"Do you?"

"Do I what?"

"Care?"

"Fuck no."

"What's next?"

"E-stim."

"Cool. I've been wanting to see how that works."

"See that red dial there? The one with the numbers?" asked Marco as he pointed to a row of small dials.

"Yes."

"Turn it to point five."

"What's it mean?"

"Half an amp."

"Doesn't sound like much."

"It is. Trust me. It will quiet her down."

Marco watched as Malum slowly turned the dial.

"A bit more. To the right of the mark. It's not exact, but close enough."

Malum adjusted the dial, and stood back.

Marco could tell he was eager.

"She's going to twitch. Not a lot, but she'll know something's going on."

"And what's this for?"

"This? It's just a predatory step. Like tenderizing a steak before you put it on the BBQ. It will add an essence to her blood. Loosens the tissues too. Something you should appreciate when you do your work. Hard to describe really, but without it, well, it's just not the same. Now watch."

Marco flipped the switch that his thumb had been resting on.

The effect was instantaneous.

Holly's screaming stopped, but her body immediately tensed as the electrical current flowed through her body. Each and every nerve was being stimulated. Her fingers and toes began to hyperextend, and the muscles in her face began to pull back creating the widest smile she'd ever experienced.

Marco released the switch and Holly's body relaxed.

He flipped it again.

Holly tensed.

"I could turn her into a marionette if I wanted to. Watch this."

Marco flipped the switch on and off every few seconds.

Holly danced in the Spot Free Rinse.

"Quiet a jig, isn't it?"

Malum laughed and clapped.

"Do it more, Marco. Do it more!"

Marco smiled.

He thoroughly enjoyed performance art.

"Turn the dial to point seven."

*

"Is she alive?"

"Yes," snapped Marco as he pointed to the beeping heart monitor. "She passed out. I know how to do my job, fuckwad."

"Oh. Sorry."

"See the valve at the base of the trap door?"

"Yes."

"Open it. But make sure the table is underneath the chute before you start otherwise you'll be cleaning up a lot of filthy water. Most of them piss themselves in there. Sometimes there's even a floater and it's not a candy bar."

"What's the valve for?"

"To drain the tank, Dipshit. The water will drain onto the table, through the diverter, and into the sump hole. You know how Jimmy Boy gets if there's a mess? Christ! I don't have time to deal with that drama so make sure you do it right."

As the water drained, Malum peered into the Spot Free Rinse's window.

"She looks dead. Her head is all slumped over and everything."

"Well, she's not."

*

After an hour hanging in the tank under the heat of the four blow dryers Boots arranged from the ceiling and daisy-chained to a single switch on the control panel, his guest was just starting to regain consciousness.

At least she was dry.

He watched as her eyes would flutter open, try to focus through the small acrylic window, her head would lift up, bob back down, and her eyes would close.

Every guest reacted the same way.

That meant it was time for him to get back to work.

Macro looked around the Opera House. He was impressed. Malum didn't make too much of a mess when he drained the tank and prepared for the second step.

"Jimmy Boy will thank you."

"Why?"

"You're definitely not the brightest one of the bunch. You didn't make much of a mess, that's why."

Malum smiled.

"Is it time? Time for the next step?"

"Yes. Are you sure you can do it?"

"I'm ready," said Malum with an ear-to-ear grin.

Marco wasn't convinced. There were things to be done before he had a chance to test his assessment of Malum, but deep down, he didn't think Malum had it in him.

Step two took finesse.

And balls.

Marco jiggled the big toe that was just barely visible from the bottom edge of the Spot Free Rinse, felt it react to his touch, grabbed it at its base, and twisted until he heard a crunch.

His guest's scream echoed within the corrugated steel tank, and she pulled her foot with the sideways toe back into the tank as far as she could.

"Hello, Holly. Welcome back. Sorry about that, but I wanted to make sure you were up," said Marco in his sweetest voice possible as he turned the switch to activate the winch. "Wouldn't work if you were still asleep. Need you bright-eyed and bushy-tailed. You're nice and clean now. Dried off. Time to get you out of there."

Their guest, Miss Holly Newcomb from St. Paul, began to descend through the tank and make her way towards the table. When her ankles appeared below the tank, she started to panic, and tried to use her legs and arms to keep from moving any lower.

No matter how much they thrashed, the laws of gravity always won. Marco smiled very slightly, and wiggled his right index finger.

"No, no, no. Can't have that now. You settle down in there."

Marco banged his fist on the side of the tank to make sure she understood he meant business.

Holly screamed and kicked with her left foot.

"Let me out of here!"

"You'll be out of there very soon. I promise. You just have to relax."

The noise of her hands and feet slipping on the tank's ribs, and the banging of her elbows concerned Marco. He didn't want her to damage any of the electronics within the tank. Each of his guests did this, but Holly was turning out to be a bit feistier than the others.

She had some spunk.

She was younger than the rest.

That could explain things.

Thanks to Boots' ingenuity with Romex and dimmer switches, he had a quick remedy for her petulance, and was ready to use it. It wouldn't take much to entice her to move her hands and feet away from the sides of the tank. All it would take was quarter-inch turn of the dimmer switch marked "Interior E-Stim."

Marco was tired of playing games.

He had things to do today besides dealing with their guest, so he rotated the switch a full inch to the right. Inside the chamber he heard a combination of squeals and sparks. Holly slid the rest of the way out of the tank and onto the table.

"Slicker than shit," said Marco. "Now get her wrapped up and secure. Put the pads under her neck and shoulders so everything goes towards the drain. I don't want her moving, and I don't want a mess."

"She's bleeding."

"Hit her head on the way down. She shouldn't have tried to hang on like that. It's her own fault."

*

Marco looked down at Holly as he walked around the table and inspected Malum's work. He tugged on the four sets of leather straps to ensure they were tight, but not so tight as to constrict the flow of blood.

"Good job. Very good job."

"Thanks, Marco. You're a good teacher."

Holly's arms and legs were strapped to the edge of the table with leather belts. Her head was secured with silver duct tape. She was facing forward with a bright pink, fuzzy tennis ball stuffed into her mouth. The ball was firmly fixed with the same silver tape that kept her head from moving.

"I used the pink ball. Nice contrast with her hair."

Marco nodded his approval, and then put his nose into the air. He took a long, deep breath. Something was different. He bent down towards the table and sniffed Holly's neck directly below her ear.

Lilacs and roses.

"Mystique. I love that perfume. Has always been my favorite."

"I know you always wash her with that after you're done, but I thought I'd spray some on her before we begin."

"Good idea. Adds to the ambiance. Nice touch."

"I knew that's your favorite."

Marco looked up on the shelf next to the control panel and saw the tall, red, plastic bottle of Mystique.

"Not much left. We'll probably have to go to K-Mart and get a few more bottles after we're done with her."

"Grab the hunting knife."

"Which one is that?"

Marco pointed to the assortment of knives organized on the back wall of the Opera House.

"On the wall over there. Third row. Second knife from the left. The one with the black leather handle."

"This one?"

"No. Your other left."

Marco was jumping the gun. There was generally a bit of pre-amble ceremony before the knife work, but he wanted to know for certain if Malum was as ready as he said he was to actually follow-through with his desires.

He was pretty sure Malum wouldn't.

He couldn't.

Macro took the knife.

"You see, the knife is sacred. It has the same curves as our guest. Thin here," said Marco as he pressed his thumb against the tip of the knife. "It widens a bit. Then tapers off."

Marco ran his thumb down the blade as he talked, and drew a thin line of blood. He let it drip onto Holly's stomach for a while, and then pushed it into this mouth. He smeared the droplets on her stomach with the blade.

"It's important. Mixing the blood."

Marco slid the blade to Holly's side and wiped it clean.

"That's the incision point. Your target."

Marco handed the knife to Malum.

"Right there. Start with the point. Make a small cut. Then press in and move upwards."

Marco turned to Holly.

*

Malum was eager to prove himself. He'd been dissecting the guests for years; his job always started after Marco finished his. Now he wanted to actually make the kill. They were always lifeless and dull when they came to his table. He wanted to see them transition from life to death.

He wanted to witness the life flow from the body and down the table's drain.

The process amazed him.

Malum took the knife in his fist.

"Not that way. You're not spreading butter."

Malum adjusted his grip on the leather hilt.

"Like this?"

"Better. Remember what I said."

“The knife is sacred.”

“Yes. Just as your knives and saws are sacred for you and what you do. This knife is sacred for the part I play. Make a small cut, press forward, and then move up. It’s easy.”

Malum walked to the opposite side of the table where Marco had smeared his blood on Holly’s side.

He pressed the point into her side and created a small, shallow, one-inch incision.

Despite being held down on the table, Holly was still able to squirm. The fuzzy ball muffled her screams. Blood tricked down her side and dripped onto the table.

Malum looked at the woman, and pulled back the knife.

Tears were flowing from both her eyes.

“She’s crying,” whispered Malum. “What do we do?”

The tears dripped onto the table just as her blood was.

Malum could tell she was shaking her head. Seemingly pleading with him to stop.

He put the tip of the knife back into the incision and took a deep breath.

*

Marco could tell by Malum’s shaking hand that he was neither ready nor willing to follow-through with his desire. He’d watched him look at Holly. Watched him look at her tears streaming down both sides of her face. Watched him contemplate the blood trickling down her side and pooling on the stainless steel table. Then finally watched Malum’s enthusiasm wilt as quickly as his dick after he took care of business.

"Get the fuck out of my lab you worthless piece of shit."

Marco was seething.

"You're such a spineless pig."

"But..."

"Put the knife down. Get out. You've wasted enough of my time," Marco spit in Malum's direction, then pointed to the other side of the Opera House Lab. "Go set up your work area like you should have been doing in the first place. I'll let you know when she's ready."

*

Marco washed and bleached the knife that he'd mistakenly allowed Malum to soil. Once it was dry and shined, he oiled the leather hilt, and then ran the blade through the sharpener that Clint had bought for the team from some ad on late-night TV. His final step was the most important. He took the bottle of Mystique from the shelf, and spritzed both sides of the blade. Within seconds, the entire room was filled with the beautiful scent of rose and lilac.

His knife was sacred.

Too sacred to be contaminated with the germs of the likes of Malum.

It would never happen again.

He held the knife in his palms, kissed the blade, let the bitter taste of the perfume linger on his tongue and lips, and walked back to the table.

He smiled down at Holly.

"I apologize for the delay. I should have never let him try."

Marco set the knife on Holly's abdomen with the tip of its blade pointing to her heart. He stripped naked, precisely folded each article of clothing, gently set them under his worktable, and covered them with a layer of plastic sheeting.

"That's for Jimmy Boy," he said as he pointed under the table. "He doesn't like to wash bloody clothes. Stains are too hard to get out. Or so he says. Won't be much longer. I promise."

*

Marco moved the knife off of Holly's chest and placed it next to her head. He hopped onto the table, straddled her, and then adjusted himself. He saw her eyes widen, her struggles amplified, and her muffled cries started in earnest.

"Don't worry. Nothing like that is going to happen. You have tits that you have to manage. I have this," he said as he pointed to his crotch. "We all have crosses to bear, don't we?"

Marco leaned forward.

He pressed his chin against her throat, and brought his lips close to her ears.

"Can you hear me?"

Holly didn't move.

He reached down to her hand, took her pinky finger, and twisted.

Even with the pink fuzzy ball in her mouth, her muffled scream echoed though the Opera House.

"I know it's hard, but try to shake your head if you can hear me."

He felt Holly try to move her head. Tears pooled on her face and table.

"Good girl."

Marco scooted closer and sniffed her neck.

"The roses and lilacs of Mystique. Do you like it? Just nod your head a bit. I like the taste too."

Holly nodded.

"Good. You've learned your lesson. I really don't like doing that, but there are times I have to make sure I'm understood. That was one of those times."

He flattened his tongue, and licked Holly from her left collarbone, up across her neck, and then finished by her right ear. He licked his lips and studied the taste in his mouth.

"Bitter from the perfume. Salty from your tears," he whispered. "It won't hurt. What I'm going to do. Won't hurt at all. I promise. No need to cry. You'll be in a better place."

Marco bit the nape of her neck strong enough to draw blood. She whimpered and tried to move away.

"Nothing more than that. I've done this a lot and it's the same thing each time. A little sting, you close your eyes, and you'll drift off to sleep. Like taking a nap. Trust me."

He put his finger on the small bite wound, swirled his finger in the blood, then drew a wide, red smile on her face from each corner of her mouth.

"Now you look happy. That's how we want things to end. Being happy with a great, big smile," he said as he cleaned his finger with his tongue. "I think we're ready."

Marco took his knife and scooted down from Holly's abdomen to her hips. He caught a quick sparkle through the corner of his eye.

"What do we have here? Did we miss something?"

*

Marco looked down at the sparkle that had grabbed his attention. It was coming from the ring finger of Holly's right hand.

"Is that a diamond?"

He looked closer.

"It's so sweet. Did your boyfriend get that for you?"

When Holly didn't respond, he began to reach for her pinky finger again. She began to nod under the strain of the duct tape.

"Good girl. See, I didn't have to hurt you."

Marco took Holly's hand in his, and reached for her finger. She resisted and made a tight fist.

"Oh. That's being bad. You don't want to go down that road now, do you?"

Marco slapped her with all of his strength. Once with his left hand then again with his right. Even under the tape, her head bounced back and forth, and left glue residue from the adhesive on her forehead.

"Now be a good girl, and open your hand."

Slowly, her hand relaxed, and exposed her finger. Marco pulled the ring off, and studied it.

"I must say, your boyfriend's a cheap bastard. This isn't a diamond, it's more like a fucking chip," Marco laughed. "Probably fake. He couldn't do better than this?"

Marco threw the ring towards one of Malum's orange buckets. It bounced off of the rim, and then fell inside. He could hear it twirl on the plastic bottom, then settle.

"Two points! Normally I can't hit the broad side of a barn. I'm not the athlete of the group."

He picked up the knife again, set it on her chest.

He looked Holly in the eyes.

"Sorry. I said this wouldn't take long, but your ring distracted me," Marco moved his hands in front of Holly's eyes and fluttered his fingers. "Sparkly things. They always grab my attention. Like little butterflies."

Marco took the knife, and placed it to the left of Holly's sternum then pulled it downward a few inches.

"Right there. Most think the heart is entirely on the left, but it's really more centered on your chest. It favors the left side, yes. But it's in the center," Marco felt the blade bounce over her ribs. "This is a good spot."

Marco leaned forward, and pressed the weight of his body downward onto the knife.

"Right here," he said as the knife slid downwards into her chest.

He kept his eyes on Holly. As the knife drove in to its hilt, her eyes widened. Her arms and legs stiffened. Her body bucked. Then he smelled the distinct, bitter smell of piss as her bladder released itself.

"That always happens too. Don't be embarrassed. That's why we have the drain."

Marco cut the tape from her mouth and took out the tennis ball.

Holly's mouth was moving.

Slowly trying to form words.

He leaned forward.

"What's that?"

There was no reply. Her mouth had stopped moving, and her eyes were staring at the ceiling.

"See. I told you it wouldn't hurt. You go to sleep now."

Marco pulled her eyelids down, and jumped off the table. He grabbed the plastic off of his clothes, dressed, and walked out of the Opera House.

"Malum. You fucking, spineless bastard. She's all yours."

He quickly stopped, and walked back into the room.

"Save her head. I want to find who gave her that hideous ring. Let him see it before I kill him. Cheap bastard. She deserved something bigger."

June 18, 2012

3:00 AM

Arvilla, ND

*

Malum was anxious to unload the cargo. He wanted it gone. Even though he'd done this more times than he could count, he had an anxious feeling that he couldn't shake. It started in his toes earlier in the day, and had worked its way up to his stomach where it was now camped and was causing some of the worst cramps he'd ever had.

He felt like shit.

He still had a lot of work to finish before he could call it a night. And for some reason, Marco had told him to exchange four of the buckets with a stack he'd left in the feed shed.

It didn't make sense as they had plenty of orange buckets in the basement not including the twelve in the bed of the pickup now. Malum looked back to make sure nothing had tipped. That had happened once before and the mess it created was nauseating – even though he'd seen worse. Each bucket contained the pieces from the last five guests at the Opera House, and each one needed to emptied.

Maybe it was six.

Maybe seven.

He'd lost count.

Parts is parts, Clint always said.

The parts that were too big to fit into the buckets were dumped in rock piles around the area, and left for the coyotes, bobcats, and crows to munch on. He and Zeke had just finished that work, and Malum put a checkmark next to that task on his To-Do List. Five years ago, he'd mapped out a six-mile radius from home, and had put a stickpin on every rock pile he could use. It didn't take long to discover that there was a never-ending supply.

"Pull up to the tree line, and stop."

"It's dark," said Zeke.

"No kidding. It's three in the morning, dumbass."

"No. I mean I can't see the tree line. Can't I turn on the lights?"

"No! You fucking moron."

Malum grabbed his stomach as another cramp struck home, and started twisting his intestines. He was breathing through his mouth now.

"It's right there," grunted Malum as he pointed out the front of the Dodge Ram with one hand and massaged his abdomen with the other. "Are you blind? It's right here. Stop!"

"Sorry," murmured Zeke.

"Just shut up. Is it in park? You didn't leave it in Drive did you?"

"It's in park."

"Good. Leave it that way."

Malum got out of the pickup, opened the tailgate, grabbed two buckets, and headed towards the feed shed.

Five more round trips to make.

*

Trude was wide-awake and studying the faint shadows on her ceiling cast from the moonlight. She was waiting for a sign. She had another banger behind her eye, and wouldn't be able to sleep if she wanted to. She took two pills from the bottle next to her bed and dry-swallowed them.

Her Savior wouldn't have used water to take his medicine, so neither would she.

When one shadow resembled a crucifix, she naturally assumed her Savior had awakened her for a purpose. She looked over at the old clock next to her bed; its glow-in-the-dark hands were on three and twelve. It was only one hour earlier than her typical time to begin her day. Instead of trying to go back to sleep, she decided to get out of bed, and get in an extra hour of prayer. Before she left her the sofa, Trude took the set of rosary beads off of the stack of bibles on her nightstand, then headed towards the kitchen for a cigarette and glass of water while whispering the Apostle's Creed as she walked down the dark hallway.

"I believe in God. The Father almighty, creator of heaven and earth..."

She knew her kitchen well, and didn't bother to turn on any lights. They would cause way too much pain, and her goal was to make it go away.

Not make it worse.

She opened her cupboard and cringed as her back spasmed. The pain took her breath away. Slowly, as if not letting her back realize she was moving, she lifted up her hand and pulled down one of three old Welch's jelly jars. Robotically, she moved to the sink and filled it with warm tap water. She didn't believe she was worthy enough for the extravagance of cold water. Jesus, after all, didn't have ice cubes or refrigerated cold water.

Normally, she wouldn't pay a bit of attention to what went on in the farmyard, that was the realm of her blasphemous, evil son. This morning, though, movement by the pigpen caught her eye – the one that wasn't in pain. She held onto her rosary, and recited more of her prayer as she studied the movement of the dark shadow.

"I believe in Jesus Christ, God's only son, Our Lord..."

She continued watching the black form continuously lift objects over the fence.

"He's fornicating with those pigs."

"Who was conceived by the Holy Spirit..."

"I hope he rots in hell."

Trude gulped down a full jar of water, refilled it, and drank another.

She stuffed a long Virginia Slim into her mouth, flicked her lighter, and inhaled.

"Born of the Virgin Mary..."

"Where's that gun. I'll teach him to be fornicating with pigs."

"Suffered under Pontius Pilate. Was crucified, died, and as buried…"

Trude stopped her prayer, put down her glass, and walked to the closet by the front door. She grabbed the twelve gauge, and three shells from the box sitting on the shelf above it next to the box of old winter scarves and gloves.

*

"Here piggy piggy piggy," said Malum as he dumped the tenth bucket of ground pieces-parts over the fence into the muddy, shit and piss-filled mire of the pigpen.

He was amazed at how ravenous the pigs were. He could barely tell that he'd already dumped nine buckets in the four troughs that lined the fence. There was barely a spoonful of his special breakfast left in the troughs. Even in the dark, he could tell some of the pigs apart. Some had been around for a while, and had become more like family members instead of something to be hickory smoked and fried on Sunday mornings and served with orange juice and eggs over-easy. As usual, the big fat sow with the notched ear ate the most.

"You guys are hungry little beasties, aren't you? I have a bit more."

He reached over and scratched the sow's ear. She pushed her snout through the fence to get closer.

"Especially you, Lulu."

When the bucket was empty, he stacked them in two groups and carried them over to the feed shed. He'd opened it so many times and knew the drill. It was a son-of-a-bitch to open. He kicked the bottom of the door in the left, middle, and right. Next, he lifted the door by the handle and yanked on it towards its metal stop with all of his strength. The metal-to-metal squeal it made sent shivers down his spine, but it gave way and slowly slid open. It smell was reminiscent of oatmeal and cornbread.

His stomach growled.

*

Trude loaded the gun, and walked down the three steps from her front porch.

"You fornicating devil!" she yelled.

The shadow kept moving around the pigpen. It had to be him. She brought the gun down like her daddy had shown her when she was eight, kept her arm steady, and pulled the trigger.

"Rot in hell!"

Trude put another shell into the 12-guage, steadied her arm, aimed, and pulled the trigger again.

*

"That crazy bitch is shooting at us!"

Malum was walking to the grinder with the last two buckets.

"She's shooting! Fuck!"

Malum ducked behind a tractor, and dropped the two remaining buckets.

"What do we do?"

"I wish Boots was here."

"Well, he's not."

Malum looked towards the house and saw the old woman standing on the porch. The shadow of a gun was at her side.

"We're going to dump the parts in the trough and get out of here is what we are going to do."

"Don't we have to grind it up?"

"Do you want lead in your ass?"

"No."

"Then we are going to dump the buckets, and run like hell."

Malum picked up the buckets.

The old woman hadn't moved.

"Go! Go! Go!"

Malum ran to the pigpen, pulled the buckets over, and dumped them into the troughs.

"Let's get the fuck out of here."

June 20, 2012

The Kinnear Farm
Arvilla, ND

*

Dirt grasped a thick shank of his long, tawny hair, shaped it into a ponytail, and wrapped it with a rubber band. He was busy making breakfast and wanted to make sure he kept any errant strands from falling into what he was preparing. He'd dealt with that before, and didn't want a repeat performance of being told he was trying to poison that woman in house with his DNA. She wouldn't say the words herself, but it didn't take long to figure out what she was trying to say when she confronted him in front of the screen door using a wooden spoon as if it were a machete.

"You. You. You," she stuttered. "I found hair. You put that in my Dinty Moore."

She jabbed the spoon at his crotch with each sputtered "you."

"You will burn in hell for what you did."

From the way she was vigorously stabbing and slicing at his dick with the spoon, Dirt had figured out what she was talking about by the time she spit out the second "you." Being the good son he always wanted to be, and understanding how much difficulty she was having communicating, he decided to help her out. He said the words she couldn't right to her face with staccato-like emphasis.

"No. I did not jack off in your Dinty Moore. But if you want me to, just let me know, and I'll be more than happy to accommodate."

He relished watching her head pulsate, and turn red. Almost burst from the building pressure. She wasn't used to being talked to this way. It was a unique experience for her. She dropped the machete spoon, gasped, turned, and slammed the screen in his face. He heard her screech once she was safe within the confines of her house, and saw her staring at him wide-eyed through the window.

"You will rot in hell you blasphemous heathen!"

Her threats didn't scare him anymore. He didn't believe in Heaven or Hell so he knew he wasn't going anywhere she wanted him to go.

The only thing the threats did was keep him warm.

And entertained.

For now though, he had another meal to prepare.

Dirt stood at his small, two-burner stove, twirled the fry pan, and let the two sausage links swim in the deep pool of hot grease. He watched the links bubble for a few seconds more, imagined that they were the meaty fingers of that woman, gingerly picked them up with his fingertips, and placed them on the plate next to the strawberry Eggo waffle he'd already warmed in the toaster. The waffle was slightly dark around the edges, smothered in melted butter, and drowned in a layer of genuine butter-flavored imitation maple syrup from a bottle that resembled a fat black woman wearing an apron. Precisely as ordered.

An expert short order cook he was not.

He was a simple farmer who lived in a twenty-foot Airstream.

He was a farmer who, despite the torment she insisted in doling out, still felt an obligation to tend to a woman who was positive he was the son of Satan. He knew better than to leave excess fingerprints on the plate as that was yet another screeching match, so he sucked the grease off each finger before handling the plate any more than he had to and lifted it with his palms.

A few years ago, his father had fucked him over big-time. Pure and simple. Yes, the dead, spiteful bastard left him the farm. Most might think that was the opportunity of a lifetime, but with a single swipe of his lawyer's pen, the mean SOB permanently squashed Dirt's dream of escaping this life. Now Dirt was stuck. Probably forever. He had 2,000 acres of land and, at last count, 68 pigs, and 24 beef cattle that needed his attention on a daily basis. The final paragraph of his father's last will and testament was the goocher though.

It said that if Dirt ever wanted to touch the monetary portion of the inheritance, almost a half a million in two annuities, he couldn't sell a thing. He couldn't leave. Instead, besides the land, cattle, and pigs, he also had to care for that bible-thumping mad woman in the main house until she was either dead or so far gone that she needed constant supervision by someone with more experience dealing with despicable bitches in their late fifties who had a penchant for wearing tilted, oddly colored wigs. If it ever came to that, his father had been kind enough to account for that with another, smaller, annuity. He'd come close many times. Close to grabbing his guitar, getting in his pickup, and heading west.

Look up Danny.

It wasn't the money. He didn't really care about that.

He just felt...

Responsible.

They'd lived like paupers all of this life. No one knew about the semi-fortune his father had stowed away. Technically he was set for the rest of his life. Realistically, he was vacationing in hell – a place he didn't believe in, but could easily describe every sight and sound.

He was trapped just as that woman in the house had predicted.

He liked dealing with the pigs so much better. They didn't curse him into the bowels of hell when they saw him.

He could at least take them to the slaughterhouse when he got tired of them, which, by the way, was one of the things on his to-do list today.

His only dilemma was that the meat house would only take pigs or cows.

Not her.

Picky bastards that they were.

He would love to see her hit by a compression gun one fine, sunny day.

Even from the grave, his father was continued to make his life miserable.

Yes, Daddy was certainly a fucking bastard.

Except for his Airstream, of course, as that was something he'd be forever grateful to his father for. If it weren't for the silver torpedo he called home, he would have chosen to sleep with the swine, as they were so much more agreeable than that woman in the house.

Dirt pushed a wayward sausage closer to the waffle, covered the plate with plastic wrap, and grabbed a fork from the clean side of the sink. This wasn't his breakfast, as he'd eaten more than an hour ago, and had already finished most of the morning chores.

Except for this one.

This was the last of the herd to be fed.

This gourmet meal was for that woman in the house.

His least favorite of the family livestock.

She expected her breakfast on the front porch by 7:15. He didn't have to worry about coffee as she had an old plug-in percolator in the kitchen, and apparently was able to manage that on her own. Whenever she needed something, she left a note tagged to a nail next to the screen door. She typically scribbled on any piece of paper she could find. Some days a yellow sticky note. Others a used napkin.

Sanka.
I don't want blueberry waffles. I want strawberry.
My waffle was cold.
Toilet paper written on an empty tube.
There was a hair in my Dinty Moore again!
Milk. 2%. Not skim.
My fork wasn't clean. Are you trying to poison me again?
Cheetos. Crunchy kind.
I said Cheetos. Not Fritos, you dumbass.

She kept face-to-face contact with her evil progeny to a bare minimum, and that was perfectly fine with him. Her handwriting was getting worse year after year though. Each request did not end with a please or thank you. Instead, if there was enough space, each typically ended with, "God have mercy on your blackened soul."

Dirt wondered how long he'd be able to hang on without going crazy himself, and hoped it wasn't hereditary. He couldn't imagine such a miserable existence.

He'd rather be dead.

*

The thick stench created by the stew of pig shit and fermented, uneaten slop created a fog that permeated every square inch around the pigpen. There was no place anyone could hide, nothing to crawl under, climb into, or stand behind to help keep the aroma from burning his nose hairs to the follicle. For the uninitiated, it was an exercise in gag reflex management to stay more than thirty seconds within spitting distance of the pen's perimeter without adding his own stomach contents to the stew. Dirt was used to it though, and breathed no differently than if he were in a rose garden.

After all of these years, it was second nature.

Today was slaughterhouse day. The day when the 6-month old pigs were loaded into the truck, taken on a one-way trip to town, and sold to be reconstituted into something more freezer-friendly. Dirt hopped behind the wheel of the old truck and using his foot, pressed the button on the floor to get it started. It was a vintage 1960's truck, whose original purpose was to haul grain, but it's hydraulic system died years ago, and fixing it was more than the truck was worth. Now, in semi-retirement, the truck hauled pigs. He slowly backed the truck to the edge of the ramp that was lined with pieces of old tires as a makeshift bumper. The ramp was an ingenious feat of engineering prowess. It was a series of narrow switchbacks that walked the pigs from ground level up five feet and onto the bed of the truck. He'd built the ramp twenty years ago under the supervision of his drill sergeant of a father. It was how he learned to use power tools without cutting off any useful appendages.

"Didn't you hear me, numbskull? How many times do I have to tell you? I know you know what I'm talking about? Know what you did wrong?"

"Measure twice..."

"...and cut fucking once. Look at this cocksucker; it's a goddamn inch short. Fucking unusable now. That damn wood don't grow on trees! Grab another 2X4 and do it over. There are two ways to do something."

"Choose the right way, sir."

"Then why didn't you?"

He didn't dare smile on the day those words tripped off his father's tongue – even though he caught its irony immediately. If he would have said anything, cracked a smile, or even hinted a burp of laughter, he would now have the scars to prove it. Dirt learned early on to keep his mouth shut – regardless of what was said or done.

"That damn wood don't grow on trees!"

Now however, more than twelve years later, that one sentence made him smile each and every time he used the ramp.

It was a nice feeling, and not a terribly bad memory.

Dirt opened the gate to the pen, and walked into the mire. His size twelve boots made a sucking sound as they sunk into the stew a good three inches, and buried them to the second set of eyelets. When Dirt turned to shut the gate behind him, he felt something bump the calf of his left leg. He looked down. He knew what it was before his eyes made contact.

"Hey there, Lulu," he said as he bent down a bit and scratched the old sow's ear. "How's the lady of the pen today?"

Lulu snorted, twitched her ears in delight, and then began to nose his thigh as close to his pocket as she could.

"You're spoiled, you know that? And smart."

Dirt pulled a carrot from his pocket, gave it to Lulu, and pushed her away with his leg.

"Now you go," he pointed to the other side of the pen – the side that he kept wet and muddy. Lulu liked the mud. Plus, he didn't want her to know that he was taking her kids on a one-way ride to the Great Northern Meat Processing Facility twenty miles east to Grand Forks. He watched as she ambled towards the mud. Her curled tail bobbed up and down with her hips as she trotted away towards her mud hole.

"Got any fries with that shake, little lady?"

*

After thirty minutes, Dirt's legs were tired of pushing two-hundred pound pigs around, trying to segregate those that were to live yet another day from those going on the road trip. Lulu wasn't going anywhere, and always the curious one, had her nose stuck between a pair of wooden slats on the gate looking and snorting at her six kids. Dicky, the youngest of the set, had already found his way to the ramp and was nonchalantly making his way to the truck. Dicky was always the explorer. Rastus, Veronica, Lindy, and Bob were easy. Dirt threw a handful of carrots beyond the entrance to the ramp, and they let their stomachs lead them. When all four were past the switchback, Dirt lowered a small metal gate, which kept them from changing their minds, turning around, and heading back into the pen. Fester, a male with a large black spot on his left hip, and another on his right cheek, was stubborn and kept running away from Dirt's attempt at corralling him towards the ramp.

But Dirt was ready.

He grabbed the Shockstick he'd hung from the wooden gate, turned it on, and walked towards the pig. Using three "C" batteries, the stick delivered eight thousand volts with a mere touch of both its probes on the pig.

"This will get you to move," said Dirt as he pushed the Shockstick towards Fester's left hind leg.

Fester squealed as the probes made contact. He ran to the other side of the pen to escape another painful shock. Dirt put up another makeshift gate that cut Fester's area of retreat in half, recharged the Shockstick, turned the dial up to the max of ten thousand volts, and walked towards the stubborn pig.

Now there was only one direction for Fester to run.

Towards the ramp.

"You're pissing me off, Fester. I hope you're first in line for the compression gun."

Dirt put the probes of the stick on the pig's forehead. He knew what he was doing wasn't exactly humane, but the pig pissed him off. What erupted from Fester wasn't a simple squeal, but more of a wail as the electrical shock coursed from his forehead, between his ears, and down his spine.

Fester had the upper hand.

Even though his legs kept his belly only six inches off the ground, he was still one hundred pounds heavier than Dirt.

Dirt assumed the pig would run to the side towards the gate. Instead, Fester's two hundred pound bulk used the space between Dirt's legs as his means of escape. Dirt toppled backwards. His hands tried to regain his balance, but they simply twirled in a useless pirouette as he fell backwards into the slurry. Instead of the slurp his shoes made when he walked in, his body made a thick splash as it landed. Large balls of muddied pig shit flew into the air, and made their way onto Dirt as he lay prone on the wet ground – several onto his face and into his open mouth. The 3-foot Shockstick twirled three times in the air, landed prongs-down onto Dirt's abdomen, and delivered the shot of electricity that was meant for Fester. Dirt screamed, and his body quivered as the volts flowed through his body. He felt as if every muscle in his body was in a simultaneous cramp.

Dirt felt his bladder empty. His ability to command his vocal chords was temporarily nonexistent so "what a fuck wad," was all he could think.

*

The Great Northern Meat Processing Facility was a nondescript building six miles north of Grand Forks placed between a soybean plant to the north, and a dog hotel to the south. The facility was a window-less, pre-fab warehouse building with concrete-slab walls secured to its metal frame and a white, corrugated metal roof. To the east, was the Red River. To the west, were four sets of railroad tracks. On the set closest to the plant were three, old, red boxcars each colored with graffiti that covered any hint of determining which railroad the cars belonged to. Two were empty. One was placed below a conveyor that ran from a hole in the concrete wall and extended to five feet above its center. The conveyor dumped every leftover hoof, ear, and snout into the boxcar destined for another facility in Fargo where it would be cooked, dried, and formed into special, dog-friendly treats. The facility smelled of death just as much as pen back at the homestead smelled of fermented pig shit.

Dirt pulled the truck onto the scale, stopped, and waited for the man in the yellow hard hat inside the scale station to give him the thumbs-up to bring the truck into the unloading pen.

"How many?" the hard hat yelled.

"Five."

"Last name."

"Kinnear."

"First."

"Dirk."

Dirt watched the man as he pressed a few keys on the vintage desktop computer in his station.

"Still in Arvilla?"

"Yes."

"Your number is one four six."

The hard hat reached up to the driver's window, and handed Dirt the weigh-slip.

"Go ahead into the pen. Gate 4."

"Thanks."

Dirt looked at the weigh slip. He, along with the truck and five pigs, weighed 13,220 pounds. Once the pigs were unloaded he'd have the truck weighed again and the difference would be the pigs. That number was then cross-referenced to the weight of each pig, and then a check would magically appear in his mailbox.

Swine accounting.

Dirt put the truck into first gear, rolled forward, and heard the hard hat yell.

"Stu! Unload at gate 4."

*

"What's your number?"

"One forty-six."

"How many?"

"I told that guy everything."

"I know. I need to double-check. How many?"

"Five."

"Ok. Back it up to gate four."

Dirt studied his mirrors as he backed the truck up to the gate. When the man at the gate gave him the clenched fist to stop, Dirt turned off the truck, and climbed into the bed with the five swine. The truck's bed was already coated with a layer of shit and piss. Nervous pigs had loose bowels.

"Go ahead and lift your gate," said the man whose name was apparently Stu.

Everything here was automated, and activated with the press of a button. The system installed here was more modern than what he had back at the farm. When Dirt removed the rail keeping his pigs contained on the truck, Stu pressed a button, which lowered a three-foot wide gate leading into the facility. A small holding fence was automatically lowered at the point where the gate met the building.

"Gotta mark 'em," said Stu as he climbed into the back of the truck with Dirt.

"What's the price today?"

Stu looked annoyed at the disturbance.

"Around ninety-two cents."

Dirt did the math in his head. He knew the truck was about 12,000 pounds. He was a scrawny six-five, and weighed a buck ninety. So that meant his pigs weighed 1,030. At ninety-cents per pound, they'd gross him almost a grand.

Stu climbed into the back of Dirt's truck with a can of spray paint and a clipboard.

Dirt knew the routine.

Within a few minutes, each pig was labeled. Rastus was marked with 146-01-05-06122012. Dirt understood enough about the processes to know that little old Rastus would likely be the first in line with the compression gun. The others were also painted with numbers cross-referenced back to his account.

146-02-05-06122012.
146-03–05-06122012.
146-04-05-06122012.
146-05–05-06122012.

As each pig was numbered, Stu nudged it with the heel of his steel-toed boot towards the ramp where it trotted off until its snout sniffed the ass of the pig in front. Rastus was the only pig without an ass-only view. Instead, he was looking inside – unaware of the fate that awaited, but already nervous. It was as if he knew that death was waiting on the other side of the wall. When all of the pigs were standing single-file on the ramp, Stu pressed a button that opened the ramp's fence leading into the facility. Each pig trotted through.

"Here's your receipt," said Stu as he handed Dirt yet another piece of paper. "Go ahead back to the scale to get the tare. Thanks for your business, Mr. Kinnear."

Unloading the pigs was much faster than loading.

And less painful.

For Dirt.

The five were now on a one-way path to a roaster, or a tasty BBQ.

That last thought reminded Dirt that it was dinnertime.

June 21, 2012

Great Northern Meat Processing Facility
Grand Forks, ND

*

“Hey Monty! Just knock ’em out. Don’t try to fuck ’em!”

“Yeah, yeah, yeah. Go fuck yourself,” he yelled without looking back as he wrangled the spiraled, tangled hose of compressed air connected to his gun. The hose was the bane of his existence.

“Serious man! Get that line moving. We’re backing up out here.”

This time he pulled down his blood-spattered facemask and turned around, albeit slowly. His gimpy left leg prevented him from moving too fast. He liked to tell everyone that it was shrapnel from ’Nam, but in reality, it was just a bad knee with sixty-five years of mileage. He got more sympathy from the ’Nam thing though so he stuck to the story. The doctor told him that it was bone-on-bone and that he needed a new one. He wasn't about to fuck-ass do that. He did have shrapnel though. It was in his shoulder and it didn't bother him a bit. When he finally remembered to take a deep breath so he could yell back, a thick mixture of coppery blood and the soupy mixture of pig shit and piss slapped him across the face and momentarily took his breath away.

"Then get me some help!"

"Ain't no one else!"

"Then fuck you guys! Quit your bitchin'!"

He took a small bottle of Old Spice from his pocket, sprinkled some on his face mask, and slipped it back on. Now, instead of being assaulted with the smell of blood, shit, and piss, it smelled more like the fragrance department at K-Mart.

Not much difference, really.

Vince Montgomery, who everyone called "Monty" to his face and "that fucking old coot" behind his back, typically worked the kill room's stun line at the Great Northern Meat Processing plant a mere six miles north of Grand Forks along the banks of the mighty Red River of the North. Today, because some pansy-wad fuck-ass didn't have the fur on his balls to say, "Fuck no" to his wife's demand to attend some fuck-ass doll collection convention in Fargo, he was doing the work of an entire kill team. Not only did he have to stun the pigs as they squealed down the line, but now he had to hook them, swing and bleed them, and then do the ass-to-throat slice. Once the cut was done, and the guts spilled into the stainless steel bins just below their snouts, he pressed a button and they swung out of his sight into another room by metal hooks from the ceiling where they'd be dipped, flamed, and skinned.

That's the way things were supposed to go.

But not today.

With his luck, and the way the day was going, some other pansy-wad down-the-line would get a call from his wife and be told that if he ever wanted to see her naked again that he would have to put down his knife and drive her to some fuck-ass butterfly and fairy convention in the hotel next to the fuck-ass doll convention. Then, he supposed, he'd have to manage the dipping and skinning too. And if that was the case, then he might as well just manage the entire line. He'd get out the fuck-ass *Shake 'N Bake*, serve them up himself at the VFW with coleslaw, fuck-ass fries, a piss-warm beer, charge 'em $16.95, and make a fuck-ass mint.

"Fuck that," he said to himself, pushed up his glasses, pulled off his "Vietnam Vet" baseball cap, rubbed his head, and then scratched his ass with his free hand.

The kill line was typically the job of three.

One for knockout, one for hanging, one for slice and dice.

Two would work if the team was good and could do what it needed without thinking.

Or talking.

Monty hated working with fuck-ass talkers who jibber-jabbered incessantly no matter what they were doing.

There was too much going on. Too many moving parts for all that jibber-jabber.

The jibber-jabberers were typically the young punks who didn't know their butt from a fuck-ass hole in the ground.

Today, thanks to that fuck-ass doll convention for pansy-wads and their domineering wives some seventy miles south, Monty was a team of one. So, from his point of view, the line would move as fast as his sagging sixty-five year old ass and gimpy knee would carry him, and the guys at the front of the line would just have to fuck-ass deal with it.

He hated fuck-ass pork chops, anyway.

He couldn't stand the smell of sizzling bacon.

And now he hated fuck-ass dolls even more.

He was sure they were all fuck-ass democrats too.

*

Monty's weapon of choice was a non-penetrating compression gun. The one in front of him was a Prescott Devices Model 345 with digital variable compression. It hung from the kill room's ceiling by a pair of half-inch wire-mesh cables and a series of counter-balancing springs.

It was the top of the line.

The Buick of compression guns.

If he were to have to wrangle the gun on his own accord day-after-day, Monty was sure he would be dead of a heart attack by now as the fuck-ass bastard gun weighed almost fifty plus pounds. He wasn't a young buck any more. If not dead, maybe he would have arms like that Governor of California who used to lift a lot of weights and now made movies.

Perhaps not.

That guy was some sort of foreigner, anyway.

The springs made the gun virtually weightless and easy to handle. He could toss it between his hands as easy as a can of Pabst Blue Ribbon and not spill a single drop. The gun did a good job and made rendering the pigs unconscious virtually effortless.

And fast.

Pull the trigger, a quick, loud bang, and the pig was down.

Not dead. Just knocked out long enough to have its throat slit a few minutes later.

The gun was made in America, of course. It had a big sticker below the "Prescott Model 345" decal that told him so.

Except for the fuck-ass hoses.

They were definitely foreign.

The hoses kept getting tangled and wrapping themselves around the gun's barrel and sometimes even his neck. If they were made in the good ol' USA, they wouldn't do that.

"Fuck-ass hoses," he said as he wrestled and untangled them. "Probably made in fuck-ass China."

After all of this time, he had to find out.

He took one of the hoses in his hand, pulled it towards his pop-bottle bifocals, adjusted them on his nose, and read the printing, “Hecho en Mexico.”

“Heck-oh en Mexico,” he said. “Where in fuck-ass hell is Heck-oh Mexico?”

Monty tossed the untangled hoses over his shoulder and pressed the button to open the white pipe gate to his left. The waiting, squealing pigs started meandering down the small three-foot wide walkway towards him. The other guys on the line called it, "The Green Mile.”

Monty didn’t get the reference.

“That movie with Tom Hanks, Monty. You didn’t see it? It’s on TNT at least once a week.”

“Don’t watch TV.”

“It was a story too. Some famous author wrote it. Lives in Maine I think.”

“Don’t read much either.”

“It’s what these guys in this prison called the hallway leading up to the room where they keep the ’lectric chair. They called it ’Wa’kin the green mile.’ I think cuz the concrete was painted green. I can’t believe you haven’t seen it.”

“Could of painted it fuck-ass pink for all I care. Sounds fuck-ass dumb, if you ask me,” Monty would glare, grunt, shrug, and limp away.

Evidently, they didn’t have much work to do.

He did.

Once three pigs entered the walkway, Monty pressed the button that closed the gate. Its springs pulled it shut and it slammed against the magnet that kept it from being opened in either direction. The noise started the three pigs and they turned around in unison. Three pairs of wide-open eyes looked back at him.

"Deal with it," he said to the pigs.

Nothing else could come in.

Nothing was getting out.

Alive.

Monty stood, slightly bent, behind a waist-high stainless steel barricade and watched the pigs walk in single file towards him. The floor was a series of puzzle-piece metal grates above a stainless steel trough that could easily be rinsed with a hose at the end of the day. Its gradual slope towards waiting stainless steel waste barrels named "The Pissers" made cleaning easy.

They had stupid names for fuck-ass everything in the plant.

The floor rattled louder as the pigs began to excite one another and walk even faster. Their ears were straight up and their pink snouts sniffed and flared in the air.

They were getting nervous.

Nervous pigs tented to shit and piss a lot.

It was as if they knew what was going to happen.

The Pissers would definitely need to be emptied before the end of his shift.

When the first, and the largest, pig was directly in front of him, Monty eased the gun towards his chest, put the barrel on the pig's forehead, squarely between its eyes, and pulled the trigger.

BANG!

The gut shot out a flattened bolt onto the pig's head and it was instantly knocked out. Sometimes the skull was fractured. Sometimes not. It didn't matter. What mattered was the pig was down. Outside, the gun sounded more like a child's cap gun. Inside, within the closed walls of the kill room, the sound was amplified and bounced between the walls. In here, it sounded more like a twenty-two.

As advertised, the pig crumbled to its knees before him.

Monty watched as the other two looked down at their compatriot then up at him.

"Yup, you're fuck-ass next."

Monty scooted to his left and placed the barrel between the second pig's eyes.

BANG!

The second pig fell.

Monty pirouetted, as best he could, to the left and pulled the gun with him.

BANG!

The third one toppled.

*

Monty hobbled towards the sets of chains hanging over the metal wall to his right and held his knee as he walked. It was getting sore, as he'd been on it all morning without a break. When he reached the hanging station, he pushed his glasses further up the bridge of his nose. He needed to be sure to use the correct chains; otherwise there'd be a fuck-ass mess to clean up.

Things were still blurry.

He pushed his glasses up further.

It didn't help much.

He looked over the black rims.

A little better.

"Fuck-ass eyes," he grumbled to himself. "Gettin' old's the shits."

At the ends of each five-foot length of chain was a 12-inch stainless steel rod that separated into two pointed hooks at the six-inch mark. At the middle point of each chain was a large connecting link that would eventually be hitched to a high-tensile cable to hoist each pig and convey it further down the line. First to the cutting station, to the dip and burn, to the sectioning room, and then to the coolers. Eventually, each pig would end up sliced into small pieces just the right size for a dinner plate.

He looked down at the pigs he'd just knocked out, then back at the set of chains. Each hook was rated for 250 pounds, but he always played it safe and assumed a max weight of 200 pounds each. Two hooks gave him 400 pounds - maybe 450 at the most. The chain itself was rated at a couple thousand pounds so he was good there. Monty looked at the crudely painted numbers written on the first pig.

06202012. The date. That sucker was brought in in yesterday.

36569. The farmer's number.

352. The weight of the pig.

The numbers on the other two pigs were identical except for the last - the weight. They were 340 and 333.

Nice sized swine.

Farmer 36569 was definitely feeding them well.

Monty grabbed the chains, took the hooks, and fished each through a thigh. He had to be sure he wove it around the pigs' femurs otherwise the hook would simply tear through the muscle as they were hoisted, fall back down, and create a mess he had neither the time nor the desire to deal with.

It was as easy as baiting a fishhook with an earthworm.

"If those pansy asses at the fuck-ass doll convention were here, I wouldn't have to be worry about these fuck-ass hooks," he grumbled. "Hate this job."

Monty pulled a control box closer that was hanging from a large black cord from the ceiling towards him and pressed the green "LEFT" button. The conveyor above him moved in his direction. Dangling down from it were a cables, each roughly three feet apart, he'd attach each chain to. As soon as three cables were above him, he pressed the red "STOP" button.

It kept moving.

"Fuck-ass thing! I told you to stop!"

He slammed the box against the metal wall, pressed the red button again, and yelled at the moving cables.

"Stop you fuck-ass thing!"

He pressed the button harder and beat it against the metal rail.

The conveyor stopped and the cables swung back and forth above his head. A bit further than what he wanted, but he wasn't about to deal with the fuck-ass control box again and have it reset to the other end of the kill room and waste another fuck-ass ten minutes of his day. There was a six-pack of cold beer with his name on it waiting in his fuck-ass fridge at home and, unless they asked him to work overtime because of that fuck-ass doll convention, his shift was over in two hours. Monty grabbed three cables in his hand, pulled them down to the floor, and attached the connectors to the middle link on each of the three chains.

Monty took the control box in his hand.

"You gonna fuck-ass work now you fuck-ass sona'bitch?"

He pressed the "UP" button.

Slowly and steadily, and luckily in the correct direction, the chains started their way up towards the ceiling and lifted each swine until their snouts were dancing in front of him three feet off of the floor.

He pressed the orange "BASE" button on the control, and the dangling pigs began moving to the far side of the kill room. It was a carnival ride made especially for them and just like everything at the plant, that area had a name too: Slice and Dice.

*

Monty didn't watch too much television. Even though he loved movie theater popcorn with extra butter and salt, he hadn't been to theater since the *Star Wars* came out in '77. He did have a television and even paid for basic cable, but it was rarely on. When he did, he looked for horror flicks. Movies like *Halloween, Friday the 13th*, and the one with the burned-up freak with the fuck-ass knives for hands, *Nightmare on Elm Street*. He enjoyed watching how the bad guy kept coming back regardless of what they threw at, shot at, or pushed through him. Plus, they always had some fuck-ass jiggly-titted hottie who romped and squealed around in her bra and panties. How bouncing boobs added anything to the plot, he didn't know, but he enjoyed the scenery nonetheless. Miss Jiggly Tits was always so fuck-ass stupid, too. Instead of running away after she impaled the bad guy with the fuck-ass machete that she just happened to have laying around, she'd go up to him and make sure he was dead.

She'd poke him with her big toe.

"Are you dead Mr. Bad Guy?"

The bad guy was never dead, of course.

Then she'd get her head cut off before her scream had a chance to leave her pretty little lungs.

Bye-bye Jiggly Tits.

It always made him laugh.

Movie bad guys always had a machete just when it was needed, and the bad guy was never dead.

Never.

No one in any of the movies he did take the time to watch though, ever had what was in his left hand.

A five-inch gut hook.

Now that would be an interesting scene.

A bad guy with a gut hook.

In his right hand was a standard-issue skinning knife with a five-inch blade.

Both were scalpel-sharp.

Technically, he could run the next station with just the skinning knife, but since he was working with something that was potentially going to end up in someone's freezer, everyone in the kill room was told to be safe. A bad cut into a stomach, spleen, or intestine, and a good portion of the meat would be tainted. A bad cut and the pig was put on the conveyor leading to the boxcars outside. The plant still had to pay the farmer so it was a cut that was frowned upon.

A pork chop that tasted like shit and bile wasn't a good thing.

So he used two knives.

The skinning knife was used first to slice the carotid.

The gut hook was used to split the pig from ass to throat without puncturing anything.

That was the theory.

Monty looked back at the five men standing at the entrance to the kill room and looked for Stu – the shift lead. He found him leaning against the main door. Monty laughed to himself. He was watching a road crew.

One guy working.

Four guys standing around scratching their balls and laughing at their own dirty jokes.

"Stu! Heading over to the slice and dice," yelled Monty.

Stu didn't look up.

"Stu!"

He finally got his attention.

"What!"

"I'm heading over to the Slice and Dice."

Stu, the kill room's day-shift lead, gave him the thumbs-up, and immediately continued telling his evidently inconsequential story to the other jack-offs at the assembly point. Monty had to notify the lead whenever he left his station and the compression gun unattended.

Not that Stu would think to come and man it himself to keep the line moving.

No. Not Stu. He was management now.

Too good for manual labor.

“Why aren’t you in some fuck-ass meeting? You and your fuck-ass blonde hair. Think you’re so high and mighty,” he mumbled to himself.

He remembered when Stu first started. The kid puked his guts up the first time he had to do the slice and dice.

Monty opened the gate out of the stun area, and looked back at Stu though the corner of his eyes, "Fuck-ass pansy-wad.”

Monty didn’t like too many people.

He really didn’t have much time for Stu.

Monty knew what they called him when he wasn’t in earshot.

He was an old coot, but he had lived sixty-five long, hard years, and deserved to live the way he wanted.

Monty had at least thirty more years than anyone else in the kill room.

“Bunch’a fuck-ass kids if you ask me,” he said as he limped to the pigs dangling by their hams in slice and dice.

*

Monty turned on the water to the hose that fed into and filled the trough under the Slice and Dice. It didn’t take a decade at the plant to understand that blood was thicker than water. He saw enough of that in ’Nam. Saw the Mekong swirl red at its shores one day and, if it were not for some fuck-ass chopper pilot named Spooncake, his blood would have surely been in the river’s mix.

It was as if the fuck-ass bastard knew where the 'Cong were.

He was a fuck-ass pilot for sure. Flew that thing by the hair on his balls.

Monty heard that he and his crew were shot down not far from Vinh Long a few days after he was pulled from the jungle. He was still doped up and never got a chance to thank the guy. Never saw them again. They found the headless body of his medic, a guy named Franklin, but there was no sign of the pilot, Spooncake, or the gunner, Hammond.

Just lots of blood, and a few dead 'Cong for good measure.

He went to that memorial in DC a few years back. Looked for the pilot and gunner's name.

Weren't there.

Poor bastards.

Monty hoped they didn't torture them.

He'd heard the stories and knew it wasn't pretty to be captured by the 'Cong.

Monty sighed and longed for the good 'ol days. He had something to live for back then.

A real purpose.

Now he was killing pigs instead of the Slopes in 'Nam.

"What a fuck-ass life," he whispered to himself.

Monty turned the faucet up higher – the trough needed more water. He had to keep it flowing. The water in the trough kept the blood moving to the drain and eventually to the Pisser. When the water had filled enough of the trough below the pigs so that the blood wouldn't stick to the bottom, he flexed his shoulders and wrapped his arms around him in a hug. He learned early on that manning the Slice and Dice did a job on his back and shoulders.

Too much bending.

Too much up and down.

Too much left and right.

Too much moving.

That's why he liked running the gun.

That was just point and shoot.

Easier on his back.

Monty started with the first of the trio – the big one. He took his skinning knife, brought it below the pig's left ear, and sliced to the other side. Blood gushed over his arm, dripped down his elbow, sprayed across the floor, and into the trough below its snout. Since it wasn't dead, its heart was still pumping.

That lasted for about fifteen seconds until there was nothing left to pump.

He sliced the throats of the next two strung up in front of him.

"Fuck-ass blood," he said as he scraped it off his arm and dripping elbow. It was already getting sticky.

It didn't take long.

Monty rinsed the skinning knife in the running water and put it back into the leather sheath attached to his belt. He moved back to the big pig now hanging completely lifeless, blood still dripping into the trough from its snout, and tossed the gut hook to his other hand. He placed the hook in the pig's ass and pulled straight down to its throat. The pig's abdomen opened up as if Monty had pulled a zipper on a winter jacket.

The remaining two split open just as quickly and effortlessly.

Monty moved three catch buckets below each of the pigs, put a hand into two of the three abdomens and pulled. As viscera of two of the pigs oozed into the catch buckets, Monty moved the last pig and started the same avalanche of guts. Once cleaned and cooked, it was future dog and cat food.

And sausage casing.

"We eat some crazy fuck-ass shit," he said as he shook his head and took a few steps back to admire his work.

Monty looked over at the catch basin below the first pig and shook his head in disgust.

His aim was off.

"Shit," he said as he walked back to the other side of the three dangling pigs. The smell of fresh meat and blood was permeating through his mask despite the additional sprinkles of Old Spice he'd just added. The big pig's stomach didn't land in the basin as it was supposed to, and was instead draped over the edge of the catch basin's metal side.

It looked like a snot-covered, grey-pink water balloon.

Distended.

About ready to burst.

Except Monty knew that it didn't hold water and getting soaked with its contents would not be pleasant.

He'd stink for days.

Monty walked over to the basin and pushed at the stomach. He could feel the contents squish between his fingers. What he should have done, is put the gut hook away and use his hand, but he didn't. It was too late as his brain was already in control of his hand, and its motion was beyond the point of return. The gut hook caught the trailing edge of the stomach, just before it transitioned into intestine, and sliced it open. It was just a two-inch gash, but big enough. Its contents sloshed onto the floor, across Monty's boots, and started to ooze in all directions.

Most of the liquid contents moved towards the drain.

All of the solids remained on the floor and around his feet.

"What a fuck-ass day," he said as he looked down at his feet – accepting the fact that new work boots were in his future.

Monty's face turned white.

He could feel the sudden increase in pressure as his heartbeat increased.

There, at his left foot, as if grasping to hang on to the tip of his boot before it was swept into the trough, was a human hand.

Monty froze.

He tried to yell, but nothing, not even a faint squeak, could escape from his lungs.

*

It was Stu that finally broke through the fog that had paralyzed Monty.

"Monty! Get your ass moving! Monty!"

Monty looked over at Stu then back down at the floor. He was breathing again, and finally found his voice. He could hear his heartbeat between his ears.

"Shut 'er down. Stu! Shut 'er down."

Besides the hand clawing at his boot, Monty saw a jawbone, an array of fingers, a nose, and an ear.

It was a royal fuck-ass day.

June 21, 2012

Grand Forks, ND

*

Grand Forks County Sheriff Gordy Albrecht was in a corner booth at *Pesto!* – Grand Forks' answer to gourmet Italian – with his wife of two years, Monica Cromwell. She always made sure everyone knew it was Cromwell, and by no means Albrecht. Now he was even in the habit of correcting those who had the misfortune of calling her Monica Albrecht, or Lord have mercy on their souls, Mrs. Albrecht. It was as if she already knew the eventual demise of their nuptials, and was making the transition from "Single" from "Married" just one checkbox easier.

Even though they were both at the restaurant and had both ordered the same thing, Gordy was the only one getting his money's worth of iced tea, and all-you-can-eat soup, salad, and breadsticks. Today, to Gordy's dismay, they were in a booth. Gordy normally preferred tables, but everything was taken, so Gordy was forced to improvise and pushed the table towards his wife in order to make room for his belly.

He was not only on his third bowl of pasta fah-gee-oh-lee (as he called it), but also his third wife, and realized that he went through bowls of soup almost as fast as he went through wives. The first two had given up on him after getting tired of his job, his penchant for bourbon, and his friendship with the "rurals." Monica, a tall brunette with the standard East-coast superiority complex, was a transplant from New York City, and was having a very difficult time adjusting to life in fly-over country. She missed the city and never failed to ensure he was punished for it. The problem was that he wasn't about to move from the country. She wanted nothing more than to return to a real city. One with sky scrapers, fine dining, and fashion besides denim and flannel. Gordy was sure he'd be single soon enough.

He wouldn't fit in the big city.

Their marriage wasn't exactly a logical pairing, and definitely not a match made in heaven as things were turning out. They didn't fight, Gordy was never mean, and the sex had stopped a long time ago so now they were basically roommates. She just didn't like her life at the moment, and Gordy knew he had to let her come to the decision on her own. Gordy wasn't even sure why they'd gotten married in the first place. But, at the time, it was infatuation at first sight. He was right off the rails from number two, five years younger, and twenty pounds lighter. She was the events planner at the conference he was attending in Dallas for FBI Academy Alum. She thought she'd get her hands on an up and coming executive. She wanted a man with a title who wore expensive suits. He was on the rebound. It seemed to make sense. They had fun together at first – until the city girl moved to Grand Forks, North Dakota. A place without boutiques catering to her every need. A place without Broadway plays. A place where lunch cost less than $5, and was made with pronounceable ingredients. They were married in the Bahamas before she had a chance to realize what his home was like, and what exactly being the sheriff of Grand Forks County North Dakota really meant.

Square peg, round hole, stuff.

"Would you like more breadsticks, Sheriff? Or another bowl of soup? Mrs. Sheriff? Anything for you?"

Gordy cringed.

"Mrs. Sheriff" was almost as bad as "Mrs. Albrecht." He knew she despised being called anything other than Monica or Ms. Cromwell. She didn't take his last name when they were married as, evidently, that's not what sophisticates from New York City do these days. Gordy looked at his wife apologetically. She shook her head, rolled her eyes, and looked out of the window without acknowledging the server.

It would be beneath her social status to speak to a restaurant server. Especially one at a restaurant called Pesto! in the middle of bumb-fuck North Dakota. At least that's what she called their home when no one was around, or when she was particularly mad at Gordy for bringing her here.

Gordy was positive she didn't want, or need, anything else from the menu or from the server who was still standing at their booth. Monica had already complained twenty minutes ago that she was full after a lettuce leaf, a nibble of her breadstick, and an ice cube.

It was a New York City thing, she always told him.

People don't over eat in New York City.

"Monica. Want another ice cube?"

His wife glared back at him and Gordy turned his attention to the server.

"No thanks, hon. We've had enough. Just bring us the tab."

Like it or not, Sheriff Albrecht was a celebrity around town. Even the people who didn't vote for him had to admit that he was just a nice guy. Generally the only reason someone didn't vote for him was easy, and didn't have anything to do with politics, botched arrests, or bad press. The "someone" was generally a neighbor, childhood friend, or family member of his opponent. It was that simple. The job was his until he retired.

Gordy was jovial.

Self-Deprecating.

Sarcastic.

He had round cheeks and a belly rotund enough he could use it as an armrest.

He was bald except for a four-inch, thinning shag carpet band of light brown hair that wrapped around the side of his head, over his ears, then worked its way up to the crown of his head to form a stripe.

Gordy was always ready to tell a joke with his slight Irish brogue and toothy grin. He would always come down with an infectious belly laugh before he reached the punch line, always unable to finish the joke. Gordy's humor wasn't necessarily in telling the joke itself or even the botched punch line. The fun and humor was Gordy himself.

His largest voting block came not from those in Grand Forks, but from everyone "out on the farms" to the west of the city. He knew most everyone by name, knew their kids, knew where they kept the hidden keys to their houses (if the house was ever locked which most weren't), and most importantly, he knew where each family kept the bourbon, the jelly-jar glasses, and was always told to help himself when he came to check on things.

Which he always did.

Gordy's problem was that he wasn't a politician.

Instead, he was a sheriff, and a steadfast friend.

Gordy loved his job, but hated the bullshit as much as a dentist's drill.

His cellphone began to whine just as the server brought the check, and set it on the table along with four chocolate mints. As he picked up the phone, Gordy looked at his wife who had already brought her eyebrows down in disapproval.

"I know it's lunch and all, but I have to answer this."

"Whatever," she said with a shrug. "One of your farmers probably needs you. A missing cow or something."

Gordy wondered if there would be a fourth in his future, or if he was better off being single. Number four would have to understand his job and not take it personally when he had to go. Someone who didn't think farmers were low-life dirt diggers, and enjoyed their company, culture, and casualness as much as he did. Number Four was likely have to be someone local, and definitely not from either coast. Maybe he should try being single for a bit.

At least a couple of months in-between three and four.

"Albrecht," he said as he answered the phone.

Gordy went silent as he listened, and slowly pulled his wallet from his back pocket.

"Shit," he said as he looked at his watch. "I'll be right there. Call the coroner."

Gordy put the phone in his shirt pocket, and looked at his wife across the booth.

"Some farmer's cat gets caught in one of those combining machines?"

Gordy threw two twenties on the table, took all of the mints, stuffed them into his pocket, and didn't bother commenting on his wife's snide remark despite the fact that she mispronounced it. Normally, he would have. But something big was happening and didn't have time to deal with attitude.

"That's for her, by the way. All of it. Every single penny."

"Our tab was what? Twenty-five max?"

"Twenty-two," said Gordy. "Something's going on at the meat plant up north. Gotta run."

"Ah. Some farmer's pig got molested."

He gave his wife a kiss on the cheek, grabbed his keys, and rushed out the door.

"Don't count on me for dinner. This doesn't sound good."

She shrugged.

Before he left, he saw her exchange one of the twenties for a ten.

"Bitch," he said to himself.

Number three was a mistake.

He knew that now, and wondered how much this one would cost him in the end.

He'd never learn.

*

Gordy parked his black, unmarked 2010 Chevy Suburban fifty feet before the yellow crime scene tape, and turned off his lights and siren. As sheriff, he didn't have to drive a regular patrol car. Instead, he was allowed to drive his personal vehicle, which the county customized with lights in the front grille, a plethora of antennas on the outside and just as many radios inside, and a siren. He had a magnetic flashing emergency dome light with a cord running into the cigarette lighter that he could quickly toss on the Suburban's roof directly above his head when he was in a hurry. When the dome was on, everyone knew he meant business.

This was the first time he'd been out to the plant. He wondered how those who made their living slaughtering pigs ever got used to it, and if they could eat a ham sandwich without imagining a slight squeal when they took the first bite. The moment Gordy stepped out of his truck, the smell of the processing plant hit him. It was a sickening, sweet smell of rotting flesh. It didn't smell like ham or bacon at all. Being a graduate of the FBI academy, Gordy knew to always look at his surroundings first. He scanned the area and saw dozens of hooves sticking up over the top of a Burlington Northern rail car as pushed the crime scene tape down, and stepped over it.

"Sir? Your badge?"

Gordy stopped, and showed the scene's managing officer his gold Sheriff's badge. The officer wrote his name, and the current time on the crime scene log. Gordy was sure it was a boring-ass job, but very important nonetheless. The crime scene log maintained a chronological list of every single person who entered a crime scene and when they left. Prosecutors used the log to question those who were on the scene. Defense lawyers used it to find holes to shoot down evidence. If someone was at the scene and not listed on the log, or if someone came in and didn't log out, it provided a goldmine of opportunities to have critical evidence thrown out of court.

He was sure the officer who he showed his badge to knew damn well who he was, but it was protocol to ask for identification, double-check the time, and write it all down. He would have chewed the officer's ass off if he wouldn't have asked to see his badge.

Gordy pulled a small notepad and pen out of his breast pocket and flipped it open to a blank page.

"Coroner been called?"

The officer looked at the log, and shook his head.

"I'm not sure if they've been called, but I know they haven't checked-in, Sir."

"When did the first officer arrive? When was it called in?"

"It was called in at 12:22 this afternoon. First officer arrived on site at 12:31. Backup was called in at 12:45 and arrived on site at 1:12. Tape went up at 1:23. You are the fourth on the list. That's all I have at this point, Sir."

Gordy looked at his watch. It was 1:52, and he'd been called at 1:39.

After all of this time in law enforcement, he'd learned to keep time by the minute, and not round up and down. He'd also learned to write every piece of information down. Lawyers and media had an annoying penchant for wanting detail.

"MD?"

The kid looked confused.

"The Managing detective?"

"Oh. Sorry. Detective Richards, Sir. He's inside."

“Right where he should be. Thanks, officer.”

Gordy clicked his pen, closed his notepad, and walked towards the plant’s main door.

Gordy stopped and turned.

“Make sure no one. And I mean not one single person, comes in or goes out without you knowing about it, and writing it down. Got it?”

“Yes, Sheriff.”

*

Gordy stepped into the plant’s lobby, quietly shut the door behind him, and headed towards a group of silver shields standing by the coffee machine. No one was talking. None were drinking coffee or eating donuts, if they had, there would have been hell to pay. They all looked pale and, at second glance, they all seemed to be holding on to the counter for support.

“Sheriff,” said one of the detectives with a nod.

“Where’s Richards?”

“Inside,” said one of the detectives as he looked past the door. “It’s bad, Sheriff. Fifteen years and I’ve never seen anything like that.”

The other heads nodded in unison.

Before anything else could be said, one of the detectives ran through the door Gordy had just used, and stumbled onto the sidewalk. The strained, painfully familiar sound of retching started before the door had time to swing shut.

"Barely made it."

No one laughed. They either stared towards the processing room, or studied the grout lines on the tile floor.

Gordy left the men in the lobby, and strode past the door into the work area that was kept open with a concrete block; evidently to allow the people working the scene easy access in and out. He saw Detective Richards standing in the corner next to three men clad in grey coveralls with "Great Northern Meats" logos plastered on the backs, and headed in his direction.

"Why hasn't the coroner been called, Detective?"

"They have. They're over there working."

"Fuck. They didn't sign-in then. They should know better."

"It was a mess, Sheriff. They probably forgot all about it."

"Won't matter to any lawyer how bad it is or how bad it was. Get someone out there. Have them sign in."

*

Gordy and the MD, Detective Richards, moved out of the way as a trio of paramedics finished packing their gear and headed in their direction.

"Medics? What were they doing here? It wasn't an active crime scene, was it?"

"No. The guy who, um, stumbled on. I mean the guy who found everything. An older guy," Detective Richards composed himself and looked at his notes. "Vincent Montgomery. Sixty-eight. Vietnam vet. Worked on the line for fifteen years. He was having trouble breathing. The plant manager thought he was having a heart attack, and called it in."

"Alive?"

"When he left here. Yes. They took him to United. White as a ghost. I'm sure if he didn't have one here, he was well on his way to something major eventually. He looked straight at me when they pushed him by on the gurney. Shit. He looked bad. They must have taken his false teeth out to make sure he didn't choke. His face was caved in. Made things look worse. But what he went through? I wouldn't wish that on anyone."

"He a suspect?"

"Montgomery? Fuck no."

"Sure of yourself today, are we?"

"I'd bet my left nut on it. Wasn't even supposed to be working today. Kept bitching about some fuck-ass doll conference in Fargo. He quit his fuck-ass job five times in fifteen minutes, and called the plant manager a fuck-ass pansy a dozen more times before they hauled him off."

"Fuck-ass? That's a new one for you, Detective."

"His words. Not mine. And by the sounds of it, his favorite two words in the entire English language. He said them a lot as the medics were checking him out, getting him on the gurney, and loading him into the ambulance. Even with the oxygen mask on, you could hear him. A real gem, that one."

"We'll have to talk to him though. Fuck-asses or not."

The floor of the plant was littered with yellow plastic triangles; each containing a unique number and placed by anything the team considered a piece of evidence. A group of men and women, Gordy couldn't tell which was which, dressed in white, disposable coveralls was taking pictures, putting body parts in clear evidence bags, and labeling each one with black Sharpies.

Gordy looked around the facility. He was eager to get up to speed.

"Walk me through it."

*

"Anything else?" asked Gordy.

"These are the knives he used," said Richards as he handed two plastic bags to Gordy. "For processing the pigs."

Gordy took the bags, and carefully turned them over a few times to get a closer look at the contents. To ensure there was no possibility of contamination, he didn't open either one.

"The old man used these?"

Richards nodded.

"These don't look like knives you get from Wal-Mart."

"The one with the straight blade is a skinning knife. Hunters use them out in the field. Montgomery used it to slit the throats of each of the pigs. The curved one is called a gut hook."

"It cuts them open. Ass to throat."

"Yes. Safer that way. Keeps the organs from getting sliced by mistake, and tainting the meat. Company protocol. Most would just use the skinning knife for everything."

"Most?"

"Hunters. Generally hunters won't use a gut hook. Too much work changing blades. Most of the guys on the line here are hunters."

Gordy gave the bags back to the MD.

"Who's here from the coroner's office?"

"Williams, Guthrie, and Volm."

"Lead?"

"Max Williams."

"Good. Max is a good guy. Knows his stuff," said Gordy as he motioned over to the trio in white suits. "Which one is he? I can't tell. They all look the same."

"In the center. The one with his head inside of the pig. At least I think that's him."

"Who's the plant manager?"

Richards looked down at his notepad again.

"Stewart Greyson. The one the old guy called a fuck-ass pansy."

"I can't wait to talk to him."

"Greyson?"

"No the old man."

"What's his story? Greyson's."

"Plant manager on duty. One of three. Been here five years. Nothing that sticks out."

"He here?"

Richards pointed with his head.

"Over there in the corner. The tall blonde with the tat crawling up his neck."

*

"Max," said Gordy. "Good to see you."

"Sheriff. I'd shake your hand, but it might contaminate things."

"You're good. Completely understand. Can you fill me in? What do you have?"

"A mess. Pure and simple."

"Can you be more specific?"

Max pointed to all of the bags that had been next to the numbered tents but where now being put into coolers. All of the necessary pictures had been taken and every bag had been cataloged and cross-referenced. It was safe to move things.

"I would say at least four different women at this point," the coroner said as he pointed to some of the bags. "Could be more. Have to do some DNA matching between the pieces."

"How do you know it's women? I mean. How can you tell?"

“We’ve found four left hands. Size is indicative of female. That or a young male, but I’m guessing female. The fingernails were too manicured for a typical male.”

“And all found stuffed in the pigs.”

“Fuck no.”

“No? I thought you found the body parts in the pigs.”

“Yes, we did.”

“But, you just...”

“Not stuffed. The pigs ate them. They were fed to the pigs. It was an active process of consumption. Some of the residual bone frags had chew marks. Indentations from porcine molars. Holes from porcine canines,” he said as he grinned to show his canines. “The pointed sharp things in our mouth. The canines. Porcine canine are three times larger. Much sharper than ours. Molars are twice as big. Can crush a small rock.”

“They actually ate someone?”

Max nodded with enthusiasm.

“Pigs. They’ll eat anything you put in front of them.”

“A body.”

“No. I mean they probably would, but not this time. These parts were already cut up before they were fed to the pigs. Cuts were clean. Very clean. They were fed to the pigs like slop. Mixed in with other stuff. Definitely in pieces prior to consumption. No doubt about it in my opinion.”

“DNA? Prints? What’s next?”

“Can I be honest with you, Sheriff?”

"Always, Max. You know that."

"This is too big for us. We don't have the equipment. We've never had anything like this in all of the years I've been here. You know that. Never."

Gordy nodded. Max was right. Things like this didn't happen in Grand Forks County. Robberies? A few. Drugs? Constantly. Murders? Not in the last decade. Body parts in a meat processing plant streaming out of a pig's abdomen?

Never in a million years.

"What do you need, Max? You name it."

"I'm going to have to send this off. Get help. There's a forensic pathologist in the cities I want to ask for help."

Gordy grimaced. County-to-county work was relatively easy to get. The cross billing was straightforward. He even had the paperwork in his drawer. State-to-state? Not as easy. He didn't have the right forms for that.

"Is there anyone local? As in North Dakota, who could help?"

Max shook his head.

"This is too big. Body parts to match. DNA cross-references. The works."

"Have a name?"

"McCorkendale. Andrea McCorkendale."

"Sounds familiar. She wrote a book, right?"

"Yup. She wrote the book on forensic pathology. Literally."

Gordy looked at Max. He looked confused.

"What's wrong?"

"She just got married. Her name changed. It's Teague now I think. Andie Teague. I've met her a few times. Gone to her seminars. Smart as all get out. She lives and breathes this stuff."

"I'll see what I can do, Max. I'll try my best."

"She'd be having an orgasm right now, Sheriff. She's that good. Body parts in a pig. She'd love it."

Gordy laughed.

"Like I said, Max. I'll do my best."

Gordy would find the paperwork and fill it out. Max was right. The county didn't have the equipment for this and Gordy felt this case wasn't going to go away quickly.

"Thanks, Sheriff," said Max as he headed back into the pig with his flashlight and magnifying glass. "There's more in here."

Before Gordy left, Max pulled himself out of the pig's abdomen, and yelled to one of the other techs.

"We'll need to get these pigs to the lab," then he turned to Gordy. "Sheriff, we'll need a refrigerated van or something to transport these. They'll start to decompose too fast. Ruin any trace evidence remaining inside."

"I'll get the MD right on it, Max. You'll get whatever you need."

Max gave him a thumbs up, pulled down his goggles, and headed back into the pig to dig some more.

*

There were three offices in the plant's primary facility. One seemed to be used as a training room as its walls were lined with card tables and folding chairs. There was a projector and desktop computer at one end of the room, and a screen pulled down from the ceiling at the opposite end. One office was for the General Manager; that one was closed, dark, and locked. The other was the office shared by the shift managers. Both of the offices had large, uncovered windows open to the processing room. The sign on the office door he was in read, "Plant Manager / Shift Manager" and below that were three names in alphabetical order:

Paul Eine
Stewart Greyson
Todd Pollock

Besides Greyson's name, was another small placard that was slid in to its right that read, "On Duty." Gordy was sure that if the old man had his way, the sign would have read, "The fuck-ass pansy is on duty, and probably playing with himself in the bathroom."

But the sign was probably too small.

Gordy hadn't met the old man yet, but it didn't take him long to determine that the old timer's assessment of others, specifically this shift manager, seemed to be spot on. Stewart

Greyson was, without a doubt, a fuck-ass pansy. After only five minutes of being alone with Stewart, Gordy came to the conclusion that he might have to start using the old man's colorful vocabulary after all in his description of others and life in general.

He and Stewart, "Please call me Stu, Sheriff," were sitting in the office shared by all of the shift managers. Gordy had already been offered a cup of coffee, a stale donut, and a gumball from the coin-operated dispenser on his desk. Stewart had even offered him a penny.

"Go ahead Sheriff. Give it a try. I'm buying."

Gordy passed on each.

"What's the difference between shift manager and plant manager?" asked Gordy.

"About four to five bucks an hour."

It took Stewart five minutes to regain control of himself after he believed he told the joke of his life to none other than the sheriff of Grand Forks County. He'd even slapped his thigh when he started laughing.

Gordy neither laughed nor slapped his leg. He wanted to slap the kid, but refrained. Instead, he thought of the old man's moniker for Stu instead. *That* made him smile.

"See! I knew that would make you laugh. Are you sure you don't want a gumball?"

"No. I'm fine. Really," said Gordy as he pulled out his pen and notepad. He looked at the time, scribbled it on the notepad, 2:41, and looked up at Stu. He wanted the kid to know it was time to get serious. “Tell me about the pigs.”

“They make great bacon.”

Stu started laughing again, but didn’t slap his leg this time.

Gordy rubbed his eyebrows with the side of his thumb and forefinger and imagined his gun.

“Today’s event. Tell me about those pigs specifically, Mr. Greyson.”

“Please. Call me Stu, Sheriff.”

“Today’s event, Stu.”

“What do you need to know? They were just, you know, pigs. As far as we were concerned, anyway. We had no idea of what was inside. Well, we do. There’s always guts and stuff. Lots of blood. But we weren’t expecting *that.* Honest!”

Stewart flailed his arms towards the room outside of his office. Gordy put up his hand to calm the kid down.

“I know. I know. I’m not saying you put the parts in the pig. How many were there?”

“How many what?”

“Pigs. How many.”

“We get hundreds.”

Gordy wanted to shoot the kid, or feed him to the pigs.

It would be both if the kid didn’t stop with the stand-up routine. If he was going to get any good information, Gordy had to think of a line of questioning that would corral the kid, and keep him on topic.

"Do you know where the pigs came from? Do you have a record?"

Gordy was ready for the off-ramp the kid was going to take.

"Please don't say from a mama pig."

Gordy watched the kid's chest deflate.

"It's called a sow."

"Focus, Stewart. How are your records kept? Can you tell me where the pigs came from? Focus."

"Please. Call me Stu, Sheriff."

"Stu. How are your records kept?"

"Umm. Yes. We use paint."

"And how is that paint used?"

"It's water-based. Safe and everything. Won't get into the meat product. You won't taste black paint in your pork chop, if that's what you are wondering."

"I wasn't wondering. So you label them when they come in?"

"Oh. That's what you meant. Yes. Each product is labeled when they come in. With a serial number."

"Can you tell me about the numbers?"

"First three or four digits represent the account. Then a sequence number. Then the total number of product brought in. Then finally the numbers representing the exact date."

Gordy relaxed a bit. Finally, he was getting somewhere.

"Good. What can you tell me about the pigs that Mr. Montgomery processed today."

"He did lots of them."

God this kid was stupid, thought Gordy.

"The ones specifically on the floor. Right. This. Minute."

Gordy watched Stu as he leaned to the other side of his desk, and looked out the window.

"There aren't many out there."

"The ones that Mr. Montgomery was working with right before he stopped the line."

"Oh. Those," said Stu. "There's only one left hanging. I think I can read it from here. Account is 146. Looks like there were five. Number four is still hanging. And it looks like they were brought in on June 12, 2012."

"That was yesterday."

Gordy saw Stu look at the calendar, and start to nod. He looked for a line of drool, but didn't see one form.

"Yup. That was yesterday. Want some coffee, Sheriff?"

Gordy ignored the offer and continued questioning.

"You said account 146. Can you tell me who that is?"

"Sure," said Stu as he stumbled on the keyboard at his desk. "Kinnear. Dirk Kinnear. Arvilla. That's about twenty..."

"Yup. I know where that is."

Gordy's heart sank to his stomach, and he felt his face redden and warm. Dirk Kinnear. Son of Tubbs and Trude. Tubbs died a few years ago, and Gordy attended the funeral. Dirk wasn't at the funeral, but he stopped by the farm to pay his respects. He shook the kid's hand, and wished him well. Trude didn't come out of the house to acknowledge him, but he saw her looking out of the kitchen window. He didn't have much of a relationship, if at all, with Trude, but he'd known the family for years. Heard of the troubles, but thought if they needed his help, they'd call. Dirk, who everyone called Dirt, ran the farm now, and was doing a good job from what he'd heard. The kid had grown the cattle herd by a dozen, more than doubled the number of pigs from ten to near twenty-five, and was managing two thousand acres.

Plus, although he hadn't seen him in person but heard he was pretty good nonetheless, he had his own band called "Dirty Deeds" and played at Butch's on a regular basis.

Gordy thought the name was unique, but if events played out the way they typically do, the press would have a field day with that and twist it in directions never intended.

Evidently, Dirt didn't maintain much of a social life.

Gordy closed his notepad, clicked his pen, and shoved everything back in his shirt pocket. He didn't want these pigs to belong to anyone he knew and was crushed the moment he recognized the name. Why couldn't they have been from someone in Walsh County up north? Then it would be Tom Quinn's problem. Or Nelson County to the west? Then Gregg Newcomb could handle it.

But the pigs came from his county.

From a family he knew.

So now it was his problem.

"Stu? Can I trouble you for a print out of account 146?"

“How much do you need?”

“Give me everything. Complete history.”

“Sure thing, Sheriff. Coming right up.”

The kid pressed a button, and the laser printer on the small stand next to the desk started spitting out paper.

“Shouldn’t take long. Only a dozen pages or so. Why not have a donut while you wait.”

*

Gordy was the last to leave. The managing officer signed him out of the scene, and verified that there was no one else around.

“Are you the last, Sheriff?”

“Yes. You can pack up.”

Gordy was back in his Suburban, notepad and pen at the ready. He looked at his watch, and wrote down the time: 5:12. He pulled his phone from his pocket, and dialed the number for his deputy whose jurisdiction included the Kinnear farm.

It rang twice.

“Deputy Thorson,” said a deep voice.

Gordy was too tired to hold the phone to his ear so he directed the call though the SUV’s speakers.

“Booker. Sheriff Albrecht. We have a situation.”

After Gordy recited everything he knew about the case, he let Booker talk. He knew the deputy and Dirt were childhood friends, and had a lot of history.

"Do you want me to keep an eye on the farm tonight? See if there's anything going on out of the ordinary?"

"Good idea. Keep it quiet though."

"Anything else, Sheriff?"

"I'll need you there first thing. Sunrise. I'll call you. I need to arrive first."

"Yes, sir."

"Keep it quiet, Booker. I don't want any press."

"Keep it quiet. I understand. See you in the morning, Sheriff. Just let me know when and where."

June 21, 2012

The Law Office of Bancroft, Simpson and Associates
Brentwood, CA

*

Daniel wanted five minutes of privacy, and needed Ben out of the office.

"What the fuck?"

"What's wrong, boss."

"Get me the entire LeCross file. Something's not right. We're missing something."

"What's the number?"

Daniel didn't have to look at his notes; he knew most of the case file numbers, and where they were stored, by heart.

"43865. Third set of laterals at the far end of the office on the second floor. Third drawer from the bottom. About halfway in from the left. Can't miss it."

"I can't believe you know that."

Daniel shrugged and continued studying the papers in front of him.

"But we've gone over this thing five times already."

"Just get the file."

Daniel got up from his desk chair and tried to stretch his legs. He'd been sitting since midnight staring at papers, receipts, telephone records, and photos. Now it was just after three in the morning in California. The sun wouldn't even begin to rise for another two to three hours. The traffic on Wilshire Blvd below his window was amazingly light, and Daniel could count the handful of homeless men with their homemade cardboard signs staked out at each street corner waiting for any potential bleeding hearts stupid enough to give them a dollar or two.

"Fucking assholes. They probably make more than I do."

"What?"

"The homeless guys. What a scam."

A single set of lights was on in the Law Office of Bancroft, Simpson and Associates and those lights were from the office of Daniel Carpenter. Daniel and his legal assistant, Ben, were working on the LeCross civil case – and had been for the past month. Both were tired, but Ben more so as he wasn't used to working this late. Daniel, wanting to prove his worth and make partner, rarely allowed himself more than four hours of sleep per day. Anything more, *he thought*, was a waste. Anything more, *he knew*, would demonstrate a weakness the other partners would be able to smell as easily as a great white could sense a drop of blood in an ocean of salt water. And once they smelled blood, he might as well kiss his ass, and his desire to be a partner, goodbye.

It didn't matter whose daughter he was fucking.

And that fringe benefit would disappear just as fast if he didn't make partner.

"Here you go, boss," said Ben as he dropped a five-pound folder onto Daniel's desk.

"Now go get me some coffee. Two pink sugars."

LeCross was a big-time Hollywood director who made lots of money. He paid Danny's employer a yearly eight-figure retainer to keep him out of trouble. Mr. LeCross is a personal friend of the first name on the firm's door: Franklin Bancroft. Evidently, Mr. LeCross had the misfortune of being accused of raping one of the female leads in a project he worked on two years ago. He was found not guilty in the criminal phase of things, but the actress immediately moved forward with a civil case. Franklin Bancroft expertly cut the woman off at the knees, and now she was hard-pressed to get a role in a hemorrhoid commercial in Hong Kong let alone a bit part in Hollywood. Everyone was sure he was guilty, as there was word on the streets that he had a penchant for having his way with the female leads. But an accusation of rape was not an easy thing to get a conviction with the heavy "beyond a reasonable doubt" rules of criminal law. It was easier on the civil side, where to win, the plaintiff only needs to prove her case with a "preponderance of the evidence."

The actress felt she had twenty-five million dollars' worth of preponderance.

"Why are we working on this? He should just settle. Everyone knows he did it."

"That's what he's paying us for."

"But the guy is guilty as sin."

"We don't know that."

"But he is, Daniel. You know it."

"No I don't. And it doesn't matter what I think. Or what you think. That's up to a jury."

"She wants a jury trial?"

"She wants his balls on a platter. Anyway, our job isn't to determine his guilt or innocence.

"Then what is it?"

"Where did you go to school?"

"Kent State."

Daniel shook his head in as he thought Kent State was supposed to be a pretty good school.

"If the law is solid. Damage the evidence. It's the first rule of a defense attorney, Ben. We have to figure out how to discredit the evidence the plaintiff is going to throw at us."

"But the guy is dirty. He raped that actress. Probably others, too. What was her name?"

"Abbey Sinclair. And I really don't care if he did it or not."

"You don't?"

"Brings in a lot of billable hours to the firm," said Daniel with a shrug. "That's what we have to worry about. Billable hours. Not some actress. They are a dime a dozen."

He really didn't care what the guy did in his spare time. It wasn't his job. He knew he didn't necessarily like Adam LeCross; thought he was an arrogant son-of-a-bitch who liked to use his dick too much. But he'd hired the firm to make this civil issue disappear as effectively as the criminal case. So that's what Daniel was going to do.

And he'd sure as hell make partner along the way. If they wanted him to bill two hundred hours a month, he'd bill four hundred. If the doctor said he needed at least five hours of sleep, he'd aim for one.

Sleep was for the weak and unmotivated.

"Our job is to defend the legal system, not necessarily the man. Rape is tough to prove on the criminal side, but easier on the civil side. We have to shoot down every piece of evidence her side throws at us. All they need is a preponderance. We, on the other hand, need perfection. What happens after that is out of our hands."

Daniel held up a sheet of paper and smiled.

"And I think we just found it."

"Found what?"

"If you don't like the answer to the question Ben, then you have to change the question to get the answer you want. Just found the new question."

Ben looked confused, sat down on the chair across from Daniel's desk, and pulled the papers towards him. Daniel looked at his assistant and saw his eyes turn to mere slits. This was the chance he was looking for. The chance to get Ben out of the office.

"Head home, Ben. Get some sleep."

Daniel looked at the clock. It was almost four.

"Be back at seven, and we'll finish things up. I'm going to head to the gym."

June 22, 2012

The Kinnear Farm
Arvilla, ND

*

It was five in the morning, and Dirt was stirring before the sun had started to poke through the shelterbelt of oaks on the east side of the farm. Faint, gray, morning shadows were just beginning to take form, and Dirt could just barely make out the outlines of the tractors, the red diesel fuel tanks, and the long, white tank filled with anhydrous ammonia across the yard. Still in his plaid boxers, his eyes a bit more than slits, he stretched, and started to turn on the small lamps he'd bought at Wal-Mart and placed throughout the camper. Now with enough light, he walked along his home's single, narrow hallway, scratched his butt, pushed all of the curtains as far as they'd stretch on their tension rods, and opened all six windows until the plastic cranks began to grind in protest. It was his morning ritual; the winter was the same minus the open windows. Dirt loved the clean, dewy morning air that June always brought – along with its slight bouquet of diesel fuel that was always present. The pigs and cattle were starting to stir, as they knew their breakfast was not too far away.

Or maybe that was that woman in the house.

Sometimes the sounds were the same.

Dirt went back to his bed, folded the small frame and mattress into a "V," pushed down, and turned it into his couch. He felt like a magician, but such was the life in a twenty-foot Airstream. Folding his bed into a couch was basically the same contortion he had to do to himself in order to use his bathroom. The camper was not necessarily built to accommodate anyone cursed with above-average height, and since the bathroom was built against one of the sides that naturally curved, its ceiling was much lower than the camper's center, and only, hallway. Peeing was a feat that would impress a yogi. At six foot three, Dirt was sure he'd soon have a bald spot. Not from age, genetics, or male-pattern baldness, but from mere friction. At least his hair was long enough to provide a kick-ass comb-over.

He *could* go out and feed the beasties now, but habits were hard to break for people and animals. If he started feeding them this early, they'd come to expect it, and pretty soon they'd be howling for breakfast at 3:00 am.

And that was not going to happen.

They would just have to wait.

He relished the time between five and six-thirty, and considered it precious. It was a time he used to relax his mind and prepare himself for the day of work ahead of him.

It may not have been their breakfast time, but it was Dirt's, and his stomach was telling him that if he didn't wet things down with a can of Coke anytime soon, there would be hell to pay. Dirt always obeyed his stomach, and because of that, his diet was something that would make a nutritionist cringe. Those that knew what he ate day-after-day, were amazed that he was as skinny as he was. Rarely was there real food, with any nutritional value, in front of him – he should be a fat. Instead, Dirt was a six-foot-three beanpole with long hair, an unmanageable carpet of scruff that splotched from ear-to-ear, around his chin, and down his neck, and eyes that always looked tired regardless of how much sleep he had. He opened his small fridge, grabbed the two cans of Coke his stomach was yearning for, and pulled out a frozen, chocolate-covered granola bar that he kept in the miniscule freezer hidden behind a small plastic door in the top corner of the fridge. Dirt had read the label on the granola bar when he bought them; they had vitamins, protein, and, above all, were all organic and natural. He opened one can of Coke, downed half of it in two, large gulps, ate two-thirds of the granola bar in one bite, and washed it down with the remainder in the can.

His stomach groaned a happy, contented sound, and he felt the carbonation bubbles tickle and swim around inside of his abdomen.

"Happy now," he asked his flat stomach as he patted its burn-scarred flesh with one hand, and itched his armpit with the other. The bubbles in his stomach finally coagulated into one giant ball of air that desperately wanted freedom. Dirt belched, and licked the Coke-flavored spit from his lips.

"One for the record books."

Still thirsty, as he knew his stomach demanded at least two full cans by six, he snapped open the second can and relished another sip. He'd nurse this one for at least an hour. Eager to accomplish something more than gastric placation, Dirt took his old guitar that was leaning against the pony wall separating his bedroom from the kitchen, flopped down on his couch, closed his eyes, and began practicing his chords.

*

Dirt walked over to the feed shed, and flexed his arms as he prepared to wrestle its door open. It was a battle he'd fought every morning for his entire life. Every year since his father died, he made a hollow promise to tear the shed down and replace it with something new and shiny. It was one of the oldest buildings on the farm, and was more reminiscent of a two-hole Korean War outhouse than anything remotely usable. It was older than the main house, and after sixty years, opening its door involved a ritual of steps. He first kicked the bottom of the door in three areas: left, middle, and right. Then he lifted it by the handle to lessen the weight on the main support rail, and finally yanked on it towards its metal stop with all of his strength. Miss one step, pull the door at the wrong angle, and it would be forever stuck and the toolbox would have to come out. Why he just didn't take the damn door off, he never understood.

"Come on you bastard. Move."

The door opened with a large squeal as its old rollers bolted to its top frame protested and were dragged along the rusted track along the top, inside of the shed. After six, almost seven, decades, he didn't think the rollers even rolled any more as every single ball bearing had probably turned to dust years ago. He also wasn't sure if the initial kick was even needed anymore, but it something his father had done the first time he helped with the chores, and it was something he continued to do more out of fear of fucking up the door's mojo than anything based on reality. Five years ago he'd dislocated his shoulder opening the bastard because he forgot to lift it before he pulled. Now he performed each and every step. Once in the morning. Once at night.

As the door opened, its familiar smell wafted into his face. Dirt took a long, deep breath and relished the familiar scent. To him, the smell was as relaxing as his two breakfast Cokes and chocolate-covered granola bar.

There were hundreds of smells on the farm. Probably thousands if he ever took the time to make a full accounting of each and every miscellaneous scent. Some he liked: diesel, old oil, the smell of freshly harvested wheat, newly cut hay, fields of sunflower, and this, the smell of the feed shed.

Others may like to bottle the smell of a new car, or the smell of roasted coffee from a corner shop. But not Dirt. He would love to bottle the smell of his feed shed. It was a combination of corn flakes, Quaker oats, and Centrum vitamins all rolled into one. Of course there were smells that made his stomach turn: the smell of the main farm house, anhydrous ammonia, the pigpen, rotted grain of any variety, and powdered malathion. The last one was particularly nauseating.

The problem with the feed shed was that it had also become the favorite spot for interlopers: mice and rats. The bags of corn and oats were strife with holes where the rodents decided to take it upon themselves to enjoy a free buffet. He tried all sorts of poisons, and every type of trap ever invented, but nothing seemed to work. Either they kept coming back, or there were too many of them to make any impact.

Now they, Dirt and the rodents, had a symbiotic relationship – he let them live until they ended up in the grinder. If they were able to escape, they'd live to see another day. If not, they were ground into mouse pudding along with the corn and fed to the swine. Dirt rather enjoyed watching the little guys scurry around the bits of corn and oats only to be sucked into the whirlpool created by the grinder.

Dirt picked up a bag of corn. He could feel the mice scurrying inside and could hear them scratch against the paper as they tried to find a way out of their ad hoc buffet.

He covered the bag holes with his arms and spare hand. He wanted to pour as many as possible into the hopper.

"Tough luck guys. You picked the wrong bag today."

Dirt ripped the bag all of the way open, then quickly dumped the corn into the grinder's hopper. A dozen mice fell into the bin, and ran in circles in a vain escape attempt. Next, he took bag of oats and did the same. Four mice came with that bag, and joined the others in their fight for survival. Finally, he topped it all off with a small scoop of veterinary-grade vitamin supplements which dusted the scurrying grey and white mice in a fine, yellow powder. He put two orange buckets underneath the chute, and flipped the switch. He wondered if they squeaked before they were crunched into paste.

At first, the meal that came out of the grinder was lumpy with a blood-red tint to it. As more of the corn and oats were ground, and fewer mice remained, the red slowly faded, and the pig's breakfast turned into the expected yellowish-brown combo of ground corn and oats. If some housewife were able to buy Dirt's special concoction at the local Piggly Wiggly, she'd think it was multi-colored corn meal on its way to becoming homemade muffins and cornbread. With a little mystery mouse protein thrown in for good measure.

As breakfast was being ground, Dirt flipped a switch that turned on the water pump that filled the two troughs in the pigpen and also the five large, corrugated steel tubs on the other side of the electric fence for the cattle. The watering system was a feat of plumbing expertise. Once Dirt had sketched the plan, and dug the trenches, everything came together; much to his surprise, it all worked.

"Hmmm. Better than buckets, I suppose," was all that his father could say the first time Dirt flipped the switch to demonstrate the automated water pump. "Better not break is all I can say. There'll be hell to pay."

That was probably the closest thing to a compliment he ever received and, at the time, was completely satisfied.

Dirt didn't have to look over at the pen to know that he had two dozen snouts, forty-eight eyes, and forty-eight floppy ears all pointed in his direction as they waited for him to head their way with the two special orange buckets filled with piggy surprise that coated their snouts with white powder and made them all look like they were snorting cocaine by the time they were done eating. As soon as he picked up the orange buckets, one in each hand, and headed their way, it became a party atmosphere in the pen. The cacophony of snorts coming from twenty-four pigs as they watched him was comical; it was as if they hadn't been fed in days.

"I'm coming guys. I know you're pigs, but hold your horses."

He saw Lulu's tri-colored, spotted nose, and notched ear through the pen's fence boards. Her snout was twitching; sniffing the air for breakfast.

"I see you Lu. How's my fat bottomed girl this morning?"

Dirt stepped on to the first fence rail, balanced himself, and then began to lift the buckets to the other side of the fence when he was told to stop.

"Dirk Kinnear. Put the buckets down, place your hands over your head, and lay face-down on the ground."

Dirt jumped at the unexpected voice. He assumed it was Booger trying to play a joke.

"Shit! Booger, that's not funny. You scared the crap outta me."

Dirt put the buckets down, turned around, and saw five guns all pointed in his direction.

"Place your hands over your head, and lay face-down on the ground."

"What's going on?"

"Do you want to get shot, Mr. Kinnear? I said place your hands over your head, and lay face-down on the ground. I won't say it again."

June 22, 2012

Near the Kinnear Farm
Arvilla, ND

*

Most people couldn't fathom living in North Dakota. Everyone had the same series of excuses: too cold, too flat, too conservative, too uncultured, too...whatever.

All Gordy could say is, "bullshit."

For every negative that someone came up with, he had its corollary.

He'd spent time on both coasts, and always came back. North Dakota, specifically the eastern side, was home. Gordy sat in his SUV, and watched the sun come up. He could smell the freshly cultivated earth that was mildly damp from the morning dew. Now it was black. In a few weeks, there would be hint of green. A few weeks after that, it would be a sea of green waving in the wind. In a few months, most every field he could see at this very moment would be full of life. They would be growing something the folks on the coasts couldn't live without, and didn't have the slightest idea where it came from or how it was made.

This was indeed God's Country.

But even in God's Country, people did bad things. And that's why he was in his SUV at 5:30 in the morning on a dirt road waiting by a mailbox in the middle of Grand Forks County.

"Assemble at the Kinnear mailbox," Gordy had told his team the night before leaving the processing plant.

"Half-a-mile east of the farm. Five-thirty. Look for my SUV."

"Press?" someone had asked on the conference call.

"Hell no. Absolutely not. This is a closed investigation, so keep your traps shut. They're the last thing we need sticking their nose into things."

Gordy knew the area well. It was a bit past five, and he was leaning against the driver's side door of his SUV watching the trees surrounding the Kinnear farm a half-mile down the road take shape as hints of dawn began. Further down the same road, he could see the lights from the Carlson farm flickering in the warming June air. Hidden within the closest group of trees, was the old Kinnear farmhouse where Trude lived and, from what he understood, continued to polish the dozens of crucifixes she'd collected since her first miscarriage. Also nestled within those trees, but opposite from the farmhouse, was a decades-old, silver Airstream that

Tubbs had bought several years before he died. It was a haven for his son. He might not have been the most loving father on the face of the earth, but deep down, he knew the boy didn't deserve the life he was living in the farmhouse with Trude.

No one did.

Even if that "no one" was supplementing his pigs' diet with human flesh.

Gordy's stomach flipped at the thought.

It couldn't be.

There had to be another explanation, but what that could be, he couldn't begin to fathom.

Gordy heard the crunch of tires of a slowing vehicle approaching behind him. In a big city, a slowing vehicle would typically raise his hackles, and he'd slowly move his hand to his gun. In the country, it usually meant someone stopping to say hi and offer hot coffee. Twelve hours later, it would have been someone slowing to say hi and offer a cold beer pulled from a cooler in the passenger seat.

"Mornin, Sheriff."

It was the coroner's van.

"Jake."

The driver turned off the van, and handed him a tall, covered cup with a cardboard sleeve.

"Coffee. Two pink sugars. Just like you ordered."

"Bourbon?"

"All out. They had some of that hazelnut shit, so I asked them to put in two squirts just for you. Thought you'd like it. Since you are so fluffy and all."

"No corpses to fuck this morning, eh?"

"All signed out by you, from what I could tell by the paperwork."

"Thanks, Jake. I owe you one."

"I told everyone the fluffy flavor was for you, by the way."

Gordy took a sip of his coffee and relished it as he felt it warm his entire body. The only flavor he encountered as he took another sip, was coffee.

"Excellent. Love the hazelnut. You prick."

June 22, 2012

The Law Office of Bancroft, Simpson, and Associates
Brentwood, CA

*

Daniel lied.

It definitely wasn't the first time and it surely wouldn't be the last. He was really getting good at it and it was becoming easier and easier.

If being a good liar was a requirement of the job, maybe being partner wasn't what he wanted after all. Daniel could only think of what his dad would say.

He didn't go to the gym as he'd said. Instead, he stayed in his office, drank the coffee Ben had given him, filled it up three more times, and, with the help of a few pieces of paper and a data back-up, secured his move to the open corner office on the next floor up. The one right next to his future father-in-law.

His business cards would change.

Lots would be changing as a matter of fact.

Maybe he'd get that black BMW 750 he'd been eyeing. But he liked the look of the six series so much better. He liked the lines. And the bike. The sweet red and white Ducati Desmosedici that he'd taken for a spin two months ago down the Santa Monica freeway.

Yes. Definitely the bike.

It was a sweet ride.

Daniel Carpenter, Partner.
Bancroft, Simpson, Carpenter, and Associates

It had a nice ring to it.

Partner.

It sent chills down his spine just thinking about it.

Almost gave him a hard-on.

The keys to his new office and title had been handed to him on the proverbial silver platter. In legal jargon, they'd been handed to him within the third folder contained in a light brown case file numbered 43865.

Everything was right there in front of him, and he wasn't sure why, or how, the prosecution hadn't found it first. Daniel was even more amazed that Ben never saw it either as it was right in front of him too.

Maybe he wasn't as good as Daniel was led to believe.

LeCross' primary alibi against the rape charge was that he was at a restaurant across town.

"I wasn't even close to where that crazy bitch lives!"

He'd even provided a receipt. Daniel was smart enough to know that receipts could be made, modified, and, if one had to, found in the garbage cans around restaurants so he didn't consider that a huge piece of evidence.

Good?

More like adequate.

The key, quite literally, was provided from the account management page on the dining site, "InfiniteTables.com" It was a site that Daniel used whenever he wanted to reserve a table at one of his favorite restaurants. For a premium membership, which he paid ten thousand a year for, he had access to tables not available to the general public. When Joe Bagadonuts tried to reserve a table at a five-star restaurant, he'd be sent away and told to come back in a year.

For a premium, certain people got in at a moment's notice.

Daniel was one of those certain people.

Michael LeCross was too.

As part of his alibi, LeCross had shown a copy of the reservation confirmation email from InfiniteTables. Federal Rules of Evidence Rule 1002 required original documents. Daniel was not looking at the original, and the plaintiff's attorney had not noticed anything at this point in time. Or at least he hadn't said anything.

But there was missing information.

Daniel used InfinteTables at least twice a week, and knew exactly what information was provided on the confirmation.

The line, “Reservation made by:” was deleted from the email before it was printed. The information was used to show who made the reservation and when. It wasn’t on the print-out, but Daniel was positive it would still be on the electronic version. People who tried to cover their tracks always miss a footstep along the path and LeCross left a big one. There was the legal concept of “consciousness of guilt.” In other words, LeCross knew he was guilty, and tried to cover his tracks. A golden ticket for a good prosecutor.

June 22, 2012

The Kinnear Farm
Arvilla, ND

*

"What's going on?" asked Dirt as a police officer patted him down.

"He's clean."

"Why are you here?"

Dirt tried to lift his head, but the officer pressed it back down. No one was answering his questions.

"You can get up. Slowly."

Dirt cautiously brought himself to his feet and brushed off the grass and gravel. Dirt saw Gordy standing by the gate of the pigpen.

"Gordy. What's going on?"

Dirt started walking towards the sheriff, when his shirt collar pulled him back.

"Ow! What the fuck's going on? Gordy?"

Finally, Gordy left his perch by the fence, and came in his direction.

"Dirk. Did you bring some pigs by Great Northern a few days ago?"

"Yes. Five of them. Why?"

Dirk saw a group of men dressed in hip boots and white coveralls walk into the pigpen. One of them kicked Lulu as she walked up to great them.

"Hey! Don't kick her!" Dirt turned back to Gordy. "Gordy. What's going on? Why are these people here? He kicked Lulu."

Another sheriff's car drove into the farmyard just as Gordy opened his mouth. The car parked by the feed shed and the deputy got out.

It was Booger.

Dirt noticed that he had his hand on his pistol as he walked towards them.

"How could you do it, Dirt?"

"Shut your mouth, deputy. Why are you late?"

"A call in Larimore I had to handle. Someone spray painted the Ice Cream Shoppe's sign. I left you a message."

"Gordy. Booger. What's going on?"

Gordy looked at his deputy.

"Let's talk by the deputy's car."

"Head over to my car, Dirt. We'll talk there."

*

"Am I under arrest?" Dirt asked as he sat in the back seat of Booger's car.

"Not at this time. They found something in the pigs you brought by Great Northern the other day," said Gordy.

"What?"

"Body parts," said Booger.

"Body parts? What do you mean?"

"Dirt. They found human remains in the stomachs of all five pigs you sold."

Dirt felt his face turn red and his stomach instantly knotted. He felt like puking.

"Human remains?"

"Yes, Dirt. Fucking human remains. Hands. Feet. Fingers. Even a goddamn fucking nose. What were you thinking, Dirt?"

Dirt was speechless and the one-sided conversation was interrupted with a bellow from the sheriff.

"What the fuck! I said no press. Thorson get over there. Now. Who the fuck notified them?"

"You stay right here," said Booger as he shut the back door of his car essentially locking Dirt inside. "You're safer in here."

Three news vans drove into the yard, circled twice, and then parked right next to the car Dirt was sitting in. Within minutes, four cameramen were taking pictures of Dirt, the farm, the sheriff, and the men in hip boots digging around the pigpen. Two more were setting up the video equipment.

"How do I look?" said one man in a polo shirt and khakis to the cameraman.

Dirt saw the cameraman give him a thumbs-up.

"Good. Let's head over to where the forensics guys are."

When the repetition of flashes started to become blinding, Dirt covered his eyes, and looked down at his feet.

*

"Sheriff. Over here."

Gordy didn't put on a white suit, but slipped on hip boots, and tucked his pants inside. He had no desire to go spelunking in pig piss and shit in his black loafers and slacks.

"What do you have, Jake."

"Look. Right by the fence post. But stay right there, we have to get pictures first."

Gordy followed Jake's finger, and saw the small piece of jewelry next to the post. He squinted as he tried to make out more detail.

"Looks like a ring."

"Yup. A small diamond ring. Like an engagement ring. Look a bit to the left of the ring."

Gordy's thought things were bad for Dirk, but when he saw what Jake pointed to, he realized it was worse than he could imagine.

Two fingers.

"Fuck me with a wooden spoon."

"They appear to have been cut at the proximal interphalangeal joints."

"English, please?"

"The joint above the knuckle."

Gordy looked at his hand, flexed his fingers, and then looked over at Dirk sitting in the backseat of Thorson's car.

"Shit. Thorson. Get him out of your car. Now. Have him stand next to it. He can't be in it."

This was turning into a real crime scene, and it was already a circus.

"Jake. Over here. We found something else."

Gordy took his cell phone from his front pocket, called the office, and asked for a team to manage the site.

It was going to be long day.

*

"What did he do? I always knew he was up to no good!"

Everyone working the scene, including the press, stopped to look at whose voice was screaming at them at the top of her lungs.

"I knew he was evil! The minute he was born. I could feel it."

The screaming continued as the woman made her way through the two policemen who tried to hold her back. She was dressed in a flowered nightgown, and was wearing black shoes with one-inch heels. One-half of her wild graying hair was brushed while the other half was matted and greasy. She had red lipstick on her top lip, but evidently missed her bottom.

"True. Shit we don't need this right now," Gordy said to himself as he left the pigpen and headed in her direction.

"Get your blaspheming hands off of me!"

Trude pushed her way through the cameras and guns.

"Where is he? Where's Satan's son? I want to see it in his eyes before you take him away to rot in hell. I want to see his black soul one last time."

"Are we getting this?" asked one of the reporters to the cameraman.

"Oh yea. It's golden."

"Trude. Let's head back into the house. Everything is fine," said Gordy as he put his hand on her shoulder.

"Don't touch me!" she screamed as she pushed him away.

Gordy saw Booker walk in his direction with his side arm at the ready.

"Deputy. Holster that weapon."

"But Sheriff."

"I said holster it. Now. Manage this scene before it goes to hell any more than it already has."

Gordy turned back to Trude.

This time he didn't touch her, but instead used his girth to prevent her from moving any closer.

"What did he do Sheriff? I see him out here in the middle of the night. I see him all of the time. I've wondered what he was doing. Those pigs don't need to be fed at three in the morning, but he's always in there. Feeding them. Up to no good, I tell you. He's evil. Knew it from the start."

"Trude. We need you to go back in the house."

"Who's we? This is my farm."

"I need you to go in the house, Trude. Please."

"He's evil, Sheriff. You lock him up for good. Promise me that. Promise me you'll lock him up."

Gordy heard one of the cameramen count off to one of the reporters.

"And we're live in three-two-one..."

*

"What's that?" asked Gordy as he pointed to one of the out buildings.

"The feed shed," said Booger.

Gordy walked over to the shed and tried to open the door.

It wouldn't budge.

"Hang on. That's tricky, Sheriff."

Booger walked over to the feed shed where Gordy was standing, kicked the bottom of the door in the same three areas that Dirt kicked an hour earlier. Lifted it by the handle, and yanked on it towards its metal stop. The door slid open, but the metal-on-metal screech caused Gordy to cringe as his metal fillings sent spikes of pain through his jaw.

"He grinds his own feed. Pours bags of corn and oats in here, puts in a scoop of vitamins, puts a bucket there, and flips a switch. It mixes everything together and turns out like chunky cornmeal. The pigs love it."

Gordy looked in the feed basin, and then back at Booger.

"Jake! Get over here."

"What do you have, Sheriff," said Jake as he rushed over from labeling the bags of evidence he'd found in the pen.

"Looks like blood to me. In the feed."

"Look at the stack of orange buckets, Sheriff. I doubt if that's red paint."

*

Dirt watched the sheriff walk in his direction, and saw his hand move to unclasp the handcuffs he kept in a leather case looped to his belt.

The sheriff wasn't smiling.

Neither was Dirt.

"Dirk. Could you turn around, put your hands on the hood of the car?"

"Sheriff. Please. What's going on?"

"Just do it, son."

Dirt obeyed the sheriff. He turned around, placed his hands on the hood of Booger's car, and put his head down. Gordy took one wrist, cuffed it, then pulled his other wrist around his back, and cuffed that. He pulled Dirt's shoulders back, and stood him straight.

"Dirk Kinnear, I'm placing you under arrest. You have the right to remain silent. Anything you say or do can and will be used against you in a court of law. You have the right to an attorney. If you cannot afford an attorney, one will be appointed to you. Do you understand these rights as they have been read to you?"

"Sheriff. I haven't done anything."

"Do you understand these rights as they have been read do you?"

Dirt nodded.

"Son, I need a verbal response."

"Yes. I understand."

"Let's walk over to my SUV."

Dirt didn't need to be dragged. He walked towards Gordy's SUV with the sheriff's hand still on his shoulder. He felt a gentle squeeze.

"Who will feed the pigs? The cows? There's work to be done."

The sheriff didn't respond.

Dirt looked over to his friend's car, and saw Booger standing next to the hood where he'd just been cuffed. He put a handful of sunflower seeds in his mouth.

Dirt's window was up, but he could read his friend's lips.

"What the fuck?"

Tears began to flow down Dirt's cheek. He was scared and started to shiver. Another picture was snapped, and the flash blinded him.

Book 3: Fall

Harvest

JOHN P. GOETZ

2012

"Anger and despair are the only harvest after having sewn tainted seed."

The Book of Lost and Forgotten Dreams

June 25, 2012

The Law Office of Bancroft, Simpson and Associates
Santa Monica, CA

*

Daniel sat in his office and watched the traffic crawling by below him on Wilshire. He'd sat behind his desk at five that morning and at that time, even in California, traffic was minimal.

It was now approaching nine; he'd already put in four hours.

For most, the four hours would represent half of a workday. For him, the four hours represented only twenty-five percent.

If that.

Yesterday was sixteen hours, and Saturday was another ten. The LeCross case was going to get him into that partner office.

Or break him if the hours kept going as heavy and steady as they had been.

His stomach growled, and forced him to remember that he hadn't eaten since Saturday at noon. He pressed the button on his phone.

"Yes, Mr. Carpenter."

"Hannah, would you bring me a couple bottles of water? Then would you head across the street, get me two of those egg sandwiches on sourdough, and some hash browns?"

"Murray's?"

"Yeah. That's it."

"Sure thing. Be right back. Let me get someone to cover your phone first."

Dan was too hungry to wait.

"No. Just go. I'll watch the phones. And get one of those cheese danishes too. And two large orange juices. And something for yourself if you want."

His stomach growled again.

"Down boy. Down," he said as he patted his abdomen.

"Do you want your water before I leave?"

"Oh. Yes. Forgot. Definitely get that in here before you leave. I don't think I've had anything to drink in two days."

"Job's not worth dying for, Daniel."

"Yeah. Yeah. Yeah. Murray's, please," said Dan as he hung up.

*

It didn't take more than two minutes after Hannah left, for the phone to begin ringing.

Daniel knew the number of the first call. It was a 310 area code, and the only number it could be was the realtor's.

Lumin Hawthorne.

He still had to sign the paperwork and provide a check for the earnest money to finalize the purchase of the house he and Ashley agreed upon. As of last week, it was the one on Laguna Beach. He knew she was frothing at the mouth for her commission that would be close to three hundred grand.

The ghost-of-second-thoughts kept haunting him whenever he looked at the final numbers. $8.5 million was a lot of money, and it was a lot of house for just two people. Twenty-five hundred square feet for each of them. Plus almost seven bathrooms to choose from.

Daniel sent the call to voicemail.

She'd have to wait.

Even though Ashley had, he still hadn't decided.

He watched Hannah cross the street, and head to Murray's 1/2 a block down, when the second call came.

"I should have waited for backup," he said as he looked at the caller-id.

He recognized the area code immediately.

701.

North Dakota.

Very simple as the entire state was covered by one. At last count, California had close to forty.

The number he also knew.

Bekks.

Daniel considered pressing the button again to send her directly to voicemail, but his stomach told him to answer. That or it was protesting its lack of food. He couldn't tell.

He pressed the button for the speakerphone.

"Hey Bekks."

"Danny. Thank God you answered. Have you heard?"

"About the farm? You told me that last time we talked. You called me an asshole and hung up."

"No. About Dirt."

"No. What's up?"

"He's been accused of murder. His in the county jail now. It's a mess. A media circus."

"What the fuck?"

"Exactly. He needs you Dan. You're his best friend. He needs you now more than ever."

"Let me check things out, and I'll get back to you. Couple of hours. This number?"

"Yes. It's not good, Dan. It sounds really bad."

Daniel hung up the phone. He could tell in Bekks' voice that she'd been crying.

*

Dan didn't want to be interrupted by the phone, so he entered the command to send everything to voicemail. At least he hoped he did.

He turned on his laptop, brought up *Google*, typed "Dirk Kinnear," and pressed Enter. By the time he looked from his keyboard to the screen, twenty-five results appeared. At the bottom, was a message indicating that he was looking at the first twenty-five entries of 500.

"Shit," he said as he clicked on the first entry.

His screen filled with an image of his friend sitting in the backseat of a sheriff's car. Below that, Dan read the story.

"Fuck me."

He clicked on the video link from the local NBC station entitled, "Gertrude Kinnear Extolls Her Son's Guilt" and watched Trude's unedited tirade about how evil her son was. It already had more than four hundred thousand views.

The video had gone viral in a matter of hours.

"He's fucked."

"Who is?"

Daniel looked up from his laptop to see Hannah coming in with three bags of food.

"I need you to make some travel arrangements. Fast."

"But aren't you hungry?"

"Famished. But it'll have to wait. Put that in the kitchen for whomever wants it."

"Where do you need to go?"

"I need to get to Grand Forks as soon as possible."

"Where's that?"

"North Dakota."

"Ok. I'll get your passport out of the safe."

"I don't need a passport."

"But you do for international travel, Daniel. Even you."

"Grand Forks, North Dakota. The United States. Airport code is GFK."

"Oh. Will you need a car?"

"Yes. A BMW. Or something close."

"GFK, you said?"

"Yes. Think of "go fuck yourself." But with a "k" at the end instead of a "y."

Daniel watched Hannah as she looked at the bags of food then back at him.

"Now?"

Maybe Bekks was right about her after all, he thought.

A poodle with training.

"Yes, Hannah. Now."

*

Within fifteen minutes, Hannah came back into his office with her notepad.

Daniel knew this wasn't a good sign.

"The only flight to Grand Forks is tomorrow. The only car I could get is a 2005 Chevy Lumina."

"Fuck me raw. I don't want a Chevy POS."

"Sorry?"

"A Chevy POS. Piece of Shit."

"You don't have to be rude, Daniel. I'm just telling you what they have."

"I know. I know. It's become a day from hell, that's all. See what's available to Minneapolis. That's in Minnesota. Also in the United States. Airport code is MSP. I can drive to Forks."

*

Daniel was on the way to the airport in the backseat of a yellow cab driven by a man whose name he couldn't pronounce without embarrassing himself in a car that needed new shocks.

He was quickly becoming carsick.

The first call he made was to Ashley telling her that he had a family emergency.

"I thought you didn't like those people anymore?"

"Ash. It's family. I'll talk to you later."

"Well, don't forget, we have dinner with daddy tomorrow night. Will you be back?"

"Ummm," Daniel rolled his eyes. "Cancel the dinner. We'll reschedule when I get back."

"I suppose you'll be seeing your old girlfriend? The one who gave you that ridiculous department store necklace you always wear?"

"I have no idea who I'll be seeing, Ash. There's trouble at home, and they need my help."

"But Daniel. This is your future."

"Ash, I gotta go. I'm at the departure gate now. Gotta run."

Daniel closed his eyes, and pressed the red End Call button.

He'd lied.

It was getting too easy.

He reached to his neck, and pulled at the gold necklace that he was wearing. He pulled it until the small gold ring fell into his palm. He twirled it in his fingers, then re-read the inscription for what he thought was the billionth time since leaving home in 1997.

Lina and Danny - 1997

Danny put it back under his shirt, and let it fall down his chest. It felt warm. There was more than a dinner with the firm's partner that he was going to cancel. His next call wasn't so difficult, and she picked up after the first ring.

"Bekks, I'm on a flight to Minneapolis. Gets in at six tonight. I'll drive to Forks. Should be there around eleven if everything is on time."

"Press is everywhere. Trude is not helping at all, Dan. They're even at the bar interviewing anyone who will talk. Vince Grier, remember him? He was on the evening news. So was Julie."

"I'm on my way, Bekks. Can you somehow let Dirt know I'm on my way? I gotta go."

Before he pressed End, he remembered something.

"Bekks? You still there?"

"Yes."

"Can I stay at your place tonight?"

There was silence on the phone.

"Why not with Mom and Dad."

"Bekks. Please. I can't deal with that right now."

"Fine. You can stay with us for a few nights. But you *will* see them, and you better not be leaving on the next flight out tomorrow."

"I'm not. It's an open ended flight."

June 26, 2012

Butch's Bar
Arvilla, ND

*

The minute he crossed the border into North Dakota, he felt a change wash over him.

He was no longer Daniel.

He was Danny.

And it actually felt good.

The prodigal son had returned.

Danny represented the boy who drove tractors, wore a baseball cap with a tractor logo on it, and chewed on blades of grass. The one who was destined to take over the family farm. The one who was swept off of his feet by his high school sweetheart. And still longed to hold her hand.

The good son.

Daniel was what he wanted to become. The lawyer on the way to becoming partner. The man who was a signature away from a seven-million-dollar beachfront home. The one who signed an employment agreement with a clause that required him to use a different last name because the one he was born with implied an ethnicity of lesser intelligence. An agreement he eagerly signed for an extra bump in salary and a written plan for a bigger office and an etched name on a glass door.

The bad son.

Danny, formerly Daniel, pulled off of Highway 2, and turned onto the dirt road that was Arvilla's main, block-long, single-sided thoroughfare. The BMW's tires crunched on the gravel and, despite his slow speed, created a comet tail of dust that whipped around the car, crawled its way through the vents, clouded the onboard camera system, and even found its way into his mouth.

Gravel roads were not commonplace in the greater Los Angeles area. He hadn't driven on a dirt road in a decade, and even after all of the time, he was amazed.

The dust still tasted the same.

At the corner, next to the highway, was the tiny post office dedicated to the three hundred and thirteen residents of ZIP code 58214. The flag was still up and flapping in the breeze, so whoever was working was still inside. Next to the post office was a small building belonging to the town's one-and-only accountant, and next to it was the Arvilla Community Club – a long, non-descript, rectangular brown box with big white letters stapled onto sheets of plywood and hung on the building's face. It was built during the summer of 1977. A big event for the town as everyone joined in to help.

It was a twentieth-century version of a barn raising.

He remembered it still looking relatively crisp the last time he saw it. It didn't look so hot right now. Its dented front door had definitely seen better days. The "A" of "Arvilla" and the "C" of "Community" were gone. He could see the shadows of the old, missing letters against the brown paint. It was now the "rvilla ommunity Club."

Dan's destination was on the corner of the small block.

Butch's Bar.

Along with a grain elevator, every town in North Dakota had at least one bar. Sometimes two. Sometimes three. Sometimes more.

Grand Forks had dozens.

Larimore had three.

Emerado had two.

Arvilla had just one.

Butch's.

Butch's Bar was Arvilla's Facebook, Twitter, Instagram, Pintrest, and LinkedIn all bundled in one site. To be connected, you just sat at a stool and within minutes you could find out what was happening around town and to whom. If you wanted to know the price of a bushel of wheat, all you had to do was read the sign next to the painting of the woman with the big tits.

The Schlitz beer sign, hanging twenty feet high on a tilted telephone pole, had been there as long as Danny could remember and was still missing an apostrophe. It was an ungrammatical sign that read: Butchs Bar.

Instead of Butch's Bar.

The Pabst Blue Ribbon sign that hung perpendicular to its ungrammatical neighbor, was splintered and had faded to the point of being barely readable. Evidently, if the lore was true, its readable life was ended by the blast of a wayward 12-guage blast. As legend had it, some guy who had a few too many barley pops had grandiose plans to light a brick of Black Cat firecrackers with a shotgun on a certain wild-and-crazy Fourth of July celebration. He threw the brick of firecrackers in the air, took aim, and shot. It may have worked, but the sign got in his way. Like the Community Club, the Pabst sign was missing letters. Instead of drinking a refreshing Pabst Blue Ribbon Beer, you were asked to enjoy a, "Pa ue on eer."

Danny pulled up to the bar's split rail fence, and put the car in park. The fence too had seen its better days as more than one drunk driving a Dodge Ram had taken his pickup's name too seriously.

Dan's silver BMW 535 seemed out of place next to the three other vehicles parked along the fence in front of the bar. A blue Ford F150. A black Chevy Silverado. And a red Buick LeSabre. All three were rusted and dusted. Each came off of the assembly line in the 80's. Each of the truck beds had a tool chest, and auxiliary diesel tank at the end closest to the cab. The F150 was additionally loaded with two pallets stacked and wrapped with fifty-pound bags of pig feed. The Ram was loaded with three, fifty-gallon barrels of 15W40 oil. The LeSabre, in all of its glory, was missing three hubcaps, had a spider-webbed front windshield, and red duct tape for its left, rear tail light. If Dan could see through its rust and into its interior, he was sure its back seat would be loaded with empty soldiers and the front ash tray would be packed and spilling over with bent cigarette butts.

Some things never change.

Even after a decade.

Danny turned the car off.

And sat.

And watched.

He was paralyzed for some reason.

He hadn't been here in almost a decade.

He felt lost.

Afraid.

The scenery hadn't changed much – the town just looked a lot smaller for some reason.

Worn.

He doubted if they'd even know who he was, but he wanted to talk to a few people before heading back into Grand Forks and talking to Dirt. He looked at himself in the rear view mirror and pushed his hair out of his eyes.

"You big pussy," he said to his reflection.

*

Dan walked into the bar. The smell of beer and stale cigarette smoke brought him immediately to his childhood when he'd come in with his father and get a can of pop and a bag of Old Dutch BBQ potato chips. The paneling was the same, but the ceiling tiles were tinged a darker shade of brown from an additional decade and a half of cigarette smoke.

"So, Number 6 returns," said an old man with his back to the door. "We watched you pull up in that fancy car of yours. Nothing like that around here so it had to be out of town. You sat in there a long time. Scared to come in or were you playing with your pecker?"

Dan immediately recognized the man and the voice.

"What?"

"You sat in your fancy car a long time."

"I had a call."

"Didn't see any phone."

"Hands-free."

Dan sat down on a stool next to he old man, and put his phone and keys on the bar.

The old man swiveled the stool around and rested his elbows on the bar.

"BMW. Is that British or something?"

"German."

"One of those kraut cars. I suppose it smells like cabbage when you turn on the heat?"

Dan snorted and shook his head.

"No. But that was funny. It doesn't smell like cabbage. Howya doin', Butch."

"Sasquatch. I'm hangin' in there."

"Good to hear. I see you're still missing the apostrophe out there."

"Go to hell, kid."

With his large, shaky hands, the old man pushed his pop bottle glasses closer to his eyes. From his side of the lenses, Dan thought Butch's eyes were as big as dinner plates.

"Can I get you something?" asked the woman behind the bar.

"Sure. A cosmo."

"Cosmo? Just a sec."

The bartender turned around to the cash register, pulled out a small red book of cocktail recipes, flipped a few pages, and looked back at Dan.

"We don't have any martini glasses."

"A Goosedriver then."

"Goosedriver?"

"Grey Goose and orange juice."

"Grey Goose?"

"Vodka?"

"We don't have that kind."

"What kind of vodka do you have?"

"We don't have any of those faggoty-ass city-boy drinks, Sasquatch," interrupted Butch before the bartender could answer.

The two men at the other end of the bar, probably the owners of the pickups, snickered at Butch's comment as they each took a long swig from their cans of Pabst Blue Ribbon.

"Hey everyone! Danny Carlson's back. You know, Skip and Sis' boy? Went off to California to be a big-city lawyer."

Dan's face turned red and he could feel the warmth crawl up his neck.

"Sabby, just get Big City Boy here a fuckin' beer. Put it in a glass if he wants," grunted Butch. "On the house."

"Do you want another, Butchy?"

"If I'm going to have to put up with Sasquatch here, yes. Fill 'er up while you're at it and make it a double. I think I'll need it," he said as he pushed his empty glass towards the end of the bar.

Butch turned his attention back to Dan, and eyed him from head to toe.

"Haven't changed much. Still ugly as sin."

"You haven't changed a bit either," Dan grinned and reached over to shake his old friend's hand. "It's good to see you."

"Screw the hand shake shit, Sasquatch. Get over here and give an old man a hug."

*

"So what can you tell me about Dirt?"

Butch pushed his glasses up with his pinky, and shook his head.

"Shit. It looks bad. It really does. I can't believe he'd do something like that."

"I've heard a bit from Bekks, but what are you hearing?"

Danny could tell that Butch was having trouble saying the words. Butch took a deep breath, exhaled a stream of smoke from his nose, and took a long slug of his rum and coke. He pushed the empty glass towards Sabby.

"Get me another," he said then turned to face Danny. "He killed some college girl and fed her to his pigs. Now they are saying there are multiple women. He'd meet them online, kill them, then, well..."

"Anything else?"

"What do you mean, 'anything else'? Isn't that enough?"

"I'm filing a *pro hac vice* tomorrow. So I want to get as much information as possible before I see Dirt."

"A pro hac what?"

"A *pro hac vice*. I'm not licensed to practice law here in North Dakota. A *pro hac vice* will allow me to be the attorney of record in this jurisdiction if I can get his public defender to agree. I'll need a judge to approve it, but I'm going to do what I need to help him," Danny took a drink and looked back at Butch. "I just hope I can."

"I think he'll need it. He won't be able to afford it, though."

"I'm not doing it for the money. He's my friend."

"Where are you staying?"

"With Bekks."

"Not with your folks?"

Danny shook his head.

"I don't think dad likes me too well. I don't want to deal with that drama right now."

"He loves you Danny. You're stupid if you think otherwise. He's always talking about his son the big time California lawyer."

Danny finished his beer, and hopped off his stool.

"I don't think he knows the whole story."

"What? About your last name?"

Danny nodded.

"He's not dumb. He knows. But don't let that stop you from seeing your folks."

"I gotta get going, Butch. I'm beat. Don't do anything you'd regret, Butch."

"Why would I stop now?" Butch said as he saluted Dan with his cigarette.

"Perfection is hard to beat, right?"

"Fuckin' right, kid. Fuckin' right."

Dan pulled the door open, but stopped when Butch called him back.

"She works tonight, by the way. Closing shift."

"Who?"

"You're still a dumb ass, Sasquatch. Even after all that school, you're still a dumb ass. Lina. That's who. The one you really came by to see."

"I came by to say hi. That's all."

"Bullshit. And yes, she's still single. Stupid girl still pines after you even after all of these years. Still wears that crazy-ass hat too."

Danny left the bar with a smile.

*

Danny sat at a stool and watched Lina tend bar. She was still just as beautiful. She still wore the brown leather hat he'd given her in high school.

"Still have the hat."

Lina looked up.

Danny noticed a slight jolt in her eyes, but evidently that was the only reaction she was going to allow herself.

Old wounds.

"Hi Daniel. Can I get you something?"

"Hi Lina. How are you?"

"Just fine, Daniel. Can I get you something? Kinda busy."

Daniel looked around the bar. Besides himself, there were four other people sitting on stools. This might not be as easy as he hoped it would be.

"Blue's good. It's Danny."

Lina reached into the cooler and pulled out a cold, red, white, and blue can of Pabst Blue Ribbon.

"Want a glass?"

"Sure."

"two and a quarter."

Daniel put a five on the bar. It was still less than what it would have cost in L.A., but it wouldn't have been served in a can. And it wouldn't have been a Pabst.

June 27, 2012

Grand Forks, ND

*

It didn't matter where the jail was. California or North Dakota. They were all the same.

Dirty.

Dank.

Depressing.

And they all smelled like someone took a bucket full of piss and shit and used it as paint. Then to make sure the job was done well, the maintenance department gave it a second coat using a bucket of vomit.

Danny sat in the interview room across from his old friend. He was dressed in a navy blue suit, white shirt, striped tie, and black shoes. He'd showered before he came, shaved, and made sure every hair was in place. He even used a spit of hairspray to make sure there wasn't a single hair out of place.

He was a lawyer now and in front of him was a notepad and his Monteblanc Meisterstück Classique.

Danny never met a client without bringing his pen – although its significance was probably lost here.

Dirt, on the other hand, looked horrible.

And smelled just as bad.

He was in an orange jumpsuit with GFCDC painted on the front and back. His long hair, which hung down to his jawline, hadn't been washed in days and draped down to his shoulders in clumps. Dirt's acne had come back, and his face was pockmarked with dozens of angry red blotches topped with white peaks. Dirt's hands where in cuffs, and secured to the table so when a mass of matted hair would fall in his face, he had to swish his head to make it fall back in line.

"How ya doing?"

Dirt laughed.

"The food is good."

"Always the optimist."

"Have you talked to a lawyer yet?"

Dirt nodded and shrugged.

"Some woman came by. Said she was assigned to my case and that she'd be getting back to me soon."

"When was that?"

"The afternoon of my arrest. The twenty-first."

"That was six days ago. No one has talked to you since?"

"She said they were very busy."

"Did she say anything about bail?"

"No. But doubted the judge would approve anything based on the severity of the crime. I think the prosecutor has claimed there'd be a flight risk too."

"Fucking assholes. Ok. Here's what I'm going to do, but I need you to approve it. Otherwise, I can't help. I want to be your lawyer."

Dirt laughed.

"I'm not one of your big time California clients who make a million dollars an episode for playing a pig farmer on some sitcom, Danny. I'm Dirt, remember?"

"Pro bono, Dirt. This is Danny your old friend. Not Daniel."

"You'd do that?"

"Of course. There's some paperwork I have to work on in order to be your attorney, but I'm moving forward with that. I have an appointment with the court-appointed lawyer in an hour. The woman you talked to."

"When can I get home? There's so much work to do."

"I don't know, Dirt. Honest. There's a lot going on right now."

"But the pigs. The cows. They have to be fed."

"Don't worry about them. I'll make sure that gets taken care of," said Danny. "Now I'm going to ask you a question, Dirt. I don't care what the answer is, but I need..."

Dirt didn't give Danny time to answer the question.

"I didn't do it, Danny. Honest. I didn't do what they are saying. I'd never do something like that."

Danny had known Dirt all of his life. He'd seen him take a lot of shit at home and school.

This was the first time he'd ever seen his friend cry.

"Keep your chin up, Dirt. I know it's hard, but stay strong. I'm going to make sure you get some shower time. Soap and shampoo. I'll get you some food too. McDonald's ok?"

"Fries. Oh. I'd love some fries. And a Coke."

"I'll do what I can," said Danny as he pushed back his chair.

Within seconds, the guard walked over, and stood next to Dirt.

"Oh. A chocolate covered granola bar. Can you get a couple of those?"

As Danny left the room, he gave Dirt a thumbs-up.

"I'll be back. Chin up."

*

Gordy sat alone in his office. His chair was pushed back from his desk, and his size elevens were resting on his desk. He'd just farted, and was hoping that no one would walk in before the aroma had time to dissipate. He could barely stand it himself, but he'd had Mexican last night, and that always sent his guts into an uproar.

His luck didn't hold out.

Deputy Anderson walked into his office, made it past the row of file cabinets, and then stopped as if he walked into a brick wall. Gordy's stomach rumbled as he pulled his feet off of his desk.

"I think something crawled behind the file cabinet and died."

"Musta been something big. I thought I heard something stirring back there."

"What'cha need, deputy?"

"The ADA's here. To talk about the Kinnear case."

"Which one is it?"

"Pete Smith."

Gordy rolled his eyes. He couldn't stand Pete Smith.

"Give it five more minutes, and send him in. Give me time to open the windows, and air this place out. Call maintenance and have them get that dead muskrat out of here."

The deputy started to walk away when Gordy called out again.

"Bring in that can of Glade air freshener from the john, I'm gonna need it."

*

The office door was wide open, and the room looked void of any human life. The office wasn't empty by any means, as there were manila folders stacked two-feet high on top of banker's boxes in every feasible piece of real estate. The smell that permeated the office reminded him of the legal library at UCLA where he spent many nights cloistered within the stacks. He loved that smell.

It brought back the memories of the late nights, and agonizingly hard work in law school.

The only indication that he was standing at the door to the correct office was the plaque on the desk that identified the occupant: Debra Atkinson. It wasn't until he saw a fluff of blonde hair move from under a stack of folders, that he realized there was life within the piles of paper.

"Ms. Atkinson?"

The woman behind the desk looked up without lifting her head; only her eyes moved. Even though she was no longer looking down at the paper, she continued to write.

"And you are?"

"Daniel Carpenter," he stuttered. "Daniel Carlson, sorry. I spoke with you earlier this morning about the Kinnear case."

Daniel saw her eyes scan him from his shoes, all of the way to the top of his head, then back to his eyes.

"You do look like someone from California, don't you? All tan and everything. Expensive jeans. French cuffs. I've heard about you west coast types."

"Grew up here though."

"Doesn't matter. Once you leave, some of it fades away, and never comes back."

"It?"

"Can't describe it. Just something we have. A shine."

"Never thought I shined."

"That was your problem."

The woman behind the desk stood up, took a pile of folders off of the only chair in her office, and pointed.

"Sit."

At six feet, Daniel had to adjust the look in his face when she came around her desk. He couldn't help but stare. She would need a stepladder to look him in his face.

Debra stood in front of her desk. Both of her hands were behind her on the desk and supported her as she leaned back.

"Yes. I know. I know I'm not tall, but I can still rip your balls out through your eye sockets, kid."

"But..."

"Are you going to sit down, or did I move those folders for nothing?"

"I want to talk to you..."

"About the Kinnear case, I know. Do you have the paperwork filled out? The *pro hac vice?"*

Daniel reached into his briefcase, pulled out the papers, and put them on her desk.

"Here you go. Everything completed as required. Notarized. Initialed. Dated. Everything."

"You're very precise, Daniel. I bet your law professors taught you that. Nice briefcase, too. You probably have a Montblanc in there somewhere I'm sure. You Californians love your pretense. And a Brooks Brothers suit. I bet that set you back a couple of grand, right? See this," she said as she opened her arms to put her light blue pantsuit on display. "Vintage department store. Seventy-five bucks. On sale. Probably a Benz or a BMW in the parking lot too, right? Drove from the cities because you could only rent a Chevy or a Buick here in Forks? Oh. And your assistant made your travel arrangements didn't she. Didn't know where North Dakota was, either. Probably thought you needed a passport. Did she ask you if they took American money here? They always think that."

"Who."

"Californians. They don't know North Dakota is in the United States. Most think it's south of Belarus or someplace like that."

Daniel tried to put the conversation back on track. He didn't really like where the conversation was headed. In fact, he didn't know where it was going.

"Will a judge approve those?"

"Am I right?"

"About..."

"The car."

"A BMW. Yes."

"Passport?"

Daniel smiled as he remembered the conversation with Hannah.

"Yes, she did. Didn't ask about the money though."

Debra laughed and shook her head.

"The pen?"

Daniel pulled out his Montblanc, and twirled it between his fingers.

"I knew it! Nice one. Meisterstück Classique. How much did that put you back?"

"A grand."

"Can't justify that on a public defender's salary, I'm afraid. Are you going to sit or what? You're making me nervous."

Daniel sat down.

He felt properly intimidated.

And amazed.

Definitely intrigued.

He was beginning to really like this woman. She'd definitely be a force in the courtroom, and would probably scare a jury into agreeing with her just with her presence.

"Ok. Now where was that folder?" she said as thumbed through a stack on her desk. "Here it is. Right where I left it."

"Dirt said you haven't been back since he was arrested."

"Who? Did you just say Dirt?"

"Dirk. Dirt is his nickname. Sorry."

"That's cute. I hope the press doesn't get ahold of that. The bastards will have a field day. I haven't had time to get back to him. So yes, he's correct. I haven't been back to talk to him in a while."

"Six days."

"Has it been that long already? Shit. Time flies," she shrugged and waved her hands around the mountains of folders. "Not much I can do about that I'm afraid. Not with this case load."

"Can we talk about the case? They haven't let him shower. I don't know if he's eating either."

"What else are we doing? Aren't we talking about the case? I bet he stinks. Six days without a shower. Jeez. How would you know if he's eating? He has a natural emaciated look, doesn't he?"

"Will the judge sign the request?"

"Hell yes. If it means getting a case off of my desk? In a heartbeat. He won't want to deal with me if he doesn't."

"How many public defenders are there?"

"Including me?"

"Including you."

Debra looked up at the ceiling. Her mouth moved as she seemed to be counting. She wiggled the fingers on both hands.

"That would be one."

"One? You have to be kidding!"

"You're looking at her. It's not Los Angeles, kid. And that's why the judge will sign your little form here. What are you going to charge?"

"Charge who?"

"Are you sure you went to law school? Us. The county. And Mr. Kinnear. We don't have a huge budget."

"Nothing. Why?"

"Even better. I could probably forge the judge's signature, and he wouldn't mind since it won't cost us anything. But I think we should do things right. I'll get this signed. You can be the attorney of record for the case. Just pay the fee, and keep me in the loop as required. Deal?"

"So I'm not charging you, but you're going to charge me?"

"Life, kid. Get used to it."

"What can you tell me? What do they have?"

"Capital murder. Four counts from the last I heard. Could go up. North Dakota doesn't have the death penalty though, so the capital part of capital murder is moot. He'll never get out though."

"Bail?"

"Denied. Prosecution got the judge to believe there'd be flight risk. I didn't fight it, as I was sure he wouldn't have the money to post anything anyhow. I'm sure it would be in the seven figures."

"What evidence do they have?"

"Here's everything I have," she pushed six folders to him. "It's not pretty. Especially the pictures from Great Northern. I've never seen anything like it to tell you the truth. If he did do this, he needs to be put away for a long time. A very long time."

"What about forensics? Anything from them?"

"Not yet. Should be getting those reports any time now. They sent everything to Fargo. Didn't have the technology here in Forks. I'll make sure they notify you. Do you have a card?"

Daniel put the folders in his briefcase, and pulled out one of his cards.

"Here you go. My cell phone is there.

"Nice card," Debra put it to her ear. "I can hear the ocean."

"Debra Atkinson. Lone public defender. What's your take?"

"Take on what? On you?"

"On the case."

"Guilty as sin."

Daniel got up from his chair and started to twirl his pen between his fingers.

"How long have you been a PD?"

"Counting today?"

"Counting today," he nodded.

Debra looked back at the ceiling again, flipped through her desk calendar, and then counted her fingers.

"Five days including today. Last week I was selling beauty products."

"Bullshit."

"Whoa. California kid has a mouth."

"I know you've been doing this for twenty-five years."

"You've done your homework."

Daniel started to walk out of the office, but turned around.

"Here. You deserve this more than I do."

Debra looked astonished as she took the thousand-dollar pen that Daniel handed her.

"Why are you giving me your pen? Won't that hurt your image or something?"

"Probably. But after talking with you, I've realized something."

"And what is that, Daniel Carlson from California?"

"Danny Carlson doesn't need that any more," Danny smiled at her. "Thanks for your time, Debra."

"Call me Deb."

"Call me Danny."

Danny smiled and left the office. Deb taught him a lot in a very short amount of time.

*

Gordy put on the best fake smile he could muster, and shook the ADA's hand. The deputy was right, it was Pete Smith. He was hoping the deputy was either blind or dead wrong.

Smith was an ambitious up and comer who had the unpleasant habit of being forever pessimistic, and being annoyingly over-precise. To Smith, the sky wasn't blue, but light cyan. Gordy wished he would have told the deputy to send him right in, instead of letting his office clear of the green fog.

"Lose some weight Sheriff?"

"Not an ounce, Pete. Gained five as a matter of fact."

Gordy really wanted to wrap his arm around his shoulder, pull him close, and say, "Fuck you, Pete. I can always lose weight, but you? You'll always be fuckin' ugly."

He refrained and decided to continue down the professional route.

Pete was a fucking prick.

Pete was one of the guys who ran against Gordy in the last election and lost.

Pete held grudges.

Gordy decided to pick the scab on the little prick's wound.

"So are you going to run again? We had fun, didn't we?"

"I think I'm going to pass this year. I heard Simmons might run."

"Good. We'll have just as much fun. You can give him some pointers," Gordy sat down behind his desk, and took a sip of his coffee. He didn't offer any to Pete. "So what can you tell me about the Kinnear case? That's why you came by, right?"

"Mind if I sit?"

"Oh. Yes. I mean no. I don't mind. Please do," said Gordy as he pointed to the chair. "Just put those folders on the floor."

"You mean the envelopes?"

Gordy smiled when Smith took the bait.

"Oh yes. I said folders, didn't I? My bad. Put the envelopes on the floor. Looks like a beautiful day out there today."

"Little muggy."

Gordy loved playing the game.

"Kinnear case. What's up?"

Smith finally sat down, and opened the case folder he'd brought.

"Forensics came in from Fargo last night. The remains were definitely human."

"Female?"

"Yes. Between eighteen and thirty years old. Caucasian."

"Just one?"

"Up to five at this point in time."

Gordy shook his head and looked down at his shoes.

His left lace was untied.

"You know the kid, right?"

Gordy nodded.

"Know most of the families out there."

"Out there?"

"By the base."

"The Grand Forks Air Force Base."

"Yes. The Grand Forks Air Force Base."

Gordy wanted to wrap his hands around the scrawny pissant's neck and squeeze.

"There's something else. Looks like it's been going on for quite a while."

Gordy pulled his left foot up onto his right leg, and began to tie the wayward lace.

"How long?"

"Years."

"You're kidding."

"No. Based on the science, it could be as much as a decade."

Gordy yanked the lace tighter. It felt as if he would cut off circulation to his foot.

"How can they tell?"

"Urinalysis, bone studies, and tooth wear. Analyzing the porcine teeth showed excessive wear caused by the consumption of bone. Just like human teeth wear over time from our diet. Bone is not a normal component of the porcine diet. The chemical analysis of the bone uncovered high amounts of Nitrogen-15. Nitrogen-15 is more commonly found in human bones. And the analysis of the urine from the pigs at the farm, not at the processing facility, was indicative of the consumption of human-based protein within the last four days."

Gordy pulled the shoelace tighter.

It snapped.

"What's the DA's plan?"

"Capital murder. Five counts at this point in time. I'm going to continue to fight bail of any amount."

"Capital?"

"North Dakota doesn't have the death penalty, but going down the capital route requires life without parole. I'm hoping one of the victims was brought across state lines. That way it becomes federal. He'll fry in Terre Haute if that's the case. I'm keeping my fingers crossed that one of the vics was from Minnesota."

"You're sounding pretty sure. How's the evidence?"

"Rock solid. There's no way any jury could find him innocent."

"Any names yet?"

"Still working on the DNA cross-references."

Gordy wanted the conversation to end, so he finished his cup of coffee, pushed his chair back from his desk, and stood up.

"Ok, Pete. Sounds like you have your work cut out for you. Let me know if there's anything my department can help with."

"As a matter of fact, there is something you could help with. It's why I came by."

Gordy sat on the edge of his desk, and set his empty coffee cup on his thigh.

"Shoot."

"How did you know?"

"About what?"

It wasn't looking good for Dirk. If there were a time for "Innocent until proven guilty," this was it. The Dirk he knew didn't have the balls to do this. And that, in Gordy's opinion, was a compliment.

"We are going to have to put down the entire porcine population at the farm."

"Porcine population. Mind putting that in English?"

"We can't let the pigs on the farm live. We can't gamble with the chance that they could get into the food chain. It would be close to cannibalism if they did. They need to be put down so can your department help with that?"

"When?"

"Now if possible."

"I'll need something from a judge."

Smith pulled a sheet of paper from his case folder, and handed it to Gordy.

"Already done."

This was going downhill very fast. If what forensics was saying was true, he understood the logic. Gordy was a natural skeptic, but when forensics came up with something, he almost always fell in line. Gordy looked at the form, saw the judge's signature, and pressed the intercom on his phone.

"Yes, Sheriff?"

"Get in here."

Gordy turned his attention back to the ADA.

"Anything else?"

"No. But I'll tell Simmons to give you a call."

Gordy shook the ADA's hand, and watched him leave.

"Fucking prick."

*

Danny knew Lina was working tonight.

But he didn't want to come too early and bail like he did his first night back. He'd intended on staying through closing.

Now the bar was locked, the signs outside were off, and everyone was gone.

It was just him and Lina.

"Want a beer?"

"I'd like a cosmo."

Lina reached behind the bar, grabbed a martini shaker, mixed a concoction, and then poured it into a chilled martini glass she'd grabbed from the freezer.

"Wow. I was really just joking."

"Butch told me."

Daniel took a sip.

"The best I've ever had."

"No one here would know what that was. They'd think you were weird for drinking something pink in a funny shaped glass."

"Let them think whatever they want."

Lina sat on the stool next to Daniel, and poured a cold Michelob into a glass.

"Tastes good. My legs are killing me tonight."

Danny reached to his neck, and pulled the gold necklace out from under the shirt.

"You still have that?"

"Never took it off."

"You said you'd come back."

"I know. I'm sorry. I thought I wanted something else."

"Did you find it? You said you had a head full of dreams."

"I still do. You said you'd come out to California after you graduated."

"Too much time had passed. Dad retired. Mom got sick. I couldn't leave."

Danny nodded. He could feel his heart racing.

He felt like he did on their first date.

"Remember our first date?"

Lina nodded and smiled.

"*Dumb and Dumber*. One of my favorites. Dad almost didn't let me go."

"Still love that movie."

"Took you forever to make your move."

Daniel nodded as he reached down, took her hand in his, pulled her towards him, and kissed her. He wasn't going to make that mistake again.

"Better?"

Lina nodded.

"Butch said you didn't learn much in school."

"Butch doesn't know what he's talking about."

June 29, 2012

Butch's Bar
Arvilla, ND

*

Dirt's band, DirtyDeeds, was booked each weekend. Both Friday and Saturday until harvest. Weekend nights at the bar were typically bouncing with live music and phhht of opening beer cans providing additional percussion to Dirt's acoustic guitar.

But Dirt was in jail.

Now only the jukebox was playing.

Everyone was talking.

Everyone had an opinion.

"I always knew he was odd," said Mike the town drunk. "He'd never amount to anything."

Lina shook her head.

"Just like you, right Mike? You are such a wonder of ambition, after all."

"I don't think it was him. Have you ever met Trude? That woman. There's something wrong with her. She drove Tubbs to have a heart attack. Maybe even lowered the box herself."

"They said the box had nothing to do with it."

"I still don't like that woman."

"Can I get another Blue, Lina?"

"No. I don't think it was Trude. Did you read the paper? Did you read what they found in those pigs?"

"Body parts."

"Lina, I'll have another Michelob. And get Mike over there another Canadian Club."

"He's pretty drunk"

"So. When isn't he?"

"I don't know. I think that someone from the plant did it. Set Dirt up. Made it look like him."

"I'll have a screwdriver, honey. What kind of pizza do you have?"

"Pepperoni and supreme," said Lina.

"Pepperoni."

"I think it was someone from the airbase."

"That's closed down, Betty."

"There are a few people there."

"I'll have a vodka seven."

"I heard there's another girl missing. Some university girl."

"Heard that Dirt had a date with her too."

"Dirt? With a girl? Whoa. She must have bad eyes."

"You be quiet. Dirt's handsome in his own way."

June 30, 2012

The Opera House Lab
Arvilla, ND

*

Things didn't smell right and it was hard to work when his lab wasn't perfect. The smell made his nausea worse. The aura of colors was beginning to form in front of his eyes.

He felt a big one coming on.

"Jimmy Boy!" yelled Marco. "What the fuck do you think you're doing? It's smells like shit down here."

Marco walked to the stairway and looked up. Jimmy Boy was nowhere to be seen.

"Jimmy Boy! Get your ass down here."

Usually the Opera House Lab smelled like Old Spice and Mystique perfume, but today it smelled like rotted meat, and ammonia.

"Jimmy Boy!"

There was only silence.

“Malum! Clint! Zeke! Someone get down here. Find Jimmy Boy.”

Marco waited a few more minutes, and then decided that he was just going to have to continue his work despite the smell. He’d deal with Jimmy Boy and the other slackers later. He rifled through the woman’s purse, grabbed the information he was looking for, and walked to stainless steel table. He’d had several women from luvafarmer.com, but this particular one was his first poser.

“What are you looking at?”

He walked closer to the table.

“Do you actually think you’re gonna get lucky tonight? A naked man standing in front of you?”

Marco laughed.

“Don’t flatter yourself. I’m naked because it’s easier to wash the blood off. It doesn’t stain skin, but it will stain my clothes. It’s easier this way.”

He saw her eyes widen even further. She started pulling at the restraints and even with the three layers of duct tape over her mouth, he could make out the muffled, "No! Please don’t!” that she was screaming.

He pushed her driver’s license in front of her face.

“Tina Evans from Williston. I’m assuming that’s you.”

He smashed the flat card against her large nose and pressed down with all of his weight.

“Not a very good picture in my opinion. Doesn’t really match the picture on your online profile. Doesn’t match at all, as a matter of fact. I don't know whether to call you Tina or not. I hate liars, you know. I really do."

She didn't respond, but simply stared at him wide-eyed with tears streaming down the sides of her face.

"You didn't answer my question. Is this you? Did you lie?"

Tina shook her head.

"Is that a no for you didn't lie? Or a no for that's no you. Let's start over."

Marco shoved her driver's license in front of her face and yelled.

"Is this you? You fucking bitch?"

Tina nodded.

"Then you lied on your profile. Because this is the picture from the site."

Marco held up a printout from luvafarmer.com. Pictures of two very different women. The picture from the site was of a blonde with blue eyes and huge tits. Tall. The woman lying on the table had red hair and mosquito bites on her chest. Average height. Fat.

"You don't even need a bra. You just buy the tiny baby bandages, don't you? I didn't even waste time, and put you in the tank," said Marco as he pointed to the Spot Free Rinse. "Nothing could clean the ugly off of you."

Marco took one of her nipples between his fingers, twisted, and pulled.

Despite the duct tape across her mouth, her muffled scream echoed throughout the basement.

“Did you lie?”

Tina nodded.

“There you go. Finally telling the truth. You’re a lying bitch in other words. You know what I do to liars?”

Marco went back to the workbench where Clint tinkered. He was looking for the pliers.

“Fuck! He never puts anything away.”

He went back to Tina, grabbed her pinky toe and twisted until she screamed again. He bent over slightly to nuzzle her neck, and bit her earlobe.

“I’ll be right back. Don’t you go anywhere.”

*

Tina was tired of being told she was ugly. She rarely received responses, but the worst was when one of the guys she "poked" actually sent her a response. She was actually excited when she opened her inbox.

Until she read what he’d sent.

“You are fuckin’ ugly! Get off of this site, bitch!”

She cried for two days.

Then she changed her picture and modified her stats.

The interest in her profile went from zero to dozens in a matter of hours. She picked a few that interested her. The guys always questioned her when they finally met, but after she convinced them that she was a good lay despite the red hair, freckles, and a nose that was a bit big for her face, they never complained.

A few even came back for a repeat performance.

Until now.

DIRTYFARMBOY poked her first with a simple "Hi. U R cute."

She responded with a ";-) Thx. So R U."

They met as agreed upon at the taco shop on Gateway Drive. She knew him immediately from his picture. He was exactly as his profile said: Six-two. One-ninety. Brown hair. Scruff.

Beautiful.

She could tell he was taken by surprise, but when she convinced him they'd have fun, he agreed and even suggested catching a movie after sharing tacos, tots, and pops.

He was nice and polite in the restaurant.

But in his car, the minute he backed out of the parking lot, he changed into someone else. He told her to be quiet.

"Sit still. Don't look at me," he growled.

"What's wrong?"

Tina didn't have time to move as his fist came toward her at lightning speed. That was the last she remembered. When she woke up, she found herself lying naked on a table in a basement that smelled of rotted meat.

The minute she heard him walk up the stairs, she started pulling on the bands that kept her arms tied to the table.

They were loose. The left more than the right, but both showed promise.

Using all of her strength, she pulled her left arm up and away from the table.

She heard a small tear.

She pulled again.

Another tear.

*

"Where are the fucking pliers?"

Marco was furious. Not only had the bitch lied to him, but one of the others had forgotten to put his tools back in their proper space. Now he not only had an ugly bitch on his table, but didn't have what he needed to deal with her.

Marco opened each of the kitchen drawers, and slammed them shut. The drawer with the silverware didn't close all of the way so he pulled it out, and threw it on the floor. The kitchen floor was littered with knives, forks, and spoons.

"Where are the fucking pliers?"

Marco moved into the living room, and kicked the utensils across the floor. Some flew into the hallway, and he heard them bounce down the stairs.

He started at the bookcase first. Pulling books off, looking behind them, throwing them on the floor, and pulling more off of the shelf.

"Where are the fucking pliers?"

*

Tina heard a noise on the stairs, and stopped pulling at the straps to avoid drawing any attention to herself. She could just barely make out the stairs leading up to the main floor. She looked for feet coming down, but instead saw a fork and knife bounce down four stairs and come to a stop.

"One more," the thought. "One more pull."

The Velcro band finally tore loose. Her arm flew up towards her face, and the screw holding the band to the table sailed across room, and hit the side of a corrugated metal tube with a rattle.

Tina held her breath.

Afraid that it had made too much noise.

Instead, she heard another wail about missing pliers followed by multiple thuds on the floor above. This time, the noise seemed further away.

She reached around to her right arm, tore the Velcro strap off, freed her legs, and then jumped off of the table.

Tina's heart was pounding in her chest as she crept up the stairs. She didn't know when he'd be back, but she knew that he wasn't planning on letting her live.

She might not be fodder for a fashion model brigade, but it didn't mean she was stupid.

*

"What are you looking for?"

It was Clint.

Marco turned around. His face red with anger. The veins on his neck were pulsating and thick.

"I'm looking for the fucking pliers! Where did you leave them?"

"You used them yesterday. You had to tighten the coax cable going into the TV. Remember? The picture kept going out."

Marco calmed, but kicked the three books that had landed at his feet.

"Here they are. Right where you left them."

Marco grabbed the pliers, started to turn back to the stairs, and then stopped.

"You guys get this cleaned up. And the kitchen. It's a mess. I want it cleaned up before I'm done with that lying bitch downstairs."

*

Tina was midway up the stairs when she saw the shadow on the brown paneled wall.

She looked up and saw his face.

He was sneering at her. His white teeth glowing in the background. The lighting from the kitchen gave his face a reddish glow, and from her perspective below him, he looked a foot taller than he actually was.

"Well, well. What do we have here?"

He walked down until he was two steps above her. His feet were level with her face.

"I found my pliers. One of the other guys used them. Said that I did, but I know better. I always put my things away. It's the right thing to do."

She watched as he took the pliers, spread them open with one hand, and then closed them with a loud snap.

"They're very effective when used correctly."

Tina felt the spittle from his mouth land on her face.

"Let me go. I won't tell anyone. Please."

"I know. You've said that before."

Tina knew the truth. He wouldn't let her go, but she wanted his attention on her face, and not her left hand.

"Too late for that."

His left foot came down one step.

His calf was now even with her face.

Tina moved to the right, brought her left hand up, and jammed the fork she'd grabbed from the bottom step into his calf. At first she didn't think the tines would break the skin, then the fork finally slid home. She forced it in as far as her strength would let her, and finally felt it scrape bone.

The man screamed, and reached down for his calf.

On his way down, Tina grabbed his hair and pulled.

He slid down the stairs and landed at the bottom. The fork was still in his calf, but it seemed much deeper.

He was moving a bit. Flexing his hands, but his eyes remained closed.

She heard him moan.

Tina crawled up the remaining stairs. When she reached the door, she looked for the others that he'd mentioned.

No one was around.

She saw the front door, and ran.

*

Booger flexed his hands, moved his legs, wiggled his toes, and finally rotated his head.

Everything was working.

Except his calf.

The fucking bitch took him by surprise.

His calf felt as if a hot poker was resting on it. He reached down, felt the source of the heat, and pulled. The skin made a squishing sound as he set the fork free.

"Shit," he said as he looked at fork. "You guys really fucked this one up."

It was always the same. When things got really bad, Booger came to the rescue. To clean things up. To make sure all of the loose ends were tidy.

Slowly, Booger stood up. His calf resisted any movement, but he knew he'd have to work through the fire.

He cautiously walked up the stairs.

He wasn't sure where Tina had gone or where she might be hiding.

He had guns in the house.

He reached the landing, and saw the front door wide open.

"Fuck. Now I have to go hunting."

*

Desolation.

There were no city lights.

No houses.

No traffic.

Nothing.

Just pitch black, and a faint echo of cows mooing in the distance.

Tina wasn't in Grand Forks.

Nor was she anyplace that she recognized.

She reached the end of the long driveway, and looked in each direction. To her right, she could detect a faint glow of lights, but no detail. To her left, she saw a set of yard lights within a dark form of trees. Maybe a mile away.

If she wanted going to live, and she did, she had to get help. The lights were the closest, and best chance for survival.

She headed in the direction of the lights.

And stopped.

She didn't know how much time she had before he came looking for her, but she knew that if he did, that's likely where he'd go first.

Towards the closest lights.

Tina got off the dirt road, crawled into the ditch, and started walking towards the glow of lights to her right.

Where that led, she didn't know.

*

Booker put on his uniform, put on his holster, grabbed his keys, and got into his car.

It was 2:30 in the morning. The last time he looked at a clock was when he saw the time on the cable box when he found the pliers that Clint had misplaced. Booker knew that it was Marco, but also knew that is wasn't worth his time to debate.

It was 1:30 then.

The bitch had at the most an hour on him.

Maybe forty-five minutes.

But she was naked and lost.

When Booker reached the end of the driveway, he looked in both directions, trying to think like a scared woman.

"Which way did you go, honey?"

Going left would take him to the Carlson's farm a mile down the road. He could see the yard lights on her farm.

"No, not that way," said Marco.

"Why not?"

"Someone would be here already. It wouldn't take her that long to get there. That bastard, Skip would have come here in his truck by now. Plus that's where she thinks you'll go. Take a right. Go east. She'll go towards the base. The glow of the lights. More people. More help."

Booger knew Marco was right.

He might have a hot temper, but in when things got really tough, he usually was able to think things through a lot better than he could.

Definitely a lot better than the others.

Booger turned on the light bar, but kept his siren off.

He headed towards the glow.

*

Tina could feel the thistle scratching her legs with each step. She'd tripped on five rocks, and twisted her ankle in a gopher hole, but she knew she didn't have time to slow down.

She wanted to sit down and cry, but she didn't have time for that either.

Not if she wanted to live.

The glow of the lights was getting brighter, and the lights seemed to be changing color.

It wasn't the glow ahead of her that was flickering.

The ditch and the road were changing color.

Tina crouched down in the tall crab grass, and looked back from where she'd come.

It was a police car. Its flashing lights were on and it was coming towards her.

Someone had called the police and they were looking for her. Tina crawled out of the ditch, and onto the dirt road. She waved her hands, and started to cry as her salvation approached.

When the car stopped, she ran towards it.

"Help me! Help me! He's trying to kill me."

She saw the car door open and stopped.

"Help is here, Tina."

How did he know her name?

As quickly as her bare feet could on the gravel, she spun around, and ran back down into the ditch.

It was him.

*

"See. I told you. There she is."

Booger smiled. Marco was right. The bitch had gone towards the glow, and was directly in front of him waving her hands like a mad woman.

"That was a smart move."

"What was?"

"Turning on the flashers. She thinks you are here to help. Good move. Mosquitoes to blood."

"Thanks," said Booger as he stopped the car.

Booger kept his headlights on the high beams to hide his face. He didn't want her to recognize him too soon. He unsnapped his sidearm from its holster, opened the door, and got out.

"Help me! Help me! He's trying to kill me."

"Help is here, Tina."

"Bad move, dude. Now she knows."

"Shit," said Booger as he watched Tina realize who had actually come to help her.

Booger watched her run into the ditch, catch her foot in a gopher hole, and tumble to the bottom.

"You don't have much of a choice. Just get it over with. Close this one out before things get worse."

"Yeah. I know."

Booger looked down into the ditch. Tina was on her hands and feet crawling in the weeds. He raised his gun, and pulled the trigger. She flipped around twice from the force of the bullet. With just the light from his car, Booger could see that blood was spewing from her neck, and pooling beside her head. Her head was writhing back and forth but there was nothing below her shoulders.

"Must have cut her cord in half," Booger said. "She can't move."

"Fuckin' good shot."

His aim was off. He was shooting for her head, but hit her neck.

Her head slowed its dance, and then finally stopped.

Her eyes were open. Aimed straight at him.

"Oh well. Dead is dead."

Booger opened his trunk, grabbed two lengths of rope, and headed towards the side of the road.

"Let me handle this."

It was Malum.

"This is what I'm good at."

*

"I'll tie this to her feet, and back the car up to get her out of the ditch. Then we'll get her back to the farm."

"You can't drive my squad car."

"Fine. Then you back it up when I tell you."

Malum respected the original, but he could be a real jerk.

Malum took the rope from the hood of the squad car, and tied a slipknot at one end. He began to whistle as he slid down the ditch. The thistle scratched his arms as he went down.

The girl wasn't as homely as Marco was bitching about.

She had a prettiness that Malum could appreciate. He'd enjoy working with her. She had delicate hands and her fingernails were each painted a different color.

He'd save those for last.

Malum picked up her feet, slipped the loop over her ankles, then pulled to take up the slack.

She had chubby ankles.

"Let's get her out of here," he yelled.

*

Booger pulled up to the front porch, got out of his car, and walked to the front. On the drive back to the farm, he was hearing a rattle that shouldn't have been there.

Despite the fact that there was a body tied to the black push bumper.

"Shit. One of her arms fell loose. I knew I heard something."

Malum tied the girl to his push bumper and had told him she wasn't going anywhere.

"Look at that mess, Malum. Shit, now I have to clean the front of the car."

"Her arm came loose. No big deal."

"Then what did I hear?"

"The rope. It came loose. Was probably bouncing up and down as you drove."

"And what about the mess? I can't go to work with blood on the grill."

"Jimmy Boy will clean it up," Malum pointed to the front door. "Go. I have work to do."

June 30, 2012

Butch's Bar
Arvilla, ND

*

It was eight in the morning, and Danny had made a temporary, makeshift office out of one of the small corner booths at Butch's. The red Naugahyde was still sticky from years of spilled drinks, and Danny could smell the sour bouquet of old beer, whiskey, and cigarettes despite the fact that he wiped down the booth and the table with a quart of Formula 409 before he sat down. It definitely wasn't his third floor office off of Wilshire, and the aroma was definitely not a good trade for the salty smell of the ocean.

It would have to do.

The papers from the case file were spread out, and his laptop was open. He sipped from his second cup of bad coffee, probably Folgers, and studied Dirt's case file with all of the evidence that had been accumulated. Debra was right, the judge had been more than happy to sign the *pro hac vice* without question. As long as he kept Debra's office in the loop, he was officially Dirt's attorney.

"How much did those jeans cost you?"

Danny looked up at Lina.

"What?"

"Those jeans. How much?"

Danny felt his cheeks suddenly turn red. He couldn't understand why he was embarrassed as his jeans were never a question at home.

"They're Diesels. Why?"

"Never heard of them. That's what you put in a tractor, not something you wear. How much?"

"They're from Italy."

"Does that make them better? How much. Come on. Spill it."

"I have work to do Lina. I have to review this evidence."

Lina pulled a chair up to the booth, rested her chest over the pile of the papers, and adjusted her brown cowboy hat over her blonde hair. She set her chin on her fists, and looked up at Danny.

"I'm not going anywhere until you tell me."

"Two hundred. Ok?"

Lina pushed back from the table.

"You're shittin' me. Two hundred? You can get a pair of Wranglers at the K-Mart for twenty-five bucks. Maybe twenty when they are on sale."

"Exactly."

"Exactly what?

"*The* K-Mart. *The* Wal-Mart. *The* Target. *The* Kohls. *The* Sears. *The* JC Penney. I don't buy clothes from those stores. Unless I'm getting milk, if a store has shopping carts lined up by the doors when I walk in, I walk out. Ok? Now, can I get back to work?"

"Were you making fun of me?"

Danny looked up at her, and smiled.

"Well, you do put *the* in front of everything."

"Your milk is probably from Italy, too."

"No. I get it at *the* Kroger."

"Have you seen your folks yet?"

Danny nodded as he picked up a piece of paper. He needed to change the subject, and wanted to get back to work.

"What can you tell me about luvafarmer.com?"

"It's a dating site. That's all I can tell you."

"You don't have an account?"

Lina stood up, and stuck out her tongue.

"For your information, I have a dozen profiles on a dozen other sites. I get propositioned at least ten times a day."

Danny nodded without looking up.

"You probably do."

*

"Want a pop?" asked Lina as she came back to Danny's office, and sat next to him. "Is this corner office like the one you have in California?"

"Close. Smell is better there. Better looking help here though. It's called soda though. I haven't heard it called pop in decades."

He looked up and tipped her hat above her hairline.

"I forgot about your eyes."

"What about them?"

"Incredibly blue," he said as he kissed her. "How about a club soda?"

"Sure. How's it going?"

"Do you know the two rules of criminal defense?"

"I've been tending bar for a decade, not going to law school."

"There's the law and the evidence. When the law is good, you attack the evidence. When the evidence is good, attack the law. Make sure they followed it to the letter."

"What does that mean for Dirt?"

"The evidence is killing us, but they did so many things wrong at the crime scene. I have to use the law against them. Make sure they followed it to the letter. I'm hoping to get most of it thrown out because of the law. I just have to have a solid strategy. The ADA is being a real prick, and not liking the fact that I'm not licensed in the state."

Danny separated the stacks of paper, and reviewed the timeline that he'd written when he interviewed Dirt. The top page of the stack next to his laptop was a printout of the access logs from luvafarmer.com.

He cocked his head, and wrinkled his eyebrows.

"What's wrong?"

"Dirt. He says he and his band were playing here the evening of the fifteenth. True?"

"I have trouble remembering what I had for dinner last night, and you are asking me about something almost two weeks ago?"

"You had a burger and fries. Then me for dessert."

Danny heard Lina laugh from behind the bar.

"I forgot about your laugh too."

"And what about it?" she asked as he walked back to the table with a tattered calendar.

"It's cute. A little squeak followed by a snort. Very unique."

Lina turned the weekly calendar back to the date Danny was asking about.

"Yup. He played that night. Started at seven. Went to closing."

"When's that?"

"One."

Danny looked back at the access logs from Dirt's computer.

"Thank you, Mr. LeCross."

"Who?"

"A case I was working in before I left. I would have never thought to look at the logs without having worked that case."

Danny organized the papers, put them back into the manila folders as neatly as he could, and put them and his laptop in his briefcase.

"Leaving so soon?"

"Gotta go talk to Dirt. We still on for tonight?"

Lina winked and formed a gun out of her thumb and index finger.

"You betcha," she said as she blew smoke from the finger-barrel of her imaginary gun.

*

It took almost an hour before they brought Dirt into the interview room, but finally the door opened and a guard walked in holding onto the shackles around Dirt's waist like a leash. Dirt knew the drill. He sat down on the chair, and put his hands in front of him so they could be fastened to the table. Danny immediately noticed that Dirt looked a little better than on some of his previous visits. His hair was still long and stringy, but it didn't hang into his face in greasy clumps.

"They let you shower."

"Every other day."

"Eating?"

Dirt scrunched his face.

"Not really hungry."

Danny opened his briefcase, and pulled out a can of Coke and two chocolate covered granola bars.

"Officer? I brought these for Mr. Kinnear."

Danny waited until the guard inspected the wrappers around the bars and ensured the can of Coke was still sealed before pushing them over to Dirt.

"We good?"

The officer nodded.

"Oh, my God. Thank you."

"The Coke is probably warm, sorry. But Lina sends you her love."

"It doesn't matter. Are you two..."

Danny smiled.

"I think so."

"But. Um. How's that gonna work? Aren't you engaged? Aren't you heading back to California at some time?"

"Those are details I haven't figured out yet."

Dirt shrugged as he stuffed a granola bar down his gullet, and washed it down with the warm Coke.

"Have a couple of questions."

Danny pushed a picture of him sitting in Booger's sheriff's car the day Dirt was arrested.

"When you were sitting in Booger's car. Had they told you that you were under arrest?"

Dirt shook his head.

"Booger told me to sit there. Thought I'd be safer."

"So when this picture was taken, you weren't under arrest. You hadn't been read your rights."

Dirt nodded.

"I want to make sure. Don't just nod. Use words."

"I wasn't under arrest. That happened a few hours later. Booger thought it was best for me to stay out of the way. Why?"

"It's called Third Party Objective. When someone, a third party, saw that picture of you in Booger's car, they'd assume you were arrested. And you weren't."

"What's the difference?"

"I have to use the law against them. The evidence they have is not good. So I have to get as much thrown out as possible. If I can show how they mismanaged the crime scene, it will help us get some of this thrown out. Or at least put doubt in the minds of a juror. And that's what we need."

"Then definitely not. I was put in Gordy's SUV after I was arrested. I wasn't in Booger's car."

"Good. The evening of the fifteenth. You said you and your band were playing at Butch's."

"Yes. Wrapped up around midnight or one. I know it was right before closing."

"Then how do you explain this?"

Danny put a sheet of paper in front of Dirt showing the access logs of his luvafarmer.com account.

"It says you were online at luvafarmer.com at 8:33 that night."

Dirt shook his head as he finished the Coke and the second granola bar.

"Couldn't be. I was at Butch's. Everyone saw me too."

"Is there a mobile app? Did you have a laptop at Butch's or anything like that?"

"They don't have any app for the phone. Butch doesn't have Wi-Fi, so I couldn't access it there."

"Then who was on your account on June 15th at 8:33?"

"Probably Booger. He has my account information."

"Why didn't you tell me that a week ago?"

"You didn't ask."

"Would Booger admit to having it? Your account info?"

"He should. I know he put it on his phone so he wouldn't forget it."

"You said they don't have a phone app."

"Not an app. He has the account info on the phone. The username and password."

Dan looked confused as he listened to what Dirt was telling him.

"Why would you give Booger your creds?"

"He was my wingman. Said online sites were full of scammers. He told me he'd do a check on anyone I was supposed to see. Use some CODIS database or something like that."

That didn't make sense to Danny. CODIS had nothing to do with online sites, and if Booger were ever caught accessing it for personal use, he'd get in big trouble.

And Booger knew that.

"All of them? All of the contacts?"

"Most. Some I forgot to tell him about. Most never even showed up. Never heard from them again. He told me that was proof that they were up to no good."

"No one has ever asked you about this before?"

"Nope. You're the first."

Dan could feel his heart racing.

This was the type of information he could use to throw all of the evidence out. Not only would everything he heard plant a seed of doubt, he was good enough to make that single seed grow into a forest. The problem was that he was moving the shadow of guilt from one friend to the other.

That wasn't a position he wanted to be in.

Now he just need to talk to Booger to make sure he'd confirm what Dirt told him.

"I'm heading over to see Gordy. I don't know if I'll see you tomorrow, but if not, definitely the day after."

"Can you bring more granola bars? And a couple of Cokes?"

"Sure thing," said Danny with a smile.

Danny looked over at the guard and nodded.

"We're done here."

"Chin up, Dirt."

As Dirt left the interview room, he gave Danny a thumbs-up.

*

They were sitting at a table at a bar and grill in the strip mall on 32nd Avenue. It was one of those chain restaurants that practically every town across the country had. Grand Forks had five. Los Angeles probably had dozens. Maybe hundreds. It didn't matter though, as they all looked the same inside and out. The bar here in Grand Forks looked exactly the same as the one he'd go to off of Wilshire back home. The only real difference was that the one he and Gordy were at had UND hockey sticks hanging from the ceiling whereas the one he went to had multi-colored beach toys hanging everywhere.

The server came by their table wearing an ear-to-ear smile and plenty of bling. Danny could tell that not only did she know the Sheriff, but also knew exactly what he was going to order.

"Bourbon and water, Sheriff?"

"You bet. Off duty as of thirty seconds ago. Bring me one of those Philly steak sandwiches too. The one with the pepper jack cheese and lots of grilled onions. California kid here is paying, so put some extra fries with it."

The waitress turned to Danny.

"For you?"

"Cosmo. With Goose."

"Anything to eat?"

"The sandwich good?" Danny asked Gordy.

"Nothing better."

"I'll have the same."

"Extra fries too?"

"Sure."

Danny waited for the server to tell him she didn't know what a cosmo was. Instead, she smiled and told them she'd be right back.

"When I first stopped at the bar, they didn't know what a cosmo was. Lina surprised me and made one the other night though."

"Different market out there. Simpler life. Simpler needs. Smirnoff does just fine, and all they really ever need is orange juice. I think he's had the same bottle of grapefruit juice in the cooler for a month. Never needs anything else."

"It was good seeing Butch. He's gotten old. Using the cane more now."

Gordy nodded.

"We're all getting old. So are you kids mending things? You were so cute back then."

"Yes," said Danny with a nod and smile. "It feels good."

"I've spent time on both coasts. It's a different life. Not bad. Just different. Maybe you are realizing it's not for you."

Danny looked at his old friend and smiled. He felt a warmth that he hadn't experienced in a very long time. He had people he hung around with in California, but he didn't have anyone he considered a true friend.

"What's wrong?"

"Nothing. It's good to see you again, Gordy. I've missed you."

"It's good to have you home. Dirt couldn't have anyone better representing him. But I have a feeling this is going to take years. It's not going to be fast. Something like this never is. All of the delays. Lawyer games."

"We'll see. I'm hoping to get a lot of the evidence thrown out."

"Is this on the record, Dan?"

Dan shook his head. He didn't want to go down that road at this point in time.

"No. But I'm going to have to talk to Booger. Apparently he had access to Dirt's online account. That luvafarmer.com site. I just wanted to let you know I'd be talking with him."

"Ok. Just make sure that if it's an official discussion to let him know. He'd be representing the department."

"No problem. I have another favor."

"Anything you need, Dan. You know that."

"Can I get your personal cell number? I won't share it. I just thought I should have it."

As Gordy clumsily thumbed a text, the server came by with their cocktails.

"Gentlemen. Here you go."

"Might as well bring us another round, Ronnie."

Ronnie nodded, and looked at Dan.

"Might as well. I'm with the sheriff, after all. What's he going to do, arrest me?"

Danny handed her his credit card.

"Open a tab for us."

*

"It's three in the afternoon and you, my friend, are already toasted."

"I'm relaxed," slurred Danny. "Not toasted."

"You're not going to last the night. We had a date."

"Boolsheet. I'll be just fine."

Danny laughed, and tried to look at his watch.

"I said boolsheet."

Lina shook her head, and escorted him to the same booth he'd used this morning as an office.

"Who were you drinking with?"

"None other than the Sheriff of Grand Forks County."

Danny started laughing again.

"What's so funny?"

"*The Sheriff of Grand Forks County*. Sounds like a reality TV show, doesn't it? Maybe right after *The Desperate Housewives of Larimore.* Since there aren't enough housewives here in Arvilla, we can't have our own show."

"You sit here. Don't move. I'll get you a club soda."

Before Lina could leave, Danny pulled out his phone. He went for the Contacts button, but the calculator popped up.

"This damn phone never works."

"Who are you calling?"

"Tim Bernstein. Friend from Hollywood. A producer or something like that. Works in the business. I want to give him my ideas about the reality show. Shows," Danny stopped, looked at his hand still holding the phone, and put up three fingers. "Plural. There are two of them."

Danny looked at his fingers and his phone again, thought about what he'd just said, and pulled one finger down.

"Sorry. I had three fingers up."

Lina took Danny's phone out of his hand, and stuffed it down his front pocket.

"You're not going to call anyone right now."

Danny smirked as his chin bobbed down to his chest.

"Keep digging while you're down there."

Lina kissed Danny on each eye, lifted his chin, and planted a soft kiss on his lips.

"You are just too cute, you know that Daniel Scott Carlson? Too cute for your own good."

Danny's eyes closed, and he slumped against the brown paneled wall.

"I love you Caroline Grace Holmes. From the first time I laid eyes on you. Always have," he whispered before he started softly snoring.

*

"How long has he been sleeping?"

"He came floating in around three. What happened to you? Your arms are scratched to pieces. Did you go and get a kitten?"

"I was clearing thistle by the garden," said Booger as he pulled his shirtsleeves down to cover the scratches.

Lina and Booger sat in the booth next to Danny.

"I should take a picture of this, and send it to his fiancé."

Booger saw the hurt look in Lina's eyes.

"Sorry."

"No. I know he has another life. It's just that..."

"He has to go back Lina. Did he tell you about the house?"

Lina shook her head as she held Danny's hand.

"Several million. Something on the beach."

"Nothing like that around here."

"He doesn't belong here anymore, Lina. You have to realize that."

Danny stirred, opened his eyes, and tried to focus.

"Who doesn't belong where?"

"Nothing," said Lina. "How are you feeling?"

"Like shit. Have any Tylenol or perhaps a shotgun?"

"I'll get you a big, tall glass of ice water."

"I have a shotgun, if you want it," said Booger.

"What time is it?"

"Almost six."

Danny leaned forward, and rested his forehead on the table.

"Damn him."

"Who?"

"Gordy. I went to talk and have lunch. We ended up having a lot to drink."

"You saw Gordy?"

"Yeah. Wanted to let him know that I needed to talk to you about Dirt's case."

"Why not just ask me?"

"Protocol. He's your boss. Wanted to give him the heads-up. I'm Dirt's lawyer, remember?"

Booger sat back, cut his eyes to watch Lina, and put clasped his hands behind his back.

"So what's your question?"

"That online site. Luvafarmer.com?"

"What about it?"

"I noticed some strange entries in the system log files. Didn't make sense. Dirt said you have access to his account."

Booger took a sip of his beer. Lina was still behind the bar.

"She sure does look good, doesn't she?"

Danny smiled.

"I think I told her I loved her. Right before I passed out."

"Well, you have to leave here, remember? Don't break her heart again."

"I know. I know."

"I doubt if she'd want to go with you to California. She's a lifer here."

Danny nodded and shrugged.

"So. What about account stuff?"

"Dirt's yanking your chain. Sending you down a rabbit hole. I don't use those sites. Never have. Never will. Don't need 'em. I saw the farm, Dan. It was horrific. Everything points to him."

*

Danny had been in the courtroom too many times and had cross-examined hundreds of people who had put their hand on the bible and professed to tell the truth only to tell the exact opposite. One of his favorite law professors once told him that a statement from a liar is just as important as a statement from someone telling the truth.

Booger was lying.

Danny didn't want to press it now, but he'd find out why.

Dirt's freedom depended on it.

"Ok. I'll talk to Dirt again. He could have been mistaken. I have to run by there tomorrow. Meeting with Gordy again too."

"Here you go, sexy," said Lina as she brought two tall glasses of club soda and set them in front of Danny. "Sorry that took so long."

"Say. It's dinnertime. Lina's shift is over. You can barely function. Why don't you two come to the farm and have dinner. We can grill some burgers have a few beers. Like old times. You can stay in the guest room. Unlike our sheriff, Deputy Booger won't let you drive drunk."

Danny and Lina looked at one another. Danny could read her mind. They had planned a date tonight, but it was ultimately Lina who made the call.

"Sure. How about 7:30? That will give me time to get this guy home and clean him up."

July 2, 2012

Booger's House
Arvilla, ND

*

"Wow. Hasn't changed a bit," said Dan as he walked into Booger's home. "Happy birthday, by the way."

"Same to you. A couple days early, but who's counting? Dirt's is tomorrow."

"Thirty-four years. We're getting old."

"Don't tell my mom that. She still thinks she's forty."

Dan looked around the house. He hadn't been inside since before he left for college.

"It's exactly the way I remember it. Same furniture and everything."

"I'm not much of a decorator. Sit down. I have mugs in the freezer. Miller Lite good?"

Danny felt his stomach flip. Not at the notion of drinking alcohol again, but the fact that he was used to micro brews. Beer with meat and flavor. He hadn't had a Miller since high school graduation.

And that, technically, didn't count.

"Sure. Need any help? I can get the grill lit."

"Nope," said Booger as he headed back into the kitchen. "It's a charcoal grill. You probably don't remember how to light those."

"How's your mom doing?"

"She's doing great. Has a small apartment in Larimore," Booger yelled from the kitchen. "She even wondered how you were doing, Lina. Asked about Glenn. Wasn't that who you were dating?"

*

"He knows," said Booger.

Marco nodded as he grabbed two mugs out of the freezer.

"It doesn't matter what he knows," said Marco as he emptied a capsule of Special K into each of the beers.

"He'll need more."

"Yeah. He's a big guy."

Marco put another capsule in Danny's beer, and stirred each of them with a spoon until everything was dissolved.

"What are you going to do?"

"I'll process her like the others. Make him watch. I'll skip the rinse though. Let's just get her on the table."

"Everything?"

"Everything. When Malum is done, when he's at an emotional edge, I'll put a bullet through his head with your gun. Malum has never done a guy before. He might enjoy it."

"We need Boots."

"He's gone. Forever."

"They're my friends though. Danny and Lina."

"Your *friend* is asking questions. The wrong questions."

Booger nodded

*

"Ok. Two frosty mugs," said Booger as he gave Danny and Lina the beers.

"Aren't you having one, Boog?"

"I have one in the kitchen. I'm getting the burgers ready for the grill."

"Are you sure you don't want any help," asked Lina.

"No. You stay out here. Make sure he doesn't get into any trouble. You know how those California lawyers can be. Keep talking though. I'm just a couple of sheets of drywall away. Drink up. There's more in the cooler out in the porch when you need them. I served the first one. Yoyo from now on."

"Yoyo?"

"You're on your own."

July 3, 2012

The Opera House Lab
Arvilla, ND

*

Danny's head was pounding. He tried to open his eyes, but his eyelids weren't cooperating as he wanted.

"What's that smell?"

Danny took another furtive breath, and held back a retch. The smell was a sickening combination of Old Spice, roses, lilac, and rotten meat.

He tried to move his arms and legs, but they were as uncooperative as his eyelids.

"Booger? Lina?"

Danny tried to command his eyes open again. He found he had to concentrate. This time he made progress. A faint slit of light registered.

"Lina?"

"She's indisposed right now, I'm afraid."

"Boog? What's going on?"

Danny finally wrestled his eyes fully open. At first everything was blurry, but as he blinked, the fog washed away, and the room came into focus. He wasn't in the living room. He was in what looked like a combination operating room, and laboratory.

And then there was the smell.

Danny blinked again.

Booger moved in front of him.

Completely naked.

"What the fuck is going on, Booger?"

"My name is Marco. The one you call Booger? He's not here right now."

"The one I call Booger? That's his name."

"He's not here."

It didn't make sense; Booger was standing in front of him.

Who was Marco?

"Where's Lina, Booger?"

"Marco! I'm Marco!"

Booger moved to the side.

"She's right there. She's our guest. You're going to watch how we treat our guests here. It will be fun. You thought you could leave and come back."

The sight of Lina lying naked on the stainless steel table wrapped with silver duct tape sent a jolt of electricity through his body.

She looked so helpless.

A wave of nausea swept over Danny. A stream of beer and bile spewed from his mouth. It drenched his lap and pooled on the floor at his feet.

"That's the drug. Special K. Hell, you lived in California. Probably did drugs all of the time, didn't you?"

Dan wiped his mouth against his shoulder.

"Lina."

"I think she's alive. I hope so, anyway. It won't be any fun if she's already dead. Then Malum has to come in. He'd get all of the fun."

"Malum?"

"You'll meet him soon enough."

Danny tried to move, but found out his arms and legs were wrapped with yellow zip ties. He was sitting on an old, threadbare couch with towels covering all of the cushions. He'd been stripped down to his underwear. His clothes were at his feet and being engulfed by the pool of vomit.

"Nice underwear. Never heard of Hugo Boss."

"Booger. What's..."

"Marco. My fucking name is Marco! If you call me Booger again, I'll rip her toes off one at time with my pliers. Do you understand, Daniel Scott Carpenter from California? Now what's my name?"

"Marco."

Danny saw Booger calm as soon as he called him Marco.

"Good."

"What's going on, Marco?"

“I didn’t think it would be right to strip you all of the way. I do it because it’s easy just to take a shower to wash off the blood. Not so easy if it’s all over my clothes.”

“That’s ok, Marco. I understand.”

Danny looked at his jeans laying on the floor soaking up the puke and saw the corner of his phone sticking out of the front pocket.

“Thank you, Lina,” he whispered.

“What was that?”

“I was just wondering if Lina was going to be ok, Marco. That’s all.”

*

“What’s that, Marco? It looks like some sort of tank.”

Danny had to get Marco’s attention away from him.

Away from Lina.

More importantly, he had to remain calm. Act like he was standing in front of a judge. Stifle emotion until closing remarks.

“Oh. That’s the Spot Free Rinse. Boots engineered that. He’s quite a tinkerer.”

“Looks interesting. Can you tell me about it?”

As soon as Marco walked to the other side of the table, Danny pulled his phone out of his pants pocket with his toes. With his big toe, he turned it on.

ENTER ACCESS CODE

“Shit,” he whispered.

“What?”

Danny looked up. Marco was still on the other side of the room, but he’d heard Danny’s little slip of the tongue.

“Nothing, Marco. I just said it looks cool.”

Danny moved his foot to the screen and pressed 0 1 1 9 with his big toe.

Lina’s birthday.

January nineteenth.

Danny moved his toe to the phone icon, and pressed down.

The calculator appeared.

“Fuck.”

He wanted to scream, but didn’t want to let Booger know what he was trying to do.

He moved his toe down a bit and pressed again.

The phone application appeared on the screen.

Danny looked up.

Booger, or Marco, or whomever was gone.

“Marco?”

“Over here.”

Danny leaned forward, and saw Booger standing at a workbench.

“What’s going on Marco?”

“Sharpening my knives. Clint bought this sharpener. Jimmy Boy is supposed to keep things tidy down here, but he’s been slacking.”

Danny looked back down at his phone. Gordy's number was the last call he'd made and was at the top of his call log. He remembered testing it at the bar and grill earlier that day.

Danny willed his big toe to tap Gordy's name.

The phone's screen changed.

CALLING...
GORDY

Danny hoped that the sheriff hadn't continued drinking, and was passed out someplace.

The screen blinked.

CALLING...
GORDY

Danny saw movement out of the corner of his eye. His stomach fell to his knees as he thought he'd been caught. He didn't realize he'd been holding his breath. The movement was Lina's hand. She'd moved it. Then he saw her toes wiggle very slowly.

She was alive.

He started breathing again.

CALLING...
GORDY

Danny wanted to yell, "Fucking answer the phone Gordy!"

TALKING TO...
GORDY

“Fuck yes!” he croaked. “The line was open.”

“Marco?”

“What! Don’t you ever shut up?”

“Where is Booger?”

“He’s not here.”

“Did you and he make this in his basement? Your work area here?”

“We all did. Him. Me. Malum. Jimmy Boy. Clint. Even Zeke, but not so much. And Boots. Boots was our engineer.”

“Who are you, Marco?

Danny saw Booger turn around. A hunting knife sparkled in his left hand.

“This was his Dad’s knife.”

“Whose dad?”

"The one you call Booger. His father. That's why we did this, you know."

"Did what, Marco."

"Killed all of those women. The one you call Booger killed his father. Watched him get chewed up in that propeller. Saw him sink into the water. That's why we use it after all. The Spot Free Rinse. We like the water. Everything needs to be clean."

"No, Marco. It was an accident. I was there, remember. The Jet Ski hit the boat. Hit your dad. Booger's dad."

"No. He saw it all happen. Watched his father drown. Saw the look in his eyes as life left him. That's why I like to look them in the eyes when they die. I want to find that look again," said Marco shook his head. "It's all Booger's fault. Then you had to come back. She was ours after you left. You should have stayed in California."

Marco looked over at Lina.

"She was ours!"

Danny stared at Booger.

His eyes were lifeless.

He started walking back from his workbench towards him and Lina.

"Who, Marco?"

"Her," he said as he pointed to Lina with the tip of the hunting knife.

"She was ours. Not yours."

"Is Lina alive, Marco?"

"She won't be in about," Marco looked up at the clock. "Twenty minutes. Maybe thirty if I'm having fun. If we can't have her, neither can you."

"Can I talk to Booger, Marco? Can I talk to my friend?"

"No. He doesn't like to come around. He doesn't have the stomach for killing like I do. I enjoy it."

Danny wanted to scream for Gordy, but he knew he had to remain calm.

"Marco?"

"What! What the fuck do you want?"

Danny heard the clang of metal as a knife fell off of the table Booger had just left.

"That better not have broken. That's Malum's favorite. He'll be very angry."

"How long did it take you to make this in Booger's basement, Marco?"

A flash from his phone grabbed Danny's attention. He looked down at the floor just as Booger was about to answer him.

VOICEMAIL BOX...

FULL

CALL ENDED

"No!"

Danny couldn't help himself.

He screamed at the top of his lungs.

"No!"

"It's too late. Scream all you want. No one can hear us down here. There's no one to help," said Marco as he hopped on top of the table and straddled Lina. "I have work to do."

"Who are you?"

Marco looked back at Danny, and opened his arms wide. His left hand was still holding the bone handle of the hunting knife.

He laughed as he started to bring the knife down.

"I am this!"

Booger's empty eyes looked at Danny again, then back down at Lina.

"I. Am. This."

Danny watched the knife fall towards Lina's chest. Fifteen minutes ago, he thought he had a plan, but that had failed. Now he simply reacted. Survival instinct kicked in. Not only for him, but, for Lina too. The table with Booger and Lina was five feet away. He hadn't played football since high school, but he dug deep for the power he once had.

Even with his legs and arms zip tied, he had to try.

His goal was to knock him off Lina with the force of his shoulder. He'd improvise what to do next, once Lina was safe and Booger was on the floor.

Danny pulled a yell from the balls of his feet and let it escape from his lungs. He stood up, and lurched towards the table. He felt his shoulder make contact with Booger's left side. Booger looked at his assailant as he lost his balance and fell onto the floor. Danny tacked him again, as he tried to get up.

"We forgot. You were the quarterback, weren't you?" said Booger as he wrestled Danny off of his back, and tossed him aside. "You forgot that we went to the police academy. Fucking dumb ass."

Booger flipped Danny onto his back, and straddled him exactly the way he'd been straddling Lina. He brought the knife above his head.

"Maybe I can see the look in your eyes first, Daniel Scott Carlson. The look I've been searching for. It won't hurt. A little pinch, and you're off to sleep."

"Booger. This is Danny. Don't. Please don't. Remember me, Booger?"

Danny saw a glimpse of life in Booger's eyes.

A faint spec of recognition.

"Booger's not home right now."

"Booger. Please, don't."

"This is Marco, motherfucker."

Danny watched as Marco brought the knife down.

He tried to resist, but the zip ties made fighting cumbersome. He bucked some more, and slammed at Booger's side and back. It was a futile effort. Booger had seventy-five pounds of muscle that Danny didn't.

"Booger. Please."

Danny felt the point of knife touch his chest.

"Just a little pinch," he heard Marco repeat. "Open your eyes Danny. Open your eyes. I want to watch."

Danny clenched his eyes shut, and waited for the sensation Booger had told him to expect.

There was no pinch.

But there was an explosion, and the weight that was on his chest fell away.

*

"Officer down. Shots fired. I need backup at the Thorson farm. And an ambulance. Two of them."

Danny opened his eyes.

Standing above him was a man he didn't recognize, but was wearing a sheriff's deputy uniform.

"Daniel Carlson?"

Danny couldn't talk, so he nodded.

"The sheriff sent me. He'll be here any minute now."

"Lina," was all he could say as he gestured with his head towards the table. "Untie her."

*

Danny watched as the ambulances were loaded with two stretchers.

One with Lina.

The other with Booger.

Both were alive.

Danny was standing on the bottom stair leading up to Booger's front porch. A paramedic was busy dabbing antiseptic on the cuts across his forehead. He had icepacks on both shoulders.

"I didn't think you got the message," Danny said to Gordy. "I thought we were both dead."

"It went to voicemail for some reason."

"How much did you get?"

"Everything."

"Dirt?"

"We'll get to the judge in the morning. I've already called him as a matter of fact. And the DA. May take a day or two, but he'll be out."

"Booger?"

Gordy looked at the ambulances as they turned on their lights and sirens and headed down the driveway.

"Don't know. I've never encountered anything like that. Sounded crazy on the message. He'll probably be referred to the psych hospital for evaluation before anything legal decision is made."

Danny's legs began to shake, and he collapsed onto the front porch.

"Deputy. Get another ambulance."

Danny put his hand up.

"No. No. Gordy. I'm fine. I just..."

A car pulled up, and turned off its lights.

The passenger door opened, and then the driver's door.

Two people walked towards Danny and Gordy.

"I called your folks."

Despite wanting to be stoic, he was a California lawyer after all, tears rushed down his face when his parents came into view.

Book 4: Winter

Rest

2012

"Winter is the time to relive the harvest. Rejoice its bounty, or despair its tainted fruit."

The Book of Lost and Forgotten Dreams

October 19, 2012

The Carlson Farm
Arvilla, ND

*

Skip adjusted the fit of his Case hat on his head, and took a sip of the black coffee he'd been nursing for the past hour.

"Cold," he said as he topped it off. "Hon?"

Sis wordlessly pushed her cup towards the carafe, and Skip topped it off for her. He preferred his coffee strong, hot, straight, and black. Sis liked hers a bit sweet so he scooped two teaspoons of sugar in hers. His coffee cup was deep red, and had, "My other car is a Case," in white letters. He had to admit that it didn't make sense being on a coffee cup, but the salesman gave it to him for free.

Skip liked free.

Sis' cup was green and had, "Nothing runs like a Deere. Except road kill," in yellow letters. The same salesman gave that to him. Just as people had an affinity to Ford or Chevy or Toyota, he was a Case-man, and would never consider owning anything green and yellow.

Not even a garden tractor.

Skip sat at the kitchen table next to his wife, and pushed the curtains to the side. He needed to widen their panorama. He looked out of the window, at the crowd growing in the central yard of the farm he'd known all of his life. He looked down at the floor, took a long, deep breath, and let it out.

Slowly.

With a slight hint of quiver.

Seeing the growing crowd had made him realize what it all meant.

He'd failed.

It was his father's farm, and was his father's before that. He was the third generation Carlson to live here. Now he wasn't sure who would own it. It would likely be owned by ten other farmers. None of which were named Carlson. When he took the farm over in 1970, he had a thousand acres to manage. Now, forty-two years later, he had more than three thousand. It was too much for one man. He had hoped Dan would take the helm, be the fourth generation, and maybe grow it to four thousand acres. Perhaps make it a father and son effort.

But that was another life that wasn't going to happen.

Skip didn't blame Dan. He knew Dan had to spread his wings. They were two different men. Apparently Dan relished the hustle and bustle of the city, palm trees, freeways, and BMW sedans – not the bucolic life of small towns, dirt roads, wheat, and F150 pickups. When he went back to California in July, he promised to come and visit.

He hadn't yet.

That was three months ago.

Skip scooted his chair closer to Sis, put his arm around her, and pulled her closer. Now they were looking out of the same window at the same people. People they'd known all of their lives who were on their farm to buy their life away from them at what they hoped would be bargain- basement prices. It was nine in the morning, and the auction was scheduled to begin at ten. The crowd was steadily growing, and already it seemed to be standing room only.

The auctioneer even had cotton candy for sale.

Farm auctions had become carnival events.

After the events of the summer, they'd decided it was time to move on. Things like what had happened weren't supposed to happen here. Serial murders happened in Los Angeles, California, not Arvilla, North Dakota. They'd known Booker all of his life. His parents were good friends. They'd known Dirk just as long and had actually doubted his innocence. Things had changed too much, too fast. The farming life was for those thirty years younger. It was time to give up the farm, and live the life they'd talked about for at least a decade.

Sis was the first to break the silence.

"So this is it."

Skip took another sip of coffee and exhaled.

"Yup. It is. So where are we going first?"

"London. I've always wanted to see Big Ben."

"London it is."

"Then Paris. I want to see the tower."

"You need to have hairy arm pits to go to Paris. You wouldn't look good with hairy armpits. I like my women clean shaven."

Sis elbowed Skip in the side.

"Someplace warm. With a beach."

"And drinks with little umbrellas."

Skip grunted, gently took his wife's face between the palms of his hands, and turned her towards his. He could tell she was on the verge of tears. After forty years of marriage, he knew she wanted to be strong and stoic, but was not having an easy time of it.

"Don't cry. Don't you worry, it will be ok. We'll still have the house. This will always be home."

"I don't know if I want it to be. It won't really be ours."

Skip felt her nod as he held her tight against his shoulder.

"Come on. Let's go say hi to everyone. I'll buy you a cotton candy."

"I want a beer."

"But it's only nine," Skip looked up at the clock above the stove. "Nine-thirty."

Sis looked up into his eyes.

"So?"

"Ok. I'll buy you a beer and cotton candy."

Sis dried her eyes against Skip's flannel shirt, laughed, and pushed back from her chair.

"I better clean up. Bekks and Erik are going to come over."

*

It was odd, but farm auctions created a party atmosphere regardless of whose farm and livelihood was being sold off to the highest bidder. Depending upon the circumstances of the sale, there were times when there was a thick fog of solemnity. For a retirement, like Skip and Sis', the auction was more like a carnival. Cars and pickups were lined up along the driveway, and on both sides of the road leading into the Carlson's farm. Everyone knew one another, and those that were in the market for farm equipment, had already scoped out what he wanted and stood next to it as if saying, "This is mine. Back-off, fuck-face."

But those words were never said, of course. There was something called North Dakota nice that prevented those words from escaping. Thinking was ok. Vocalizing was frowned upon. Instead, simple nods were exchanged in acknowledgement of the dibs one had along with a very simple, generic conversation.

"Bill."

"Jim."

"How's the wife."

"Good. Yours?"

"Just fine."

"Too bad about Skip. He loved his farm."

"Ya. He deserves to retire though. He's worked hard."

"I hear he and Sis are going to travel."

"She's always wanted to do that."

"He has to keep it slow after that heart attack scare."

"I'm sure he will."

"Ya. Skip's no dummy."

"Good looking plow."

"Ya. Gonna be a big help."

"Good for you."

"You thinking of anything?"

"Maybe the cultivator. Gonna check it out."

"Talk to you later."

"Ya. We'll talk later."

"Let's have a beer at Butch's."

"Ya. Let's do that."

October 20, 2012

The Carlson Farm
Arvilla, ND

*

It was almost four in the afternoon, and Skip was sitting at his typical spot on his usual chair at the kitchen table. The afternoon October sun was already low in the western sky, and was creating eerie shadows of bare tree limbs on the kitchen's floor and walls. Today it was still relatively light outside, a week from now when daylight savings started, it would already be getting dark. The shadows signaled that the serenity of fall with its crunchy leaves, wind breakers, and quilted flannel shirts was making way for the gale forces of winter and its snow, parkas, boots, gloves, and stocking caps.

Even though Skip was in his typical spot, he wasn't drinking his typical coffee. At sixty-seven, he'd learned that drinking anything with caffeine past noon made sleep practically impossible.

Getting old definitely sucked.

So, instead of a cup of coffee, there was an empty can of Pabst Blue Ribbon, and a cold, frosted glass in front of him.

It too was empty.

He might was well help sleep come a bit faster.

"Anyone want another?" he said to his wife, daughter, and son-in-law as he leaned over, and opened the fridge.

No one accepted the offer, but he still grabbed two cans.

He tossed one to Erik.

"It looks like you need a refill."

Erik smiled.

"Thanks, Dad."

"Bekks? Sis?" Skip asked as he held up another can of beer.

Sis shook her head as she raised the glass containing the bourbon she was drinking.

"Needed something stronger," she said. "And we're out of Everclear."

"I'm on the hard-stuff too, Dad," said Bekks as she held up her green bottle of Perrier.

"Oh. Yeah. Forgot," said Skip with a smile. "I'm gonna be a grandpa. Your grandmother drank Canadian Club when she was pregnant with me. She did mix some ice and water with it though. Smoked Virginia Slims, too. Your grandfather was a two-pack-a-day Winston man, and drank Windsor. Just so you know."

"I guess that explains things then, doesn't it Skip?"

Bekks raised her green bottle to toast her mother.

"That's enough from both of you."

There were simultaneous snaps as each man opened his can, and a solitary glug as Skip poured the beer into his mug with the Case logo on it.

"Has anyone figured out what happened yesterday?"

"Corporate farms. Had to be. From up north. Cavalier. Bottineau. Grafton. No one recognized the bidders," said Erik. "But there were a bunch. Only some of the small stuff went to the locals. Butch bought that mounted deer head, and is going hang in the bar next to the Busty Broad painting."

"I've heard the same. Had to be something corporate. No one was able to buy a thing. Outbid every time."

"Shit. I didn't want that. I wanted folks from around here to get the things they wanted. I'm gonna call the auction house, and see what they say."

The conversation was interrupted with the chime of Bekks's cellphone. After five rings, Skip chimed in.

"Gonna get that?"

October 20, 2012

Arvilla, ND

*

The house had been abandoned for years. After Old Man Eisenberner died, a few families from the air base rented it, but they were only temporary. No one had called it home in a long time. After so many years of neglect, most of the exterior paint had fallen off, and accumulated in a line of white paint chips along its foundation. The front screen door hung by one hinge, and sat lopsided in its frame. Most of its windows were broken, and the asphalt shingles were dried and curled.

Bekks turned her white Ford Explorer onto the pitted, dirt driveway, stopped, and then held on tight to the steering wheel. She wasn't sure what to do next. Her instructions were simple, "Come to Old Man Eisenberner's house." When she asked what to say if she was questioned, she was told, "Tell them it's about the auction. That will work."

Now that she'd delivered her family to the house, she was at a loss for words.

"Well, we're here."

"I'd still like to know why you brought us here," said Sis.

"All I know is that it has something about the auction. Let's go in. It's cold out here."

"Probably warmer here in the truck than it is in the old house."

"Daddy, you are becoming an old woman. You know that?"

The four walked into the old, abandoned house. The screen door came off in Skip's hands, and he set it on the ground next to the concrete steps.

"Poor old house. Everyone always thought that Old Mr. Eisenberner was mean, but he wasn't. He was a good guy. Bad rap because he was alone. He'd hate to see his home look like this."

When they walked in, the rickety front door, barely more stable than the outside screen, slammed behind them, and left another pound of paint chips on the stoop; its clamor reverberated off of the plastered walls. The previous owners, a family of five who were stationed at the base, had left the walls painted a rainbow of colors. Two ceiling fans, one in the kitchen and one in the living room, were hanging from single wires with their lopsided, broken blades covered in dust and cobwebs. Although still early in the afternoon, it was cold, and a fog quickly formed from their combined exhale.

"Someone's been in here. Recently," said Skip as he pointed to the two sets of footprints visible through the years of dust that had accumulated on the hardwood floors.

"Smells bad in here."

"The ghost of Old Mr. Eisenberner."

The house had an old musty smell. The smell of an old man in a nursing home. If you asked any kid around town, it was because the Old Man Eisenberner's ghost still haunted the house, and on Halloween there were unexplained lights flickering in the living room and kitchen.

"Happened right over there," said Skip.

"What? Old Man Eisenberner murder someone?"

Skip shook his head.

"Neil was a good guy. Liked cigars and vodka. Told great stories about the Korean War. Made incredible meat loaf."

"His name was Neil? I never knew that. It was always 'Old Man Eisenberner'."

"What happened?"

"Years ago. Before you were born. Julie lost control of her Ski-Doo. Ended up in his living room?"

"You're kidding! That really happened?"

"Yup. Right there.

Skip pointed to the front window.

"See how that window is newer than the others? Came right through there and, from what I saw, the right ski stopped a few inches from where he was sitting on his recliner. He told me he was sipping scotch, and watching Lawrence Welk when it happened. Practically had a heart attack."

"Julie?"

"Yup. Boobs and all. Too many beers. Went for a ride and picked up a bit too much speed. She fell off before it when through the wall. Landed in a snow bank, and her Ski-Doo kept going."

"Anyone hurt?"

Skip shook his head.

"Nope. Amazing. Not a scratch."

"I bet the lawyer sharks had a field day."

A voice came from the back room.

"Hey. We're not all bad."

Everyone stopped gawking at the scene of the ancient crime, and turned around; their eyes wide when they realized the source of the voice.

Except Bekks.

*

"Follow me," said Dan as he led everyone down the hallway. "I've set up a table and chairs in what I think was the master bedroom. I had the electricity turned back on, but I didn't flip any breakers for the whole house – just the master. Who knows what wires would catch fire? It's nice and warm back here tough. I brought in a space heater."

"What's going on?"

Dan ignored his mother's question, but when he looked to his father, Dan saw the look of resentment in his eyes.

A look of lingering disappointment that had grown over the years and had only grown since he left in July.

"I have a cooler of cold beer. Bourbon for you, Mom," Dan looked at his sister. "And some cold, bottled water for you. Go easy on the liquids though. Bathroom doesn't work."

Dan waved his hands at the five chairs in front of the small table.

"Sit down. Please."

Dan sat down at the single chair behind the table.

"There's an extra chair."

"Oh. That's for me," came a voice from the doorway. "I had to walk over to Butch's and use the little lady's room."

Lina walked into the room, sat down, and winked at Dan.

"I need a beer. Anyone else? Sis. Bourbon?"

Lina didn't wait for an answer. She handed Skip and Erik a beer, gave Bekks a bottle of water, and poured four fingers of bourbon into a red plastic Solo cup.

"Here you go. Bourbon neat. Right Sis?"

Sis wordlessly took the cup, but moved her eyes from her son to her bartender.

"I'll take some bourbon too," said Dan.

*

"Dad. Do you remember when I was young? What did I call driving the tractors?"

"Piloting. You called it piloting the tractors. What's this all about, Dan?"

"I was thinking. It's time. I'd like to learn to pilot if you'd teach me again."

Sis took Skip's hand in hers.

Skip looked at his wife, then back at his son.

"Do you mind telling us what's going on?"

"Too late, Dan. We sold everything in an auction yesterday. We don't own a thing," said Sis. "The farm is gone."

Dan looked shocked; he turned to his sister then to Lina.

"I know."

"Then you know there's no family farm to come back to, Daniel."

Dan's stomach knotted.

Maybe this wasn't a good idea after all. Too much time had passed. Too many scars had formed and scabbed over. His dad never called him Daniel unless he was mad. It was Dan or, when he was young, Dan-the-Man. Sometimes Danny. Right now he wanted to be Dan-the-man again.

But this wasn't anger.

Despite the mild reconciliation over the summer, his father's heart was still bruised.

"I know because I bought everything," Dan reached into his leather messenger bag and pulled out a brown manila folder. "Well, almost everything. I let some of the smaller things go. Figured we could replace a lot of that stuff. But not that funky-ass deer head. Butch can do whatever he wants with that."

Dan took a sip of his bourbon.

Sis downed hers, and held her glass out to Lina.

"Lina. I'm going to need some more, please."

*

"I formed a corporation. Carlson Farms, LLC," said Dan as he separated some of the papers from the folder.

"Why not Carpenter Farms, LLC?"

Dan felt the arrow of words pierce his stomach. He knew this was coming eventually.

Now he knew it was time to say what needed to be said.

"Mom and dad. I'm sorry. I made a mistake. Never meant to hurt you. I thought I wanted something else. I thought I was someone else. I was for a while. Thought I wanted the big life in the big city. It just took me a while to come to my senses. I realize this is home. My real home."

"Bekks. Can you take your mother and me home? I don't know what's going on here, but I don't want anything to do with it. We have things to pack."

Skip started to get up off of his chair.

"Skip. Sit down," said Sis.

"Dad," said Dan. "I'll ask again. Will you teach me how to pilot? You and I. The way it was supposed to be."

Dan looked at his mother. She was quietly wiping tears off of her cheek. His father was looking at the floor; his face was red. Dan hoped it wasn't the red of anger as the preamble to an emotional explosion.

"Dad?"

Dan watched as his father slowly looked up.

It wasn't the red of anger.

His face was wet with tears.

Skip nodded.

"I always knew you'd come back. I always knew it."

*

Dan finished explaining the details of the contract.

The farm was split in three ways: his parents, him, and Bekks. He and his father would rent Bekks's third from her as she and Erik had their own farm and couldn't handle any more land. Dan and his father would become the partners they were meant to be.

"Will you be moving into the house?"

"No Mom. You and Dad will pay the corporation $1 a year for rent. The house is yours for as long as you want it.

For as long as you need it. The corp pays all of your expenses. Everything. It's right here in the contract."

"Where will you live?"

"I bought the old Englestadt ranch. Mile down the road. We're gonna tear the house down. Rebuild it."

"We're? Who's 'we're'?"

Dan smiled. He was waiting to break this news.

"Come here," he said to Lina with a smile. "Lina and me. That's who."

Skip and Sis turned to their daughter.

"You knew about this, didn't you?"

Bekks smiled and nodded.

"Some of it. Dan asked me about the land rental part. Erik and I talked it over. Dan's right. We can't take anything more."

"Why here then? Why Old Man Eisenberner's?"

"The future site of the Law Office of Daniel Carlson. Opens next year. I'll run it part time. Farm comes first. There's one stipulation though. Something you all have to agree on otherwise the deal is off. I have a partner."

"A partner? Who?"

"The public defender. Her name is Debra Atkinson. She worked with me on Dirt's case."

Dan looked at everyone in the room.

"Lina. Go ahead. It's your show," said Dan.

Lina got up from her chair, and took two brown folders from Dan's bag.

"That is such a girlie bag, mister," she said. "We're gonna have to work on that."

"Just," Dan wiggled his fingers at Lina and smiled. "Just do what we talked about, and forget about my bag. It cost a lot of money by the way. It's Italian leather."

Lina rolled her eyes.

"Dan and I talked about another contract we want you involved with," she said as she handed one folder to Skip and Sis and the other to Bekks and Erik. "There are two tickets to St. Lucia in each of your folders."

"What's St. Lucia's? Why do we need tickets to a church?"

Dan laughed, and shook his head. He kept forgetting about whom he was dealing with. Besides venturing into Minnesota every now and then, no one in this room had ever left the state.

"St. Lucia is an island in the West Indies. We want you all to come to our wedding. Next year. February 14th. All expenses paid. Lina's folks are coming too. And Dirt. He's going to be my best man."

Dan looked at his father. He had a slight smile and he was looking out one of the broken windows facing the old school across the street.

"Dad? What's wrong?"

"Nothing. Just ready to get working, Dan-the-Man."

Dan took a pen, signed his name on the contract, and then passed it and the contract to his parents.

"Just need you to sign and date right below your names. Makes everything legal."

Skip looked at Sis.

"Both of us?"

"Both of you. We're all in this together," said Dan. "Bekks and Erik have already signed it. When Lina and I are married, I'll work up an addendum that we'll all sign. She's in this too."

Dan looked at everyone in the room, assembled the papers, and put them back into the folder.

"We're a family, after all."

October 28, 2012

Grand Fork County Psychiatric Hospital
Grand Forks, ND

*

Booker, dressed only in a hospital gown and socks, slowed his pacing somewhat as he watched the woman in a white lab coat who, in his opinion, smelled as April Fresh as a big jug of Downy. He'd paced across the room a dozen times since the woman came in. She had a guard, who wore a huge key chain that jingled incessantly, with her who carried the two chairs, set them where she pointed, then left. Booker noticed that the same man came back every ten minutes, looked through the door's window, evidently ensuring the woman was still alive, then left.

The woman hadn't said a word since she arrived. She just sat in her chair with her notepad and pen. Once in a while, she'd write something down, but most of the time, she just sat without saying a word. Without looking at him. Booker wasn't sure what he was supposed to do. All he knew was that his feet were finally getting tired as pacing on a tile floor with bare feet became very uncomfortable.

His toes hurt.

He was very curious.

He sat down on the only other chair; the one directly in front of her, crossed his legs, and kept surveying his surroundings.

He noticed that she wrote something on her notepad the moment he sat.

He was nervous.

He had to pee.

"What did you say your name was?"

"I haven't said anything. But I'm Dr. Leslie Meacham. We've met before."

"We have?"

"Yes, several times. Who am I talking to?"

"What do you mean?"

Booker looked perplexed.

He wasn't sure why this woman was asking who she was talking to if they'd met before. To him that was a stupid question. She seemed to know who he was, but he could not recollect ever meeting her.

"Who am I talking to?"

She kept asking that same question. Over and over again.

It was really getting annoying.

"Who am I talking to?"

She asked again.

"Who wants to know?"

"I do. Dr. Leslie Meacham. Remember? I just told you that. We've met before. I've introduced myself. Now, can you tell me who I am talking to?"

How many times is this bitch going to ask?

He watched as she wrote something on the notepad she kept on her lap.

"What are you writing?"

"Just taking notes. Who am I talking to?"

Fucking annoying.

Booker looked around, put his feet down on the floor, and his hands on his thighs. As if an internal switch had been flipped, his legs started to bounce the minute the pads of his feet touched the tile. It was a habit his mother detested.

"Would you sit still!" she always said. "You're shaking the entire house for Christ's sake."

The room had a hint of familiarity to it, but its exact details and the reason he was here, kept slipping away. Each and every time he felt a memory form and begin to clarify, it would evaporate into smoke and wither away until the next one started and disappeared just as rapidly. The place had the feeling of a hospital, but the gray cinderblock walls made it seem more like a prison. The guard that kept looking in the window in the door didn't help alleviate that perception as Booker thought he saw a gun when he carried in the chairs.

People in hospitals don't carry guns.

In the corner, directly above the door, was a small glass dome with a camera, and right below that was a battered clock with a broken second hand that dangled downwards at the six. There were two small windows behind him, near the top of the eight-foot ceiling, that were the dimensions of one of the blocks. The small windows let in a few rays of sunlight and allowed Booker to see the cloudless sky.

"What time is it?"

"There's a clock on the wall. Who am I talking to?"

"I don't think it's working. Can't you tell me what time it is?"

The woman relented and calmly looked at her watch.

She wrote something down again.

"Almost three in the afternoon," she said. "I told you the time. Will you tell me who am I talking to?"

The room smelled like bleach and piss at the same time. Booker didn't think that was even possible, but the people behind the doors seemed to have made it happen very effectively.

It burned his nose and tarnished the smell of the woman.

And he rather liked her smell.

There were barely any furnishings; the chair the woman was sitting on, another smaller one for him placed directly in front of her, a trashcan, and an old record player set on a rolling cart. Where her chair was adult-sized, his chair reminded him of the small, Munchkin-sized chairs from first grade. The floor was a simple black and white checkered tile that desperately needed cleaning.

"The floor," he said as he pointed. "Is really dirty."

"Jimmy Boy?"

Booker looked at her again.

Bewildered.

"Jimmy Boy? Who's that?"

Booker watched her write some more, and then cut her eyes in his direction when he asked a question.

"Why am I here?"

"You're under observation. To see if you can stand trial or not. Who wants to know? Who am I talking to? Booker? Zeke? Jimmy Boy? Marco? Malum? Clint? Someone else? What about Boots? Who am I talking to? Tell me."

*

Marco pushed the Original aside. He'd had enough of this little charade. The bitch was pissing him off. He looked up at her.

"Is Boots here, Dr. Meacham."

He saw her put down her pen.

"You tell me."

Marco looked around.

"Don't see him."

The muscles in his neck were taught, and his legs stopped bouncing to some unheard beat. His hands were still on his thighs, but instead of resting palms-down, they were balled into tight fists that flexed back and forth as fast as his legs used to bounce.

"Who am I talking to?"

"Why do you fucking care who this is?"

"Who am I talking to? A simple question."

Marco spread his arms wide and smiled.

"Why me, of course. I am this!"

She flipped a few pages backwards in her notebook, return to a blank page, wrote some more, then finally looked him in the eye.

"Marco."

"Bingo! Give the good doctor a prize."

He saw fear. Smelled it. He'd seen that look before, and smelled that bitter scent from a woman who was scared despite outward appearances.

Several women.

And liked it.

"Smells like piss and bleach in here. Fucking burns my nose. Can you do something about that? I must say you smell much better than this room. Wearing a different perfume," Marco raised his nose and sniffed the air. "Fruity. Peaches. You're not the least bit trouty this time. I take it you're done with your period. Last time. Whoa. Right in the middle of it, I'd say. You smelled like a beached walleye."

Marco picked up the bottom of his hospital gown, rubbed his nose, and then blew it as loudly and as hard as he could. A string of snot clung to the cloth, and trapezed back to his top lip.

"Please put that down."

Marco spread his legs wider. He didn't have anything on under the gown. It was against the rules to have anything but the gown and socks; they didn't want any suicides using blue jeans or shoelaces.

He wanted to see her reaction.

"Enjoying the scenery?"

Marco closed his legs when saw a guard walk up to the window, look in, then leave.

It was 3:00.

The last time the guard came by was 2:50. The guard had a pattern and was keeping to his schedule.

He spread his legs again.

"I am this," he said as he opened his arms as wide as his legs.

"What does that mean?"

"It's simple if you think about it. Give it time. You'll see soon enough. You have all of those degrees, don't you?"

Marco smiled.

"Happy? You just smiled."

"Very happy, as a matter of fact."

"How so?"

"I have ten minutes. Wait," Marco paused, and looked at the clock. "Nine. Nine minutes before the guard comes back."

Marco watched as her pen wiggled across the paper.

"Nine minutes for what?"

"To kill you. Completely doable. Believe me. I'm good at what I do."

*

The woman didn't react the way Marco wanted.

He wanted overt fear.

Not nonchalance.

But she was scared.

Inside.

"I don't think that will happen, Marco."

She clicked her pen, and put it in the pocket next to her ID badge. Then, with her free hand, Marco saw her reach down the left side of her jacket into the large, pocket of her white lab coat.

Marco looked at the clock.

He'd wasted four minutes.

Only six minutes left to get things done.

He didn't like wasting time.

He was cutting it close.

"I'm afraid you're gravely mistaken, doc."

While her one hand was busy, he noticed her eyes momentarily focus on her pocket.

It was now or never.

Despite the casualness, Marco knew she was scared. He could see the new, small drops of sweat above her eyes.

He could even smell it.

It was a scent he knew all too well and it was getting stronger.

Marco made his move.

He stood up just enough to ease his weight off of his small chair, and grabbed it by its two front legs. In one swift, powerful drive, he swung the chair around, and aimed for the good doctor's face.

He was playing baseball again.

Hadn't done that in years.

He felt like a kid again; one who could hit a homer better than any major leaguer.

Except his ball was a woman's head.

Marco saw her look up just as the chair's wooden back made contact with her face. Her cheeks fluttered as her head pivoted from the impact. He heard a dull crack, and wasn't sure if it was her skull or the chair's wooden back. Her hand fell to her side, and she dropped the two items from her pocket: a palm-sized, battery-operated stun gun, and a thumb-sized can of pepper spray still in its leather case.

Except for the clamor the clock was making, the room was now silent. Marco could hear the clock's movement reverberate in his head. He was amazed at how loud the tick-tock actually was; it seemed to grow louder with each heartbeat.

"Fuck, that thing is loud."

3:08.

Marco still had his chair dangling in his right hand by one of the legs. He tossed it upright, caught it in mid-flip, and placed it back in front of the doctor; precisely where it was before he used it as a bat. Its wooden back was still intact, so the crunch he heard was definitely her head. He was glad he didn't break the chair – he'd grown fond of the little thing. He stood still for a few seconds, and focused on the doctor; her chest moved slowly in and out. Her breathing was slow, and rhythmic – just like the clock. Just not as loud.

She was alive.

Good.

That's what he wanted.

"Can't have you slumped over though," said Marco. "Wouldn't be theatrics right now."

Marco grabbed the doctor's shoulders, and placed her upright in her chair. He put her hands on her lap, picked up her notepad that had flown to the other wall, and even smoothed her long dark, brown hair that had swung around and become stuck on the blood streaming from her nose. He even put her hand into a makeshift fist, and put her pen in-between her fingers.

3:09.

Marco smoothed his gown, sat down on his tiny chair, and pasted a fake, toothy, smile across his face. The guard would be by soon so he started his monologue.

"Why yes, doctor. That's an excellent observation. What? You want me to fuck you in the ass? Wring your little titties off your chest? Well, I don't know about that. You seem like such a sweet thing. Are you sure? We can talk about it later when you are dead. Does that sound like a plan?" Marco leaned forward a bit. "What was that? Oh. You are such a funny, naughty woman..."

Marco faked a laugh.

He was an excellent actor.

Marco continued repeating the pattern of babble, smile, laugh, babble, smile, laugh until he saw the guard peer into the window for a few seconds, and then disappear. He even slapped his leg once or twice.

Marco had ensured that everything from the guard's point of view appeared completely normal. The guard would see Marco sitting in his chair. He would see the doctor's backside sitting in her chair. He would perceive a completely normal, happy scene of a doctor and her adoring, and very attentive, jovial patient apparently telling her stories that he couldn't hear on the other side of the large metal door.

Everything was good.

The patient was laughing and talking up a storm; the doctor seemed perfectly fine.

Check.

What the guard couldn't see, from Marco's perspective, was the doctor's bleeding nose; its constant flow onto her white coat that was making quite a mess and had even made a small, red pool on the black tile by her left foot. He also couldn't tell that the left side of her face was turning blue, and beginning to swell.

Marco watched the window out of the corner of his eye and saw the guard look in and pause. He held his breath and fingered the stun gun he took from the doctor when she dropped it.

He was prepared.

Finally, the face left the window.

Marco looked at the clock and smiled.

He was right on schedule.

3:11.

He had nine minutes.

Time really did fly when he was enjoying himself.

Just like the old days in the Opera House Lab.

*

Marco sat face-forward on the doctor's lap. He straddled the chair and her legs.

He slapped her face: left, right, left, right, left, right.

"Doc. Hey doc. Wake up."

3:12

The doctor's eyes flickered open, and she tried to wrestle Marco off of her lap.

"No. No. No. There's no time for that."

He felt her reach for her pocket again.

"Those aren't in there anymore, I'm afraid."

Marco moved closer to his prey.

His nose touching hers.

"You smell. You smell like," he took another deep breath. "I thought it was peaches, but its roses. And lilacs. Is that Mystique? It's nice. My favorite perfume. You shouldn't have worn it just for me."

Marco licked the right side of her face. He kept his tongue flat and moved it up slowly from her chin to her hairline.

"I can taste the roses."

Marco took his finger, wetted it in the blood dripping down her nose, and brought it to his mouth. He wiped it against his lips as if he were putting on lipstick, then ran his tongue back and forth to wipe off the blood.

"Sweet. Coppery."

He licked her again.

"Dying isn't so bad. Really, it's not," he said as he nuzzled her neck, and bit her hard enough to make her flinch. "Just like that. A little pinch of pain, then. Then, nothing. Body goes into shock. You don't feel a thing. I've made it happen a lot. Watched it happen. Most of the time it's like falling asleep."

The doctor tried to move her head away.

She squealed as Marco slapped her back in his direction.

"Look at me," he said as he gripped her face in both hands and squeezed her cheeks tight enough to make her pucker.

3:14.

"I've made it happen more often than you know. Death. More than anyone will know I suppose. Dozens. Probably much more. I've lost track. Doesn't matter. They're dead. What difference does it make?"

Marco looked at the tools he had at his disposal: a small can of pepper spray, a stun gun, a pad of paper, and a pen.

"Fuck. None of this shit is going to be of much help. I'm not MacGyver."

He adjusted his position on her lap.

"Guess I'll have to do it the hard way. The old fashioned way. I'm sorry, but this might hurt a bit."

Marco licked her again. This time on each of her eyelids. Then he kissed her where he planned on placing each of his thumbs. He could feel the beat of her heart on his lips.

"I can feel your heart. You're scared. Don't be. But that's where I'll start," he lightly pressed her throat with his thumbs. "Right there. Right where I kissed you. Ready?"

Marco took his hands and placed them around her neck. Each thumb was directly on top of her windpipe as that was what he needed to crush.

Right were he kissed.

He began to squeeze.

Marco brought her close.

"Don't struggle. Just let it happen. I am this. I am death."

The doctor began to thrash under his weight, but Marco pulled her tight against his body, wrapped his legs around her and the chair, pressed his thumbs deeper into her throat, and squeezed his hands tighter.

Hers was such a small throat too.

He could wrap his fingers together on the back of her head. He could feel the tiny neck bones on her spine.

He pushed them towards his thumbs.

Her free right hand beat against his back. At first with rhythmic force. Then, slowly, the beats faded to mere taps. Then, finally, stopped as her arm fell lifeless to her side.

Marco kept pressing until he felt the telltale snap under his thumbs.

3:18.

Time of death.

Marco let her body slump to the side, and kissed each of her eyes as he dismounted. He took the can of pepper spray out of its leather case, made sure the stun gun was charged and ready, and waited by the door. The guard would be by in less than a minute. He'd look through the window, see the poor doctor slumped over, notice that her patient was nowhere to be seen, maybe even see some blood, and come in to investigate.

*

Marco stood with his back against the wall; he tried to make himself as flat as humanly possible. When the guard came in, the door would swing open, and the guard would have to walk right past him. If the guard were more interested in finding out why the doctor was slumped in her chair, and head in her direction first, then everything would be fine. If the guard had his hackles raised, and decided to poke his head into look around the room before entering, he'd see Marco then his plan would have to change.

Basically, he'd be fucked.

*

Ray Youngman hated his job.

It was boring. It was the same thing day in and day out. Carry a chair here. Carry two chairs there. Look in this window. Look in that window. Is anyone dead? No. Move on to the next door. Is anyone dead? No. Move on. Fifty more doors to go.

He actually wished that one day he'd come across someone who was dead. Or dying. Just to get a bit of excitement. Then, maybe, he'd actually be able to unholster his gun for once and actually shoot someone. He always thought that shooting one of the whack-jobs here would actually help society out.

"Like that's gonna fuckin' happen any time soon," he said as he scratched his balls.

He also hated the smell of the place; it always smelled of piss and bleach. He didn't know how it could be possible, but it was. After a while, even his clothes smelled like it. Except for Doc Meacham. Today, she smelled especially sweet.

And her door was coming up next.

Ray didn't wish for her to be dead.

She smelled too good.

But the guy she was with was a total nut-job. He's the one who cut up those college girls, fed them to some pigs, and framed his friend.

He even heard that they had to kill all of the guy's pigs.

What a fuck-wad.

It was in all of the papers, and reporters still came by and tried to bribe him to take a picture of the most famous whack-job Grand Forks County had ever given birth to.

Someday, he'd take them up on it.

But for now, he had to check on Doctor Meacham.

*

Marco could tell the guard was getting closer as the telltale sound of his keys was growing louder. The small gap between the door and the floor carried sound into the room, as the guard grew closer.

Marco looked at the clock.

3:20

The jingling stopped.

Marco could even hear the man's breathing and whisper as he peered through the window.

"What the fuck?"

Marco heard the key as it was pushed into the door's lock, turn, and then disengage the deadbolt.

Marco fingered the trigger on the stun gun, and held his breath.

3:21.

*

Ray looked through the window into the room where Doctor Meacham was working.

"What the fuck?"

The whack-job wasn't in his chair, and from what he could tell from his vantage point behind the door, the doctor was slumped forward in hers, and her arms where dangling at her sides. He could even see a pool of blood seeping from a black tile into one of the white tiles.

Now he'd have a floor to clean too.

"Fuck this shit," he said as he opened the door and unsnapped the leather strap holding his gun into its holster.

Ray moved half of his foot into the room and stopped.

He could hear breathing, and he knew it wasn't his.

Ray looked up at the clock in the corner of the room next to the camera encased in the glass dome. The camera hadn't worked for years, but it was the movement in the reflection of the small glass case that caught his eye.

Mister Whack-job was standing next to the door.

Ray pulled his gun from his holster, turned the safety off, held the gun at ready, and walked in.

*

Marco saw the guard's foot glide past the tile threshold then stop.

"Fuck!" thought Marco.

He looked around to see if there was any sign he'd left to give him away. Any reflection anywhere that hat was giving him away.

There was nothing.

3:22.

Marco saw movement again as both feet moved past the threshold. Then a shoulder. Then an elbow. The guard was coming in after all. At least enough of him to use the stun gun on. Marco brought his hand up, put his finger on the trigger, and eased his hand and the gun's probes towards the guard's shoulder.

*

Ray had never encountered anything like this before. His training hadn't covered: "What to do when a Whack-Job kills a doctor and is lying in ambush by the door you are going to walk though."

Or maybe he missed the day that was covered.

There was no one else he could call for back up. Budget cuts only allowed for one security guard on this floor during this shift.

It was all his.

And it was his boring-ass job.

Ray looked up at the dome again. Whack-job was still standing next to the door.

No more than two feet away.

It was now or nothing.

Instead of walking in straight, Ray moved his body in the direction that the door swung open – away from the wall where Whack-job was standing. Once in the room, Ray pivoted on the heels of his black boots, and brought his gun up level to where the reflection had shown Whack-job to be.

*

Marco wasn't prepared for the guard to move the way he did. Instead of walking in straight, he veered away from where Marco was standing.

Maybe the guy was smarter than Marco gave him credit for. It was as if the guy knew exactly where he was.

It wasn't a huge distance, but enough to throw his balance off as he lunged for the guard's shoulder.

Marco was off by one-half of a step and as he tried to regain his aim and stance, he heard two explosions and a bolt of lightning strike his right shoulder. The momentum of the concussion threw Marco back against the concrete block wall; he felt himself slide down towards the floor.

Stunned.

Not from an electrical current, but from a bullet.

His back was wet. He felt as if his shoulder was on fire, but he still held the stun gun in his left hand.

*

Ray saw Whack-job lunge for him, and even had time to recognize what he held in his hand: a company-issued stun gun. He knew how that particular model worked and knew that if it's two metal prongs made any contact anywhere on his body, he could kiss his ass good-bye.

Ray pulled the trigger.

Twice.

One bullet missed, but one found a home in Whack-job's right shoulder. He watched as the man slid down the wall leaving a path of blood behind him.

"Fuck, more to clean."

"Don't move," said Ray as he took aim again.

Whack-job started to work his way up the wall, smearing more blood in the opposite direction. He held the stun gun out in his left hand.

"Don't move."

Whack-job lunged towards him and he could hear the clicking of the stun gun as the electrical current pulsed between the two metal probes.

Ray pulled his trigger again.

*

Booker was back.

He always came forward when things got bad – when things looked like they were getting out of control. Everyone else could be such chicken shits. Even Marco despite all of his macho talk.

Like now.

As soon as he felt the heat of the bullet enter his abdomen, Marco retreated. Now it was his mess to clean up. But, he didn't think there'd be much left. Booker also realized that he'd been lying all of this time.

What he and the others had told all of those women was completely wrong.

It did hurt after all.

Dying.

It was more than just a little pinch, and then falling off to sleep.

Booker started laughing.

He choked on blood and coughed.

Red spray flew up, and rained back on his face as he rolled onto his back.

His head lolled to the side, and his eyes focused on the glass dome over the camera.

He saw his reflection.

"That's how you knew," he said as blood spurted from his mouth. "That's how you knew we were there."

Booker squinted as he looked at the dome again.

He tried to concentrate, but it was hard. His body felt as if it was on fire, but it was calming as the pain transitioned to numbness. The images in front of him were losing focus.

The curve of its shape of the camera's dome caused his reflection to be multiplied and bent.

He counted six images.

Six skewed images of himself.

Marco, Malum, Zeke, Jimmy Boy, and Clint looked back at him.

"I am this," he whispered.

He liked that line.

Something Boots always said.

"I am this."

He looked at the clock, and closed his eyes.

3:26.

Time of death.

October 31, 2012

Larimore Cemetery
Larimore, ND

*

Dan held Lina's hand as they stood next to the fresh grave. The sun was kissing the horizon and the three friends had come to the site to say their last farewells to their childhood friend before the day's sun set. They wanted private time with their friend – away from the scrutiny of a priest or photographer. It was time that no one else could ever understand or even comprehend why they would come in the first place. The sod the groundskeeper had laid over the grave was still wet in the center but was curling up at some of the edges that had prematurely dried. Dan pressed down an end down into the soil and tried to make it stick, but as soon as he moved his foot, the sod rolled back up. Booger deserved a clean grave. He felt a tear tickle his eye, and used his shoulder to sop it up before it drizzled down his cheek.

He didn't want anyone to see what he'd done. It wasn't a tear for the Booger at the end of his life. It was a tear for the Booger he'd grown up with.

"I saw that. It's ok, you know. He was your friend," whispered Lina. "We all loved Boog."

Dan felt her tighten her grasp on his hand. He shrugged, and swallowed the peach pit that was stuck in his throat.

They had been at the service earlier that day. Besides Dirt, the priest, and a photographer from the *Herald*, he and Lina were the only ones there. No one dare come to the funeral of a murderer. No one dared be seen in a picture. The person they knew as Booger was dressed in a blue, pin-stripe suit in the casket that was now encased in a concrete vault six feet below them. Before they closed the casket, Dan and Dirt slid a memento under Booger's stiff arm. Dan put in the baseball cap that Booger had given him as a birthday present. Dirt put in an old guitar string and a pick.

Dan, for one, was trying to remember him exactly that way – as Booger, the childhood friend. The person who killed all of those women, the person who almost killed him and Lina, was not Booger. In the end he was a conglomeration of people – of personalities – bad ones. Evil ones for the most part. Those others not only killed the women, but killed Booger in the process. The real Booger had probably died years ago.

"We had some good times."

"We did. Got into some trouble too," said Dirt.

Dan could tell that Dirt was having trouble maintaining his composure too, and tried to lighten the group's mood.

"Remember when he brought that M80 to the sand pit?"

"Yeah! Almost blew my fucking arm off."

"That was all on you. You should have just left it alone. But no. You had to go all Army on us and show us how you were gonna be an Army Ranger and throw grenades at bad guys one day."

"Wasn't one of my most intelligent moments in life. I still have the burn marks," said Dirt as he rolled up his sleeve and exposed the disfigured skin. "See?"

"Shit man. Still hurt?"

"Not that much. When it gets cold I can feel it. Other than that, no biggie. The ones on my back are much worse."

No one commented on Dirt's last statement, as they all knew where the other burn marks came from.

"I remember Dad put bag balm on it after hitting me across the back of my head, yelling at me for an hour, and telling me how much of a waste of human flesh I was. Probably should have gone to the doctor, but that woman figured it was penance for my evil soul, and wouldn't let him."

"Don't know how you did it, Dirt. Growing up like that."

Dan noticed Dirt's face change, realized he brought up a touchy subject, and quickly brought the conversation back to the day of the sand pit.

"Sorry."

Dirt shrugged his shoulders and smiled a very faint smile that was typical Dirt. Not many people knew what was going on inside of his head.

"You brought a pack of your dad's cigarettes," said Dan.

"His Camels. Unfiltered menthols. The only thing he'd smoke. We all turned green when we lit up. I don't think you even inhaled. You wuss," Dirt said as he nodded. "And, if I remember, you brought tequila."

"My throat clenched up. Couldn't bring myself to take a breath. I had fur on my tongue for days. And it was my dad's bottle of Patron, not just tequila."

"You and Booger puked your guts out."

Dan looked back at Dirt with wide eyes.

"So did you! You blew chunks right alongside of us. Corn and all."

"Oh. That's just gross, you guys. Too much information."

"I couldn't eat for days after that," said Dan. "Mom and Dad thought I had the flu."

"Yeah. Right. Their little boy wonder would *never* be drunk. *No. Never*," said Dirt with a large dose of sarcasm.

"He hit on me after you left for California, you know."

"Who? Dirt?"

"No Booger!"

"Booger hit on you?"

Lina nodded and smiled.

"He was so cute. Didn't know what to say. Kept looking down at his shoes."

"What did you say to him?"

"Told him that I was a lesbian."

Dan and Dirt both roared in laughter.

"And what did he say? How did he take it?"

Lina's smile spread further across her face so far her eyes were mere slits.

"He gave me one of those golden retriever looks. You know. The kind with the cocked head and lost eyes. Then he said, 'Does that mean you don't want to go out with me?'"

"That's so mean!"

"I thought for sure you were going to come back with your tail tucked between your legs. I didn't know it would take so long for you to come to your senses."

"My tail isn't tucked between my legs."

"Bullpucky."

"Sun's down. Wow, look at that moon," interrupted Dirt. "It's fucking huge."

The three friends looked up at the full moon's ghost that was just beginning to show itself. Dan still held Lina's hand but put his right arm over Dirt's shoulder.

"Booger always loved the moon."

He saw Dirt slowly nod, then felt Lina shiver.

"You cold?"

"Yes. All of the sudden. A breeze just wrapped around me. Cold. It's the last day of October what can I say."

"It's Halloween and were in a cemetery. How stupid is that?"

Dan let go of Lina's hand and pulled her closer to his side.

"I felt it too," said Dirt. "But please don't pull me in any closer. I don't swing that way."

"That's so weird. I didn't feel anything."

Dan looked over at the tall grasses at the edge of the cemetery, up at the trees, and then crunched his eyebrows.

"What's wrong?" asked Lina.

"Do you hear that?"

"Hear what?" asked both Dirt and Lina simultaneously.

"Exactly. Everything went quiet. The birds. The frogs. Everything. They were all making quite a ruckus a few seconds ago."

Another breeze whipped around their legs.

"You had to have felt that," said Lina.

"That one. Yes."

"Do you smell that?"

Dan and Lina put their noses into the air and sniffed.

"Old Spice. It smells like Old Spice."

"That's what I thought too. Booger used that in the basement. You know. To hide the smells."

Another breeze wove itself between the trees and within the cusps of the granite headstones; Dan heard a man's voice.

"I am this."

"Did you guys hear that? I could have sworn..."

Dan paused, looked into the forest of granite, and shook his head. Confused.

"I am this."

"Booger?" asked Dan. "That you?"

"Don't be ridiculous, Dan," said Lina as she hit his shoulder with her fist.

"Yeah. Quit fuckin' around, Dan. Not funny, man."

Dan felt goose bumps travel up his spine, over his neck, and down both arms as the chill engulfed him. He didn't care what his friends thought but he was being completely serious. He knew that voice. Recognized its pattern. His old friend, and perhaps what he became, was here.

"There's the cold again. And the Old Spice."

"I am this," repeated the wind. "I am this I am this I am this I am this I am this I am this I am this."

October 31, 2012

Butch's Bar
Arvilla, ND

*

Dirt, Danny, and Lina sat in the corner booth at Butches. None of the three had anything in front of them except club soda.

"So you two are really gonna buy this place?

Danny and Lina looked at one another.

"How did you hear?

"We haven't told anyone," added Lina.

"You forget. Butch is my boss and he can't shut up after a couple rum and Cokes. So does this mean you'll be my bosses?"

"Guess so," said Lina. "We'll have to talk about how much you charge for your band. A bit pricey."

"But I'm famous now. I could charge double if I wanted to. People just want to look at me and point."

"But Dirt, *everyone* looks at you and points. Even those who don't know what you've been through."

Dirt gave her the finger.

"I talked to the therapist who was evaluating Booger for trial. She said he suffered from multiple personality disorder. He would have never stood trial."

"Is that why you said he kept telling you to call him Marco?"

Danny nodded.

"Besides himself, there were five that she talked to: Marco, Malum, Jimmy Boy, Clint, and Zeke."

"She actually talked to them?"

"Yes. She never knew which one would talk until he came forward. They each had very distinct personalities. She said she liked Jimmy Boy the best. He was cute. Always asked for his Twins baseball cap, and wanted to keep things clean."

"That doesn't sound like Booger at all. He could be a slob."

The three laughed.

"I want a beer. Or something stronger."

"I could use something too."

"Dirt? Want a beer? Dan? A cosmo?"

"Yes. That would taste wonderful."

"Goose?"

"Only the best for my California man."

Danny nodded as Lina went up to the bar, and ordered their drinks.

"She said there was another."

"Another what?"

"Personality. One that everyone talked about, but never came through. They all seemed to admire him."

"She say why?"

"Probably because he wasn't fully formed. Wasn't ready. She said every personality is different. Different timing. Different mannerisms."

"Did he have a name?"

"Here you go, gents," said Lina as she put two beers and a martini glass on the table and sat down.

"Even have martini glasses now, Dirt. We're gonna be cookin' with gas," said Danny as he sipped his cosmo. "Oh. That tastes good."

"Danny told me the doc said Booger had another personality that wasn't ready to 'come out'."

"What was his name?" asked Dirt.

"Boots. They always called him Boots."

Book 5: Epilogue

JOHN P. GOETZ

2013

"The grain is stored, the tractors are parked. Yet work is never done. It's time to prepare for the toil, pain, and sorrow the next year foretells."

The Book of Lost and Forgotten Dreams

February 2, 2013

Kinnear Farm
Arvilla, ND

*

Maggie Johnson was Trude's nurse since she became a patient in the home hospice program six weeks ago. Trude was waiting for death to take her. A stroke and lung cancer that metastasized throughout her body, was putting a period at the end of her life's sentence.

She was terminal.

"It can be any time now, Dirk. I'll be back tomorrow at the same time to put on a new bag of saline and morphine. Just call if you need me, and I'll be right here."

She looked solemn, and tried to make sure Dirt knew she cared about his mother.

She didn't know their complete history.

Maggie didn't know what kind of royal bitch she was keeping alive with her nursing skills.

"Sounds good, Maggie. I'll head back in there. Keep an eye on my mama."

Maggie opened the door to her car, sat down, and started it. This time of year, everyone let cars warm up a bit before putting them into gear.

Just a habit.

"She's in and out of consciousness. Give her more morphine if you think she's in pain. Just press the button on the pump."

Dirt waved as he watched her drive through the canopy of lilacs covering the driveway. In the spring and summer, the lilacs were green with hundreds of clumps of light purple flowers that scented the entire farmyard. In the winter, the lilacs bushes provided a skeletal canopy of brown sticks that didn't smell like anything.

*

Dirt pulled a chair from the kitchen, and sat next to the woman he'd referred to as "that woman in the house" for so many years. He held back the bile that crawled up his throat after telling Maggie he'd, "keep an eye on mama."

Like hell he would.

She'd caused so much pain.

There was too much history to ever forgive her.

Too many scars.

Too many burns.

Dirt reached over to the nightstand next to the hospital bed the hospice program delivered, and almost toppled the three red, plastic bottles of Mystique sitting between two novels that had been there for decades and were probably never opened. Two bottles were completely empty. One was half-full. He could smell the perfume from where he sat.

It made his stomach turn.

He opened the drawer and reached in.

They were still in there. Her last pack of Virginia Slims. There was one cigarette left.

Dirt popped it into his mouth, flicked the lighter, and lit it. He inhaled as deeply as his lungs would allow. It tasted wonderful, and even gave him a slight buzz. He didn't smoke too often. He preferred Camels when he did. Had some Silly Weed every now and then, but never in public.

Only in his Airstream.

When the tip of the cigarette was hot and glowing, he pushed her head to the side, pushed down the collar of her favorite nightgown, and moved her hair. He brought the cigarette closer, and watched her react to the heat. There were four other marks in the same area he'd put there over the last couple of days.

No one would notice.

He sucked in again to make the tip red-hot, then placed it on her neck directly above her hairline.

Even this close to death, and as weak as she was, her hands clenched into fists. The smell of burning flesh and hair filled the room.

"How does that feel?"

Dirt looked at the morphine pump next to the bed. The IV bag was full.

"Maggie said I could give you as much morphine as you needed. Want some? Does it hurt?"

Trude blinked.

Dirt perceived a very weak nod.

"No. You don't deserve a single drop."

Dirt watched her eyes.

"What? Are you wondering what's going on? Why? I am this! You made me. Like it? I. Am. This. You fucking bitch."

Dirt wanted to scream in her ears. He wanted her soul to hear his anger and rage.

"An evil son. You always called me that. I guess if you wish for something long enough, it eventually comes true. What do you think the bible says about that? Huh, Trude? Gertrude? Mommy?"

Dirt poked her chest after each name he called her.

"Cancer has eaten you up, hasn't it? Can't call you a fat bitch any more. You are as skinny as I am."

Dirt pulled at her nightgown.

"Gonna finally bury you in this. This fucking ugly thing you've worn all of your worthless life. I'll feed your slippers to the pigs too."

Dirt saw her eyes slowly move towards the stack of bibles against the wall.

"Do you see your bibles? I never knew how many you had, Trude. But you had a lot. They're all here. I gathered them from around the house. I even weighed all of them."

Dirt yanked Trude's head to the side so she could see all six stacks of bibles against the wall. Her eyes were only slits. He was sure that even though her brain was turning to pudding, she understood what he was saying.

"I weighed all of them. That's almost two-hundred pounds of praise the lord you're looking at there."

*

Dirt put a bath towel over his mother's chest, tucked it below her chin like a bib, and then pulled it straight down to her knees.

"I don't want someone to find sawdust or anything. Don't want you to get a sliver either. This is for you too," he said as he placed a rectangular piece of plywood over the towel.

Dirt looked under the piece of wood to make sure it was properly placed and not pinching any IV lines. There couldn't be anything awry for the nurse to find.

"You always shamed me with your bibles, Trude. Now you can die with them."

Dirt began stacking the bibles onto the wooden platform he placed on his mother's chest. He counted off each one as he added it.

"One. Two. Three…"

He watched her breathing when he reached forty.

It was becoming labored.

"Having trouble breathing Trude? What passage would help you? How about Psalm 34:18. Do you know that one?"

There was no response.

"You don't know it? Let me refresh your memory. Psalm 34:18. *The Lord is near to the brokenhearted and saves the crushed spirit.*"

Dirt stacked another five bibles onto her chest, then pushed her eyelids open with his thumbs.

"I think that is very appropriate don't you?"

*

She stopped breathing at seventy-five bibles, but Dirt continued until ninety just to make sure. As he unassembled the bible stand on her chest, he picked up his phone and dialed her nurse.

She answered on the second ring.

"Dirk?"

Dirt tried to convince his voice to crack before he started talking. He wanted to sound upset, but still be careful not to over-do anything.

"Maggie."

Dirt paused to take another loud breath.

"Yes, Dirk. It's Maggie. What's wrong?"

"Maggie," he said as he paused for effect. "I think Mom is dead. I don't think she's breathing. What do I do? I'm scared."

Dirt took a few deep breathes and sniffled.

"Sorry Maggie. I knew it was coming. I guess I wasn't as prepared as I thought."

"I'll be right there. I'm so sorry, Dirk. But she was in a lot of pain."

Dirt hung up the phone, and set it on the nightstand next to the red bottles. Over the years, Dirt had become an excellent actor.

"I certainly hope she was," he said as he continued unloading the bibles. "I certainly hope she was."

*

When all of the bibles were out of sight, the platform was off, and the towel was put back in the bathroom, Dirt came back to the chair. He leaned back, pushed it onto its two rear legs, and put his feet on top of her chest. He scratched one of the zits on his nose, drew blood, and wiped his finger on her nightgown. He looked at his shoes, his boots, resting on her chest.

Boots.

They were big.

Size twelves.

He hadn't been called that in a while.

Boots.

Booger came up with it years ago.

"Christ man, you have some big ass feet."

"They get in the way."

"That's your new name from now on."

"What is?"

"Boots."

Dirt smiled.

He had to admit, Boots was a lot better than Dirt.

ACKNOWLEDGMENTS

I dedicated *Dirt* to Arvilla. Arvilla, as you have read, isn't a person, but a town, my hometown. Its locale is exactly as I described – as is its population. It was a wonderful place to grow up. Just as *Dirt* has special characters, there are a few characters from Arvilla, who will always hold a special place in my heart. Growing up, Bob "Bumps" Baumgartner owned the one bar in Arvilla called, "Bumps Bar." Yes, it was really missing the apostrophe. Bumps was a special man with his own foibles, but he was a truly wonderful person. Bumps taught me a lot about life. I will never forget him, and I miss him to this day. You can read more about him here:

http://chesfilms.com/2014/12/05/what-do-stories-mean-to-you-john-p-goetz/

Several other people in and around Arvilla are just as special. Some are making heaven a happier place because they have been given their wings. Every single one of them is likely enjoying a beer or a glass of Windsor as I write this: Dad, Gordy, Bob M., Margaret, Julie, Jr., Bob B., Sis, and Pete H. These are just a few of the souls that helped me along the way. As for the good people still alive and well in Arvilla, and still regulars at The Hitching Post Saloon? There are way too many to thank, but all of you influenced me in one way or another. I thank you all for that. I hope to see you all again soon at The Hitching Post. Ruth and Dennis? Please make sure you have at least two martini glasses ready. And Goose, of course.

I want to provide special thanks to my good friend, who is now an attorney, Cindy Thompson English. Cindy provided me valuable insight about the life of an attorney, what it's like to be in a law firm, and what the law school experience was like. I definitely took liberties with Daniel's life as a lawyer. Anything that is incorrect, is totally on my shoulders. Cindy and her husband Loren are "lifer" friends. They are friends that no matter how far away you live from one another, and how long it's been since you've seen each another, are always there when needed.

Another very good friend, Jerry Seevers, answered all of my questions about law enforcement, and the life an officer lives. After his twenty-eight year career, he knows a lot. Believe me. He and his wife Jil are more of those lifetime friends that will always be connected no matter where our families live.

Gregg Gibbs provided valuable information about the anatomy of a crime scene, how they are managed, and even told some amazing stories about incredibly stupid criminals.

ALZHEIMER'S DISEASE

Many of you who know me, have read my books, and have followed my blog, know that Alzheimer's has affected my family in many ways. My grandfather, Peter, died in 1986 from the disease. In 2007, my mother was diagnosed, and as of this writing, is in Stage 6C. She lives in a memory care unit in Fargo, ND and I talk to hear each weekend. I'm blessed that she still knows me, and recognizes my voice.

"Hi Mom! Do you know who this is?"

"My baby."

My mother, Helen, as many of you know, is a beacon of light and an important part of my life. She has one of those North Dakota nicknames. Most know her only as Squirt. Many don't know her real name. You can read about her, and also learn more about Alzheimer's Disease on my blog at www.johnpgoetz.com.

When I first started outlining *Dirt*, I held a silent auction to raise awareness of the disease, and to benefit the

Alzheimer's Association of Minnesota and North Dakota. One of the items on the auction block was a cameo part in *Dirt*. The person who won the bid that evening was Debra Atkinson. You'll recognize her as the over-worked defense attorney who was assigned to Dirt's case. She ultimately helped Danny see the light, and come to the realization that the big city, big lawyer life wasn't really what he was cut out for. It was fun creating this character. My favorite line of hers is when she's talking to Danny about leaving North Dakota...

"You do look like someone from California, don't you? All tan and everything. Expensive jeans. French cuffs. I've heard about you west coast types."

"Grew up here though."

"Doesn't matter. Once you leave, some of it fades away, and never comes back."

"It?"

"Can't describe it. Just something we have. A shine."

"Never thought I shined."

"That was your problem."

I hope I made the "character" of Debra as powerful and unselfish as the "real-life" version is.

ABOUT THE AUTHOR

Award Winning Author John P. Goetz: Crafter of Intrigue, Master of Storytelling.

John P. Goetz is a driven writer, crafting compelling stories that grab a reader's attention with intense, ingenious plots, and clever characters.

The disparate worlds of John P. Goetz collide in stories that are rife with realism, authority, controversy, and adventure. Audaciously original novels spotlight the author's pervasive curiosity and his artistic eye for fascinating twists and turns that delight and captivate readers. You will be frightened. You will be moved. You will also be teased, surprised, and horrified. And, after reading just one John P. Goetz book, you will become a fan for life.

John lives in Golden Valley, MN.

Follow John P. Goetz on Twitter @JohnPGoetz. Look for John's postings to his blog and for updates about his new books at johnpgoetz.com. You can also follow him on Facebook at facebook.com/jpgoetz.

PRAISE FOR JOHN P. GOETZ' AWARD WINNING NOVEL, "DOORWAY TO YOUR DREAMS"

"A thriller with a touch of the supernatural and a rock-solid pace."

Kirkus Reviews

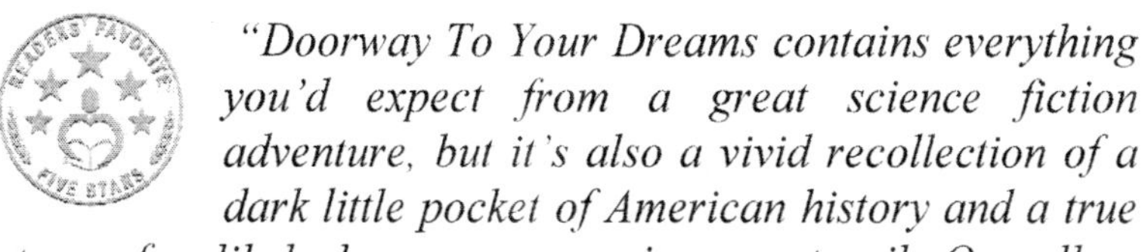

"Doorway To Your Dreams contains everything you'd expect from a great science fiction adventure, but it's also a vivid recollection of a dark little pocket of American history and a true story of unlikely heroes overcoming great evil. Overall, a recommended read for action, wartime and sci-fi fans."

K.C. Finn, Readers' Favorite

"The book is definitely a must-read for all those who enjoy action, war and thrillers. With its three-dimensional characters and action, this story has an esoteric vibe that grabs the attention of readers and keep them glued to the pages."

Mamta Madhavan, Readers' Favorite

"This complex and harrowing thriller is thought-provoking and, ultimately, very entertaining. Doorway to Your Dreams is highly recommended."

Jack Magnus, Readers' Favorite

"If you like your fictional warfare to be gritty and graphically violent, Doorway to your Dreams by John P. Goetz contains enough scenes that will keep you teetering on the edge of your seat, but not all of its battles take place on solid ground and in the here and now. The story matches outer struggles with groundbreaking inner exploration. One aspect that sets the book apart is some truly top-notch characterization. While the hero is portrayed as a multi-faceted individual who is easy to root for, readers will also gain insight into some of the events and factors that shaped the story's villains and, ultimately, the darkest corners of the human psyche. A well told story."

Carine Engelbrecht, Readers' Favorite

Available now in softcover and ebook.

Enjoy A Sneak Peek from *Doorway to Your Dreams*
By John P. Goetz
Available now in softcover and ebook.

Vinh Long, South Vietnam

July, 1967

*

If given five days of R&R, most men stationed at an army helicopter base and mobile hospital in the middle of Vietnam would eagerly forgo a month's salary and their left nut for a seat on the next sixty mile trek to Saigon—even if that seat was on a rickety, splintered cart pulled by a pair of yak, guided by a blind rice farmer named Ving. Their goal would be to not only get away from the aromatics and sights of war, but also to get drunk, fuck whatever had two legs, sober up, and do it all over again. If things were really bad, the legs were optional.

Most would.

But not Spooncake.

Helicopter pilot Tim "Spooncake" McAllister preferred the near-quiet solitude of his small plot of sand on the banks of the Mekong to the cacophony of thought-noise and intrusive color spikes he'd be subjected to in the crowds and bustle of Saigon.

Spooncake was heading to his beach fully equipped for the day. He carried what the camp cooks concocted and called a lunch wrapped in his beach towel. Five amber bottles of warm beer were securely nestled in the pockets of his flight jacket. In his left hand was a bottle of gin, and in his right was a tattered lounge chair. The camp's mascot, a black and brown shepherd mix named Dinner, bumbled a dozen feet ahead of him through the overgrown elephant grass, joyously sniffing everything. The dog had, after all, been to their solitary campsite dozens of times before with Spooncake and knew the way. As always, a spike of happy, white light bounded above the dog's head.

Spooncake jealously relished the quiet serenity of white.

Dinner wasn't *his* dog. He was the camp mutt who just happened to shadow Spooncake's every move. It was a one-way adoption that Spooncake had just learned to accept. Legend has it that some anonymous lieutenant rescued the dog from the local butcher two years ago. He bought him right off of the chopping block for five bucks and, until now, Dinner had meandered around the camp begging food from whoever would spare a scrap. The name started as a joke, and stuck. Somehow, for some reason, Dinner found Spooncake irresistible. The dog escorted him to his chopper each day and napped under the fuel tanks until his rotors stopped turning. When he wasn't flying, the dog was never more than three feet away at any given moment. If anyone wanted to know where Spooncake was, all they had to do is look for Dinner.

Spooncake could smell the stench of his approaching salvation and quickened his pace in anticipation of his imminent relaxation. As he crested the small hill, the thought-noise from camp a little more than a mile away in Vinh Long, diminished from a roar to a mere buzz, and he exhaled a long sigh of relief; the quiet already felt good. By the time he reached his destination, the noise created by the hundreds of men and women at the base would taper to a slight, yet manageable, hum. A sound he could easily sleep through with a bit of help from the bottle of gin he carried in his left hand. Even though his grandfather had taught him how to control the volume of the thoughts travelling into his brain, when combined with the chaos and emotion of war, the thought-noise worked its way through regardless of what he did to lock it away.

The colors he saw were different; they never went away. Unlike the thought-noise, the colors, thankfully, were silent and relatively unobtrusive. He turned back towards camp and saw hundreds of colored spears stretch into the cloudless, cyan morning sky of Vietnam. Most of the shards of light were a mixture of orange confidence and the hurried intensity of turquoise. A few lights were angry crimson. Since it was a helicopter base and hospital taking care of wounded soldiers was its function, too many lights were pink transitioning to the black of death. As each person faded, so did his light.

It was a pattern of color, he'd learned that was common to everyone—regardless of where they called home.

Spooncake stopped walking when he heard a torrent of explosions behind him. He turned and eyed a column of thick, silvery black smoke billow and grow in the sky north of the Mekong towards the jungle canopy several miles away. He heard the distinctive roar of the F-4 Phantoms, then craned his neck and waited for the jets to appear behind the scream of their engines.

Even from this distance, the F-4 pilots' emotions were clearly on display. The orange shards beaconed from each cockpit, broke through the black smoke they'd created, and streamed into the blue sky above them. The pilots' colored spears announced the jets' approach before he could even see their triangular forms.

As the colors foretold, a quartet of silver-gray ghosts appeared over the tree line with the orange bolts of light bouncing above each pilot's canopy. In unison, the aircraft pulled a stiff 45-degree turn then disappeared into the blue as wraithlike as their namesake implied. Their orange lights transformed to creamy yellow then faded to nothing as Spooncake's perception of the pilots' emotions faded.

Spooncake looked back towards the pillar of smoke and saw dozens of crimson, pink, and black pins of light climb from the jungle floor and pierce the smoke curling higher into the sky. Spooncake knew what the lights were. It was war after all, and he'd become very familiar with this particular light sequence. He called it the colored dance of death. He'd seen the lights of friends follow the same path: from the anger of crimson, to the "am I dying?" confusion of pink, to the quiet acceptance of black. Each crimson pin represented the anger of individual Vietcong who survived the attack just moments ago. The black bolts of lightning belonged to the men on the edge of death who were likely still burning from the package delivered by the phantoms he'd just seen. As Spooncake continued to watch the cavalcade of light and emotion, several crimson shards lightened to pink then turned dark, as the blackness overcame them. At the moment of death, each black light dissipated into nothingness and was replaced by the cloudless blue sky. Only two crimson shards of angry revenge remained. Each one furiously pulsated with life.

Within minutes of the attack, the acrid scent of the petroleum-based payload delivered by the American pilots assailed Spooncake's nostrils. He shook his head in a fruitless attempt to avoid the smell the morning breeze tossed in his face. Even from this distance, the smoldering, heavy odor of burning napalm bit his lungs with each breath. Aiming his nostrils away from the smoke didn't help, as the equally offensive, humid aroma of the slurry of yak shit that comprised the Mekong, flowing a hundred yards further ahead, immediately accosted him. The morning smog of Van Nuys, California, the place he called home, was a bouquet of roses in comparison.

Spooncake turned back onto his path, accepting that this was the freshest air he was going to get on this otherwise beautiful morning, and continued his trek through the green grass towards the small patch of sand he'd claimed as his own almost two years ago.

He was technically on vacation, after all.

Dinner stopped and turned, sniffed the air, sneezed, then feverishly shook his head. His tail, or what remained of it, wagged furiously as he checked his friend's progress.

"Bless you," said Spooncake. "Napalm. Shit reeks."

The dog muffed in reply then turned and continued towards the riverbank and their private Eden with his beam of white light following his every move.

Spooncake hitched up the tattered lounge chair closer to his armpit and continued down the path to the river. The sun began to break through the spreading smoke, and even though the morning temperature was mild, the humidity made the sweat rain down his forehead and trickle down the bridge of his nose. Spooncake licked salty droplets from his top lip as the river finally came into view—the yaks already cooling themselves and wading in the river appeared drier than he felt. However refreshing it may appear, Spooncake wasn't about to join them. Unless he wanted his dick to fall off, Spooncake wasn't about to step into the gray-brown slurry of the Mekong. Despite the fact that he chose not to have it exercised with the others heading to Saigon, he still liked having it around when he needed it.

*

Spooncake pulled off his fatigues and stripped to his red and white striped boxers. He balanced himself across the few intact plastic straps holding the lounge chair together and stretched out along the river's murky bank to relish the sun and solitude. His pale, near-naked body appeared as a beacon next to the grass and dark brown water in the river. Anyone passing by would likely mistake him for a corpse. A corpse who wore gloves.

Everyone thought he wore the glove because of a case of contagious meningeal psoriasis, a disease he made up. Most laughed it off. Some crinkled their faces in worried concern and backed off, afraid they'd catch what he had. Spooncake knew the real reason: he couldn't touch anyone with his hands without having their thoughts broadcast through his mind. Hearing them was one thing, seeing them was something he could not tolerate.

The past few months had been hectic and harrowing. His team had pulled in more than four hundred wounded soldiers, a camp record. His gunner, Hammond, had likely killed just as many of the enemy, and his new medic, Franklin, had washed gallons of blood off of his hands and face. Franklin's fatigues were now more red than green. He looked like a watermelon at times.

He and his chopper crew had earned the five days of R&R that Uncle Sam had graciously provided them, but now Spooncake's only goal was to diminish the constant din of thoughts flowing into his brain. The DNA handed down to the McAllister Men was a curse he had to endure.

Spooncake reached down to his knees and brought the bottle of gin to his mouth, pushed its neck between his lips, and took another long pull. Dinner, who was now relaxing next to him and chewing on one of his old socks as if it were a T-bone, looked up with wanting eyes as the hand that had been scratching his single ear stopped the massage in order to raise the bottle. The gin burned on the way down, and he was sure he heard the faint echo as it splashed in the pit of his empty stomach.

"Shit. That's bad," he said through his clenched jaw and looked at the dog. "I don't think you want any of this, my furry friend. It's the local stuff. Formaldehyde and yak piss with a tinge of pine."

Dinner ignored him and returned his attention to his sock.

Despite frequent experiments with alcohol intake, he had yet to find a way to totally silence the constant invasion of thoughts. The gin helped somewhat. At best, it helped him fall asleep. At worst, it just muffled the noise rattling between his ears.

Even after two years, the smell at the riverbank was something that took a bit to get used to. He'd tried to unwind the secrets of the fragrance but had yet to discover its exact formula. Dead fish, sewage, and yak shit were primary ingredients, as he could see them floating with the current, but there was something missing. There was an aromatic high note he just couldn't place.

He could tolerate the smell better than the noise from the base camp almost a mile away. That's why he liked this particular spot. The thought-noise down here came from the fishermen and arrived in an odd dialect of Vietnamese. It wasn't at all like the parlance he'd grown used to at the base from the locals. That was a concoction of Vietnamese, American English, British English, and a bit of French all rolled into one giant barely comprehensible ball. Even though he'd been stationed here for two years, he couldn't follow their speed-of-light thoughts, and he certainly didn't want everyone to repeat themselves just so he could listen to them think.

One pass was enough.

The fishermen's thoughts flowing between his ears now were like listening to a heard of cows bellow in a far off pasture.

It was a sound.

Incomprehensible yet almost as relaxing as a mother's hum.

Just white noise from a television left on after midnight.

When he was at the base, the noise was different. It was prime time with all three channels on at the same time.

The individual words were understandable, but they were usually garbled into a jumbled, never-ending paragraph. American thoughts at the base were primarily English. There were some Spanish transmissions. Some even came with a southern twang or "wacha tawkin' bout" Brooklyn emphasis.

His brain continuously and involuntarily deciphered each and every brainwave, whether it was something he wanted to know or not. And because of this, he knew many of the inner most secrets and desires of almost everyone at the base. Luckily, his grandfather had taught him how to create and use a "psychic volume" knob. It wasn't 100% effective, but it helped dim the noise when it became unbearable. Since coming to 'Nam, he found that even when the volume was cranked all the way down, the noise still made it through, just as his grandfather had warned.

Right now though, McAllister found the random baying of the fishermen to be relaxing and didn't bother tuning anything out. He put his hand back on Dinner's head and shut his eyes in desperate search of sleep with hopes of dreaming of the days before everything went to hell. The day, nineteen years ago, when his father decided to put the barrel of a 12-guage to his right eye and pull the trigger.

*

With his eyes still shut, Tim felt for the reassuring neck of the gin bottle between his knees. He didn't want to turn into his father, but he had to admit that the booze did help quiet the clamor. He had a better understanding of what his father went through now. He doubted that he'd put the barrel of a shotgun in his eye socket to quiet things, but perhaps that's why he volunteered for Vietnam and kept re-upping time after time. Maybe he wanted someone else to pull the trigger.

"It's amazing you're not as red as a boiled lobster, sir," came a voice from behind.

McAllister's eyes fluttered. The voice belonged to Franklin, his medic. He forced his eyes to open into slits expecting to shelter them from the sun he last remembered somewhere else in the sky.

It wasn't where he left it.

Instead, it was beginning its journey to the western horizon. He'd been asleep for several hours.

"Don't burn. I tan," he mumbled.

Franklin noisily unfolded the lounge chair he was carrying and sat down.

"Hey there, Dinner," he said as he scratched the dog's notched, floppy left ear. "He sure does seem to like you. Follows you everywhere."

"Yup," mumbled McAllister as he tried to fall back to sleep and ignore the intrusion.

Too late.

The thoughts began to flow as soon as McAllister's consciousness was awakened. Even though Franklin was just one man, it didn't matter. One man acted like a giant antenna and the thoughts from those at the base, although garbled, came flowing across the span of grass, through Franklin, and into his brain. If he told Franklin to lift up his left arm, stand on one leg and turn sideways, the reception would likely improve. He'd have to lower the volume himself, after all.

Spooncake sighed as he concentrated on volume control the way his grandfather had taught him. "Lock it away," he always said. "Lock it away and never let it out."

"Base is quiet."

"Yup. S'pose so."

"Not as quiet as you think," thought Spooncake.

"What's wrong?"

"Nothing. Just trying to concentrate."

"Ah. What about?"

"Theory of Relativity and such. Just give me a sec."

In less than a minute, Spooncake stretched his neck and turned his attention to Franklin. He knew the kid wasn't about to leave and something was on the kid's mind.

Spooncake knew what it was but had to carry on the conversation as if he was clueless.

"What's up?"

"They brought in about a dozen wounded a few hours ago. Two didn't even make it past triage."

Spooncake knew that. He'd seen the lights. He lay back down on the lounge chair.

"That's why I came down here. Need a break."

"What do you think Hammond is doing in Saigon?"

McAllister kept his eyes closed but held up his hand and extended three fingers.

"I will drink them dry. I will punch someone. I will find new and exciting ways to get VD," said McAllister as he counted down each of Hammond's goals with a finger. "His words. Not mine."

"That sounds like him, alright."

McAllister heard Franklin take off his shirt and stretch out on the lounger he'd brought. If McAllister knew which lounger it was, it was in worse shape than his, and he wondered how the kid was balancing himself on its torn straps and not falling through. Specialist Andrew Franklin was still technically a green bean, just six months into his first tour. He was the fourth medic he'd had on his team. The other three he'd trained and had to watch die. He hoped Franklin would not be just another name on someone's report.

Yes, Franklin was new.

Yes, Franklin was afraid of his own shadow.

Yes, Franklin was barely nineteen.

And yes, Franklin was thin as a rail and had acne that made McAllister wince at times. When it was bad, Hammond couldn't resist a running commentary.

"Damn, kid. You gonna pop those things or what?"

Hammond loved to taunt the kid but the kid never said a word and that pissed Hammond off to no end.

The kid was good.

Franklin was one of the best medics that McAllister had ever worked with, and he was glad to have him on his crew. Many men were alive because of the skills the kid had out in the field. He could stop a bleeder with his left hand and simultaneously inject morphine into another soldier with his right.

The kid had become a surrogate little brother.

The problem for McAllister was that he didn't want a little brother right now.

He wanted solitude.

He wanted quiet without having to manage the volume.

"Give me some of that," Franklin said as he reached for the bottle of gin still clasped between McAllister's knees.

McAllister heard Franklin take a long gulp, wheeze, and try to catch his breath. The kid had probably only tasted gin once before in his long life.

"Go easy on that shit. It'll kill you if you're not careful, or worse yet, your dick'll fall off."

Franklin coughed and nodded.

"Have you…"

"For as long as I can recall. And please don't think of me as lucky. You don't want what I got."

When Spooncake was tired and not in the most communicative of moods, he rarely let anyone finish sentences. Conversation went much faster when he could move things along.

Like now.

Franklin pushed the bottle back between McAllister's knees.

"It's just that…"

"I know what they say. Don't fucking care, really. Just ignore them and focus on your job."

Spooncake never advertised his intuitive abilities. But he couldn't avoid the fact that Hammond, the pampered high school football jock he was, had a mouth the size of a large mouth bass that he used quite often, spectacularly often when he was drunk, and Spooncake's abilities were often the topic of conversation during Hammond's drunken monologues.

"Goddamn. Motherfucking McAllister. He took us right to those gooks. He can see them you know. He can see those short little motherfuckers in his head. Then I just point and shoot."

That was Hammond. Even when it had the two-inch nub of a spit-soaked cigar in it, his mouth was generally open when it shouldn't be. More brawn than brain.

Spooncake had acquired the genetic trait from his father. He called it a curse that was passed down to the men in the McAllister family tree. Everything in life was good until his father decided to blow his head off by pressing a 12-guage into his left eye socket and pulling the trigger. Spooncake heard thoughts as clearly as a radio disc jockey queuing up the next set of tunes. It seemed to be evolving, though, and had changed since he arrived in Vietnam. His ability to perceive feelings instead of just thoughts was growing stronger; a trait his grandfather never described. The curse seemed to be gaining strength.

Everyone was accompanied with color. Good news brought yellow. Exciting news was sun-bright yellow. Sadness was dark blue. Crimson was anger. Pink generally displayed itself when a soldier had accepted the inevitability of his death and was replaced by a black so dark that no other light could penetrate it as death approached. Ultimately, as death overcame life, the black faded and dissolved to emptiness. It didn't matter which side of the war you were on, either. The colors were the same, regardless of the shape of anyone's eyes, or whether the corpse-to-be had tits or a dick.

The colors helped him know where the enemy was even through the dense jungle canopy. Angry red flashes of lightning seared up through the jungle wherever the VC were hiding. When he was in the air, the enemy was almost always blood red. There was never the ecstatic happiness of yellow in combat with the other side thinking, "Yeah! McAllister's coming to shoot us!"

"Over there," he'd say, as he'd see spears of crimson rise through the jungle canopy. He'd point and rotate the Huey so Hammond could check his straps, position himself on the strut, pivot his gun, and start his barrage.

"I don't know how you fucking do it," Hammond would say as he pulled the trigger and poured a couple hundred rounds into the jungle. "But I sure like it. I like it when my mail comes special delivery and unannounced."

Hammond loved his job.

He considered himself a mailman and was performing a service to mankind and delivering their mail.

McAllister never considered Hammond the perfect human being.

As each of Hammond's bullets found its target, the red shards turned instantly black without the pink interlude, until they eventually disappeared. Typically, when gunfire was involved, there wasn't time for the acceptance of pink to appear. The lights went from crimson, to black, to dead.

Then gone.

"I think we got 'em," Spooncake would say as he turned the chopper back on course.

Spooncake preferred white.

White implied normality, calmness, and serenity.

People didn't die when things were white and Spooncake was tiring of red of any shade.

Bright green was sometimes as bad as red. Bright green was jealousy. It didn't take McAllister long to learn that men with bright green spikes of light above their heads and carrying assault rifles were not generally a good combination.

He felt Franklin grab the bottle again. This time he took a smaller pull that didn't steal his breath.

"Why do…"

"It's a dessert. That's all."

The kid had wanted to ask about his odd nickname since the moment he arrived at the base and had been introduced as a member of his crew. Most at the base called him Spooncake—very few knew why. Franklin still insisted on calling him "Sir," probably because he was too afraid to call him Spoon or Spooncake as everyone else did. Hammond had the uncanny ability to never refer to him as anything but his name.

He was named "Spooncake" during basic training, and the name had followed him across the globe to the hellhole he now found himself stranded in. During flight school at Fort Rucker, Alabama, his mother would send him a care package that always contained a new four-pack of *Fruit of the Loom* underwear, three pairs of socks, and a tinfoil tray filled with squares of strawberry spooncake—his favorite dessert.

To everyone's delight, he always shared his mother's baked goods and in time, when his trunk couldn't hold any more underwear and socks, he gave that away too. Within a short time, everyone asked when the next delivery was set to arrive. Soon he was no longer Tim, but Spooncake. Leave it to a group of drunken grunts in flight school to turn Spooncake the dessert into Spooncake the man.

To them it was a natural progression.

"Hey, Spooncake, pull back on the goddamn fucking stick! You're gonna auger the motherfucker!"

"Not so quick, Spooncake! This bird isn't a forty-year old Saigon whore you're screwing. Think of flying this thing like you are fucking a virgin. Slow. Easy. Little moves. She'll do what you want."

"Hey Spooncake, wanna go to the officer's club tonight?"

Pretty simple.

Regardless of where he went, there was always someone who knew him as Spooncake, and it only took someone saying it once to make everyone else follow suit.

Some didn't even know his real name. Tim.

Spooncake considered himself lucky, though.

They could have called him "Fruit of the Loom," as over time, he gave away just as much underwear as dessert. His mother always thought he should wear briefs instead of boxers and wanted to make sure he was properly covered and supported where it counted most.

"If they find you hurt and some nurse has to see you without clothes, I hope you are in clean underwear and not wearing those ugly boxers! I didn't raise you like that, Timothy."

His mother called him Timothy.

He hated that.

His grandfather called him Tim, Kid, or Kiddo.

Those were acceptable.

Franklin coughed as he took another swig of gin. Spooncake saw him eye the remainder of the sandwich.

"Yes. You can have it."

"Thanks. I'm starving. They sure make great food, don't they?"

Even without having taken a mouthful of gin, it was Spooncake's turn to choke; the kid was a walking food vacuum despite being so skinny he could hide behind a fence post without an inch of overhang.

He could tell the kid was nervous and had good news he desperately wanted to share.

"Spill it, kid."

"Spill what?"

"You came to tell me something. Didn't you?"

The kid laughed through his nose.

"Can't hide anything from you, sir."

Franklin was surrounded by light as bright and yellow as the morning sun, and Spooncake would be sure to feign surprise when Franklin broke the news about his newborn daughter.

No. You couldn't hide anything from Spooncake.

Most of the time.

You had to be really good at lying.

*

"Received a letter from home today," said Franklin.

McAllister sat up, pulled his legs to the side of the lounger, felt a lone strap slide up his ass, adjusted his balance, and looked at Franklin.

"Everything ok?"

"Couldn't be better."

Franklin's light became a solar flare.

"What's up?"

Franklin handed him four black and white pictures.

"I'm a daddy! My wife had the baby. Kristy Rae Franklin," Franklin said. "But you probably already knew that didn't you."

Spooncake didn't acknowledge the question. Instead he found himself having to squint from the pulsating light emanating from the kid, preventing him from looking directly at him.

"That's wonderful news, Andy. Congrats," he said as he stood up and shook the kid's hand then gave him a warm, brotherly hug.

"Thanks, sir."

"This news deserves a drink," he said as he passed the gin to the kid. "What are Kristy Rae Franklin's stats?"

"Stats? Well, she's a girl."

McAllister laughed.

"No. When was she born?"

"Oh. June 17th."

"Height? Weight?"

"Gee. I don't know."

"Well, you better find out because all of the nurses will ask you, and when you don't know, they'll make your life a living hell."

"How do you know? Do you have kids?"

"No. I've just seen what others have done wrong. The nurses hate it when guys think this is no big deal. Just have the info. Makes life so much easier. Trust me."

McAllister returned his attention to the pictures and studied each one. He didn't fake interest—it was genuine. He longed to be a father; he just didn't want to potentially pass on his cursed genes, so he assumed his desire for fatherhood would always have to be lived vicariously through others. He stopped at one picture with the mother cradling her new daughter, looked up at Franklin, then back to the picture.

"She has your nose."

"My wife said the same thing in her letter."

"I know these are black and white, but I can still see that hair! Is that your red mop?"

"Yup!"

"I suppose I'm destined to be Uncle Spooncake?"

Franklin took another swig of gin, nodded, and smiled like every new, proud father was supposed to smile.

Franklin nodded. "I'd like that, sir. That would be great."

The color around Franklin pulsated with the pride of fatherhood.

Spooncake preferred white, but right at this moment, he decided he liked yellow, too.